CW00522042

It has been beyond words
spending time with you and
knowing you.
You are so lovely and I'm
going to miss you loads!
Many thanks and boatloads
of love,

Claire M x

Claire Merchant is an author from Western Australia. She began writing in high school as a means of commenting on her surroundings, which soon developed into a passion for storytelling and character building.

Claire attended university to study English Literature, Communications and Education, and has used skills she learnt, along with personal experiences, to help her in her writing.

She has written several stories surrounding the residents of the fictional *South Coast*, in themes ranging from fantasy and supernatural fiction, to adventure, action, drama and romance.

South Coast Son

Sunset... son rise

Also by the author

Mistry by Moonlight
(Vanguard Press, 2013)
ISBN: 978-1-84386-757-9

Claire Merchant

South Coast Son

Vanguard Press

VANGUARD PAPERBACK

© Copyright 2014
Claire Merchant

The right of Claire Merchant to be identified as author of
this work has been asserted by her in accordance with the
Copyright, Designs and Patents Act 1988.

All Rights Reserved

No reproduction, copy or transmission of this publication
may be made without written permission.
No paragraph of this publication may be reproduced,
copied or transmitted save with the written permission of the publisher, or in
accordance with the provisions
of the Copyright Act 1956 (as amended).

Any person who commits any unauthorised act in relation to
this publication may be liable to criminal
prosecution and civil claims for damages.

A CIP catalogue record for this title is
available from the British Library.

ISBN: 978-1-84386-820-0

All of the characters, names and events in this publication are products of the
author's imagination or if real, are used fictitiously. Any resemblance to real
person, living or dead is purely coincidental.

Vanguard Press is an imprint of
Pegasus Elliot Mackenzie Publishers Ltd.

www.pegasuspublishers.com

First Published in 2014

Vanguard Press
Sheraton House Castle Park
Cambridge England

Printed & Bound in Great Britain

For everyone who has the courage to follow their dreams

Acknowledgements

Firstly I'd like to extend a special thank you once again to my friends who make it so easy for me to live in reality when I'm not caught up in fantasyland. You are all such an inspiration to me, thank you for giving me strength, hope and reassurance in this crazy world.

To my High School and University—Corpus Christi College and The University of Notre Dame Australia—I cannot thank you enough for your continual support and encouragement through my post-graduate ventures.

To everyone at Pegasus Publishers I extend a heartfelt thank you for your guidance, faith and patience. I couldn't ask for a better publisher and it means the absolute world to me to have your belief and support.

A special mention must also go to One Direction for supplying me with music that inspires so many scenarios in my stories. Big love to you lads, thanks a bunch.

To my mum who is my angel, my dad who is my saviour and my brother who is my protector—you're my entire world and I'm so lucky to have you. Also to my Nonna, Granny and Granda, and the rest of my wonderful family—I'm so blessed to have you all.

Last but definitely not least, thank you to everyone who reads this book. All I've ever wanted is to share my stories with people and to be able to do so with you is a dream come true. I hope that in some way my books might inspire you to pursue your own dreams. You can do anything you set your mind to, so go and make it happen!

Much love. Cx

Preface

And End All

I don't believe in happy endings. I believe in endings, but that's because they happen so regularly. After all, every single day there is an ending. Sunrise, sunset.

But then there are the other endings—relationships, dreams and my favourite, respect.

Everything ends, there is no denying it. What goes up must come down. If you want to bet on anything, bet on that.

Knowing this and believing this doesn't make me a negative person though, in fact it makes me rather positive. It allows me to live every day to the fullest, to make the most of the time I have with people and fight like hell to make my dreams come true whilst I have the power to.

As for respect, well, that's something that doesn't have an expiration date, but once it's gone, it's generally gone forever.

I might sound as if I'm brimming with sage wisdom but the truth is that I only discovered all this as a result of my own ending—or endings.

"Samuel, this isn't the end, it can't be."

Yes, it can. Yes, it is.

"Sammy, you need to keep trying."

No, I don't.

"Sam, you can't give up."

But is it giving up when it's inevitable?

I did try, I fought hard. But sometimes it's high time to accept that it's healthy for some things to end. Sometimes you need to move on with life and find a new girl or a new dream, a new you.

In the end, you only really find out who you are and what you have when you lose it. It's only then that you can focus on rebirth, rebuilding, and reinvention.

Tomorrow's sunrise.

But sometimes—sometimes when things end, they end for good.

Sometimes you're really only left with nothing.

Nothing but a sunset.

I

Of the Round Table

She sighed and I frowned.

"You're quiet today," Paige murmured, glancing up at me through her long eyelashes. She didn't smile; Paige hardly ever smiled but it didn't really make a difference. She was beautiful either way.

"I've got a lot on my mind," I answered. It wasn't really a lie, but my silence had more to do with the guilt I felt because I knew what was coming and it wasn't going to be pleasant.

"Okay," she nodded, her cloudy blue eyes searching the silver and navy coloured cafe we sat in. I liked it at Lunar; it had the best burgers in South Coast. I picked at my hot chips.

"Do you have training this afternoon?" Paige asked, letting the spearmint milkshake drain from the black straw as she lifted it out of the glass.

"No, it's Tuesday," I replied. "Training is on Mondays and Thursdays."

"Right," she sighed, dropping the straw back in the thick liquid. I never understood why girls did that—ordered something then let it sit there until it's no longer consumable.

"And Wednesdays I guess, if you count basketball," I shrugged.

She nodded, reaching out to run her soft index finger down my thumb. I liked Paige when she was like this—introspective— but as strange as it may sound, sometimes I wished she'd just tell me what she was thinking. Her eyes were sage and wise, complex,

15

like her mind was always ticking. She was intense and guarded, but then there were times when those walls came down and it was just her and me. No thoughts, no defence. Some of my mates didn't understand Paige because they never saw that side of her. Lately that carefree Paige seemed to all but disappear, and after almost a year, those walls were getting harder to break through.

I cleared my throat, dusting the salt off my hands.

"Okay, there's something I need to say," I said, ripping off the proverbial bandaid.

Paige looked up, her overcast eyes wide and deer-like; I nearly lost my nerve. What was it I heard recently? Six percent of guys broke up with girls over the telephone? Or maybe that was propose—no, wait, it was propose. Crap.

"What's wrong Sam?" she asked. "You look… weird."

I looked down; clearly she wasn't going to make it easy for me. Not that she really ever had—I tried to love her, to be with her, but Paige never needed me. She had this bizarre way of shutting people out and at first I found it refreshing because unlike other girls, she didn't feel the need to talk about everything—but then I realised she just didn't talk about it with me. It was Liam Archer she turned to, her *friend* from when they were young. I was supposed to be her boyfriend so why did she shut me out? I took a steadying breath.

"I think we should break up," I answered. My words, though only slightly above a whisper, seemed to sound loudly in my ears. The silence that followed was unnerving and I looked up to see if she'd heard me.

Paige blinked in confusion before running her fingers through her brilliant red hair.

"You want to break up," she repeated.

"Yes," I nodded. There was no going back now. The words were out.

16

She exhaled. "Why?"

"It's almost been a year," I shrugged. "And nothing has really changed between us. I just don't really see a future here."

Paige bit her lip. She looked incredibly sexy when she bit her lip. I dropped my gaze back to my chips.

"I'm sorry. I didn't want to hurt you," I murmured. "I hope we can still be—"

"Don't," she sighed. "Don't say it Samuel."

I looked up. Crap, she was crying. Paige hardly ever cried. Why do girls do that? To make us feel worse? Mission accomplished. So how do I make it stop?

"Paige—" I started, reaching across the table for her hand. I wasn't sure what I was going to do with it but it didn't matter. She pulled it away.

"Don't touch me," she snapped. That was more like it. That was more the Paige I knew.

"I'm sorry," I said helplessly. What else could I say?

She shook her head. "Sure."

I rubbed my forehead.

"Is this about that girl? The brunette?" she asked suddenly.

I looked up, feeling the blood drain from my face. "Who?"

"Don't play dumb Sam, you know the one," she sighed, sounding more fed up than angry. "The *princess* with blue eyes who's been texting you."

"Have you been going through my phone?" I frowned.

"You're really going to get mad at me when you were the one cheating?" she replied flatly.

Fair call.

"I wasn't cheating," I answered. "It wasn't like that. We never—"

"I don't really want to know," she interrupted.

I blinked in confusion. "Why didn't you say anything then? If you suspected something, why didn't you just talk to me about it? You never talk to me; I bet you spoke to Archer about it."

"Seriously Sam…" She exhaled, gathered her things and pulling some money from her pocket; she threw it on the table in front of me.

"Paige," I groaned.

Paige stopped mid-step and raised her eyebrows incredulously at me before leaving without another word. Independent to the very end—why wasn't I more surprised?

I scratched my forehead and peered around the diner but everyone else was wrapped up in their own worlds, at least they hadn't caught the show. I glanced down at my phone and saw I had two missed calls from my best friend Marcus Saxon, also known as Sax, and a text from Isobel. I wasn't sure what Marcus was calling about, probably something to do with the fact it was student night at Crescent—one of the bars near uni—and he needed a wingman. Sax didn't study at South Coast Uni with me but he made sure he completed a unit a semester at tafe to qualify for a card just for discounted beers once a week. I wasn't sure whether to shake his hand or shake my head.

I opened the text from Isobel and frowned: *Good luck today, let me know how it goes. Ix.* Isobel. I did not see her coming.

It was true that I'd broken up with Paige because she was too guarded and it was that distance one evening that had led me to confide in Isobel. I never planned on falling for her when I was already with Paige but Isobel opened up to me in a way that Paige didn't. Maybe now that I'd broken up with Paige, she might be compelled to break up with her boyfriend and we could finally be together without the guilt hanging over our heads.

I hit reply as my phone rang again and listened as the score to Darth Vader, The Imperial March, began to play. Arthur Saber: good old Artie, I wonder what he wanted.

"Dad," I sighed. "What's up?"

"Samuel, where are you?" he asked. All business as usual.

"Out, why?"

"When will you be home?" he grumbled. "The reporter from *South Coast Courier* will be here in half an hour. They want to interview the whole family which includes you."

"Uh ha," I sighed.

"I'll expect you to walk through the door in ten minutes," he finished. My father didn't believe in negotiation—as the mayor of South Coast most people just tried to compromise with whatever he wanted.

"I'm more than ten minutes away," I answered. "So just a heads up."

"Samuel, don't get smart with me," he snapped. "Everywhere in South Coast takes ten minutes. I'll see you at five forty."

I glanced at my watch. "That's in eight minutes."

"Stop wasting time then."

The line went dead and I shook my head, pulling my wallet out of my back pocket and throwing a twenty beside Paige's ten. That would more than cover the meals and give a decent tip for the staff. Tipping wasn't a custom around here but I got some kind of satisfaction in throwing away my father's money. He took enough away from the noble citizens.

"Leaving so soon?" a voice called as I stood.

I turned and smiled at Demi, one of Lunar's wait staff, as she cocked a black eyebrow at me.

"Where's your friend?"

"She had to leave," I answered as she sauntered over; her black skirt was just that little bit too short to pass off as a uniform for the place but who was I to complain?

"She didn't look too happy," Demi smirked, tucking her red pen behind her ear as she leaned over to clear the table.

Her skirt hiked up her tanned thighs and I tipped my head back in silent appreciation. Demi had great legs.

"She wasn't," I answered, snapping out of it.

"Aw Sammy," Demi pouted, her blood-red lips plumping. I forced a smile and she beamed a grin, tucking the cash into her apron. "Thanks for the tip; I knew there was another reason why I liked seeing you here."

I laughed.

"Do you have to leave?" she asked. "I knock off at six; we could grab a drink somewhere if you like."

I bit my lip. "Would love to but duty calls. Raincheck?"

She closed one eye. "I'm going to hold you to that."

"Sure," I laughed, raising a hand to wave. "See you next time."

"As always, Mr Saber, it was a pleasure," she smiled.

I nodded and glanced down at my watch as it ticked over onto five forty, and made my way down the street to my 1962 almond-green coloured Morris Minor 1000. Artie tried to buy me another car a few months ago but I knew it bothered him that I drove a vintage car rather than some slinky new hybrid sedan like he insisted on my mother and sister driving—driving being a relative term since the chauffer was usually the one behind the wheel.

I pulled up the driveway to our castle-like house at ten to six, the front door opening before I'd even stumbled out my car.

"Samuel you're late, your father is terribly upset with you," my mother sighed. Angela Saber was, in plain terms, the closest thing to a living angel I'd ever met. Her patience and tolerance were golden.

"Sorry, I got caught up," I replied. "I did tell him I was more than ten minutes away."

Angela smiled weakly. "Come inside please. The reporter will be here soon, they're never late."

I dragged my feet up, kissing my mother on the cheek as I passed, and swaggered through the living room. I could see three of my father's men pacing the room and paid them the same ignorance they showed me.

"Samuel! Get changed and get back here!" Artie growled. "And for goodness sake son, would it kill you to shave?"

I ran my hands over the stubble on my chin—stubble that had been there for several months and not caused an aneurism before.

"Well go on then, move!" he demanded. "God almighty, that boy."

I continued through the house, yawning as I made my way up to my tower and I ran my hands though my jaw-length hair. It could probably do with a wash but I wasn't going to push it, Artie was already on edge. Besides, if a clean shirt was all that would appease the man I wasn't going to argue. I was pretty sure that the housekeeper had ensured I had one of those.

I kicked open my door and stumbled over a pair of football boots I'd left on the floor, catching my shoe on another shirt that had fallen off my bed. At least the man still gave me my privacy— nothing was ever touched or cleaned in my room. As I straightened, my eyes were drawn to a coat hanger of clothes covered in plastic. Apparently I was wrong about the former. On them was a note: *Samuel - Courier interview clothes.*

I sighed and pulled off the plastic, kicking off my shoes, and dragged my T-shirt off over my head. The blue shirt that had been picked out for me felt new and crusty, the sleeves a little tight for comfort over my upper arms. I'd been doing more weight training in the lead up to football season and I guessed whoever chose

21

them didn't factor that in. At least the black slacks fit. I hated new clothes; I didn't really see the point in them. Every time Artie had some press thing on I got them and they were practically disposable. I'd picked out a small handful that I liked and didn't really bother about others. I never really understood girls who had wardrobes full of clothes they never wore; it annoyed me to have excess crap lying around, there was enough of that already.

I heard voices downstairs and yawned again, heading out to the bathroom before making my way down for the show.

This whole day had felt like a show. Class, Paige—Paige. I could still remember the time when she had been responsible for making me smile but lately someone else had claimed that position, and she didn't even care enough to mention noticing it.

I rested my hands either side of the sink and took a few deep breaths.

"Hi Sammy," my sister Amelia called.

"Hey."

"What's wrong with you?" she asked, appearing in the doorway.

I sighed. "Nothing. I broke up with Paige."

"Really? I liked her."

I looked up to find her face in the mirror. "No you didn't."

She shrugged. "That's because she moved my stuff in the shower all the time. I like her better than some of the other girls you've dated."

"There haven't been that many," I replied, turning the tap to splash some water on my face.

"Hm," Amelia shrugged. "So why'd you break up with her? I guess she was a bit pouty... and poor."

"Be quiet Millie. Don't talk about her like that," I answered.

"It's true and everyone knows it," Amelia said unapologetically. I wish she'd keep her opinions to herself, but my sister seemed to think that she was entitled to be honest with everyone despite the fact her honesty was sometimes obnoxious.

"Not everyone," I grumbled, reaching for the hand towel to dry my face.

She rolled her eyes. "You're such a guy."

I threw the towel at the rack and ignored the fact it didn't stay. "So do you know what this is about? The reporter thing?"

Amelia seemed to sober. "Something about that new entertainment complex Dad built in the city."

"So why do we have to be here for it?" I frowned.

"United front," she offered. "Family perspective. I don't know; who knows with Dad?"

"Sounds like a pile of crap to me," I shrugged, heading out to make my way down. "What does South Coast need another entertainment complex for anyway? We need another sports ground. The one in Iris Cove is all beaten up and not even half the size of some of the grounds over east."

"Don't let Dad hear you say that," Amelia warned as she followed me downstairs.

"Say what?" Artie asked, painting on the most pleasant politician facade I've ever seen. "Alex Marrone, you remember my children: Samuel and Amelia."

"Of course," Alex nodded. Alex had been with the *Courier* for over twenty years now. He worked in general news so often covered stories about my father. I was glad they sent him rather than one of the girls; it was embarrassing seeing them try and charm Artie—or worse, me.

"Something on your mind, son?" Artie grinned. I'd come to learn over time that this was not an invitation to speak, rather the opposite. It was a hard learned lesson.

"Nope," I answered, forcing a smile back. "Where do you want us?"

Artie had us well trained.

"Alex?" Artie asked. "Shall we go into my study?"

"Whatever suits, Mayor Saber," Alex nodded. Apparently he had Alex well trained too. I had the urge to pat the guy on the back in sympathy.

Artie smiled but didn't correct the title with a polite *Please, call me Arthur* like you would expect after the several years of acquaintance—he was too arrogant for that.

"Alex, how's the family?" Angela asked. "I haven't seen Krystal in a while down the club."

My mother and Alex's wife play tennis together on Wednesdays. I used to help out as a coach down there during first year uni but had to stop when I picked up basketball. Krystal is a nice lady but she's far more consumer driven than Angela—the complete opposite to their husbands it seems.

"She's been a little unwell actually, Angela," Alex answered, giving my mother a warm smile. "I expect she'll be back for next week though."

"I'm sorry to hear that, please give her my best," Angela replied as we all settled down on the couch around an oak coffee table in front of Artie's desk. I could see Artie getting jittery that the limelight was shifted from him.

"Well now, let's get down to business," he said. A typical phrase of his.

"Certainly, Mayor Saber," Alex nodded. "Why don't I start with your lovely family then we can talk one-on-one?"

"Sounds fine," Artie affirmed, looking at me pointedly. The warning shot, the non-verbal *behave Samuel.* It was practically an endearment from Artie.

Alex took his recorder out and pressed the red button, setting it on the table between us all.

"Samuel, Amelia, you two must be very proud of your father, what with all the milestones he's accomplished whilst being in office," Alex began. "I know that there are a lot of exciting things planned for South Coast in the future, including the completion of the new entertainment complex which is being unveiled this weekend, on the anniversary of Mayor Saber's indoctrination into office."

I resisted the urge to roll my eyes and I felt my phone vibrate in my pocket and pulled it out. Artie took it from my hands before I got the chance to check it. My mouth opened to protest but I was silenced by his glare which was followed up with a suggestive glance at the recorder.

"Do you have any comments you'd like to make regarding his achievements?" Alex finished.

I eyed my phone and contemplated mutiny.

"Sam?" Alex prompted.

"Yes?"

"Anything you'd like to say about your father?"

Where to begin?

"I for one am so proud of what he's done for South Coast," Amelia interrupted, the dutiful daughter. "People used to ask me if I think it's weird to have a father as the mayor but I love it. I never feel embarrassed or ashamed of anything he's done. He's a great father and the greatest mayor anyone could hope for."

I looked at Artie who was beaming with pride over Amelia's little speech. I wondered who had written it for her.

"Sam? Care to add anything?" Alex asked.

Artie's expression hardened as his brown eyes turned on me. I drew in a breath and shook my head. Alex pressed his lips into a tight smile.

"I heard through the grapevine that you're one to watch this season," he said. "A friend of mine who works for the RedBacks implied there might be some interest in adding you to their line up."

That got my attention. "Really? Who's your friend?"

Alex smiled. "I shouldn't name names."

I nodded, still feeling elated by the revelation. The RedBacks were the state major-league football team based in South Coast. I currently played for one of the local minor league teams called the Iris Cove Suns. I'd been a RedBacks supporter since I was old enough to walk.

"We should probably stay on topic," Artie chuckled, claiming back the attention. Of course.

"Certainly Mayor," Alex murmured. "So Sam, what do you think of the new entertainment complex designed by *Freeze Frame* Architecture? At your age no doubt you've been to a few concerts, do you think it will add to the existing culture in our city?"

I looked at Amelia then Artie and their varying expressions, amusement, caution. Amelia knew my opinion and Artie could only havoc a guess in the line of my thinking.

"I don't attend too many concerts so I'm probably not the best person to ask," I replied, keeping it pragmatic.

"Oh," Alex answered. "Amelia?"

"I think it will add to the culture, for sure. South Coast isn't exactly the largest city and I think being so isolated from other cities, if there was a venue that allowed for more people to attend it might attract more performers here. I definitely don't think building it will have lessened the culture."

Artie glowed with satisfaction again.

"One final question for the kids then I'll have a chat to you, Mr Mayor, and Angela," Alex said, glancing at his notes. "From a youth perspective, Sam, since we haven't really heard from you, what do you think—if anything—that South Coast needs more of?"

Snookered.

"I'm not sure how to answer that question," I replied honestly.

Alex smiled in encouragement. "There are no wrong answers."

Artie shifted in his seat and Angela gave me a reassuring nod. There were no wrong answers, only wrong ideas. If I told Alex what I really thought, it would mean I thought Artie was neglecting an area of South Coast; if I didn't, I'd be lying. My father doesn't consider everyone in the city, he doesn't even consider half of the people, he only considers those who are loud and opinionated enough to complain about things; hence the new building—even if we already had two appropriate venues for musical acts.

"Well, I never really thought about it before I guess," I shrugged.

"Never?" Alex asked. "You wouldn't change anything or add anything? What if you were mayor for a day?"

I couldn't think of anything worse to be for a day.

"I'm not too sure," I chuckled.

"Go on Samuel," Artie encouraged with a false laugh.

I threw caution to the wind.

"Well I can't speak for all of the youth in South Coast," I sighed. "But personally I think it wouldn't go astray to look at what we've got here to offer in terms of sporting venues and funding. There is a lot of focus on the arts but that only covers a small percentage of what you might call *culture*."

Artie laughed and it was the most disturbing of sounds. He sat forward to clap me on the back and I almost choked on my tongue.

"What my son is saying is quite accurate and we have plans in place to look at the allocation of funding in the way of sporting and fitness," Artie bluffed. "Of course we're still in the planning phases right now and we're focusing on one project at a time, but I can assure the fine people of South Coast that we are looking at a holistic approach to bettering the city in a multitude of categories."

Smooth. I was going to pay for that later, I was sure.

Alex reached to stop the recorder.

"Thank you Sam, Amelia," Alex nodded. "Mayor, if I could speak to you and Angela now?"

Artie nodded at Alex then looked at Amelia and me, raising his eyebrows in silent dismissal.

I stood and cleared my throat.

"Can I have my phone back please?"

Artie rested it in my outstretched hand, letting it linger a moment as he stared me square in the eye, sending a chill through my spine. He released my phone with more force than was necessary. Yep, I was dead.

I pushed the phone back in my pocket.

"Good to see you again Alex," I smiled, extending my hand towards him.

"Likewise Sam, all the best this season," he nodded. "I'm sure you'll be a household name before we know it."

Bet Daddy will be proud.

"Cheers," I replied, following Amelia out. When we were out of earshot she started to laugh.

"You are so dead, brother," she sighed. "I thought Dad was going to have a stroke."

I frowned, checking my phone. It was Marcus who had called.

"You think it was really that bad?" I asked.

She looked at me, questioning my sanity. "Yes."

"Great," I groaned, hitting redial. Marcus answered straight away.

"Sammy."

"Sax."

"Where've you been?" he asked.

"Sorry, family commitments, what's up?"

"Keen to come out tonight? Tuesday is student night at Crescent," he said. "Or do you have plans with Paige?"

Paige.

"Nuh, we broke up," I answered flippantly. "Sure, Crescent sounds good. You driving or should I meet you there?"

"Cool, I'll come and get you," he replied.

I looked down at the clothes I wore. Contemplating whether I could be bothered changing.

"Sure, I'll see you when you get here," I sighed.

"Be there in ten."

Dial tone.

"Are you going out?" Amelia pouted.

"Yep," I nodded, heading towards the stairs.

"Dad's not going to be happy about that," she taunted.

I laughed. "He can add it to the list."

***

I didn't end up changing my clothes, mostly because I couldn't rationalise changing more than once in a day after only wearing these threads for half an hour. I didn't feel so bad though because Marcus was a tie away from looking like he was going to a funeral. I don't know what his deal was—for a concreter he sure was compensating for something. What he did for a living didn't make a whole lot of difference to me; I wasn't really one to talk. I was a full-time student who just happened to be born with a golden spoon.

"Yo Sammy," Marcus called. "You suited up."

"Like I said, family commitments," I answered, opening the passenger door to his rose-taupe, sleek-style utility coupé.

"Ah Artie," he chuckled, flooring the accelerator so the wheels of his ute skidded and fishtailed down the circular driveway. I could hear his concreting tools slide in the back of the flat-bed tray.

"Geez Marcus, I'm in enough trouble as it is, ease up would you? The reporter's still inside," I groaned.

"Whoops," he chuckled. "Oh well, give the old man something to talk about—tightening the speed limits."

"He's not the police commissioner."

"Right," he sighed. "So did you say that you and Paige broke up?"

"Yeah."

"Why?"

"Wasn't really working out," I shrugged. "She didn't seem to care much about what I did. Plus she spends more time with Archer than me anyway."

"Yeah I always thought that was a bit weird," he nodded. "You okay?"

"Yep," I sighed. "Hey, the reporter that was at the house said he got word from someone at the RedBacks that they might be interested in taking me in. Wouldn't say who but sounds promising."

"Wicked, bro," he grinned. "I wonder if they'll take me too."

"Nuh, Sax, you're not as good as me," I laughed and glanced at my phone, remembering I hadn't replied to Isobel's text from earlier. "*Sax and I are heading to Crescent, come and have a cocktail with us.*"

"Good team this season though, Sammy. With you, me, Macca and Elliot we'll make the finals for sure," Marcus continued.

I looked up at him curiously, having only been half listening. Me, him, Louis McKenzie—or Macca to his teammates when he's here. He was a few years older than us and worked fly-in-fly-out up north. Then there was Elliot. I felt my frown deepen as my phone vibrated.

"*Hey, I'm out with Elliot, call you later. Ix.*"

Elliot was Isobel's boyfriend and the team captain of the Iris Cove Suns—and so the plot thickened.

"We'll definitely make the finals," I answered belatedly, dropping my phone into my lap.

We arrived at Crescent shortly after; my castle wasn't too far. Marcus bypassed the bouncer because they were old friends now. We headed straight for the front bar and found a stool down the end. We usually started off here before heading into the main bar, it was quieter and although he doesn't drink much, Sax claimed he liked to finish at least two pints of liquid courage before trying his luck with the ladies. He usually didn't have to try hard though—a lot of the girls in South Coast craved attention and the fact he was an athletic tradesman weighted heavily in his favour.

Three hours and around five beers later to my name, we were in the back bar which had more of a club feel to it with the in-house band playing. It was a new group called *Damage Control*— three brothers—not bad.

It was a pretty full house with not much space to move. I was glad I had that burger and chips earlier because I could feel the alcohol taking affect. I wasn't much of a lightweight but generally tried not to drink so much because I was in training. No club wants another kid with a dream and a drinking problem.

I grabbed a glass of lemonade from the bartender and settled on an empty stool, taking a breather from the sweaty, intoxicated bodies rubbing up against me.

As soon as the stool beside me was free, a girl with raven black hair sat down, her curves brushing against my arms as she passed me.

31

"Hey I'm Sadie," she smiled, her white teeth glinting in the neon lights.

"Sam," I nodded, looking at her properly for the first time. She looked familiar. "Aren't you Nathaniel Blake's sister?"

"No, Nate is my brother," she replied.

"That's what I said."

"How do you know Nate?" she asked, tipping her head so her black hair fell over her shoulder. She was beautiful, but tried a little too hard to get attention. Not really my type.

"My girlfri—uh, I know someone who's friends with his best friend," I answered.

Sadie thought for a moment. "You mean Liam? Did you used to date *his* friend—the redhead?"

"Her name is Paige," I mumbled reluctantly.

"Right, Paige," she laughed. "I don't know what the hype is with her."

I frowned. "What d'you mean?"

"Nothing," she answered. "She just seems a bit moody and temperamental."

I laughed. "She's not like that all the time."

"If you say so," Sadie shrugged. "So you're here alone then?"

"No, I'm here with a mate."

"A boy mate?"

"Yep."

"Cool, guy's night," she grinned.

I took a sip of lemonade. "I 'spose."

"I was here with my friend but she left with her boyfriend," she explained. "She's got work tomorrow."

"You don't?"

"No, I mostly work weekends," she answered. "Besides, I'm sort of dating my boss so he's lenient—actually not really, but I don't care. He can be a jerk anyway."

"Okay," I nodded. I never understood why some girls feel the need to tell random guys their life story after only just meeting them.

"We're not exclusive though," she continued. "Me and my boss."

"Right," I replied. "Bet that's not awkward at work."

"We don't really talk in lengths about it," she shrugged. "Sometimes secrets are important in relationships."

I laughed humourlessly.

"So what's your story then?" she asked.

"My story?"

"Yeah, tell me about Sam."

I shrugged. "Not much to tell."

"Sammy, who's your friend?" Marcus asked, hanging off my shoulder. I shrugged him off.

"This is Sadie," I answered with a small smile. "She's—I mean, Nate's her brother."

Sadie smiled.

"I'm Sax," he grinned.

"Sam and Sax—cute," she noted with a raised eyebrow.

Marcus glanced at me with that look—that 'dibbs' look.

"So what are we talking about?" he asked.

"Well Sam here was just about to tell me his life story," she giggled.

Marcus ruffled my hair and I elbowed him. "Did he tell you that his dad is King Arthur?"

Sadie straightened, her chest becoming more prominent. "Like, of the round table?"

I rolled my eyes. "Like of the small South Coast."

"Your dad is Artie Saber?" she half choked. "So you're like a knight? Do you have your own sword?"

Marcus started laughing and I couldn't help but join in—so many ways that could be interpreted.

"Nah," I replied, deciding to take it literally. "I'm not one of his swordsmen."

"You should totally get one," Sadie smiled, sliding her finger across my left bicep. "Right here."

Marcus' eyes lit up. "Oh let's do it! There's a tattoo place not far from here."

"I'm going to need a few more drinks before I do something that stupid," I answered.

Sadie grinned, a glint of mischief twinkling in her impossibly violet-coloured eyes.

"Next round's on me."

I I

With the Iron Fist

I kept my eyes closed as I assessed the damage. I was lying on something cold and hard, my feet and lower legs felt wet, my head felt like it had been run over by a muscle car, my left bicep stung and there was something slobbering on my face.

I opened my eyes.

"Dalziel, stop," I grumbled, pushing my beige Staffordshire terrier's muzzle away from me. Artie was still convinced that I'd named him after Ian Dalziel, the British politician and businessman, but really it was after Scott Dalziel: the Scottish footballer born in 1985. Dalziel sniffled excitedly that I was awake and returned to lick my face with more zeal.

"Dally!" I complained, pushing myself onto my back. I had somehow lost my shirt between Sadie's round and now. No wonder I was cold. Dalziel practically leapt onto me, standing on my sore arm. I winced, pushing him off and ignoring how my head spun as I sat up. I was lying out on my front porch, the wetness on my feet caused by a late night shower. The rest I could pretty much attribute to Marcus and Sadie.

I turned my arm over, and frowned at the white patch running from my armpit to my elbow and pulled back the medical tape.

Oh crap, Artie is going to go ballistic.

In plain black ink was the drawing of a sword, slightly reddened and scabby but well drawn. A tattoo, I had actually gotten drunk and got a tattoo. Of a sword.

I groaned and rubbed my sore eyes, pushing myself to lean against the wall as Dalziel gave a silent whimper and walked over to lick my face again.

"Dally," I complained. He sat down beside me and I ran my hand down his coat.

The front door opened.

"Samuel? What are you doing out here? Where is your shirt?" Angela asked.

"Hi Mum," I murmured. "I don't quite remember."

She pursed her lips. "Come inside before your father sees you, he's mad enough that you disappeared last night."

"Sorry, blame Sax," I yawned.

Angela sighed. "Go and take a shower, I'll get Marion to fix you some breakfast."

I pushed myself up and walked passed her into the house. "What time is it?"

"Seven thirty," she replied. "Arthur is in his study so go through the kitchen."

"Thanks Mum," I answered, stopping to kiss her cheek before hurrying through. Marion looked up as I passed but otherwise ignored me, the fifty-something-year-old lady was already desensitised to my miscreant behaviour.

After my shower I ate the omelette she'd prepared and grabbed an apple before heading into uni just in time for my eight thirty class. I was in my third year of Engineering Technology and it definitely wasn't something to try and learn with a hangover. I don't know how I'd passed so far, call it a fluke or luck, the only thing I had going for me was that I attended most lectures. Artie was big on keeping up appearances so as long as I was there, I was fulfilling my duty. I spent most of the time in class designing things to make though; I'd built a lot of my furniture and made the odd sand board and birdhouse. It kept me busy during the football off season and it kept me out of trouble—mostly—when Artie flexed his iron fist.

My head throbbed all through the morning and even after downing two bottles of PowerAde I still felt pretty seedy. Marcus texted me at around eleven, after just waking up, and I cursed his laziness since last night was his big idea and I was the one paying for it.

I headed down to the esplanade at twelve thirty to try for a nap between lectures then decided I'd get more benefit from staying here than going to class. At three o'clock I dragged myself back to the library to download the notes I'd missed, I checked my email while I was there and almost spat out my mouthful of the third bottle of sports drink. What was this?

To: South_Coast_University_all_students
From: anonymous

Hey everyone, did you hear about Samuel Saber dumping Paige Stewart? I wonder who had that in the pool. Can't believe it lasted that long to be honest, I don't know who I feel sorrier for—him or her. Guess South Coast's son is on the prowl again. Ladies start your engines!

Oh crap.

Poor Paige.

I glanced around me and noticed for the first time that people were staring and muttering. Who would have done this? Who knew about us from yesterday afternoon? I'd told Marcus but even he wouldn't stoop that low, and I know Paige wouldn't make it common knowledge—I mean surely she would have told Liam but I knew the guy and it wasn't in his nature. He was too noble.

I packed up my stuff, throwing it recklessly into my bag and headed for the exit to get to my car, nearly walking into someone as I blew out the library door.

"Watch it!" the girl shrieked.

"Sorry," I mumbled, stepping around her.

"Hey, wait," she called. "You're Sam Saber, right?"

I turned. "Yeah?"

The blonde girl I'd never seen before smiled sympathetically. "Sorry to hear about your breakup."

"Err, thanks," I sighed before walking hurriedly in the direction of my car.

What the hell was going on?

I threw the door open and piled in, running my hands through my hair before jabbing the keys in the ignition, ready to start it.

There was a knock on my passenger window that made me jump and I looked up to see Isobel. She opened the unlocked door.

"Hey," she smiled. "Are you okay?"

I shook my head. "I've got to get out of here."

"Okay, let's go," she said, climbing in and buckling herself.

I looked at her curiously. "Are you sure you want to be seen with me? Haven't you read the email?"

"Are you going to drive or not?" she asked, shuffling down in the seat so her head was below the window.

I started the car and pulled out onto the road.

"So, how'd she take it?" Isobel asked, looking up at me awkwardly. Even like that she looked beautiful, radiant.

"Not well," I sighed. "She actually asked if it was because of you. I think she went through my phone."

Her blue gem-like eyes popped. "What?"

I glanced at her briefly as I slowed for a red light. "Relax; I don't keep your messages just in case the lads at the club get a

38

hold of my phone. She just knows we've been in touch from the call log."

"Good," she exhaled, moving to sit properly. We were out of the university vicinity now and heading for the river where we sometimes met under one of the bridges near my castle.

"So how come you weren't in the philosophy lecture today?" she asked. "I waited for you."

"I fell asleep at the park," I replied. "Woke up a bit worse for wear this morning."

"Marcus?" she frowned. "Every time you go out with him you end up worse for wear."

I smiled. "He's harmless."

"Are you okay though?" she asked. "About Paige?"

I looked over at her then turned my attention back to the road. "Yep, fine."

"You can talk to me you know," she said, putting her hand on my hand that rested on the gearstick. "It's okay to be sad, you and her were together a while."

I exhaled. "I'm more angry actually; break ups are hard enough without everyone talking about it. Whoever sent that email was just trying to cause trouble."

"Yeah, I read it, I don't know who would do that," she frowned.

I cleared my throat, pulling into park. "What about Elliot?"

"What about him?"

"You're still with him?"

"Yes," she replied, looking over her shoulder before unclipping her seatbelt. She climbed across the front seat to sit on my lap, pinning me against the chair. I unclipped my seatbelt and ran my hands down her arms.

"We can't keep doing this," I sighed.

"I know," she smiled, kissing me hotly. Her small hands balled up the collar of my shirt, pulling me towards her; I was at her complete mercy.

I moved my arms around her and winced as my fresh tattoo scraped against her blue woollen cardigan. Isobel sat back.

"What's wrong?"

I exhaled. "Nothing."

Her eyes traced to my hand as I pressed it to my bicep.

"Nothing?" she asked. "What's that?"

Busted.

"I might have gotten a tattoo last night," I laughed. "Want to see?"

Isobel sat back against the steering wheel as I peeled back my hand to reveal it.

"A sword," she mused, running her finger across it. "Why?"

"Just something Sadie said," I answered. "Or Sax—I can't remember."

"Who's Sadie?"

"Sadie Blake."

"As in Nate Blake?"

"His older sister," I replied. "She's nuts by the way. More tolerable than Nate though."

Isobel nodded slowly.

"What?"

She shrugged. "Nothing."

"I don't believe you."

She ran her hands up my chest and they settled around my neck.

"I just don't like to think of you being out drinking with another girl," she pouted. "A girl who you'll remember forever now because you got a tattoo with her."

I laughed. "I didn't get a tattoo *with* her and I did invite you out last night but you were with Prince."

"I know," she frowned, resting her forehead on mine.

I brushed her hair back over her shoulder. "If anyone has a right to be jealous here it's me. The thought of him touching you and kissing you... it just feels wrong."

"I know," she sighed, her fingers running through my hair. "I am going to break up with him but if I do it now, people will talk and Elliot will know it's because of you. You guys are friends and I don't want to ruin that."

"We've already ruined that," I answered, even if Elliot and I were more just civil teammates than actual *friends*. "And we'll ruin it further if you and I ever officially get together."

"Don't say that," she breathed, clutching my shoulders.

I shrugged. "I'm okay with it."

"No," she frowned. "I don't want it to be something you're okay with, I'd be ruining your friendship."

"Isobel, we knew it would be like this," I answered. "Prince isn't just going to be okay with you and me. If any of my friends or teammates hooked up with Paige, I wouldn't be okay with it either."

"Samuel," she sighed. "Stop talking like this."

"I'm just telling you how it is," I replied. "But like I said, I'm okay with it if it means we can be together."

She bit her lower lip as she traced mine with her finger and I could feel my body reacting to the two.

Then her phone rang.

"Hey," she said flatly. "What's up?"

My brow creased.

"No I left, why?" she continued. "I'm not home yet, I had to make a stop... maybe half an hour, an hour, why? Oh... yeah, I just forgot that's all... okay... I'll see you then."

She hung up.

"What's up?" I asked.

She shook her head. "I promised Elliot I'd go to dinner with his family tonight."

"Oh, so you have to go?"

"Soon," she nodded.

She still seemed to be upset so I tipped up her chin.

"What's wrong?"

"Nothing," she mumbled.

I sighed. "Are you having second thoughts?"

"I just wish things were different."

"Different how?"

"I wish it didn't have to be this way," she explained. "Us in a car under a bridge and Elliot… and you… and it's all so hard."

"It's not hard, don't over think it," I shrugged. "It'll sort itself out."

"How can you be so casual about this?" she asked. "Aren't you worried about what will happen if he finds out?"

I smiled. "Isobel, if I worried about all the 'ifs' and 'buts' of the world, I'd be a cot case."

"Boys are so strange," she mused. I couldn't understand how girls agonised over non-existent issues, yet *we* were strange.

"Are you going to be okay?" she asked. "I mean, about Paige and the email?"

I'd completely forgotten about that.

"Yeah, I'll be right," I replied. "It'll blow over."

She shook her head incredulously.

"I wish I could be more like that," she sighed.

"More like what?"

"Carefree."

I smiled because it wasn't hard—it wasn't even a choice.

She traced my lips again with her finger then leaned in to kiss them.

"I wish I didn't have to go," she whispered.

"Then don't."

She moaned, the sound stirring something inside me.

And then her phone rang again.

I exhaled.

"Hello?" she answered. "Oh, hey Liam—"

Liam? What was Archer doing calling her?

"Um, no sorry I'm in the middle of something actually. Yeah, I'll call you later. Okay. Bye."

She hung up and sighed.

"Liam?" I asked. "As in Paige's Liam? Liam Archer?"

She shrugged. "We had world history together last semester, he's nice."

"Nice," I mumbled, feeling like cold water had been thrown over me. What was with this guy always interfering with my relationships?

"Are you jealous?" she grinned. I never understood why girls found that cute.

"No, talk to who you want; Prince is your boyfriend, not me," I shrugged.

Isobel frowned. "Don't be like that. He's just a friend."

"Okay," I nodded.

"Sam," she murmured, moving her hands down my chest and under my T-shirt.

I swallowed. "When do you have to be home?"

"By six."

"But it's only four."

"Then we've got two hours to kill."

***

After I dropped Isobel back at uni, I headed home to change for basketball practice. Artie wasn't home so I dodged another bullet for my absence the night before. I hoped by the time I saw him he'd be mad at me for some other reason and my chances were pretty good. I tended to be in strife on any given day about any given topic. I eventually realised that he thrived on it—so I'd be the delinquent if that's what he needed—work kept him distracted from any real punishment anyway.

I usually liked Wednesdays because they were a different change of pace. I loved football but there was a lot less pressure at basketball.

Plus, I got to hang around a different group of guys so that kept things interesting.

"Hey Saber," Bryce Watson grinned as I dragged my heels onto the indoor courts. I was feeling the interrupted sleep by now and wished I'd at least made it into bed last night. I made a mental note to not get *blind* drunk with Marcus again.

"Watson, how's it going?" I answered, accepting his hand to grasp.

He slapped my back and chuckled. "You sound a bit rough."

"I feel it," I grumbled. "Big night."

"Sax?"

"Yep."

He laughed.

I threw my bag down and stretched my arms above my head, aware of the slight sting of the new tat on my bicep but ignored it—it was getting easier to ignore.

"New ink?" Bryce asked, dribbling the ball around me.

"Yeah, wasn't planned," I sighed.

He chuckled. "Are they ever?"

I smiled, glancing over as another one of our teammates wandered in. I felt my brow draw.

"What's Nate Blake doing here?"

Bryce took a shot and scored. "He joined a few weeks ago, remember?"

"Nope."

"Guess you spent most of the time on your phone texting," he smirked. "Speaking of, how is Paige?"

I blinked—it hadn't been Paige I was texting.

"Uh, we broke up," I mumbled. "Surprised you didn't hear."

His eyebrows furrowed. "Oh, why? When did that happen?"

"Yesterday—but somehow the whole of SCU got the memo," I answered, rolling my eyes.

"Sucks," he frowned. "You good?"

"Yep," I shrugged.

He threw me the ball and I took a shot; it bounced off the hoop. I cursed under my breath.

"So anyone new on your radar then?" Bryce asked.

"Nuh," I lied. "Think I'm going to have a break from girls for a bit."

He laughed. "Right."

I eyed Nate as he stretched, trying to remember why I'd ignored the fact he'd joined the team. I know that he and Paige never got along, which was a large reason why I never had time for him. She was never really one to talk about her feelings but she made her feelings of distaste for Nathaniel perfectly clear. If he and Liam weren't such good friends, and Paige and Liam weren't as close as they were—I groaned internally—I would have happily smacked the smirk off his face a long time ago.

"Hey, I met Nate's sister last night," I said to Bryce. "She's not bad—bit crazy though."

Bryce's auburn eyebrows lifted. "For real?"

I nodded. "She was the one who suggested the tattoo then filled me full of booze."

Bryce huffed a laugh. "It was a big night then—did you hook up?"

"Nuh," I shook my head. "I could have but she was a little too desperate."

He chuckled. "Ruins the fun?"

"Exactly."

"Hey, I saw you in the paper today," Bryce said, a glisten in his eye. "Talking about how South Coast needed to spend more on sports."

Oh crap, I'd forgotten about that.

"Oh yeah," I nodded. "Artie might just kill me before sundown."

Bryce laughed. "He comes off looking the hero as always. Actually makes him sound like he's 'in touch' with the people."

"Of course," I groaned. "Wonder how much he had to pay for that one."

Bryce huffed as we wandered over into the huddle, ready for the game to start.

***

The game was not going well. We were twenty-seven points down with five minutes to go and not only that, Nathaniel Blake was proving to be more of a hindrance than anything else—as usual.

"Damn it, Nate, pull your head out, you're on our team," I groaned.

"At least I'm trying, moron," he mumbled. "Are you going to break up with me too?"

"How did Sadie scrub up this morning?" I answered. "You never told me she had a tattoo on her hip."

And then he lunged at me.

Bryce couldn't stop laughing as he helped press the icepack onto my swollen face.

"You did make a remark about the guy's sister," he chuckled. "What did you expect?"

I shook my head, pushing his hand away as I pressed the pack on myself. If I didn't hate him before, I really hated Nate Blake now. I know I deserved the punch—you never talk about a guy's sister—but after he made that comment about Paige, I wanted to hurt him.

I threw the pack down.

"I've got to go."

Bryce ran his hands through his short auburn hair and frowned. "You all right, bro?"

"Yep," I sighed. I was getting sick of being asked that. "I'll catch you next week."

He nodded. "You keen for fishing on Sunday?"

"Uh, I'll let you know," I replied, grabbing my bag and raising my hand in a wave.

Bryce gave a two-finger salute in response and I left, heading home for round... whatever I was up to.

When I finally got home and my face was pulsing, and when I opened the door and heard Artie's voice I knew that the inevitable high-and-mighty routine lecture was most likely in the cards.

"Samuel," he bellowed from his office. "Come in here, son."

Son? My lectures didn't normally start with 'son'.

I inhaled and headed down, half shading my swollen face from view. I heard another murmur and figured he wasn't alone.

"Hey," I mumbled. "What's up?"

"*Hey, what's up?*" Artie imitated. "Samuel, you remember Judge Armelle and Police Commissioner Prince."

Snookered.

"Yes, hello Judge, Commissioner," I nodded, hoping it was a personal visit and not some kind of intervention.

Judge Lance Armelle was Isobel's father and the Supreme Court Judge in South Coast. If there was any high profile case or any issue that was worth anything, he had the final say. Police Commissioner Prince was Harvey Prince and—as it turns out—Elliot's father. If there was anything like royalty in South Coast, these two men were it. Artie liked to consider himself part of the boys' club but unlike the judge and police commissioner, he didn't own his title—he could be knocked off as easily as he was voted in. The fact that Isobel and Elliot were dating was something of a coincidence which suited both Judge Armelle and Police Commissioner Prince. If I likened it to anything it would be like opposing royal families marrying their children to acquire more power. Isobel and Elliot was a match made in social climber's heaven.

"What happened to you?" Artie asked disapprovingly.

"Basketball," I answered. "Did you need me for something? I was about to take a shower."

Artie gave me a stern look that told me I would pay for whatever I'd offended him with this time, later.

"We were just discussing your idea to expand our sporting and recreation facilities and funding here in South Coast," he said abrasively.

"Oh," I nodded. I wasn't sure what it had to do with the police or the justice system but I wasn't about to question him.

"Considering it was your idea, and it seems to be such a passion of yours, I thought you would like to be a part of the planning," Artie said smugly.

This had *payback* written all over it.

"Oh, err…" I frowned. "I don't know if I have the time."

He huffed. "Surely you can give up a few nights a week with Marcus for your city."

Lance and Harvey chuckled.

Apparently this was war.

"It's not Sax—I have training and uni commitments."

"Well, this is disappointing," Artie sighed almost theatrically. "Why don't I give you a couple of days to think about it before you give me your final answer?"

I couldn't see how a couple of days would change anything. "Sure."

I took a step back.

"Big season this year, Samuel," Harvey noted. "Elliot thinks you lot can go all the way."

"Yes, sir," I nodded. "That's the plan."

"And last year it was so close," Lance agreed. "I remember watching it with Isobel from the stands; she was so devastated for you boys. Missing out on the finals in the last ten seconds…"

I laughed bitterly in reminiscence. "I know, brutal."

"Well now, son, why don't you leave the adults to talk?" Artie interrupted, claiming back the limelight.

"Actually, Artie, I should go, I'm already late for dinner with the family," Harvey sighed. "Including your lovely daughter, Lance."

"Ah yes, of course, I remember Isobel mentioning that," Lance nodded.

I found myself nodding along too.

"Well, I might go and take that shower," I smiled tightly. "Judge, Commissioner."

"Good to see you again, Samuel," Judge Lance grinned.

"See you on the field," Commissioner Harvey replied.

I chuckled to myself as I left Artie's office, feeling a strange sense of victory in the exchange. I bet he didn't factor in that his accomplices were as big a football fans as I was. I doubled back through the kitchen and grabbed an icepack from the freezer—something I made sure was always on the ready due to the amount of sport I maintained. My cheek was sure to bruise but I managed to get in a few shots of my own before the team dragged Nate and I apart. At least it put an end to the agony of the three dying minutes left in the monstrosity that was the game.

"Sam," Amelia called from the top of the stairs.

"Hey."

"Paige called," she replied. "She sounded mad."

The punches kept rolling.

"She called here?" I frowned, fossicking through my bag to find my phone. I had four missed calls.

"Oh crap, thanks Millie."

"What's that about?" Amelia asked. I could hear a smile in her voice. "What did you do?"

"Nothing, it wasn't me," I mumbled. "Someone sent this email about us breaking up to everyone on campus."

Amelia laughed and then sobered. "Crap, who?"

"Don't know," I sighed. "I'm getting a shower."

"Okay," she nodded. "How was the rest of your day? What happened to your face?"

"Got into a fight at basketball."

"Not fairing so well today, brother."

I dragged my feet into the bathroom. "That would have to be an understatement."

She giggled, Amelia did that a lot; it reminded me of when she was a kid. "Don't worry, the day's almost over."

"Good, not sure if I can take much more," I smiled, closing the door and reaching for the tap.

My shower was quick despite the fact I needed to wash my hair and my tattoo needed attention. Apparently fresh tattoos sweat ink for the first week and a half, so I decided it was in dire need of disinfectant cream and new gauze. Mission accomplished.

Wednesday evenings didn't only mean basketball, they meant family dinner. Angela tried to ensure that we all ate together Wednesdays and Sundays and of course that suited Artie for happy family perception purposed, though lately we'd missed a lot due to Artie working late on the preparations for the opening of the new entertainment complex. It was a big deal.

"So how was everyone's day?" My mum smiled enthusiastically as she glanced around the table. She'd been the only one not to ask about my puffy face but I suppose she was good at ignoring things that were unpleasant—after all, she'd been married to Artie for over twenty years.

"Good," Amelia answered. "We got back our English essays; I got seventeen out of twenty."

"That's wonderful Amelia," Angela grinned. Amelia was in her final year at South Coast High School; she'd always been good at school—or at least she applied herself at it. I still managed to do pretty well whilst not really bothering much with it. I think that frustrated her sometimes.

"Well that's great Millie," Artie nodded—*Millie* was a nickname Amelia had come up with when she was a baby and couldn't say her name. "At least one child of mine is applying themselves."

I groaned into my mashed potato. Typical.

"Arthur," Angela warned. "I'm sure Samuel is doing his best."

"His best to create more work for everyone else," Artie retorted.

And here it comes.

"You know half of my day was spent trying to fix what *Mr Culture* over here went *on record* saying yesterday?"

"What about the other half?" I mumbled.

51

"I *beg* your pardon?" Artie asked.

"Please," Angela sighed. "Please can we have a civil family dinner without the two of you arguing?"

I shovelled another forkful of peas into my mouth.

"Samuel, what about you honey? How was your day?" she continued.

I shrugged. "Average."

"Average? Why?" Angela asked. "Did you and Paige have a fight or something?"

"Sam and Paige broke up yesterday," Amelia interrupted. "Didn't he tell you?"

"Oh, Samuel, why didn't you say?"

To avoid this discussion. Why couldn't girls understand that guys didn't need to talk everything out?

"Didn't come up," I replied.

Angela frowned. "Paige was such a lovely girl."

Thanks Mum.

"So where did you get to last night then if not with her?" Artie asked almost forcefully, and then rolled his eyes. "Or do I need to ask?"

"Arthur," Angela sighed. "Please."

"You were busy with Alex so I didn't think you'd even notice if I wasn't here," I answered.

Artie stared me down. I didn't blink.

"When did you get in?" he asked.

"Late."

"Or early?"

"Does it matter?" I shrugged. "I didn't wake you, did I?"

"We have a responsibility and a reputation to uphold in South Coast, Samuel," he replied.

"No, *you* have a reputation to uphold," I clarified. "*We* are just along for the ride."

"You, *son,* are a part of this family," he growled. "And you'll do well to remember who supports you and funds your little *fun rides* with Marcus."

"Whatever," I mumbled.

"What's that?" he asked.

I looked him square in the eye. "What. Ever."

I could almost see the blood beneath his reddening skin rise to his ears and steam over.

"Angela!" Artie bellowed. "Do something with your son."

"Samuel," Angela exhaled.

I dropped my fork and stood up. "I'm not so hungry."

"Samuel," she continued. "Please stay."

"I'm not staying just to be lectured by him," I shrugged. "I may be a part of his family but I'm not one of his staff that he can order around. If that's what it means to live here then it's not worth the strings attached."

"You're not moving out, you've got no money boy," Artie scoffed. "Now *sit down* and finish dinner."

He raised his fist and dropped it on the table.

I considered leaving, I wanted to more than anything. But what was it worth?

It was Angela who swayed me, I found it hard to say no to my mother—a woman who was just a casualty, caught in the clutches of King Arthur. She looked up at me with her pleading big brown eyes and I sat back down, folding my arms as everyone returned to their meal.

III

In the Stone

"Paige," I sighed Thursday morning as my phone rang. My voice was thick with sleep after only just waking up; uni didn't start until ten thirty this morning. It was just after nine.

"Have you been screening my calls?" she snapped.

"No."

"Then why weren't you answering?"

"I was busy," I yawned. "What's up?"

"Did you see the email?"

"Yes."

"Well do you know who sent it?"

"No."

"Who did you tell?" she pressed.

"Not the entire campus if that's what you're getting at," I answered. "Did you actually read it?"

"Yes, of course I did!" she said impatiently. "Why do you think I'm calling?"

I sat up. "Well, if you *had* read it, you'll notice it doesn't exactly paint me in a good light. Maybe it was someone *you* told."

"Impossible," she sighed. "I only told Liam."

"Uh-ha, and he doesn't speak to anyone?" I asked.

"What are you implying, Sam?" she said pointedly.

"Maybe you should be speaking to him instead of me," I shrugged. "Was there something else you wanted?"

She exhaled. "Is that it? That's all you've got to say?"

"I don't know what you want me to say, Paige, what's done is done," I replied. "It's not as if we can make everyone unread it. Just let it go."

There was silence.

I took a breath and let it out.

"It sucks for me too, okay?" I answered calmly. "But don't worry, it'll blow over. We're not that interesting."

"Right," she sighed. "Well I've got to go."

I rubbed my eyes with one hand. "Okay."

"Bye."

Dial tone.

I dropped my phone onto my bed and sighed. Thursday. Right. Come at me.

＊

My day didn't seem to improve after Paige's phone call. I'm not one to normally be a downer or pout about the world hating me, when my car wouldn't start and it started to pour with rain, I began to question my existence. Artie had taken his car to the office and Angela was out shopping, so short of calling a cab or hiking to the bus station which was about as far as SCU anyway, I was going to get soaked.

I tried calling Marcus, in case he had a late start, but he was at a job. So I tried Isobel. She didn't answer.

I didn't have a lot of cash left and I hated asking Artie for anything so I just walked.

The rain wasn't too bad but it was enough to soak me through to the bone.

"Saber," a voice called from a slowing car. I squinted through the rain and frowned.

"Prince, hey," I replied. Awesome.

55

"Want a ride?"

"Uh, sure. Thanks."

Elliot pulled over and I waited while he laid out a towel over the luxurious seat covers before he unlocked the doors to let me inside.

"Sorry, the interior is expensive."

I sat down carefully. "Sure."

"Nice day for a walk?" he noted sarcastically, pulling back into the traffic faster than was safe considering the wet weather and his concern for the vehicle.

"Car wouldn't start this morning," I sighed. "Think it's the alternator."

"Don't tell me there's not a better alternative to walking in the rain," he huffed. "You're Artie Saber's son; money is as much an issue for you as it is for me."

"Mm," I nodded. "So how was dinner last night?"

Elliot's dark brows furrowed. "How'd you know about that?"

Whoops.

"Erm, your dad was at mine when I got home yesterday."

"Right," he yawned. "Yeah, it was good."

I nodded and Elliot glanced sideways at me, shaking his head.

"What happened to your face?" he asked.

"Walked into a door."

"Didn't take you for being clumsy," he replied. "But I guess you have been known to trip over your feet on the field."

I don't know where he got that idea; I hardly ever lost my footing. I didn't reply and we drove on for a little while. We weren't far from uni now, thank goodness. Walking in the rain wasn't nearly as uncomfortable as being in the same car as Elliot Prince. I don't know what I was thinking in accepting the ride. I guess I was curious about what Isobel saw in him—and late for class.

"Heard you and the redhead broke up," he said after a moment. I think I preferred the awkward silence.

"Yeah, apparently word gets around fast," I mumbled.

He laughed. "She was a bit moody anyway, you're probably better off."

I frowned in annoyance.

"What you need to do is find someone similar to you, in your own social circle and status. Someone—someone like Isobel. She and I are good together because we're from similar standing."

"Someone like Isobel," I repeated in irony. He'd probably kill me if he could read my mind when I thought about her.

"Yeah, someone who doesn't need me for my wealth."

Is that all she was to him? A convenience who wasn't a gold digger? Was he implying that Paige only wanted me for my status and money? That wasn't true at all. She hated being in the limelight and I lived on a student budget and hardly played a role in Artie's social functions unless I was emotionally blackmailed by Angela into being there.

"You can drop me here," I sighed in relief as the streets of SCU came into view. "My class is in the nursing building."

"Okay," Elliot replied, pulling sharply into the curb. "I'll see you later at practice."

"Yep, thanks for the ride," I nodded, slipping out the seat into the drizzle. I pulled the collar of my damp jacket up and closed the door behind me as Elliot swerved back into the traffic.

I dragged my feet to my class ten minutes late, only to find the tutorial had been cancelled. I cursed under my breath and started heading towards the library. The rain got heavier, I got wetter. It dampened my mood.

When I reached the library, the rain had separated my hair into cord-like spikes that dripped onto my supposedly water-resistant coat. If I wasn't so lazy I'd write to the company telling them what I thought of their product.

I made a quick right once inside and headed down to find a desk to shake out the water lodged in my ears. I got midway down and stopped at one with no one either side and dropped my bag, removed my jacket and flapped my arms around, no doubt splashing water droplets on everyone in a three-metre radius.

"Hey," a few people murmured around me. Whoops.

"Well, hello swordsman," a voice of amusement whispered. "How's the tat?"

I looked up at Sadie who sat two chairs down and smiled. "Healing."

She laughed. "What happened to your face?"

"Your brother."

"Really? Why?"

"You," I shrugged, pulling a chair around to straddle in front of her desk. "Apparently he's not keen on us hanging out."

She rolled her eyes. "Little brothers."

I looked over at the book in her hand. "What are you up to?"

"I've got a gap," she explained, turning the book over to reveal some trashy girl's novel. "Light reading."

I laughed. "Educational?"

"Very," she smirked. "What are you up to? Apart from sharing the rain with everyone?"

"My tute was cancelled so I'm just waiting until it clears up a bit to walk home," I yawned.

She nodded. "That sucks."

"Yep," I sighed. "Want to grab a coffee? Or a bourbon, considering my week so far."

Her eyebrow rose. "And risk another black eye?"

"I can handle Nate."

She closed her book. "Why don't you let me handle him?"

58

I shrugged and stood. "Whatever."

"Lead the way, Saber," she smiled.

I grabbed my bag and coat and we both headed out into the elements. Despite the rocky start, my day was beginning to look up.

***

"So how long have you been seeing your boss?" I asked, leaning back in the chair in a small pub on the corner of one of the several streets that SCU stretched over.

Sadie took a sip of her coffee.

"Not long, like I said we're not exclusive or anything. We more just hook up on occasion. He doesn't want anything serious."

I smiled. "Sounds like a keeper."

"You sound like Nate," she groaned. "He hates Simon."

I made a face.

She rolled her violet eyes. "He's not so bad."

"Who? Nate or your boss?"

"Both," she shrugged. "Either."

I tipped my head. "Each to their own."

She smiled. "So why'd you and the redhead break up?"

"Things just weren't working," I sighed, gulping a mouthful of mocha.

"Why?"

My shoulder lifted. "She didn't seem into it."

"Were you?"

"Yeah," I replied. "I mean I *was*."

She tipped her head. "What changed then?"

I spun the mug in my fingertips. "Nothing—I think that was the problem."

"Did you tell her?"

"Paige never really talked," I frowned. "She talked to Archer but never really to me about stuff."

"Ah Liam," she smiled. "He's sweet."

"So I hear," I grumbled.

She laughed. "So she turned to him, it bothered you but you never told her, and then broke up with her?"

I looked up. "Sounds about right."

"Such a boy," she sighed.

I laughed lightly. "Hey, I tried. I was there for her but she never needed me."

"Sure she did, or she would have broken up with you first," she replied.

I blinked then shook my head. "I don't want to talk about Paige."

Her head tipped, causing her black fringe to sweep across her eyes. "Fair enough."

"So what are you studying?" I asked.

She moistened her full lips. "Business and public relations."

"Cool."

"It's not really as fun as it sounds," she smiled.

"Jobs never are."

"What about you? Politics so you can take after Daddy?"

"Hell no," I laughed. "Mechanical engineering."

"Wow," she nodded. "For real?"

"Yeah, it's not as fun as it sounds," I grinned.

"Touché," she sighed. "So where will that get you?"

"Not sure yet," I shrugged. "I only really did it to get Artie off my back. I'd have preferred to focus on footy or just be a simple motor mechanic. This was the next best thing."

"So now you'll be like a super mechanic."

"Right," I smiled.

She shook her head. "You are a smart boy Samuel Saber."

I huffed as something caught her eye.

"Hey Ruby," she beamed. "Hey Oliver."

"Hey Sadie," the pretty blonde smiled. Linked to her arm was a tanned-looking guy who looked like an athlete. "Who's your friend?"

"This is Samuel Saber," Sadie answered.

"Saber?" Ruby repeated, her artificial blue eyes tracing to me. "As in…?"

"Don't hold that against me," I smirked.

Ruby laughed. "Nice to meet you—this is my boyfriend, Oliver."

"Hey," I nodded.

"How's it going?" Oliver replied, shaking my hand. "Hey, I know you. You play for the Iris Cove Suns, right?"

"Right," I nodded. Cool.

"Yeah, Jason's mentioned you," Oliver said. "Ruby's dad Jason Cobalt works for the RedBacks."

"Yeah, I've heard of him, he's the assistant coach," I answered, feeling a lift of elation. "No kidding, that's your dad?"

Ruby nodded. "So how do you two know each other?"

Sadie smiled. "Sam knows Nathaniel."

"Oh you're friends with Nathan?" Ruby asked.

"I wouldn't go that far," I sighed. "Sadie and I met at Crescent the other night."

Ruby bit her lip. "Oh, right."

"I should go actually, my class starts in ten and it's across campus," Sadie groaned, finishing the remainder of her coffee.

I gulped down my mocha. "I'll walk you; I'm headed in that direction anyway."

"Thanks," she grinned. "You can shield me from the rain."

We stood, said goodbye to Ruby and Oliver, and headed back into the moody weather. Sadie wasn't kidding about her class being across campus, and through dodging the showers and cars she ended up getting there about ten minutes late. She didn't seem fazed.

"Well, swordsman," she smirked. "Thanks for being a gentleman."

"You're welcome milady," I nodded. "Maybe I'll see you around Crescent sometime."

"Probably," she shrugged. "I'm there a lot."

I smiled. "Yeah, Sax likes to go there every Tuesday for cheap beer."

She giggled. "He's so funny."

"He likes to think so."

"You two are cute, kind of like brothers," she noted.

"Mm," I agreed. "Anyway, you'd better get inside or you will've gotten soaked for nothing."

She exhaled. "I suppose. Thanks again for the coffee—and for walking me here."

"Anytime," I nodded. "Take care."

She winked. "Bye swordsman."

I chuckled and turned back to head home. The rain had calmed down some from when I'd left this morning but I didn't expect to get dry anytime soon. I pulled up my collar and stabbed my hands in my pockets, cursing that I'd made the stupid journey in for one class that wasn't even on. And what was up with my car? I'd just given it a once over and now it was playing up again. I didn't think it was the spark plugs or the battery since I'd just replaced them, but the alternator could've died then the car just run off the battery until that eventually went. Crap, I needed a job. I didn't want to keep hitting up Artie for money because, judging by my behaviour recently, it was likely to run out in the very near future. Alternator… stupid electromagnetic device causing all sorts of problems. I only hoped it was that simple.

"Sam, hey," the soft voice murmured, interrupting my reverie.

I looked up and narrowed my eyes. "Hey Isobel. Archer."

"Samuel," Liam nodded. It annoyed me how he said my name. What was she doing with him?

"You're all wet," she frowned. Her perfect lower lip jutting out, I wanted to bite it.

"Yeah, crappy weather."

Her lips pulled in a half smile. "Why are you walking?"

"My car wouldn't start this morning," I shrugged. "I'm about to head home and have a look at it. What are you doing?"

"Actually, we were just going to grab a coffee in the break," she explained, glancing back at Liam cautiously, as if only remembering he was there—or hoping I hadn't seen him. "Um, did you want to join us?"

"No, I just had one, thanks," I replied, continuing walking. So they were an 'us' now.

"Sam," Isobel said, almost in desperation—or maybe that was just wishful thinking.

I stopped, looking through my drenched hair as droplets ran off the daggered ends.

"I'll see you soon then," she whispered.

I gave a nod and continued into the rain, wondering whether it was ever going to stop.

***

The battery was drained thanks to the malfunctioning alternator so I needed to replace that, plus, upon further scrutiny, I discovered that the water pump was broken which caused the head gasket to blow, which had in turn leaked engine oil all through the cylinders. Awesome.

I was elbow-deep in metal when Amelia appeared in the garage doorway.

"Don't you have training tonight, Sammy?" she asked. I could smell the hot chocolate she drank even from there.

"Yes, crap, what's the time?" I grumbled, wiping my hands on an old tea towel I used as a cloth.

"Almost five," she answered, stepping back as I squeezed passed her.

"Thanks."

"Sammy," she called. "How are you getting there if your car's broken?"

I cursed under my breath. "Where's Mum?"

"Out."

"This is not my week," I sighed, taking out my phone, black grease blotching the screen as I thumbed it. "I'll ask Sax to get me on the way."

Typical Marcus, of course he was running late.

"Sure, be there in a few," he replied almost instantaneously.

Crap, I needed to change.

"Thanks Amelia," I breathed, darting inside and up to my room. I tore my clothes off and pulled on my jersey, yanking on my shorts and grabbed my shoes, almost stumbling back down the stairs.

"Son," Artie bellowed, causing me to drop my shoe.

I cursed and picked it up. "Yes?"

"Where are you going?" he asked.

I looked down at my footy clothes then back to him. "Football training."

"Ah," he nodded. "Thursday night."

My eyebrows rose expectantly.

His brow drew. "What's that thing under your arm?"

Crap. The gauze covering the tattoo.

"Uh."

There were two short horn beeps then a long one, as if someone was holding down the horn, then my phone rang. I exhaled at the distraction.

"Is that Marcus?" Artie near growled.

"I should go," I answered, jogging towards the door.

"I'll talk to you later Samuel," he warned.

Swell. "Sure."

"And Samuel, tell Marcus I don't want him behaving like—"

"Later," I called, closing the door behind me. Marcus was laughing from the car as I shook my head, making my way around to the passenger side.

"Dude, you're going to give Artie a stroke from all your crap," I sighed, leaning over to pull on my shoes.

He just laughed. "So what's up with your car?"

"Battery, alternator, water pump, head gasket," I groaned. "I think I need to get a job if I have a prayer of fixing it anytime soon."

"Don't think Artie will foot the bill?" he asked.

"Nuh, I'm not in his good books after the interview," I answered. "He'd sooner give me a company car, he hates the Morris."

"Sacrilegious," he mumbled.

I breathed a laugh.

"Did'ya end up getting to uni all right?" he continued.

I huffed. "Yeah, Elliot drove me."

"Who? Prince?"

"Yep."

"For serious?"

"For serious," I laughed. "Saw me drowning and stopped."

Marcus chuckled. "Well there you go."

"Mm," I nodded. "Made me wait in the rain while he water-proofed his fancy seat covers though."

"That's sounds more like the Prince we know and... well just know," Marcus smirked.

I shook my head incredulously. "I have no idea what she sees in him."

Marcus frowned. "Who? Isobel?"

Crap. I said that out loud.

"Yeah," I shrugged. "She's seems pretty cool but he's a bit of a dick."

"Just a bit," Marcus agreed. "But at least he can kick a football straight."

"Mm."

"Maybe it's the money thing?" Marcus shrugged.

I hated him talking about Isobel like money was the only important thing to her. Sure, it was important to people knowing that they could afford stuff but she wasn't one to pick and choose a guy based on his income—or family income. I didn't think.

"Who knows?" I answered abrasively. I didn't want to talk about Isobel; it only made me think about her with Elliot—then her with Liam. What the heck was going on there? I knew they knew each other, they had some world history class together or something, but coffee?

"When's Macca back?" Marcus asked. "Is he going to make the first game Saturday?"

"Who Louis?" I frowned. "Not sure if this is his in or his out week."

Marcus shrugged.

Training was tough—but the first few training sessions for the season were always tough trying to get back in the swing of things. My body was in royal protest after the late night—early morning pub crawl with Sax, and admittedly I had slowed down on the gym in recent days. I was sure I had a good reason at the time but right now, with the aches in my muscles, I couldn't for the life of me remember.

***

"Pull your socks up Saber! You're struggling out there!" Coach Wesley yelled. He wasn't wrong. Ah crap, this wasn't how it was supposed to go. This was my season.

I stopped midstride and rested my hands on my knees, my breath catching in my throat, tearing my windpipe like a cat's claws down a curtain. My chest was on fire.

"Keep up Saber," Elliot taunted, passing me with laps.

I glanced up and saw Marcus frown at me and dragged my feet to catch up with the team. I powered through the pain, gaining my second wind and managed to finish the laps. By the time Wesley blew the whistle I felt like collapsing—and then did.

"Mate," Marcus sighed, cowering over me. "What's going on?"

I tried to catch my breath. "I'm just knackered."

"From running?" he frowned. "Not like you."

I groaned and he offered me his hand. I took it and he pulled me up.

"Right, that's all for tonight lads, see you Saturday," Wesley bellowed. "Saber, stay behind."

Ah crap.

Marcus patted me on the back as he left and I folded my arms as Wesley paced towards me.

"Sam, bit of an off night, lad?" he asked. I wasn't sure why he posed it as a question; the answer was as obvious as a brunette amongst blondes.

"Sorry."

"Everything okay?"

"Yeah, I'll be fine for Saturday," I nodded.

He frowned. "I'm going to be honest Sam; I've had some sharks circling you, looking to maybe promote you to a senior line-up. I'd hate for a few off days to get in the way of that."

"It wasn't a few days, it's one training session," I replied. "Trust me; I've got this, coach."

Wesley looked at me through a drawn brow then nodded once and I turned to make my way to the locker room. I knew I had stuffed up and the reminder that I couldn't afford to do it again was a harsh but fair awakening. To play for the RedBacks has been my dream and it was my way out from under Artie's iron fist. It was my sword in the stone that would free me and I couldn't—and wouldn't—let anything stand in the way of that.

IV

From the Tree

I got home to find Isobel's blue ribbon tied to a branch overhanging my doorstep. She was here. I waved to Marcus and dropped my bag at the foot of the stairs, heading around the back to the garage where Isobel stood leaning against my Morris Minor which sat naked and in pieces.

"Hi," her soft voice murmured.

"Hey," I sighed. "What are you doing here?"

"I wanted to see you," she shrugged. "You looked a little weird today."

I looked at my car and frowned. "I had a few things on my mind."

She pushed off the metal and wandered over. My head tipped back as her fingers walked up my collar.

"Anything I can do to take your mind off it?"

I exhaled as her cool skin brushed across my face, over my swollen eye.

"Who hurt you?" she pouted. That lip again.

"Nate Blake," I murmured, guessing she meant the black eye—the obvious mark of inflicted pain.

"Why?"

"Doesn't matter," I sighed. "You're not with Elliot tonight?"

She shook her head slowly.

"What about Archer?"

She frowned. "Liam?"

I watched her jewel-like blue eyes flutter with confusion then understanding. "Liam and I are just friends."

"Okay."

"Are you jealous?" she smirked.

"Should I be?" I asked. "Should I be jealous that there's another guy in your life that I have to compete with?"

"Who's competing?" she asked, settling her hands at the back of my neck as she pulled herself up to kiss me. Once her sweet lips met mine, I was in her mercy, under her spell. She had a way about her, a kind of black magic that gave her an unfair advantage over suckers like me. That was evidenced to the line of guys after her.

"He will kill me, you know," I murmured when she pulled back to catch her breath.

Her brow puckered. "I won't let him."

I smiled at her idealism. "He won't let you go without a fight—no-one would."

"I'm not something that he can fight for," she replied. "I'm not some property or country that he can claim."

I dropped my head. "I'm just saying."

"I know," she answered. "But it's between me and him and if there's no me *with* him, there's no us."

I laughed. "I'm going to trust that whatever you said makes sense."

She sighed. "I miss your smile."

"I miss you."

"I know," she nodded. "I'm going to end it with him soon, I just don't want anyone to say I left him for you or he *will* kill you."

I blinked. It was confronting hearing the words come out of Isobel; she was too sweet and innocent to even think of something as gruesome as death.

"Okay, um, thanks I guess."

She kissed me again, her hand slipping to clutch at my shoulder, pulling my body against hers. She pushed against me, my knees hitting the bench behind as I fell back with a groan. She smiled and climbed on my lap.

"Isobel," I sighed, resting my hands on her shoulders. "Don't start something you're not prepared to finish."

She smiled as her fingers laced through my hair like a comb, tipping my head back as her lips lowered to my throat. My eyes closed.

"Samuel?" Angela called.

I cursed.

Isobel sat back. "Is that your mum?"

"It's okay, she never comes in here," I breathed—or more panted.

"Samuel, is that you?"

"Yep, only me," I called back. "Just give me a minute."

"No rush honey," she replied. "Your father just wants to start dinner."

"You can start without me," I answered, rolling my eyes. Isobel tipped her head as her fingers moved from side to side around my collarbone. I caught her hand.

"I'll get Marion to keep your plate warm in the oven," Angela said. "And I'll put your bag inside the door in case it rains again."

"Thanks Mum," I sighed.

There was silence and I exhaled. Isobel smiled.

"Maybe I should go," she whispered.

"No, stay."

"I should go," she pouted, running her hands up my torso. If she was really planning to leave, she wasn't playing fair.

"Are you going tomorrow night?" she asked.

I frowned. "What's tomorrow night?"

"The opening of the entertainment arena," she smiled. "Really, Samuel."

"Oh," I groaned. "Yeah, I'll probably have to then."

"Well I'll be there," she grinned.

My eyebrow rose. "With Elliot?"

She shrugged. "I'll still be there. We can sneak off."

"Lord above," I groaned. "Just leave him already; this is going to end very badly for me otherwise."

Actually, it was going to end badly whether she left him or not—though at least if she did I'd be with her which was better than things were now.

"I know," she nodded. "I'm working on it, promise."

"I don't want to hide anymore," I frowned. "I want to be able to have you stay for dinner with my screwed up family and not have to sneak around in garages or under bridges."

She smiled. "Me too. Even if it is fun sneaking."

"There are better ways to have fun," I answered.

She laughed and stood up from me and I grabbed her wrist.

"Don't go."

"I can't stay."

"But we never got to finish," I sighed.

She smiled and pulled me up to stand. "Next time."

I shook my head. "Never happens."

"I don't want to do that while I'm with Elliot, you know that," she answered, reaching up to move her fingers through my knotted hair.

"So quit teasing me then," I groaned. "It's hard enough without you being so... you."

She laughed. "I didn't mean to get you all riled up."

"Sure you did."

"Maybe a little," she breathed, rising to her tiptoes to kiss me. Her breath was hot and sweet as she sighed against my mouth then stepped back.

"I'll see you tomorrow night then," she said, planting a parting kiss before slipping out the side door.

I exhaled, running my hands through my hair, trying to pull myself together before heading back inside.

"Sammy," Amelia hissed as I pushed open the front door. "You're naughty."

"What are you on about?"

"Isobel is with Elliot," she smirked. "What's she doing sneaking around with you?"

I frowned. "Keep whatever you think you saw to yourself."

"Oh brother," she sighed. "Is that why you broke up with Paige?"

I walked passed her. "Enough, Amelia."

"Son!" Artie bellowed.

I groaned. "Yes?"

"Come here," he demanded.

I dragged my feet into the dining room. "Yes?"

Artie straightened. "Tomorrow night is the opening. You will be there."

I noticed that it wasn't a request.

I shrugged.

"You will also be delivering a speech," he said.

I frowned. "What? Why?"

"Because, son, your enthusiasm was not well demonstrated in the interview Tuesday so you'll make it up to the kind citizens of South Coast at the opening," he answered sternly.

"Why does it matter what I think?" I shrugged. "No one actually cares."

"I care."

Conversation ended.

"Whatever," I groaned.

"Wait!" he snapped. "Come here."

I rolled my head and walked in, folding my arms. "What?"

"I beg your pardon?"

"Is there something else you wanted?" I clarified.

I could almost see the steam coming out of his ears. He stood up and walked over to me, meeting me eye-to-eye then grabbed my wrist, holding up my arm to reveal the bandage.

Oh crap.

"What's this?" he asked, jutting a finger towards it.

"Nothing," I shrugged.

He tore it off. Busted.

"A tattoo?" he fumed.

"Oh, yeah."

"Let me guess," he sniped. "Marcus."

I pressed my lips together.

"I'm banning you from going out with him if this is what kind of influence he's going to have on you," Artie growled.

I laughed and then realised it was the wrong reaction to have. His eyebrows lifted.

"You can't stop me from seeing him," I answered. "And he doesn't influence me; I'm capable of making my own bad decisions."

"Well fine," Artie snapped. "Then you're grounded."

I laughed again. "I'm twenty-one. You can't ground me."

His jaw hardened and I pulled my arm free.

"I'm going to get a shower," I murmured. "I'll do the speech tomorrow night."

It was the least I could do—you're welcome King Arthur. Nothing more was said.

***

Fridays were the greatest because I didn't have class. I did, however, have my work cut out for me with my car and I started my day off trekking to my go-to mechanic, Austin, to see about the multiple parts I'd need to fix her.

"What were you going to start with?" Austin asked, rubbing grease through his scruffy light brown hair. I wondered fleetingly if he noticed.

"Water pump or alternator," I mused. "Probably water pump though since it's quicker."

"Okay, sounds like you've got a plan," he nodded. "Hand me that wrench?"

I placed it in his palm. "Are you the only one here today?"

"Yeah," he sighed to the sound of protesting metal. "Short staffed."

"You need some help?" I shrugged. Maybe this was my answer to earning some money.

Austin straightened. "You serious?"

"You know that I know this stuff," I answered. "I could help out on the smaller jobs if you're worried about liability."

He looked down thoughtfully. "Like an unofficial apprentice."

I laughed. "I know almost as much as you."

"I wouldn't be able to pay you much."

"I'm just looking to fix the Morris so whatever you can offer is more than I've got."

Austin leaned against the car contemplatively.

"Tell you what," he mused. "What if in exchange for your extra hands and know-how, you get free reign of the garage and the parts you need to fix her?"

"For real?"

"You'd have to work for it though," he replied. "To cover the costs."

"Done. When do I start?"

"What are you doing today?" he smirked.

I grinned. "Put me to work."

It was pretty awesome to work in the garage fixing stuff with everything I needed at my fingertips. Austin was a cool guy and decent company too; he wasn't complicated like most people, didn't buy into all the politics I was normally surrounded by. For a twenty-eight-year-old, he was someone who I aspired to be like. Living the life he wanted on his own terms—everything made sense to him so long as he had oil under his nails and grease in his hair.

Another thing I liked about him is he didn't ask questions. Straight up. Not that a lot of my friends did, I mean guys don't dwell on the deep and meaningful like girls do, but Marcus knew me too well. Even if he didn't ask, sometimes he didn't need to, but I could see the curiosity burning behind his eyes.

"Solid effort today mate," Austin nodded, patting me on the back. "I'll organise a tow for your car so we can work on it here. When can you come in next?"

"Tuesdays and Thursdays after uni and Friday all day is normally good for me," I shrugged.

He smiled. "See you Tuesday then."

I walked home in the light rain feeling the water mix with the sheen of oil on my skin, resigned to the fact that all the soap in my house probably wouldn't get rid of it—kind of like when you break a glass in the kitchen and still find shards years later.

"Samuel, honey, where have you been today?" Angela asked as I sauntered into the kitchen in search of food. "What are you covered in?"

"Um…" I mused, looking around before eventually grabbing an apple. "I've been working with Austin today. That's probably engine oil."

My mother's brows lifted. "Engine oil?"

"I got a job, I guess," I shrugged. "Helping Austin in the garage."

She blinked. "A job?"

"Yeah, pretty cool, huh?" I smiled.

Angela frowned. "Working in a garage?"

"Did Sammy just say he got a job?" Amelia asked, walking through to grab a bottle of water from the fridge. "Like work?"

I wondered if I was still speaking English—or maybe the mention of manual labour was a foreign concept around here considering we had someone on our payroll to cover all the tough jobs.

"Why is that such a shock to everyone?" I frowned.

Angela and Amelia exchanged a look that made me feel like I was missing something.

"What?" I asked, rubbing the apple on my chest.

"Honey, I know what your father will say about you working in a garage," Angela answered.

"Are you kidding? He's always telling me to take responsibility for myself," I replied, taking a bite. "That's just what I'm doing."

Amelia smirked.

Angela shook her head. "No honey, I mean you were only just saying to him that you couldn't help with promoting sports in South Coast because you were too busy, and then you get a job?"

"Oh," I sighed. "Well, don't tell him."

"Samuel," she warned. "I won't keep secrets from your father."

Amelia pulled a face I wasn't sure I was supposed to see. If I remembered I'd ask her later what it was about.

"Just let me talk to him first okay?" Angela sighed. "Why don't you go and take a shower. Arthur will be home soon and he's anxious enough about tonight without you looking like a grease monkey."

I gave a nod and wandered up to get clean and found a dinner suit laid out on my bed. Great. From grease monkey to monkey suit. Sometimes I hated being Artie Saber's son.

***

It didn't take me long to get ready but I ended up getting distracted with texts from Isobel so was the last one to join Artie, Angela and Amelia in the entrance before we all headed out to the limousine to take us to the opening. I actually hated arriving in a limo; it was far too Hollywood for me and tended to give Artie more of a celebrity complex than was warranted for a politician.

"Here, memorise it," Artie murmured, handing me a wad of cards as we drove. I took them and glanced down at the speech that had been written for me about how wonderful the entertainment complex is and tried not to roll my eyes. There was no way I was going to memorise it and he knew that—I couldn't even remember what I'd eaten for breakfast this morning.

"Couldn't you have done something with that black eye?" Artie scolded. "For goodness sake, son, you look like a thug."

"In a thousand-dollar suit?" I scoffed. "Lucky thug."

"Samuel," Angela warned.

I looked back to the cards. *Good evening acclaimed guests and fellow South Coast citizens...* oh for the love of all that is—

"Samuel?"

I looked up. "Huh?"

"Here's some concealer for your eye," Angela said, holding out some powder attached to a mirror.

"What? I'm not wearing make-up, you've got to be kidding," I answered. "Sorry Mum, but no."

She sighed, closing the lid. I wondered if she actually thought I'd take her up on the offer but could see resignation in her face.

Amelia was snickering into her palm.

The silver limousine pulled up against the curb outside the entertainment arena, an extravagantly sleek and futuristic style building positioned in the heart of South Coast City. I still wasn't convinced that it was necessary at all—South Coast had a perfectly fine old theatre with miles more character than this thing. Nevertheless, apparently it was what the people wanted; who was I to deny them that? It was well designed, I suppose. The *Freeze Frame* architect had done a good job.

I still couldn't understand why photographers cared about us—why everyone cared—but we arrived to the same bright flashes and fake smiles as always, and show time began.

"What's Liam Archer doing here?" I asked Amelia as we were ushered through the door.

"His mum is the caterer, I guess he's helping out," Amelia shrugged, looking over at him appraisingly. I made a face and looked back to him—he was wearing black pants and a white shirt, like the other waiters, like the redhead girl standing beside him... like Paige standing beside him.

"What is Paige doing here?" I hissed.

Amelia looked up and frowned. "Guess she's helping too."

Great.

Artie stood up in front of the crowd and said his bit, cut the ribbon and smiled for the masses before stepping down.

"You're up, son," he murmured.

I glanced at him and rose to the podium. "Um, hi everyone, I'm Samuel Saber."

Artie cleared his throat and I glanced back at him as he nodded pointedly towards the cards in my hand. Right, don't improvise the speech.

I looked down and sighed. "Good evening acclaimed guests and fellow South Coast citizens…"

***

"Nice speech," Marcus smirked after all the pleasantries, as the food started circulating. I gave him a look and reached for a *hors d'oeuvre*.

"Not that one Sammy, try the quiche," Marcus interrupted.

I frowned and picked up the quiche and the waiter disappeared.

"Thanks for coming, Sax," I mumbled. "At least it makes it a little more bearable."

He chuckled. "I'm surprised Artie let me in—how'd you swing that?"

"I made a call and got you on the list," I shrugged. "If anyone asks you're a distant cousin."

He laughed and reached out for a drink as another waiter passed. "Well this is South Coast, anything is possible."

"Hey, did I tell you I've figured a way to fix the Morris?" I said, taking a glass from the extended silver tray.

"No, how?"

"I'm working for Austin a couple of days a week," I replied. "He's going to let me fix her up and get the parts in exchange for helping out."

"Awesome," he nodded. "What does Artie think of that?"

I shrugged and Marcus laughed.

"You haven't told him."

"Nope."

He laughed. "The mayor's son doing manual labour, alert the media."

"Shut up Sax," I mumbled, taking a sip of the wine. I cringed at the rancid acidic taste and put the glass down on a table beside me.

"Up for something a little stronger?" Elliot asked, sauntering up to us.

I raised an eyebrow. "What did you have in mind?"

"Thought we'd start the after party early at my family's beach house," he shrugged.

"Does the police commissioner know that?" Marcus asked. "Or coach? I'm sure he'd be pleased if we all rock up hung-over tomorrow morning."

Elliot laughed. "Can't hold your liquor, Saxon?"

Isobel appeared beside Elliot and he put his arm around her, pulling her recklessly against his side. Isobel made a quiet noise of complaint that made me want to rip Elliot's arm from its socket.

Marcus cleared his throat and finished off the glass of cola he held, placing it on a passing tray that belonged to Paige.

"Oh, hello Marcus," she murmured.

"Paige, hi," he answered as he gave a sideways glance at me. I reached back to the wine I'd set down and took another sip, choking as I swallowed.

Isobel took the glass from me and smiled.

"So? What do you say, Saber?" Elliot asked. I'd forgotten he was still waiting for an answer.

I frowned. "I can't leave yet, my dad will go spare."

"Yes Elliot, can't we just stay for a while longer?" Isobel pouted. "I'm rather enjoying myself."

"Fine," Elliot sighed, pushing her away before leaving.

Isobel exhaled and took a mouthful of the wine as I shot her a private smile.

"So, how are you, Paige?" Marcus was saying. She was still standing here?

She bit her lip. "Fine. Is everything okay here?"

"Yes, thank you," Isobel answered.

I glanced up at her. "You wouldn't happen to have any bourbon out the back there by any chance?"

Paige's brow twitched. "I'll check with Liam."

"Liam?" Isobel frowned. "Do you mean Liam Archer?"

I gritted my teeth.

"Yes, Liam Archer," Paige nodded. "Excuse me."

I watched her go and exhaled.

"Should you really be drinking during the football season?" Isobel asked, tipping her head cutely.

I shrugged. "Probably not."

"Shouldn't you really be lecturing your boyfriend instead of us?" Marcus countered. "He's the one encouraging it."

I fleetingly wondered how Elliot would take it if Isobel was to take Marcus' advice. Her dainty shoulders lifted.

"I'm just saying," she murmured, taking another sip of the wine. How she could drink it was beyond me, it was horrible stuff. I'd prefer to drink battery fluid.

"Ease up, Sax," I sighed.

Marcus shrugged and walked away, heading in the direction of the toilets. I glanced back to Isobel.

"Sorry about him."

"He's not wrong," she replied. "You look very handsome tonight."

I smiled. "And you look like a princess."

She blushed, brushing her cheek on her shoulder.

"Hey, Saber," Elliot interrupted, literally appearing out of nowhere. He draped his arm around Isobel, nearly crushing her with the bottle he held and set two shot glasses down on the high table beside us.

"Fancy a shot?" he asked, taking the bottle from the arm around her to pour the liquid into the glasses. "While your keeper is away."

I saw Paige walk up from the corner of my eye and reached towards the shot as Elliot took the other one between the fingers of his free hand.

"On the count of three," he smirked. "Two."

"Sam, don't," Paige warned.

"It's fine," I groaned. Why won't everyone just leave me alone? Her hand gripped my wrist as I lifted the glass.

"No, it's not."

"Leave him alone red, he's a big boy now," Elliot chuffed.

I looked at Paige and her eyebrows lifted. "Don't."

Her hand dropped as she shook her head. I looked back to Elliot, ignoring her protest—ignoring her warning and not stopping to question the concern.

"One," Elliot finished, throwing the caramel coloured liquid back with his head. I mirrored the motion, smelling the hazelnut as the liquor touched my lips, circulating my mouth and searing down my throat. I dropped the glass, feeling my wind passage swell as I folded, my lungs collapsing within me making me choke as it tried to eject the oxygen I craved. I fell to my knees with the spasm of my abdomen, the liquid knocking over the dominos in my body as it made its dangerous course though my system.

"You really are an idiot Sam—it's Frangelico," Paige murmured, dropping to her knees beside me. "Where's your EpiPen?"

"Don't... have," I choked, wheezing for breath.

She reached behind her to grab something small and black— her bag maybe, I couldn't really see as my face began to swell and the bitterness rose in my throat, threatening to surface. I heard her exhale then felt a stabbing to my thigh and a click, gasping as the epinephrine shot through my veins.

I coughed, swallowing back the bile and clutched at my abdomen, pulled myself up to sit and she slammed something into my chest with more force than was necessary—it was an EpiPen.

"I meant to give this back," she said through gritted teeth. "You're really stupid, Sam."

"Thanks," I gasped, not sure whether I was annoyed at her anger or relieved that she'd just saved my life.

She shook her head and walked away, her red hair flowing behind her like a cape.

"You all right Saber?" Elliot laughed, leaning to slap me on the back. I felt like I was going to be sick.

"Yep," I coughed.

"Lightweight."

"Nut allergy," Marcus interrupted. "You are an *idiot* Sammy."

"Shut up Sax."

Marcus glared at Elliot. "Are you trying to kill him?"

Elliot scoffed. "Ease up Saxon, I didn't know he was deathly allergic."

I lifted my hand to look at it, noticing the reddish rash through the tremor. Marcus grabbed it and pulled me up.

"Come on, enough for you," he murmured.

I clutched at my head—it felt as if it was increasing in size by the second.

"You're leaving?" Isobel frowned.

"Apparently."

"Let him go, princess," Elliot sighed. "We can have our own party."

My jaw clamped shut as the nausea rose, I would not be sick in front of them. Marcus draped my arm over his shoulder and began walking me swiftly to the exit.

"What is wrong with you?" Marcus groaned.

I exhaled. "I have a tree nut allergy which makes me go into anaphylaxis."

He opened his car door and stuffed me in, disappearing to grab something from the back tray and thrust a bucket under me.

"Exactly," he snapped. "So why are you trying to kill yourself to try and impress that douche?"

"I'm not trying to impress anyone," I grumbled.

Marcus slammed the door shut and took his place in the driver's seat, barely starting it before he was accelerating out of the park.

"You're just lucky Paige was there with your EpiPen," he muttered. "You're really, really stupid Sam."

I sighed. "So everyone keeps saying."

I lurched forward, finally throwing up as it burnt up my throat. I could feel my heart palpitating and cursed the side effects of the shot of epinephrine. Sure, if just saved my life but I felt as if I was going to have a heart attack.

Marcus made a quick turn, speeding down the dark street.

"Where are we going?" I groaned.

"Hospital, you just stopped breathing," Marcus said sternly before muttering a string of expletives under his breath.

The doctor in emergency kept me in observation overnight. An overreaction and overcautious decision on his part since in the past I'd only required between four and six hours of medical babysitting and oxygen. So it was a complete waste of a night all because my usual allergy doctor, Dr Frost, wasn't there and wasn't answering their calls. Thanks, doc. Aces.

Marcus stayed with me for a while but ended up leaving a little after midnight. It had been a long day for him and I told him to go and rest up for our first game of the season tomorrow. I hoped no one would tell Wesley about my episode so he'd let me play still but I wasn't optimistic.

I still felt nauseous and my head was pounding but I managed to get some sleep, though South Coast Memorial Hospital was notoriously busy because it was the main public hospital in town. If I had any sense I would have told Marcus to take me to Iris Cove Private Hospital because at least that was a little quieter.

Angela picked me up early on the Saturday morning in one of the company cars and I could see the concern and disapproval in her expression as we rode home in silence. I took a shower right away, changing out of my dinner suit from the night before and into my team colours, and waited for Marcus to come by and pick me up on the way to the game.

"Better?" he asked. His tone was light and normal—the best thing about guys is that we don't tend to hold grudges for the trivial things; we can't be bothered.

"Yep."

"Think Wesley will let you play?"

I shrugged. "Hope so."

"Me too."

When we got to the oval, Wesley told me to make myself comfortable on the bench thanks to Elliot who had expressed his concerns as captain about my condition following last night. I told him I was fine—that it wasn't the first time it had happened and that I was discharged from the hospital with a clean bill of health. Wesley said he'd consider it depending on how we went because he'd prefer I miss one game than half the season. I wondered if he actually understood what having an allergy meant.

At half time, we were down by two goals and I was chomping at the bit to get a run. Finally my voice was heard and I was sent out in the second half, feeling a little winded but pushed through the burn in my chest. We ended up winning three-two.

"Sammy!" Louis 'Macca' McKenzie howled excitedly. "You little ripper!"

I rested my hands on my knees as the siren sounded and our team song bellowed through the speakers around the ground, almost drowned by the cheering crowd.

I could hardly breathe having only just scored the winning goal in the dying seconds of the game and was suddenly knocked off my feet by my teammates as they piled on excitedly, showing their appreciation in a way I didn't quite appreciate.

Elliot kept his distance, not sharing his joy of our first victory of the season—but somehow that made it all the more sweet. I wasn't sure what I'd ever done to him to make him standoffish of me, well, apart from sneaking around with his girlfriend, but arguably he didn't know about that. I didn't much care though; it was easier to be with Isobel knowing she was with someone who wasn't exactly a stand-up guy. Can't say that made it suck any less when she met him with open arms outside our change rooms after the game—or the way her forget-me-not blue eyes cut through me as she did.

"I'm starving," Marcus groaned. "Lunar? My shout?"

Louis looked at me in disbelief. "Won't say no to that—Sax never offers to pay."

I breathed a laugh. "Sounds good."

"Just for that Macca, you can pay for yourself," Marcus retorted.

Louis huffed.

Marcus slapped my shoulder with more force than necessary as he steered me towards his car. I glanced back at Isobel as we left and nearly turned back as Elliot shrugged her off, pulling his hand away as she tried to hold it. She looked at me and turned away, heading after him in the opposite direction.

V

Of Your Own Medicine

Before I opened my eyes, I already regretted the day ahead of me. As awareness seeped back to me slowly I began to feel the pulse of my sore, heavy limbs that felt as if they had been implanted with diving weights.

My head felt like it was in a clamp with someone pounding rhythmically on my temples and I was pretty sure that opening my eyes would cause a decent amount of pain, which would only add to the throbbing sensation I currently felt. What happened last night? How did lunch at Lunar turn into the most monumental of hangovers? I couldn't for the life of me remember.

"Oi Sam, you're lying on my arm," Louis' croaky voice mumbled.

I groaned and willed myself to roll over, feeling him yank his arm out from beneath me.

"How much did you let me drink last night?" I grumbled.

"How much did *I* let you drink? One beer," he sighed. "How much did you *actually* drink? A few pubs dry."

I groaned and rolled to my stomach to avoid the dull sunshine I could make out behind my closed lids. As the movement jostled my frame, my insides churned, swishing around whatever poison I'd ingested—and it certainly *felt* like a few pubs' worth.

"I think I'm going to be sick," I moaned, patting for the side of the bed. Once I found it I dragged myself over to the edge just in time for the acidic liquid to upsurge, burning its way up my oesophagus.

"*Sam*-uel," Louis complained.

I choked and wiped my mouth. "Oh God, I'm never drinking again."

He chuckled once. "I'd believe that more if it was the first time you'd said it."

I groaned and sat up, cringing away from the light that seemed too bright in the small room.

"Where are we?" I asked, looking around curiously. I didn't recognise anything.

"Uh, that black-haired waitress' place," he answered. "Remember?"

I clutched at my head and rolled over. "No."

Louis laughed. "Geez Sam."

"What?" I murmured, sounding like a chain smoker. "Err, what waitress?"

Louis yawned. "Now *that* I'm surprised you don't remember."

I frowned, thinking back through the muddy memories of the night before. Waitress... waitress... oh he must mean Demi. Ohhh crap.

I smacked my hand to my chest and felt down my body. I was missing my shirt but I was still wearing my pants. Well, nights had ended worse with Marcus and Louis.

"Sammy?" Marcus' voice slurred. "What's that smell?"

"Sam spewed," Louis answered.

I blinked slowly wondering where Marcus' voice was coming from. "Sax, where are you?"

"Here," he replied and I saw his hand flapping around beside Louis' side of the bed. I couldn't help but feel relieved that he wasn't on my side or that smell might be a lot worse.

"Morning all—oh, ew," a female voice said as a shadow appeared in the doorway. I half rolled to see Demi. At least I remembered her—though given we'd gone to Lunar I wasn't giving myself too much credit for that.

"Sorry about your carpet," I groaned.

"It was you?" she asked and then tipped her head. "Can't say that I'm surprised, I've never seen anyone drink so much in my life."

Marcus chuckled. "He is the heavyweight champion."

"And you're the lightweight champion, Sax," Louis joked.

I groaned. "My head is pounding."

"Got any food Demi?" Marcus asked, hoisting himself up on the side of the bed. Louis gripped onto the comforter to keep from falling off.

Demi thrust a thumb behind her. "There is black coffee and raisin toast in the kitchen."

"Sweet," he sighed, rising to his feet and crawling across the bed. I groaned as it jostled and clutched at my head. Everything hurt and everything felt like it was going to start oozing from my pores. My stomach lurched again as Marcus bounced off and slid passed Demi to the kitchen.

"Food sounds good," Louis mumbled, rolling over. I groaned as the bed shook again and Louis sidestepped my vomit to follow Marcus out of the room. I peeked around at Demi and closed my eyes again, hoping the opportunity for more sleep would present itself given the departure of the others.

"Can I get you anything?" Demi asked. I felt the mattress beneath me shift and opened my eyes to see her sitting beside me. She reached over and brushed a piece of my hair behind my ear and if my body wasn't pinned to the bed in weakness, I might have dismissed the gesture.

"No," I croaked. "Thanks."

"Water? Coffee?" she offered. "A shower?"

I closed my eyes and exhaled—a shower sounded good but I didn't have the energy to move. I guess that's what people referred to as opportunity cost.

"I could give you a sponge bath?" she mouthed by my ear.

"You know, a shower sounds good," I murmured, clutching my head as I tried to sit up.

"Do you want me to join you?" she asked.

I frowned. "Nuh, I'm right."

She smiled as I moved towards the corner of the bed and exhaled, feeling a sense of motion sickness wash over me.

"Where's the bathroom?" I sighed.

"Just off the bedroom," she answered, nodding towards a door I hadn't noticed before. "Do you need help walking?"

I shook my head—bad idea. "Just give me a sec."

She smirked. "Maybe next time you should pace yourself."

"Yep," I groaned, standing up slowly. It was harder than a marathon to walk the five or so metres to the bathroom and once inside, I leaned against the shower door as Demi reached in to start it.

"Do you need me to finish undressing you?" she asked, sounding as if she was trying to be alluring. It was a wasted effort.

"Nuh, I'll be right now," I mouthed.

She shrugged. "It's not as if I haven't seen it before."

"Uh ha," I mumbled, stepping under the water flow in my jeans. It was freezing cold, a result of frozen winter pipes, and I struggled for the hot tap, though it seemed to be colder—if that was even possible. My body shuddered as I cringed away from the chill, making me feel sicker than I already did.

I saw Demi hesitating by the door and frowned as she turned back towards me.

"You don't remember last night, do you?"

I blinked. "Erm, not really."

91

She shook her head as blood rushed to her cheeks. "Wow, I feel stupid."

I watched her as the words seemed to sink in slowly, like a drop of wax on a sponge, and realisation struck me like lightning—suddenly all the offers of help made sense.

"Oh crap," I groaned. "Did we…?"

Demi's eyebrows rose. "*Oh crap?* Gee, thanks Sam."

I tipped my head back in the water.

"I'm sorry," I groaned. "I didn't mean how that sounded. I just…"

She smiled and it looked broken. "It's not me."

I looked at her sadly and shook my head.

"She's a lucky girl," Demi answered quietly. "I guess it was her who called last night."

I nearly choked. "What?"

"Right, you don't remember," she sighed. "You took a call at Lunar before we left to go out clubbing. You seemed pretty upset when you came back."

I ran my hands through my wet hair and tried to think. Isobel. Isobel. I did have a feeling I'd spoken to her but I couldn't remember what was said.

"I was upset?" I frowned.

"Yeah," she huffed. "You seemed keen to forget something after that."

I sighed. "I'm really sorry Demi. I didn't mean to…"

"Yeah," she breathed, turning to leave. She pulled the door closed and I dropped my head, owning the pounding ache it brought with it because it was the least I deserved. I mentally took back thinking that nights had ended worse with Marcus and Louis because waking up and *not remembering* being with a girl and not even being able to walk properly to commence a walk of shame was pretty bad even for me. I wasn't normally the guy who did stuff like this. That was usually Louis' thing since he was away so much. Not me. What had happened with Isobel to make me lose the plot? I wished now more than ever that I remembered so I could add it to my list of regrets for the past twenty-four hours—or heck, forty-eight hours.

Demi returned my shirt to me which she'd apparently hung out to dry since it ended up drenched in spirits. I was too afraid to ask how it got that way so just thanked her and headed out to Marcus' ute in my dripping jeans.

"Couldn't remember how to unbutton pants, Sam?" Louis asked, cocking an eyebrow. "You seemed to do all right last night."

"Shut it Macca," I groaned.

Marcus pursed his lips. "You're not getting in my car like that, you'll wet the seats."

"Geez Sax, you sound like Prince," I grumbled, walking to the tray to climb up. Marcus and Louis exchanged a look of amusement.

"You're riding in the back?" Marcus asked. "Of my ute? In the back of my ute with my tools?"

"He'll fit in then," Louis laughed.

I shoved the leveller over and squeezed in. "Beats walking."

"You're a dope."

"Shut up and drive, Sax," I yawned. "I'm probably in enough trouble already."

Marcus sighed and climbed in the car as I pulled over the cover to conceal me from sight—and anything else I should be hiding from that I didn't remember.

***

When I got home, the house was quiet but that didn't mean anything at the Saber estate. Artie preferred it that way so he could squash anything that threatened his peace. Guess that was me today.

"Son," his voice bellowed as I kicked the door closed. The thud it made echoed through my middle ear and into my brain, squeezing it tight. I dragged my wet jeans into the door of the study and waited.

Artie took pause from his papers to glance at me. "How was the game yesterday son?"

"Yeah, really good," I answered. "Coach almost wasn't going to let me play but at half time we were down by two so he ended up letting me have a run."

There was a pause then Artie looked up. "Well done then."

I frowned—well done what? Was he even listening? Why did parents do that? Ask a question then not care about the answer? Was it their way of just filling a pleasantry quota or proving that they care, just not enough to spend another twelve seconds to drive it home?

"Yeah, right," I grumbled, walking away. Sometimes I wondered why I even bothered. I knew what he was like—why even open myself up for it? Oh right, because I'm his son.

I headed upstairs to brush my teeth then went straight to my room, prying off my clinging soaked jeans and alcoholic T-shirt and kicked them to the corner before crawling into bed. If I could, I would stay here all day—though even I knew better than to expect that.

My door flew open after what felt like a minute and a half but my clock said I'd been dozing for a couple of hours.

"Sammy, where have you been?" Amelia's shrill voice demanded.

I groaned. "Go away."

"Samuel, seriously," she screeched.

I wrapped my pillow around my head then felt it being ripped away.

"Geez Amelia—what!?" I spat.

"Mum has been looking for you," she replied sharply. "You didn't come home yesterday and she was worried since you spent Friday night *in the emergency department.*"

"I'm fine," I grumbled, snatching my pillow back. "Now leave me alone."

I closed my eyes but didn't hear movement. When I opened them she was still there—all judgemental with her arms folded.

"What?" I groaned. "Why won't you leave me alone?"

"I was worried Sammy," she pouted. "You weren't answering your phone; I thought something had happened to you."

I frowned at her jutting lower lip. I hated seeing my sister upset, especially when I was the cause. It looked like I was disappointing people all around this week.

"Naw Millie," I sighed, sitting up. "I'm fine, really."

She looked down. "You should have answered."

I looked around me for my phone and realised I hadn't seen it since—since when?

"I don't actually know where my phone is," I sighed, rolling out of bed. I walked passed her to find my footy bag and pried it open. Sure enough it was tucked in one of my boots.

"Oh crap," I groaned, glancing at the twenty-five missed calls and eight text messages I had. "I'm really sorry Amelia."

Amelia and Angela's attempts accounted for around twenty of the calls and three of the messages. The rest were from Isobel. Man, I was in trouble.

"Don't do that again, Sammy," Amelia murmured. "Seriously, you're a complete idiot."

I seem to be hearing that a lot lately.

"Sorry Millie, really."

She pressed her lips in a tight smile and headed for the door.

"Where were you anyway?" she asked.

I scratched my cheek. "Sax and Macca—"

"Say no more," she groaned, walking out the door. "You need to find more responsible friends, Sammy."

I almost wished I could blame them but this was all on me. I leaned over and nudged my door closed before heading back to bed with my phone. Isobel hadn't left any voicemails so I began flicking through the five texts from her:

"Sam, I'm sorry for what I said, you were right. Please answer your phone—we need to finish our conversation. Ix."

"I didn't mean how it sounded before. I really do want to be with you. I'm sorry, okay? Call me. Ix"

"Sam, why are you dodging my calls? Please talk to me. I don't like how we left things. Ix"

"If this is you trying to teach me something then it's not working. I'm trying to apologise to you and you're being really childish in avoiding me."

"Seriously, please call me. I need you Sam. You know I do. Ix"

I sighed. Whatever passed between us, clearly it ended badly—which would explain why I wanted to drink South Coast dry.

I hit the reply button. *"Hey, clearly we need to talk. I'm home if you want to come around or I can meet you somewhere. Let me know. SS."*

I barely had the chance to rub my forehead when I got a reply. *"Give me ten minutes. I'll meet you in the usual spot. Ix."*

The bridge.

I fished some jeans off my floor that looked relatively fresh and a clean white T-shirt and dressed, stepping into my shoes and nudging them on as I strode down the stairs on my way out.

"Heading out Amelia," I called for good measure, grabbing an apple I'd eat on the way. "Got my phone."

"All right Sammy," she replied from upstairs. I didn't even bother with Artie.

I arrived at the bridge in just over fifteen minutes to find Isobel's blue fully restored 1978 Lancia Beta coupé parked and empty. I kind of dug her car—it had character. It definitely wasn't the type of car you'd expect for the princess of South Coast but Judge Armelle was a car enthusiast so she grew up going to car shows. Another completely hot thing about her was her know-how of cars—as if she wasn't already the perfect girl.

"Sam," she called, appearing by the pearly-looking bridge. It was cloudy again today, making the silver concrete look almost white.

"Hey," I replied, heading over to her. "Thanks for meeting me."

She shrugged. "Thanks for finally replying to me."

I shook my head. "Sorry about that, I misplaced my phone."

"You had me really worried," she frowned, stepping forward to hug me tight. "I thought I'd lost you."

"Lost me?" I repeated. "Why?"

"You were so angry when you hung up on me," she pouted. "I'm really sorry for what I said."

I pulled back to look at her. "Look, to be honest, I got a bit hammered last night after we spoke—"

"This is all my fault," she sobbed, running her hands through her long brown hair. "I wish I could have explained myself better but you know I get sensitive about Elliot. I know he cares about me in his own way even if he doesn't always show it, but I shouldn't have said what I said."

"What did you say?" I asked.

"You know, about Paige? I didn't mean that you never cared for her, I just mean that it was different between you two because like you said she never really needed you," she explained. "But

Elliot needs me in his own way so just walking away from him isn't as easy for me."

"You think that it was easy for me to leave Paige?" I frowned.

She sighed. "I don't want to fight—"

"Because it wasn't," I interrupted. "You know as well as anyone that I cared about her; I wished I could've been that guy for her but I wasn't."

"I know," she sighed. "And *you are* that guy for me."

I exhaled. "So what's the problem then?"

"Why are you trying to simplify this? It's not that simple."

"Why are you making it complicated?"

"Because it is complicated."

"No it's not—he doesn't care about you, Isobel," I groaned. "Why can't you see that? He treats you like a trophy, like some kind of possession; you're just another achievement to him."

She recoiled. "No I'm not—he doesn't, stop saying that."

Oh, so apparently this was the conversation we'd had last night.

"Are you kidding me right now?" I asked. "You can't tell me you don't see it."

She shook her head more out of stubbornness than disagreement.

"When have I ever pushed you away?" I pressed. "When have I ever spoken to you the way he does? Or dragged you around like some rag doll? When have I ever made you feel like you're not more important than some game?"

"Football is important to Elliot," she sighed.

"It's important to me too," I answered. "But I would give it up for you."

"I'd never ask you to give it up."

"I know," I nodded. "But I would."

She looked down, stepping forward to wrap her arms around my neck as she nestled her face into my collar.

"I hate fighting with you," she murmured against my skin. I felt the hair rise on my arms from her warm breath.

"I know, me too."

She sniffled. "I will leave him, I promise. I just need to pick it right."

"It's never going to feel right," I replied. "Breaking someone's heart never does."

"I wish I had known you first," she breathed, peering up at me with her gemstone blue eyes. "Then it wouldn't be this hard."

"Yeah, things would definitely be simpler if it happened that way," I nodded.

She pulled herself up to kiss me and her lips seemed to send a fire through my entire body.

"So you were out with Marcus and Louis last night," she said—she was probably the only one who called them both by their first names. "Did you have fun?"

I frowned at the blurry memory. "Not so much."

"Because of me?" she pouted.

"Because I drank too much," I replied honestly. "And I don't remember a lot of it."

"I don't want to lecture you but I don't think you should drink as much as you have been lately," she whispered.

"I don't disagree with you on that one," I sighed, my mind wandering back to Demi. I should probably tell her but I didn't know how she'd take it. Did it really matter? She was with Elliot and they were together all the time—plus the whole thing, whatever it was with Demi, didn't actually mean anything because I didn't even remember it.

I felt my forehead pucker.

Isobel blinked. "Is something wrong?"

"No—well maybe—I don't know," I answered, scratching my brow. "I think I have to tell you something and I think... I just don't want you to get mad with me, okay?"

"Mad? What do you mean, Sam? What is it?" she asked. "Did something happen?"

I exhaled. "That's just it; I don't remember but... apparently it did."

"I don't understand."

"I slept with someone last night," I murmured. The words were harder to hear than they were to say—I'd slept with someone else, someone who wasn't Isobel.

She took a step back and folded her arms. "You—you slept with someone?"

I knew she'd heard me so I didn't reply.

She breathed out. "Who? Paige?"

"Paige? No," I frowned. "No, she's just a waitress. I don't even remember it."

"Then how do you know you did it?" she asked.

"She told me," I replied. "I don't think she'd lie about something like that."

Isobel scoffed. "You're Sam Saber, of course she would."

I cleared my throat. "Okay."

"Why?"

"Why what?"

"Why did you do it?"

"I told you, I don't remember," I shrugged. "I was really drunk—like really drunk. Like, I don't even remember talking to you—drunk."

She frowned. "Okay."

"Okay?"

"Okay," she nodded. "What do you want me to say?"

I lifted my shoulders. "I don't know, I just thought you'd want to know."

"Why?" she asked. "We're not dating. You can do what you want—or who you want."

I sighed. "You're mad."

"I'm not mad," she snapped.

I rolled my eyes. "Yes, you are."

"No I'm not," she said, beginning to pace. "Why would I be mad? You break up with your girlfriend and say you want to be with me then sleep with the next slag to batt her eyes at you."

"Geez Isobel, it wasn't like that," I groaned. "And yes—I did break up with Paige to be with you, but like you said *we're not dating* and you're still with Elliot. You don't see me getting annoyed every time you blow me off to be with *him*."

"That's not fair," she answered.

"No, it's not," I sighed. "Because I'm just the sucker waiting around for you to make up your mind on who you want to be with. If I'm not mistaken, it was after our argument last night that I decided to drown my sorrows—an argument about how Elliot isn't the complete tool I think he is. You were defending him because you're still into him. Face it Isobel, you're never going to leave him, not for me, not at all."

Her mouth opened then closed. "I told you it wasn't as easy as that."

"Whatever," I exhaled. "Do what you want."

"Sam."

"Seriously Isobel, I'm fed up with having the same conversation over and over."

"What? What do you mean?" she stuttered. "Sam."

I started in the direction of home.

"Samuel."

I stopped and turned.

"Don't walk away," she pouted.

I sighed. "What do you want me to say?"

"Do you still want me?"

"Yes."

"Even if sometimes I make you angry?"

"I'm not angry at you, I'm frustrated at the situation," I shrugged. "I don't understand why you want to stay with him when he treats you the way he does—but you already know that because I seem to be saying it a lot lately."

She looked down.

"Do you still want to be with me?" I asked.

"You have to ask?"

"Yes."

"You know I want you."

"Do I?" I half smiled. I couldn't see why she could question my feelings for her but I couldn't do the same. Out of the two of us I'd given up more for whatever we were doing here.

She lifted a shoulder. "You should."

I nodded, tucking my hands in my pockets.

"I know he treats me like one of his possessions," she murmured. "I know he does but I care about him—I wouldn't be with him otherwise—and maybe he doesn't care about me in the same way but I know he does in *some* way."

I knew she cared about him but it was hard to hear the words out loud regardless. I hated to think about her with him; it didn't feel right because he didn't deserve her. I didn't know whether the fact that she saw how bad he was for her was worse or better, since she still hung around.

"You can't be mad at me for that," she shrugged. "Just like I can't be mad at you for what you felt for Paige."

"Paige? Damn it Isobel, Paige and I are over," I replied. Why did girls always do that? Bring up the past when it's completely redundant and out-dated.

"I know, I'm just saying," she sighed. "Neither one of us can judge on jealousy because we started this when we were both with other people."

"Who said anything about jealousy?"

"Come on, Sam."

I rolled my eyes. "I just really hate the guy. I hate him even more for having you."

"He doesn't have me," she disagreed.

I sighed. "Yes he does—you just said it yourself."

She frowned and it was only after she raised her hand to wipe her cheek that I realised she was crying. That did it. I was over to her in two strides, encircling her in my arms and protecting her from the world.

I didn't understand why girls made things so hard for themselves. I didn't understand why she was causing herself so much heartache when she knew what she wanted but was too afraid to go after it. From the moment I fell for Isobel, I knew I couldn't stay with Paige. Even if Isobel and I didn't start off with anything more than being each other's confidant—a shoulder to lean on because our respective partners couldn't offer that to us— as soon as that morphed into something more, I bit the bullet and pulled the trigger. Pretending didn't help Paige and expecting something from her that she wasn't willing to give didn't help me either. It was better for the both of us that I ended it, just like it's better for Isobel in the long run if she leaves Elliot. He's never going to be the guy that she needs and even if it wasn't me she wanted, it definitely wasn't him.

***

When I got home Sunday afternoon, Angela was waiting for me on the porch.

"Son, you're alive," she sighed.

I laughed. "Sorry about the missed calls and stuff. Amelia's already expressed her concerns about my inability to answer a phone."

"Where were you all afternoon?" she frowned. Clearly I was going to get two bad cops on this one.

"I went out with Sax and Macca."

"Where?"

"Lunar, then just out," I shrugged. "Why? What's the big deal?"

"The big deal, *son*, is that you are not long out of hospital, then run around in the rain all morning and head out drinking all night," she answered. "And to top it off, you don't answer your phone so we don't know if you're still alive or not and you roll into bed mid-morning without any explanation."

"I didn't think I needed one to hang out with my friends," I replied. "Dad didn't seem to care."

"You know he has enough on his plate to—"

"To notice I didn't come home last night?" I finished for her. "Yes, I know."

"Sam," she sighed. "I'm just worried about you."

"I know Mum, but I can take care of myself."

She pressed her lips together and frowned, walking forward to capture me in a bear hug.

I groaned. "Mum."

"I'm always going to worry, Samuel, you're my son," she replied. "And especially this time of year after what the Stewart family went through. Such a tragedy."

Stewart family? Paige's family?

"What tragedy?" I frowned, pulling back to look at her. "What are you talking about?"

She shook her head sadly. "You know, honey, what happened to Paige's sister."

"Paige doesn't have a sister."

"I know honey, she died—drowned. Didn't Paige tell you?"

I blinked. "No."

"I can't even imagine losing a child," she sighed. "It's a terrible thing. I don't wish that upon anyone."

"When was this?"

"Oh, ten years ago now. I'm surprised Paige never mentioned it."

"Mm." Typical Paige: never talking about anything personal. I felt like I didn't know her at all.

"I suppose it can't be easy to talk about," Angela mused. "She and Paige were close—identical twins too, inseparable."

"Paige is—was—a *twin?*"

"Yes, the poor thing took it hard. She was there when it happened—didn't speak for a long time. Her parents moved schools because of it since they thought a fresh start would help. If it wasn't for that friend of hers, the Archer boy, who knows where she'd be? He really helped her through."

"Who? Liam?"

"That's right, *Liam* Archer."

I felt a fresh surge of jealousy, humiliation and understanding for the guy who always seemed to be the guy I wanted to be for Paige. Turns out I didn't know a thing.

"What I'm trying to say is that you need to be extra careful due to your allergy because despite what you may think, you're not immortal, son," she finished, cradling my cheek. "I know you can take care of yourself but I want you to promise me that that's what you are doing—*taking care.*"

I barely heard her speaking, I was too deafened by her earlier words—Paige was a twin? Her sister died? She didn't speak? Why didn't I know this? Why didn't she trust me enough to say something? *Ten years?*

"Sure, Mum," I nodded absently as she looked at me expectantly. I was relieved it was the right answer to whatever question she'd asked because she just smiled her small accepting smile and turned towards the house.

What else had Paige kept from me? And why did it bother me so much that she'd never told me? We were together almost a year and nothing was ever said. Nothing. I couldn't even remember anything being remotely wrong or ever bothering her, I couldn't remember anything being implied or any photographs around her house. But then how could I know if they were identical twins, especially if I wasn't looking for it?

My reality felt as if it had been sucked into a black hole—a vortex that led to some other world where everything made sense. I felt like I didn't know what was real anymore—or even if the people around me were real. I couldn't remember when everything felt normal, and that was a very strange and unsettling feeling.

Sunday night family dinner was just Angela, Amelia and me since Artie had some business meeting at the office. I didn't care; I was too busy being disillusioned with the world and trying to think back to whether I'd missed everything with Paige if she'd ever tried to tell me about her twin. And then there was Isobel—and I wasn't sure why she had been so calm about me shacking up with another girl. I thought it would bother her more—don't girls usually get mad about that stuff? It drove me crazy that she was with Elliot and she was with him even before we started hooking up. I didn't even want to think about Demi and how badly I'd screwed up there. I guess I'd probably have to avoid Lunar for a while and that bummed me more than everything. Their burgers were the best. Well done Samuel. Aces.

I had class Monday from eleven thirty to three thirty so I took advantage of the late start to catch up on sleep. Monday night I went to football training with the weight of consequence on my shoulders. I decided to do the only thing I could do and channel all my pent up rage and uncertainty into training—running the heats and gunning for that score like it was the last hope. Everything seemed to make sense on the field, like I was untouchable—because I was. I was better than everyone out there and anyone who had a set of eyes and a brain could see and appreciate that.

Except one person of course, Elliot Prince... more like Prince Elliot. He was the only player that played selfish, swaggering around like he owned everyone; and the ironic thing was that he pretty much did. Everyone was scared of him and he fed off that fear—everyone except me. I wanted to teach him a lesson, to find his weakness and give him a shot of it in a shooter glass and watch him collapse, but I'd made a mental promise to clean up my act after the talk with Angela and Isobel.

"Whoops, sorry Saber," Elliot chuckled, after crunching me into the grass. He slapped my shoulder as he stood up and I groaned, trying to move my limbs that felt twisted in wrong directions.

Louis extended his hand towards me and I grabbed it as he yanked me to my feet.

"I'm going to melt him," I grumbled. "No way that was an accident."

Louis laughed. "He's on your team."

"Ever heard of friendly fire?" I asked, shaking out my arm. I cringed as my right shoulder cracked.

"You good Sammy?" Marcus frowned.

I nodded, stretching it out. It was almost the end of practice and we were playing the equivalent of half-court in basketball. Elliot was supposed to be on my side but lines seemed to be blurred for him. I didn't even have possession of the ball when he drilled me into the floor.

"Right lads, let's call it a night," Wesley called. "See you lot Thursday."

I hesitated before heading to the change rooms, paranoid that I'd be called to stay behind again. Wesley turned his attention to his playbook so I just followed Marcus and Louis back.

"What's up with you and Prince? Did you sleep with his sister or something?" Marcus laughed.

I glanced at him. "Elliot doesn't have a sister."

"Then what put you on his hit list?"

I shrugged, a little bothered that I wasn't the only one paranoid enough to notice his specific reserved hatred for me lately. I'm actually miffed he didn't just hit me with his car when he offered me the lift since he'd tried to kill me twice since then.

"Hey, you keen for Crescent tomorrow night?" Marcus asked, elbowing me in the arm as we settled in front of the lockers. I pulled my jumper over my head.

"Are you kidding? I'm still healing from last week," I huffed, lifting my arm. "Literally."

Marcus grinned. "Oh I forgot you got that."

"You got a tattoo?" Louis laughed. "Of a sword. Why a sword?"

"Something a girl said about being one of King Arthur's knights," I shrugged.

"Swordsmen," Marcus corrected.

I rolled my eyes, heading to the showers.

"Oi, Sadie might be there again," Marcus called. "She was fit."

I laughed, stepping under the water to rinse off and then returned to dress.

"Sadie? Did you sleep with her too?" Louis asked, turning to me.

"Unlike you, Macca, I don't feel the need to sleep with every girl I meet," I replied.

He chuckled.

"Your loss then Saber," Elliot added, pulling a shirt on.

I frowned. "What are you on about, Prince?"

He smirked and I stepped forward to lunge and beat it off his face. Was he implying he *cheated* on Isobel? Louis nudged me back.

"Dude, you have the hottest girlfriend in South Coast," Marcus added. "And she's like, what, eighteen and the Supreme Court judge's daughter?"

Elliot nodded. "I'm not saying she doesn't have her perks."

I balled my hand into a fist and felt the blood pulsing in my ears.

"Idiot," I mumbled.

"Beg pardon, Saber?" Elliot asked. "What did you say?"

"I said—"

"Lancelot," Louis interrupted. "He said Lancelot—that's Isobel's dad's name isn't it?"

Elliot pulled a face. "Lance Armelle."

"Right," Louis laughed. "There you go Sam, all this King Arthur talk has got you thinking medieval."

I looked at Louis as he pulled on his jacket.

"Come on, let's get out of here, too much male bonding going on," he noted, pulling the strap of his bag over his shoulder.

I pulled on my shirt and followed suit as he pushed me towards the door.

"Sax, I'll take Sam home," Louis called.

"Sure, sure," he yawned. "Later."

We got outside and I exhaled.

"You didn't have to do that, I don't need you to speak for me," I muttered.

"Right, because I'm going to let that tosser beat you to a pulp over a girl," he answered. "What's going on with that? You keen on his little princess or something?"

"Isobel is not—" I stopped and sighed. "I don't know what you're talking about."

"Sure you do," he nodded, all traces of humour gone. "Sax mentioned you and Paige broke up—then you sleep with that waitress which is not like you, and now you're angling for a fight with Prince. What gives?"

He folded his arms, stopping by his twilight blue 1973 Ford Falcon GT.

I looked at him in annoyance—Louis may not be here a lot but he was the only one to see past my facade. I wasn't sure if I resented that or not.

"You're right," I sighed.

"About what?"

"All of it."

"All of it," he mused. "You mean you're keen on Elliot's girl?"

I shook my head. "We've been… seeing each other I guess for a couple of months."

Louis laughed. "Have you lost your mind?"

I shushed him.

"Damn, Sam," he groaned, running the tips of his fingers through his short dark blond hair. "Of all the girls in South Coast—of all the girls you could have—you pick the one who's dating Prince?"

"I didn't really pick her," I frowned. "We just sort of started talking one day and… I don't know."

His brow furrowed. "You were cheating on Paige?"

110

"Isobel and I never slept together—"

"That's not what I asked."

"Define cheating."

"And to think you were going to beat him for the same thing," Louis sighed.

I gaped. "What?"

"You're as big an idiot as he is," Louis noted. "Paige was a cool girl; she didn't deserve that from you."

I pressed my lips together. His comment confused me. The way he and Marcus used to make comments about her, I used to think that he didn't like her all that much. Sure, she wasn't a girly girl but they didn't see the side of her I got to. Guess they were just teasing.

"I know she didn't."

Louis shook his head. "Anyway, keen for a feed?"

I looked up. "Sure, but I don't want to go to Lunar."

"I was thinking Camelot," he grinned. "Their burgers might suck but they make the best fried chicken in the state."

I breathed a laugh. "Yeah, sounds good."

VI

In Your Court

I was restless all through class on Tuesday morning. I watched Isobel from the corner of my eye for the duration of our philosophy tutorial, wondering if Elliot was serious about his implications of cheating on her. I wanted to ask her but I knew if she confronted him about it he'd suspect something since only a handful of people were around to hear it.

After class she waited behind for me.

"What's wrong?" she asked. "You look like you're waiting for me to snap or something."

I smiled. "No."

"So what is it?"

"Nothing."

Her eyebrow rose. It was incredibly hot.

I shook my head. "Really, it's nothing. I'm just... thinking about my car. It's getting towed this afternoon."

She frowned sceptically. "Okay."

"So did you see Prince yesterday?" I asked as we walked out towards the student common room.

"Yes, before training," she answered. "Why? Did something happen at practice?"

I shrugged. "Nothing out of the ordinary."

"Sam, what's going on?" She frowned, catching my elbow.

I turned towards her. "Same story Isobel, you're too good for him."

"Where's this coming from?"

I kept walking. "Nowhere new."

"Sam," she called, skipping to keep up. "Sam, wait."

I slowed.

"What happened?" she whispered. "Did he say something to you?"

"You mean before or after he minced me into the grass?"

"What?"

"Nothing."

She sighed. "Is there something you want to tell me or not?"

I exhaled. "I just... he's not good enough for you. You need someone who sees only you."

She gave a laugh. "Like you? Didn't you sleep with some waitress a few days ago?"

"Ouch," I breathed.

"And what does that mean?" she asked. "Do you know something?"

My forehead flattened. "No."

"Sam?" she pouted. That pout.

"I don't know anything, honestly," I shrugged. "He just implied something like that yesterday."

"Implied?"

"He said something about me missing out by not sleeping around," I groaned, breaking my plan not to mention anything specifically.

"Oh."

"I'm sure it's..." I began to say then stopped. Why was I defending him?

She laughed, doing the absolute last thing I thought she would—as usual.

"What's funny?" I frowned.

"If it is true, I can't really complain," she replied. "Or I'd be a hypocrite."

"Oh, right," I smiled. "But we've never slept together."

"Well that's true," she nodded. "Anyway, I've got to go."

"Okay."

She laughed. "I'll catch you later."

"Okay."

I watched her leave, feeling as if I'd been the punch line in a practical joke, then gave up and turned my attention back to the common room. Right, breakfast then a workshop until one thirty, then—finally—back to the garage with my beloved Morris to try and fix something I actually had the means and knowledge to.

***

"Where were you?" Artie asked as I dragged my feet in later that evening after spending the latter part of the afternoon with Austin.

I looked up. "Out."

"Don't be smart with me," he growled. "Out where? Not with Marcus again?"

"No—not that it's any of your business," I grumbled, heading towards the stairs.

"I beg your pardon?" he sniped. "Samuel?"

"What?" I groaned.

"*Where were you?*"

"At the garage trying to fix my car," I sighed.

"Garage?"

I nodded. "Anything else?"

"Why were *you* trying to fix it? Aren't you paying someone to do it?" he frowned.

"No," I replied—annoyed that he picked now to ask me about my life. I really wanted a shower.

"Why not?"

I shrugged. "Don't have the money to."

He smiled ironically. "So instead of asking for it you're doing it yourself?"

"I want to do it myself," I answered. "Plus Austin is letting me help out with some other jobs."

Artie's amused expression darkened. "I beg your pardon?"

I hated when he said that; it made him sound pretentious.

"I guess Mum didn't mention it," I sighed.

He gawped. "Angela knew? How long has this been going on?"

"Since Friday," I shrugged. "I'm sure you were probably just too busy to notice."

"Watch your mouth, son, you're not too old to be belted," he warned.

He'd have to catch me first.

"Okay," I yawned. "I'm getting a shower."

"Just a minute," he bellowed. "You don't think you're going to keep this—this job, do you?"

"Sure I do."

"Do you know how it will look if my son is working as some blue-collar worker?" he asked.

"Like you're teaching him the value of honest work?" I offered.

He frowned at the thought. "That's one spin."

I mashed my lips together and turned.

"Samuel," he called.

I sighed. "Yes?"

"Have you thought any more about my request for assistance?" he asked.

"Not really."

"Well, since you have time for a job, you must have time to help your father better your city—at your own request I might add."

I blinked. "I don't quite see that logic."

"I'll tell you what, you come work for me, on my payroll, and you can earn the money to get that heap of metal fixed by a—erm—professional," he said, folding his arms.

I could just see it—him actually being the boss of me. The thought repulsed me more than anything else in the world, including Elliot Prince and his hold over Isobel.

"No thanks," I answered.

"No?"

"No thanks."

"No."

I looked to the side, wondering what he wasn't understanding.

"Is that your final answer, son?" he asked, cocking his head. "No?"

"Y-yes?"

Artie's eyebrow rose. "Yes?"

I shook my head. "Yes—no is my final answer."

He considered that. "I see."

"Is—uh, is that all?"

"Yes, son, go take that shower," he nodded.

"O-kay," I said slowly, progressing upstairs. I couldn't help but feeling I'd just blindly signed a contract of an unknown nature. Arthur Saber didn't let things go and he wasn't one to lose a fight or not get what he wanted. He was a politician after all—and trained as a legal counsellor—failure was not an option. It wasn't in his vocabulary. He had a way of outsmarting his opponent which was how he got elected as mayor in the first place. Artie wasn't the most well-liked person, but he was the smartest contender. He had a way of outwitting people and I could've almost sworn that I was his most recent victim.

I had another early start on Wednesday morning and I hated to admit that it was a welcome distraction and alternative to being at home. After my morning class I went and grabbed a mocha before heading to the philosophy lecture. I was interested in catching up with Isobel after yesterday since she hadn't gotten back to me after our chat about Elliot, but she didn't show up in the end.

I texted her but she didn't reply. She didn't do geology like Paige who had an excursion today—which I only remembered because I happen to pass the notice on the School of Arts and Sciences board on the way to class.

I kind of wanted to talk to Paige too since I hadn't had the chance to after finding out about her past. In hindsight, I felt a bit guilty about it all—about how it ended and how I'd missed it all—but in the same respect, she never mentioned anything to me. She hadn't trusted me enough to let me in.

At quarter past three, I finally got a reply from Isobel asking for me to meet her under the bridge after class. Philosophy was almost finished so I just left, using the head start to my advantage since I was still on foot. I had managed to get good leeway into repairing the water pump and gasket on my car yesterday so at least it wouldn't be out of circulation for too long.

It took me about twenty minutes to walk there and when I arrived, Isobel was waiting, leaning against the bonnet of her car.

"Hey," I called. "I missed you in the philosophy lecture."

This seemed to be the habitual start to all our Tuesday afternoon encounters.

She looked down. "Yeah, I skipped it."

"I noticed," I nodded. "What's up? Is everything okay?"

"I broke up with Elliot," Isobel said.

"Really? That's great."

"He didn't take it well," she continued. "Actually, he said everything to try and make me reconsider, including bringing up how disappointed our parents will be."

I scoffed. "You're kidding."

"He's right though."

"But is that enough?"

"No."

I exhaled. "So what now? I suppose we have to be smart about this and not tell people—"

"About that," she interrupted. "Given how delicate the situation is, and the fact that you and him are teammates, I don't think we should push it."

"What do you mean?"

"I mean, maybe we should cool things for a while."

"Why?"

"I don't want Elliot to find out about us, and he'll be extra paranoid right now. I don't want you to get drawn into this."

I blinked. "But I already am."

"Sam, please. We will be together; I just think we need to give it more time."

"Then why do we have to cool it? We don't have to go public or anything but—"

"I just think it's for the best."

I shook my head in frustration. "This is crazy. We've been seeing each other for ages while you were with him and now that you're *not*, you don't want to *push it?*"

She sighed. "I'm only thinking of you. Do you know what Elliot would do if he found out?"

"I don't care, I can take it."

"What about football?" she asked. "Or your dad?"

"Don't you mean *your* dad?"

"My dad?"

"It reflects more on *you* if people find out."

"Nice, Samuel," she sighed. "I wasn't the only one cheating."

118

I shook my head. "Sorry, this just epically sucks. It just feels like there's always something standing in the way."

"It won't be for long," she whispered. "We've come this far."

"Yeah, right," I breathed.

Isobel pressed her lips together. "Well I'd better go."

"Go? Why?" I frowned.

"I'm... I'm meeting Liam for coffee."

"What?!" I exclaimed louder than both of us expected.

"Don't Sam," she exhaled. "Liam is just a friend."

"But you'll go out with him and not me?" I asked. "Aren't you worried what Prince will do to *him*?"

"Maybe this will throw Elliot off the scent?" she shrugged, pacing around to the driver's side.

"Do you hear yourself right now?" I replied. "Do you know how crazy-paranoid you sound?"

She shook her head. "I'll be in touch."

"Isobel," I groaned.

"Goodbye, Sam."

"Isobel."

She climbed in her car and I ran around to grab her door before she could close it behind her.

"Don't make this harder for me," she sighed.

"It doesn't have to be hard, you're making it hard," I answered, kneeling between the open door and the car. The ground was damp and hard on my knees.

"I don't want you to get caught in the crossfire," she pouted. "I do want this, I want us. But not yet, okay? Just be patient."

I've been nothing but patient.

"I don't care what happens to me," I breathed. "I just want to be with you. We've waited long enough."

"So wait a little longer," she replied, pressing her palm on my cheek. "I care what happens to you."

My shoulders fell.

"Now please let me go," she whispered, moving her cool fingers over my lips before they moved back to her steering wheel.

I bit my lower lip and rose to my feet. "So that's it?"

"For now," she frowned.

I nodded and stepped back, closing her door.

The sound of her engine starting and the pebbles scratching beneath her tyres as she pulled away were perhaps the hardest things I'd ever had to listen to. Something inside told me that it was her way of letting me down easy—not that it felt easy, it felt as if my heart had been punched. After all, we weren't a couple—we never were—we'd never even been on a real date. This was clearly her way of saying we should stop pretending and that she wanted Liam all along. She was willing to risk the wrath of Elliot for him but not me. She had broken up with Elliot and picked him—just like Paige always did. I wish she'd just have spared me her carefully crafted excuses and lied to me instead.

I dragged my feet into the house, hoping that I was the only one home or at least that no one would notice and try and talk to me. I wasn't in the mood.

"Oh good, son, you're home," Artie's voice bellowed.

Perfect. Just freaking perfect.

I looked up at him and kept walking.

"Son," he called, clearly missing my disinterest in whatever he had to say. "Samuel."

I exhaled. "Yes?"

He smiled. "I just wanted to let you know that it's all taken care of."

"What is taken care of?" I frowned.

"Your truck."

"My truck?" I repeated. "What about it?"

"It's repaired."

"What?" I groaned. "Why?"

"I took care of it."

"I don't understand."

"I paid someone to fix it," he explained. "So now you can come and work for me."

I blinked, feeling the rage building up inside. "No. Just no."

"No?"

"Seriously, what don't you understand about the word 'no'?" I fumed.

He huffed. "No one says 'no' to me."

"Well I just did, so… just no."

"No son of mine is working as a common mechanic," he growled.

"Well bad luck," I snapped, stomping up the stairs. "No one asked you, it's not your decision."

"*Bad luck?*" he growled. "Hey, don't walk away from me, boy."

Uh-oh.

I stopped and rolled my head around to look at him.

"Now you listen to me, son," Artie said very calmly, in a low voice. "You will not fight with me on this, you will not be ungrateful and you will not, *you will not*, speak to me the way you just did again or there will be consequences, do you understand?"

My eyebrows rose. I didn't reply.

"*Do you* understand?" he repeated.

I looked to the side. "I'm not going to apologise for who I am."

He huffed. "Well sometimes you need to."

"No I don't," I frowned. "Maybe for what I do, but never for who I am."

"Is there a difference?" he asked.

"Is that a legitimate question?"

121

"Son, what you do defines who you are," he explained insultingly. "Not what you say."

I folded my arms.

"You will do this—you will do what I tell you to do," he continued. "You're a Saber, it's your obligation."

I felt like I was freefalling into a fire pit. "You can't make me be something I don't want to be."

Artie smiled hauntingly. "We'll see."

I never thought it was possible—I never wanted to believe it—but I could safely say that in that moment, I was ashamed of my name, ashamed of him, and ashamed that deep down, I knew that he was probably right—that he would make me into this person, this stranger that I already hated.

I was barely home five minutes when I headed back out again—just to get out. I went running and didn't stop because I didn't want to go back there, to go *home* and feel like a stranger who couldn't make any decisions for myself. Artie ruled my future; Isobel toyed with my feelings; Marcus told me what was best in social situations; Elliot called the shots to Wesley in football... the only person who let me be me was Paige and it turns out, I didn't know her as well as I thought—or really appreciate her, I guess.

It was only after being out for hours that I realised I'd missed basketball so rounded back and caught Bryce leaving the courts.

"Hey Watson," I sighed. "How'd you go?"

"Hey Saber," he nodded. "Yeah, not bad considering we were two down."

"Two?"

"Nate wasn't here either because of that excursion," he explained. "You all right? You look a bit beat."

I nodded, not sure which I was agreeing with.

"Hey, sorry I bailed on fishing Sunday," I sighed. "I was horizontal pretty much all day."

He huffed. "Sax again?"

"And Macca," I cringed. "Not good."

Bryce looked behind me. "Did you walk here?"

"Ran."

"Do you want a lift home?"

I shook my head. "Don't want to go home yet."

He frowned. "You good, bro?"

"Nuh, not really," I sighed.

He nodded. "Want to come to mine for a bit? Think the missus is cooking."

"Sure, that sounds good," I smiled.

He laughed. "Don't get too excited, she tries but… well you'll see."

I chuckled and followed him to his car.

Constance Watson was a lot of things, but gourmet chef was not one of them. Regardless, I enjoyed her take of spaghetti bolognaise and was humbled by her and Bryce's hospitality.

"Jennifer, can you say hello to Sam?" Bryce said, catching his three-year-old daughter and propping her on his knee. She had tumbles of strawberry blonde curls, completely adorable.

"'llo Sam," she squeaked in her little voice.

Constance smiled, cradling her pregnant belly as she sat down beside the two.

"So Sam, Bryce tells me that you want to be a professional footballer," she murmured. "You must have quite a talent."

I took a sip of water. "I hope so, I do okay."

"He's lying, he's incredible," Bryce grinned, looking down at Jennifer. "Can you say incredible?"

"Ick-redim-bull," she giggled.

I laughed.

"Your parents must be pretty proud," Constance sighed pleasantly.

123

I frowned. "I don't know if proud is the right word. I think my dad has other plans for me."

"I'm sure he is," Constance nodded. "Parents just want the best for their kids. As long as you're happy, I'm sure that's enough."

I smiled tightly, wondering if that was actually enough for regular people. It took me a long time to realise that not everyone was brought up the way I was. But how could any kid know that it took more than the occasional family dinner, weekly allowance and housemaids to make a home when they didn't experience it first hand?

"So Sam, do you have a special girl in your life?" Constance asked, unwrapping a silver lolly from the bowl between us.

"Uhh," Bryce interrupted, shaking his head as she turned to look at him.

"No, it's okay," I breathed. "Um, actually I just broke up with my girlfriend."

Constance frowned. "Anyone new on the horizon?"

"Babe," Bryce groaned.

I chuckled. "Um, well, I don't know actually. I thought there might be but it's all up in the air right now."

"Oh," she sighed. "Well I'm sure everything will work out."

Bryce laughed. "Babe, you can't just say that. Sorry Sam."

I shook my head. "It's okay."

Despite the awkward questions, I was actually thoroughly enjoying myself. It felt good to be around normal people—a normal family for a change.

"See, it's fine," Constance shrugged. "Ooh, he kicked."

I glanced down at her belly. "How long do you have to go?"

"Three months," she smiled. "I can't wait."

"And it's a boy?"

She nodded. "Bryce is glad—it'll even the numbers up around here."

I huffed a laugh.

"Excuse me, I don't mind either way," Bryce replied. "I'd be just as happy with another girl."

Constance grinned up at him. "Sure you would."

"How long have you been together for?" I asked, tipping my head. Bryce was only a few years older than me but seemed miles ahead in maturity. He supported a family for one—I could barely support myself.

"Uh, eight years?" Constance answered. "We started dating when we were—what sixteen?"

"About that," Bryce nodded. "Who am I kidding? We were definitely sixteen; I remember that as clear as anything. I'd been begging you long enough."

Constance smiled so her nose wrinkled. "And I finally said yes and haven't looked back since."

I breathed a laugh and glanced down at my water as Jennifer yawned, her little mouth stretching as wide as the moon.

"Tired little girl," Bryce crooned. "Bedtime, hmm?"

I sighed. "That's probably my cue."

"No, don't feel you need to leave, Sam. I'll take her," Constance said, standing and picking the little girl up from Bryce's arms.

I stood up and glanced at my phone. Amelia had already messaged me twice—I made sure this time I replied in a timely manner.

"No, I should go," I frowned. "It's getting late."

"I'll drive you," Bryce replied. "Babe, do you mind?"

Constance shook her head.

"Oh hey, that's not necessary," I answered.

"Nonsense," he shrugged dismissively. "It's no trouble."

I smiled tightly. "Thanks—and thank you for dinner Constance, it was great."

She laughed. "Well now I *know* you're just being polite."

"Seriously," Bryce chuckled.

Constance pushed his arm playfully as Jennifer rested her head down on her shoulder.

"I won't be long," Bryce said with a wink. He leaned down and kissed Jennifer on the head and then kissed Constance's cheek. "Love my girls."

"I'll see you soon," Constance nodded.

"Night Daddy," Jennifer murmured.

"Say goodbye-bye to Sam," Bryce said to her.

"Good bye-bye Sam," she squeaked, burying her face into her mum's neck.

"Goodnight Jennifer," I waved. "Bye Constance, thanks again."

"You're welcome, anytime Sam," she grinned. "Good night— and I hope everything works out with your girl."

I sighed. "Thanks."

Bryce rested a hand on my shoulder, turning me towards the door. We headed out to his station wagon in silence.

"You have a great family Watson," I mused. "You're really lucky."

He nodded. "I know. Thanks."

"No, thank you for having me over," I answered. "It was real decent of you."

He smiled. "Anytime."

***

When I got home, my parents were nowhere to be seen. Amelia, on the other hand, seemed to be waiting up to make sure I didn't pull another all-nighter. Little sisters are weird.

"Hey," I sighed.

"Hi," she smiled. "You're out late—you missed family dinner."

"You knew where I was," I yawned.

"I know," she nodded. "Did you have fun?"

"Yep."

"Are you okay, Sammy?"

I shrugged. "Why wouldn't I be?"

"I don't know," she replied. "You've just seem... not yourself lately."

"I don't know what you mean."

"Is this about Paige?" she asked.

"No."

She looked down. "You just seem sad since you broke up with her."

"I've just had a lot on my mind," I sighed, forcing a smile. "I'm okay, really Millie."

She frowned. "I'm just worried about you."

"Join the queue," I laughed. Her frown deepened and I rolled my eyes. "Seriously you don't need to worry."

"Okay," she nodded, returning to her room. She peeked out her half-closed door. "Goodnight Sammy, I love you."

I smiled. "Love you too. Goodnight."

Amelia closed her door and I headed to my room to grab a change of clothes to get a shower before heading straight to bed. It wasn't late but it wasn't early—and I was knackered after the long day and afternoon run.

***

Thursday morning I didn't have class until ten thirty but I walked in early, ignoring my repaired Morris Minor in protest. It felt like blood money.

"Hey swordsman," Sadie grinned as I headed to class.

"Miss Blake," I nodded. "You got a break now?"

She flicked her hair over her shoulder. "Yep—you got class?"

"Just for an hour," I sighed.

"Well I'm headed to the library if you want to do coffee after," she offered. "I don't have class until twelve thirty."

"Okay, sure," I replied. "I'll come find you."

"I'll be in my usual spot," she winked. "See you later."

I gave her a two finger wave and continued on my way— guessing that her *usual* spot was where I'd stumbled across her last week. I had to admit, I didn't expect to like Sadie as much as I did—in a purely platonic way, of course.

"How was class Mr Saber?" she smiled as I walked up.

"Don't call me that," I grimaced.

"You have a daddy complex, huh?"

"No—do you even know what that means?" I laughed. "I'm not interested in older men."

She giggled. "Sure."

I cleared my throat. "So are you hungry or anything or just wanted coffee?"

"I could eat," she shrugged. "If you're buying."

"Sure."

She grinned and bounced up, skipping towards the exit. I followed her less enthusiastically.

"So I missed you and Sax at Crescent Tuesday night," she noted, turning and raising an eyebrow.

"Yeah, I'm still recovering from last week," I replied.

She laughed. "Lightweight."

"Well that's something I've never been called," I sighed. "So where are we going?"

"I was thinking *Cafe Excalibur.*"

My eyebrows rose. "Excalibur? Are you being serious right now? Or are you just trying to be funny?"

She shrugged. "Bit of column A, bit of column B."

"Right."

We walked in comfortable silence to the corner cafe and found a table by the window. I didn't need to look long at the menu to decide on what I was getting—I'd missed breakfast and a bacon and egg anything would go down great with my mocha.

"So what's new, swordsman?" she smiled. "Anything interesting happen in the last week?"

I smirked at her, thinking back through my murky memories from our last meeting: got a job, lost a job, won a game of football, slept with a random, got rejected by Isobel, got bought by my father and worried my mum and sister.

"Not really," I shrugged.

"Fix your car yet?" she asked, popping a hot chip into her mouth as the waitress set them in front of us—Sadie's request.

I huffed. "Sort of."

"What does that mean?"

"I started to fix it, even got a job at a garage to pay my way and King Arthur swooped in and saved the day," I groaned, shoving some chips in.

Sadie smiled. "Hail King Arthur."

I shook my head.

"You don't seem happy about it," she noted. "What's the big deal?"

The waitress placed my bacon and egg roll in front of me and I nodded thanks.

"His motive—he only did it so I wouldn't work at the garage," I explained, trying to pick it up without everything falling out. "He wants me to work for him instead so it's his way of backing me into a corner."

She shrugged. "Maybe he just wanted to do something nice?"

"Artie doesn't do anything without a motive," I mumbled with a mouthful. "Not when it comes to me anyway."

"Are you sure you're not being paranoid?"

"Yes."

Sadie bit her lip. "That looks good, does it taste good?"

"Yes."

"Can I have a bite?"

My eyes widened. "Excuse me?"

"Please? I let you have some chips," she laughed.

I took another mouthful. "I paid."

"Come on swordsman, you probably shouldn't be eating so unhealthy—aren't you supposed to be in training?" she reasoned.

I frowned. "Nice try."

She pouted, glancing up at me through her long black lashes, her violet eyes penetrating in their hypnotism.

I rolled my eyes and passed it across the table to her. "Fine."

"Yay," she beamed, leaning forward. She took a massive bite and wiped the barbeque sauce from her chin.

"I said a bite, not half the thing," I laughed.

She chuckled, her amused expression turning to surprise as her eyes panned towards the door.

"Crap," she mumbled.

"What?" I smiled, turning to see Nate and Paige walk in— hand in hand. I dropped my roll in shock. Paige and Nate? Nate and Paige? Holding hands? Didn't they hate each other? What the heck was going on? First Isobel and Liam, now *Nate and Paige*. The world was going crazy.

"When did that happen?" I asked, turning back to Sadie who was looking squeamish. "What's wrong?"

"Sadie," Nate's voice grated. "What's going on?"

Her expression turned pleasant. "Hi little brother, we were just thinking the same thing. Hello redhead."

"It's Paige," she answered. "Hello Sadie; Sam."

I frowned at them—something crazy must've happened on their excursion to the caves yesterday because Paige even talking to Nate was astonishing enough. She absolutely hated the guy and I didn't blame her for it. He had always been a complete jerk to her.

"Sadie, what are you doing here with him?" Nate barked.

Sadie wedged another couple of chips in her mouth. "Eating."

I couldn't help but laugh at how annoyed he was and her childish response. He was acting more like her father than younger brother.

"What are you laughing at, Saber?" he snapped.

"This is all a joke, right?" I asked. "I mean, you bossing Sadie around and you and Paige being all chummy."

Paige shuffled uncomfortably beside him but kept her hand in his. I wanted to tear them apart.

He glanced sideways at Paige before returning his burning gaze to me.

"The only joke here is you."

I laughed harder. "Okay."

Nate stepped forward, releasing Paige's hand and readying himself to fight.

"Looking for another black eye?"

"Ah, no," I replied. "Do you mind though? We're actually in the middle of something."

"Not anymore. Sadie, come on get your stuff," Nate muttered, clutching her arm.

131

Sadie smacked him off. "No, leave me alone."

"Nate, let's just go," Paige pleaded.

He looked into her eyes, his face alarmingly close to hers. "I'm not leaving her with him."

"Sam's harmless," she answered earnestly. "And she's not the one—remember?"

My face screwed up in confusion. Remember what? What was she talking about?

"Sam and I are just friends," Sadie interrupted. "You don't have to freak out."

Nate looked from Paige to Sadie then glared at me.

"If you try anything, I will—"

"Yeah, yeah," I sighed, picking my roll back up and taking a bite. "Always a pleasure, Nathaniel."

I saw him hesitate from the corner of my eye but didn't risk a look in case I turned to stare at his fist again. Paige's feet disappeared first and I turned to see them leave before glancing back to Sadie and smiling.

"Nice," she groaned.

I shrugged. "Your brother's a jerk."

"He means well," she replied. "I'm sure he does anyway. He really doesn't like you."

"Yeah," I mused. "Not sure what I ever did to him though; he hated me long before you came along."

A smile stretched across her face. "Are you serious?"

"What?"

"You really don't know?"

I frowned. "Know what?"

She bit her lip. "I don't know whether I should say."

"Well you've got to tell me now."

Sadie reached in for another chip. "Nate's had a crush on her since we moved here eight years ago."

"What?"

Oh. Now it all made sense—her comment at Crescent about how she didn't know what "all the hype" was about Paige. It was because she'd heard it all from her brother.

"No," I groaned. "Really? He used to tease her all the time. Paige hated him."

Sadie huffed a laugh. "Come on swordsman, you're a guy."

I finished off my roll and dusted my hands. "Are you saying he hated me because he was jealous?"

"Boom goes the dynamite," she sighed. "Don't tell me you've never hated a guy for dating the girl you had a crush on."

I thought about Elliot and Isobel.

"Only because he was a complete arse," I answered.

"Maybe he thought you were too?" she grinned.

My eyebrows rose. "No, not possible."

She laughed.

After we'd eaten as many chips as we could fit, I walked Sadie to her class before heading to the library to find a textbook for secondary reading.

"Hey Samuel," someone murmured as I entered the courtyard. I looked up to see Liam.

"Archer," I frowned.

He breathed a laugh that aggravated me.

"Something funny?" I asked, spinning around to confront him.

He looked up, a blond eyebrow rising. "Nope."

"That's what I thought."

Liam chuckled. "You get what you give, you know."

"Excuse me?"

"Paige didn't deserve how you treated her," he answered. "Neither did Isobel."

I frowned. "What do you know about it, Archer?"

"Enough to know that they're both better off."

133

"And you think that Isobel is better off with someone like you?" I asked. "You, the son of a caterer, rather than someone like me, her equal?"

I hated myself as I spoke the words—words of those aristocratic jerks that I resented—but I wanted to hit him where it hurts and not even he could deny that a girl of Isobel's standing had certain needs and expectations.

Liam rolled his blue eyes. "Not everything is about money, Saber."

"*I* know that," I smirked. "But does she?"

Liam scoffed, turning his back on me.

I began to walk off.

"You know, she picked me," Liam called back. "She could've had you but chose me."

I glanced over my shoulder and he shrugged arrogantly. It took everything I had not to go and break those shoulders.

"I'm not the one you have to worry about, Archer," I huffed. "If I was you, I'd be more concerned about how Prince is going to react seeing you two together so soon after their break up."

Liam's smugness darkened into unguarded fear and I smiled at his discomfort. Idiot. At least his dumb face would probably end up being rearranged eventually, whether that was by me or Elliot was irrelevant.

I didn't know what Isobel saw in him—maybe some girls found him attractive for his floppy blond hair or clean-cut preppy dress sense, or maybe she just wanted to slum it for a while? No, Isobel wasn't like that. At least I thought she wasn't.

"Hey Sam," a voice whispered through the books. "I have a proposition for you."

I looked up through the shelf and spotted a blonde girl and frowned. "Do I know you?"

"I'm Ivy," she answered.

She looked familiar—why did she look familiar? Oh, she was the girl who'd given me her condolences for the breakup last week after I'd walked into her.

"You don't know me," she said, reading my thoughts. "But your ex is dating mine."

I blinked. "Do you mean Paige and Nate?"

She tipped her head.

"Word travels fast around here," I mumbled, glancing back to the books. "What are you talking about, a proposition? What kind of proposition?"

"I thought we could help each other," she answered. "Because you seem to be in a right fix with love these days."

My brows drew. "What do you know about me?"

She disappeared and walked around the aisle so she wasn't shielded by shelves and ambled towards me.

"I know you broke up with Paige then hooked up with that Isobel girl," she explained. "Who then left her boyfriend and is now with Liam."

Her knowledge took me aback. "So? What of it?"

She shrugged. "So, jealously is a powerful motivator."

"Jealousy?" I frowned. "What are you on about?"

"We could help each other," she repeated. "All she has to do is see you with someone else and she'll come running back to you."

"Who?"

"Whoever you want," she shrugged, running her finger up my shoulder. I caught her hand.

"What's in it for you?"

She frowned. "I made a mistake when I broke up with Nate. I want him back but he'll never leave Paige."

"Well if you think Paige will leave him for me then you're delusional," I huffed. "Besides, Isobel is only with Liam until things blow over with Elliot."

I realised how naive I sounded and hoped she didn't notice.

I exhaled. "Regardless, I don't like games so you'll have to find someone else to play."

She rolled her golden eyes. "You do know that Isobel is playing you though, right?"

"What are you talking about?"

"Please," she groaned, flicking her blonde curls over her shoulder. "She breaks up with her boyfriend and begins seeing another guy and her excuse is she's waiting for things to blow over." Her fingers air-quoted the last six words. "Open your eyes, Sam, she was never going to be with you—if she was she wouldn't be with Liam right now—she's be alone if anything."

I folded my arms.

She shook her head. "Look, just think about it, okay? What have you got to lose?"

I considered that for a moment—I had already slept with another girl since breaking up with Paige and Isobel didn't bat an eye; she didn't even bat an eye when I mentioned my suspicions of Elliot cheating on her.

"What if it doesn't work?" I asked. "The jealousy thing I mean."

"Then she never wanted you at all," Ivy answered, lifting a shoulder as she reached into my pocket for my phone.

I frowned and made a mental note to activate the screen lock.

"Your call," she finished, sliding it back in my jeans. "Let me know what you decide."

VII

The Harder They Fall

I couldn't get Ivy out of my head—everything she was saying about Isobel, in a weirdly stupid and complicated-girl-way—made sense. But I didn't know how hooking up with her, or at least pretending to, would change anything. I mean, sure, she was attractive but she wasn't who I wanted and it just seemed like being with someone else who wasn't Isobel again was just going sideways rather than forward.

I headed over to Austin's garage in the afternoon, I felt like I needed to explain myself to him—or at least not leave him high and dry like Artie intended me to.

"All good, bro, your dad's cheque more than covered the cost of your car," he laughed. "Actually it covered your Morris Minor about eighty times over. I hired a couple more guys off it so we're doing good now."

"Oh," I frowned. I had kind of hoped he'd need me regardless so it bummed me to not be required. I'm sure Artie had thought of that when he paid Austin off. Cut all ties, eliminate all threats. He's nothing if not thorough in covering his tracks.

"I guess I should thank you," he smiled, sliding back under the old MGB GT coupé.

"Thank me?"

"For your help last week," he explained. "And for choosing me as your mechanic. That money saved my business."

I nodded. "No problem. Erm, happy to help."

"How is the car running now anyway?" he asked. "I don't see it out front."

I scratched my neck. "Yeah I walked, trying to keep fit."

"But it's all good?"

"I'm sure it's great," I answered. "How'd you get it fixed so fast? I thought we were waiting on the new alternator."

"Turns out money is a powerful motivator," he chuckled. That's all that was said.

"Okay well, I've got to get to football training," I sighed. "Thanks for... stuff."

He rolled out from beneath the car. "No need to thank me, bro—thank your dad."

I grimaced. "Yeah."

"Don't be a stranger, Saber," he smiled.

I nodded and turned, heading towards home. I resented the fact that Artie always seemed to come off as the hero almost as much as I resented that no one seemed to understand that he was only motivated by his own interests. Like a selfish Santa. I couldn't help but laugh at the image but it was no laughing matter at all. It was concerning: the blind faith everyone seemed to have in Arthur Saber.

***

"Sammy, you ready?" Marcus called from his ute as he held his horn down.

"Hey Sax," I waved.

"Your Morris is back?" he frowned, glancing at the truck. "Is it fixed?"

I rolled my eyes. "Thanks to Artie."

"Why am I picking you up then?" he laughed.

"I'm in silent protest."

"Why?"

"Because he went behind my back and paid Austin a pile of money to fix it so I wouldn't have to."

"Master of puppets," Marcus sighed. At least he understood.

"Is Macca still here?"

"Yeah, until Sunday."

"Oh good, we could use him this weekend," I nodded.

"We're not going out again," Marcus replied. "I think you should go on a liver cleanse."

"I didn't mean you and me—*we*, I meant *the Suns*—we," I groaned. "Besides, it's always *your* bright ideas that land me in an alcohol-induced coma."

Marcus laughed. "You can lead a horse to water…"

"Shut up Sax."

He chuckled harder as we pulled up at the oval and headed to the change rooms to get kitted up and met the rest of the guys on the ground. Louis jogged up behind us as I frowned at who Wesley was standing with.

"What's he doing here?" I muttered.

Marcus looked at me then followed my gaze. "Who?"

"Nate Blake."

Louis' face pinched. "Who?"

"Nathaniel Blake," I grumbled. "Come on, you've heard of him."

"Oh, Blake," Marcus nodded. "He used to play for the Bandits, I heard coach talking about recruiting him as a rookie."

"You're joking, right?" I asked. "He's not joining the team."

"What does it matter to you Sam?" Louis shrugged.

"He's not a team player, the guy hates me," I explained evasively.

Marcus smirked. "I heard he's shacked up with Paige."

"Ah, now I get it," Louis laughed.

I rolled my eyes and shook my head as we joined the circle.

"Listen up, lads," Wesley shouted. "This is Nate Blake; he'll be joining us at training tonight to see how he goes. Nate plays for the Hawthorn Bandits, local team, so we're going to see how he goes at state level."

I exhaled, feeling my heart sink to my heels. If Nate joined the Suns, it was pretty much guaranteed that my chances at impressing the RedBacks' scouts were shredded. Nate hated me, that much was clear—whether it was because of my former relationship with Paige or my friendship with Sadie remained to be seen. Maybe it was both. I didn't get it personally, it's not like I did anything too bad to either of them. I mean, sure, I broke up with Paige but anyone who played witness to our relationship could see that it wasn't founded on openness and honesty anyway—she kept just as many secrets from me as I did from her, the only difference was mine were formed over time whereas she was apparently insincere from the beginning.

"All right, let's pair up and run some drills," Wesley clapped. "Saber, you're with Blake; show him how it's done."

I opened my mouth to protest and felt an elbow in my ribs coupled by Marcus' chuckle.

"Have fun, Sammy."

"Shut up, Sax."

Louis thumped a ball into my chest and I gripped it. Nate glanced over looking about as excited as I was to be paired with him. I cleared my throat and sauntered over.

"So, uh, we normally start with rolling the ball between us then move onto kick-to-kick," I explained.

He shrugged. "Sounds easy enough."

"Good," I sighed, throwing him the ball. "You'll have no problem keeping up then."

Nate and I didn't talk. That suited me. But practice felt longer than usual and I resented that he was imposing on a place where I normally found refuge. Everything that was mine was being stripped away before my eyes and I was beginning to think that I'd wind up with nothing.

"Saber, stay behind," Wesley called at the end of practice. I half expected it. Marcus saluted me as he passed; Louis slapped my shoulder.

"Coach?"

"How'd Blake go? Did he keep up with you?"

I shrugged. "I guess."

"I think he shows promise," Wesley nodded contemplatively.

I looked to the side and spotted Paige in the parking lot, my brow furrowed. I still couldn't understand it—I couldn't understand girls and the stupid decisions they made and the idiot guys they chose. Why did they insist on picking the guy that was the worst for them?

"Sam," Wesley said.

"Sorry?"

"What do you think?"

I blinked. "About what?"

"About taking him under your wing, I think he could learn a lot from you," Wesley replied. It was a compliment but I felt like I'd just been sucker-punched.

"I don't know if I'm the best person for that," I answered.

"Why not?"

"He and I…" I sighed. "He's dating my ex, coach."

Wesley laughed. "I see."

"Maybe Prince or Sax will do a better job."

Wesley shook his head, rubbing his leather-like neck.

"Prince and Saxon are not as skilled as you," he mused. "And both lack the focus you have on the field."

I smirked at the accolade but realised it came with strings.

"Look Sam, you're a good player and I'm going to be honest, I don't think you'll be hanging around here much longer what with the interest from the senior clubs," he explained. "So, I'm kind of hoping you'll put your differences with Blake aside to impart some of your knowledge on him before you go. You'll be hard to replace, Samuel, but I see the same promise in him I saw in you when I first saw you play."

I pressed my lips together—what could I say to that? It was as difficult to say no to Wesley as it was to Artie; the only difference was their bargaining tools. Although I preferred Wesley's it didn't make it any easier to swallow the lack of choice I was being offered.

"Have you spoken to him about it?" I asked.

Wesley shook his head. "I wanted to speak to you first."

I huffed a laugh. "Well, I'm not sure how keen he'll be to work with me."

"If he knows what's good for him he will," Wesley chuckled. "Is that a yes?"

I shrugged. "If it's okay with him, I'll help out. I don't want to leave the team high and dry if I do go."

"What's this *if?*" he asked. "My boy, you're going places whether I have to send you there myself."

I smiled.

"Now get out of here," he chuckled, tipping his head in the direction of the change rooms. "I'll see you Saturday."

I nodded and turned, glancing up as Nate walked into Paige's welcoming arms. It shouldn't have bothered me to see, but it did. Paige had never come to training, she hated this kind of thing—team sports. I thought it was maybe because she'd never understood the significance of being able to rely on someone else to have your back—Paige never liked asking for help.

"Sammy, I'll wait in the car," Marcus called. "All good?"

"All good," I replied. "Won't be long."

"Hey, heads up," Louis said as he passed me coming out the change rooms. "Prince is throwing a shindig for Blake Saturday night—I think it's just an excuse to have a party."

"Right," I sighed. "You going?"

He shook his head. "I'm flying out tomorrow."

"Bugger."

He nodded. "I heard he broke up with his girlfriend."

"She broke up with him."

"For you?"

"I don't know, she's sort of seeing some other guy," I shrugged. "Something about throwing Prince off the scent."

Louis frowned. "Well that's messed up."

"Tell me about it."

Louis laughed. "Good luck with that."

"Thanks Macca, see you when you're back next."

"Yeah, you know the drill, a couple of weeks," he sighed, extending his hand towards me. I gripped it and gave it a squeeze and he nodded, heading back towards his car. I pushed open the change room door.

"Hey Sam, your car fixed yet?" he called.

"Kind of, why?"

"Well I was going to say you can use my car while I'm gone if you're without," he shrugged. "It'll give it a run."

"You serious?" I asked with a laugh.

He nodded.

"That'll be great."

"Okay, well if you want you can have it now if you drop me home, my brother can give me a lift to the airport tomorrow."

"Yeah, just let Sax know he's right to leave," I replied. "I won't be a sec."

"Sure thing," Louis nodded, heading towards the car park.

The good thing about staying back is most of the guys had cleared out by the time I made it to the rooms. Elliot was still there allocating who was bringing what to his party—and whom. Louis was right about one thing: this was just an excuse to rally a heap of girls to get over Isobel. At least he wasn't dwelling on the breakup—I wondered if he knew about Liam.

I dropped Louis home and detoured to the bridge to park for a while before going home myself. I knew what was waiting for me and I didn't want to face it—rather, I wanted to put off facing it for a while longer.

I got in late but Artie was still up, well at least I saw the light in his office still on from under his door. I saw Angela on my way through and said goodnight before heading to bed. I didn't actually have anything planned for Friday considering Artie had made me redundant at the garage, but when I got to my room and saw the business suit laid out I knew that he had other plans for me. I wish I was more surprised but everyone knew that my father didn't know the meaning of the word 'no' when it was directed at him.

***

"Samuel, up," Artie bellowed from outside my room Friday morning. I stirred and sandwiched my head between my pillows.

"Samuel, five minutes and I'm sending Marion up," he added.

I considered that and wondered if he'd actually do it—or if she would come. Did I want to risk it? I groaned and dragged myself to get shower. Twenty minutes later I sauntered down.

"Well, don't you look the part," Artie noted. "Ready for work?"

"No."

"Great, let's go."

I thought about making a run for it but my legs were too sore. Instead, Artie ushered me out to the company car, frowning at the addition of the '73 Ford in the driveway.

"What's that doing here?" he asked.

"I'm looking after it for a friend."

"Who?"

"Louis McKenzie, he works away."

"I see," he nodded sternly.

I yawned and sat back in the seat.

"Get comfortable now son because once we get to the office it's all business," he sighed.

"Not my business."

"Yes your business," he growled. "You got yourself into this."

I glanced up at him. "All I meant by that comment was that there's more to culture than the arts. Building more entertainment things is just spending resources; if you want to actually enhance the city you have to allocate your spending more evenly around."

"Well thank you for the budget advice," he murmured. "For someone who has no interest in city planning you sure have an opinion on it."

"People have opinions on everything," I shrugged. "That doesn't mean they have an interest in it all."

Artie exhaled and his phone rang. I closed my eyes and rested my head back.

"Arthur Saber," he said in his most businesslike tone. "Yes… what? I see… where was it scooped? …have you managed to get a hold of Angela? …well find her and double her security, take her to the house and keep her on lockdown there… no, don't make any comment, I'm on my way in now with my son… I agree, a united front is of utmost importance right now. Exactly."

He hung up. One of my eyes opened.

"Problem?"

"You could say that," he sighed. "There's been a change of plans for the agenda today."

"So sorry to hear," I grumbled sarcastically.

Artie huffed. "Not for long."

I frowned.

"A story has broken that I have been unfaithful to your mother," he explained. "There is no truth in it, I can assure you."

I sat up straight. "Well who's making the claims?"

"An airhostess from a flight I went on a few months back," he explained.

"So why'd it take her so long to come forward?"

"She is making allegations that she's pregnant."

"Allegations," I repeated narrowing my eyes. "Did you sleep with her?"

"No I did not," he snapped. "Honestly, Samuel, I expected more support from you."

I shrugged. "I wanted to hear you say it."

"Angela doesn't deserve this," he muttered. "Or Amelia. Oh gosh, Amelia."

"Well if you didn't do it, just get her to take a paternity test," I answered. "Mystery solved."

"Yes, but mud sticks, son," he groaned. "And if I ask for a test it still looks bad."

I exhaled. "Well then good job Dad."

"I beg your pardon?"

"Well, you must have done something to make her think she can pull something like this," I replied. "I mean you don't need a test to confirm or deny her accusations, you've got witnesses—clearly you did or said something that seeded enough doubt for her to lie about it."

The car stopped outside of government hall and I looked out the window, spotting a swarm of photographers and press hovering around the entrance. When they saw us, they near mobbed the car, shouting so many questions that they were all unintelligible.

"Don't say a word and stay close behind me," he said sternly. "Apologies, this is poor timing."

Apologies—not sorry, he wasn't sorry—and *poor timing*—when is the right time for a sex scandal to break around your father? My day just got interesting.

The twenty-five-year-old woman in question, whose name was Regan, was a politics and journalism graduate from Iris Cove University who decided to throw her qualifications to the wind—in a literal sense—and became a flight attendant. She met Artie, as he said, on a trip for a conference over east for work which Angela, Amelia and I were not invited to. The liaison between them reportedly continued after they actually landed for the layover—layover indeed—and three months later she claims she is carrying the next addition to the Saber legacy.

Artie spent the day perfecting his frown and going over the official release with Lawson and Perry—his head of security and head of marketing respectively. I, on the other hand, spent most of my time Friday making coffee and talking to Willow, Artie's secretary. She was a cool, thirty-three-year-old with hair the colour of sunset. Willow had worked for him for about nine years, so had kept tabs on my impending football career and studies over the time. When I was younger, and more idealistic about my father's priorities, I used to talk to her almost as much as Artie from checking in to see whether he'd make my presentation nights or junior league games. I quickly realised that if a conflict in his schedule occurred, it was me who got bumped. For Arthur Saber, spending money was a lot easier than spending time.

We headed home mid-afternoon to find a camera crew at our house and after a very brief reassurance to Angela, Artie and her sat hand in hand and addressed the circulating rumours. I was glad that Perry decided it would look better without Amelia and I on side because regardless of whether the allegations were true or not, I didn't want to be associated with it. Life was going to be hard enough without being on the evening news.

Marcus called to see how I was but we didn't talk long. We didn't tend to dwell on all the warm and fuzzy deep and meaningful stuff. Besides, talking doesn't often help matters and sometimes things are what they are and no amount of expended oxygen can change the facts. Isobel also called but I didn't answer. I didn't want to talk to her, I wanted to be with her, and I knew that wasn't why she was calling me.

When the house got quiet, I snuck out with Dalziel to give him a run. I felt kind of bad that I'd ignored him in the past few days so figured he'd enjoy the fresh air. Angela was pretty good with him and loved his company almost as much as me, but I tended to keep a faster pace than she did. By the time we got back, we were both knackered so I got him a fresh bowl of water and headed up for a shower. When I reached the top of the stairs, Amelia was waiting for me on the landing between our rooms, her face deep-set in a pout.

"Hey, what's up?" I asked, slowing to a stop. She kept her eyes lowered.

"Do you think he did it?"

"Who, Dad?" I frowned.

She nodded.

I scratched my brow. "Well he said he didn't."

"But do you think he did?" she asked. I knew what she was thinking—it was the same thing I was thinking. He was a politician, an expert at lying and persuading people to have faith in him. Defending his wrongful actions was as second nature to him as the breathing reflex. Amelia looked up when I didn't answer and I saw the shadow of hope in her light brown eyes. Hope I wanted to reciprocate but couldn't. I knew my father too well. I knew what he was like when it came to charming women—but whether he actually cheated on Angela was another question all together.

"I hope he didn't," I answered finally. "For Mum's sake."

"What do you think will happen if he did? Do you think they'll get a divorce?" she frowned, the darkness of despair snuffing the faith. My heart sank.

"I'm sure it won't come to that," I replied. "They've gotten through bad stuff before and for all we know Dad is telling the truth."

She nodded glumly.

"I wouldn't worry, Millie," I sighed, stepping up to capture her in a hug. She clung to me desperately, despite the fact I was still a bit sweaty from the run with Dally.

"I love you Sammy," she murmured.

"I love you too."

"I miss you sometimes," she said, squeezing me tighter. "We used to hang out more."

"I know, things have been crazy lately."

She sighed and pulled back to look at me, her eyes looking blotchy and glassy. "You're not going anywhere are you?"

I frowned. "Where would I go?"

"Away," she shrugged. "I know you and Dad don't get along sometimes but I don't want you leave."

"I don't plan on going anywhere," I smiled weakly. "Don't worry about anything, okay? We'll be fine. We Sabers always are."

Amelia smiled her cute little mashed-lips smile and nodded. "Thanks Sammy."

"Get some sleep," I whispered.

She waved and stepped back towards her room. "Goodnight."

"Night."

***

I couldn't sleep that night and I blamed it all on Artie. I hated him for being him and making Amelia worry, and I hated him for what he had now inflicted upon Angela. My mother deserved better than him. We all did.

I wasn't looking forward to facing what was to come because I knew that scandals like this didn't just disappear. Artie was right—mud did stick—and regardless of what happened now, he'd forever be known as the guy who was accused of impregnating a young airhostess on a business trip—an airhostess young enough to be his daughter. If I was honest, I didn't care who said what about the South Coast Mayor and former Man of the Year, I cared about what they'd say about Angela—the doting wife who got dragged along for the ride and got the raw end of the deal. Now amongst all the other crap I had to deal with right now, I had to be strong for them because Artie was too cowardly and selfish to do it himself.

I fervently regretted not getting enough sleep Friday night because Saturday morning at football was simply brutal. My only saving grace was hoping the scouts weren't here to see it since I barely got a touch, never mind a scoring shot. It was a losing battle from the very beginning, before we'd even stepped on the emerald green turf. Artie's indiscretions, whether true or not, seemed to paint a target on my back, opening up the field for a repertoire of snide remarks and side-bumps. All game I was triple teamed and drilled into the dirt whenever the ball came within three feet of me. It certainly didn't help that Artie decided to come; it just gave

150

the guys more ammunition. But Perry thought it would be a good press thing to appear unaffected by the scandal and as a family man, continuing life as normal. I couldn't understand how this was normal considering he hadn't been to a game of mine since I was eight.

Everything hurt when I dragged my sorry self into the change rooms. It was a bitter pill to swallow on our second week—our first loss.

"Next week, lads," Wesley sighed as he left. "Tough game. Get yourselves cleaned up and I'll see you Monday."

No one spoke as he left and I felt like all their silent rage was directed at me. I didn't really blame them though, I felt responsible for it—today I was the weak link, the cheap shot, and it worked since I was usually our strongest player.

"I'm fully game to drown this week tonight at my family's beach house," Elliot announced. "If you're not feeling too delicate, Saber, you should come."

I glanced up at him. "Maybe."

"You of all people need a few shots," he huffed. "After the last time I'm not entirely convinced you can hold it but I'm willing to give you another chance."

I looked at Marcus who frowned down at me.

"You going?" I asked.

He shook his head. "Can't. Family thing—my cousin's birthday or something."

"On a Saturday night?"

He shrugged.

"I can't stay at home, it's mental there at the moment," I mumbled. "But I don't want to go on my own."

"Ask Sadie," he joked. "Or that waitress from Lunar."

I narrowed my eyes. "Funny. Nate is probably going—he'd love that."

Marcus started laughing and I envied his energy to do so.

"Do you think he'll bring Paige?" he asked after a moment.

Paige.

"I don't know, maybe," I frowned.

He ran his hands over his shaved dark brown hair. "Well, you can always come with me but I can't guarantee it'll be fun—the food's always good though."

"I don't want to impose."

Marcus shrugged, heading to the showers. "Well the offer is there."

I sighed and hung my head, trying the rub the dirt-stains from my hands and arms as I scrutinised them; I could see some bruises begin to form on my forearm.

I knew straight up that I was not going to spend the night at home. Amelia had even arranged to stay at her friend's house so I wouldn't even have her to keep me sane—but to go to Elliot's beach house on my own with Nate and Paige seemed just as nuts. And then it struck me—the other alternative and the ultimate payback to Nate bringing my ex-girlfriend to the party.

I picked up my phone and scrolled through to her number, not thinking twice about what a mistake this could be before hitting the call button.

"Hello?" the smooth voice echoed down the handset.

"Ivy," I answered. "It's Sam Saber."

"Sam," she replied, and I could hear the smile in her voice. "Have you made a decision?"

I exhaled. "Got anything planned tonight?"

***

Ivy was more than happy to step up as my date for Elliot's party. I was just happy to be out my house. Artie had been nauseatingly

152

pleasant to me since the scandal broke but as far as I was concerned, it was too little too late. I kept the peace though; it was in my best interest to let him do whatever he needed to while Perry spun his magic with the public relations stuff. That guy was like a warlock with his words; he could make anyone sound like a saint.

"So are you ready for this?" Ivy asked as we pulled up in front of the South Beach house.

I exhaled. "I suppose."

"So what's the plan?"

I shrugged. "Go in?"

She rolled her eyes. "I mean, how couple-y do you want to be? Are you comfortable with hand-holding?"

"Err, I guess."

"What about kissing?"

I bit my lower lip. "Why'd you break up with Nate if you're still into him?"

She looked down. "At the time there was someone else."

I scratched my brow. "So why pick me to make him jealous?"

"It's got to be you," she smiled. "You're the only one who can make him mad enough."

I blinked. "Right."

"Besides, the fact that he's with your ex has a kind of poetic element to it," she grinned. "I'm sure you can't be happy seeing that regardless of whether you still have feelings for her or not."

I tipped my head.

"Get your game face on, Saber," she grinned. "Let's do this."

She climbed out of Louis' car and paced around to me as I followed suit, her hand slipping in mine before I even had the chance to tuck them in my pockets.

"So where were you with the whole kissing thing?" she asked, cocking a brow.

"Hey, you're making the rules, I'm just playing by them," I shrugged.

She chuckled. "I think we're going to get along just fine."

Half the football team were already there when we got in and the fact that I had Ivy by my side didn't go unnoticed. She was hard to miss. Her normally curly hair was in large silky waves, glistening like pirates gold in the dim lights. Her smile was dazzling—it was the only word for it—and lit up her golden eyes. She wore a tight white strapless dress that hugged her contours in all the right places. When she walked in the room, she turned heads, claiming their attention with the air of elegance she carried—plus she was hot as hell. I honestly didn't know how Nate managed to score all the good-looking girls.

"Saber, you made it," Elliot smirked. "Who's your friend?"

"This is Ivy," I said, glancing down at her as her hand moved up around my arm to hug my bicep. "Ivy, this is Elliot Prince."

"Prince," she noted. "It's nice to meet you."

"The pleasure is all mine," he replied. "Can I get you a drink?"

Ivy laughed, it sounded like a bell. "Sam has already offered."

I glanced down at her curiously as she released my arm and lifted her eyebrows.

"Oh, right, I'll be right back," I stuttered, glancing over to the kitchen where an entire liquor store seemed to be set up. "Any preference?"

"Surprise me," she winked.

I couldn't help but laugh. Even I was convinced by her performance.

Ivy was a natural and as soon as Nate and Paige arrived, she turned up the charm. Nate could hardly take his eyes off her—amongst other guys in the room. I kind of enjoyed the attention of being her date rather than attention for other reasons. It made for a nice change of late.

As the night went on, people began to become less and less coherent—or conscious—and by about eleven o'clock, I took the opportunity to break away from the golden girl to head to one of the many bathrooms of the Prince Palace. The "holiday house" was huge, almost as big as our home, and was only a stone's throw from the South Beach foreshore. I figured police commissioners must be well paid—I wasn't sure what Elliot's mum did.

I walked down one of the corridors and stopped short as I nearly collided with someone. I stepped back and saw it was Paige.

"Oh, hey," I murmured. "How are you?"

"Hi," she nodded.

"Funny to see you at one of these things."

"Nate asked me to come," she shrugged.

"Right, Nate," I answered. "How'd that happen? I thought you hated him."

"Things change," she shrugged. "I see you're here with Nate's ex. Classy."

I shook my head and stepped around her. I didn't want to fight with Paige and I could see that was exactly where it was heading.

"Sorry to hear about your dad," she exhaled. "That must suck for your mum. I always liked her."

I turned and nodded. "Sorry to hear about your sister."

Her brows puckered. "Who told you? Was it Nate?"

"Nate?" I frowned. "No."

She mashed her lips together, shaking her head dismissively.

"Why didn't you tell me?" I asked.

She shrugged. "I didn't want you to know. It was in the past, I didn't need your help."

"But you need Nate's help?" I said bluntly. "You never needed me, did you?"

155

Her expression changed and she blinked. "No. But I did *want* you Sam. Just not in the way you wanted me to."

"Right," I exhaled. "You know, I really tried with you. I would have done anything for you at one point but you never asked for anything so I never knew where I stood with you."

She looked down. "I've been told that my walls are hard to break down."

"Did Nate tell you that?" I huffed.

She didn't reply—she just bit her lower lip. Ugh, that lip.

I turned and continued to the bathroom. Things were never easy with Paige—at least not towards the end.

I dawdled on my way back to the party, dragging my sore legs back down the rabbit warren to the main room. I almost didn't hear it over the blaring music and chatter but Paige's voice made me stop dead in my tracks. I paused for a moment to make sure I wasn't just hearing things and then heard her protests again—and then I was moving very quickly back down the hallway. There were three doors that were all closed over and I nudged two of them until the third opened to two figures. I don't know what I was expecting—maybe Nate cowering over her or maybe her on the phone; regardless, answering her duress was like second nature to me.

It was Elliot who was the threat and he had her hands pinned above her head as he stood between her legs, she was struggling against him—putting up a decent fight—but he was stronger and had her easily restrained. Her silence was due to his free hand being clasped over her mouth.

I saw red.

Elliot turned as I burst in, and Paige, taking advantage of the distraction lashed herself free, kicking him away as I threw a punch in his direction. He faltered drunkenly and tried to fight back, stumbling about in an attempt to keep his footing. He was still strong though and managed to grip me in a headlock; it was only Paige's right hook that halted him, sending him flying unconscious to the floor. Some right hook.

"Thanks," I sighed, brushing my hair back.

I glanced over at her and she nodded mutely then burst into tears. I'd never seen Paige cry so openly before, on principle she didn't. It scared me a little.

"Hey," I soothed, walking towards her. "It's okay, you're okay now."

She looked at me with an almost confused expression then walked into my chest; instinctively I moved my arms around her, holding her tight to shield her from the world.

After a few minutes had passed, she stopped crying and stepped back.

"I'm sorry."

"For what?" I laughed but it was humourless—more incredulous.

"Crying," she frowned. "I don't know what came over me."

"You're allowed to cry."

She shook her head. "He just came at me and grabbed me… I tried to fight him off but he's strong."

As she spoke, she wound her fingers around her small wrists and I could see the reddening marks beginning to form.

I wanted to continue thumping him into the floor. My head turned to make sure he was out and I was kind of disappointed that he was. Paige must've guessed my thoughts.

"Don't Sam," she murmured. "Let's just get out of here."

I looked longingly at his slumped figure but listened to her—the last thing I needed was Elliot with more reason to hate me, I was already in pretty deep with throwing the first punch but I'd do it a hundred times over given the chance.

"Thanks for saving me," Paige whispered as I followed her out the room and closed the door.

"I'm not sure I did."

"You found me, if it wasn't for that…" she stopped and squeezed her eyes closed, raising her hand to her reddened cheek. I hadn't really noticed it before.

I frowned. "Did he hit you?"

"Don't Sam," she pleaded. "He's not worth it."

"Are you *kidding* me?" I sneered, resting my hand on the door. Paige clutched at my arm.

"I mean it, just leave it," she begged. "It's over with."

I glowered at her angrily, wondering when she'd become the person to back down, to cry, to open up—she'd completely changed in the past week and it both surprised and awed me.

"What's going on?" Nate's voice echoed, cutting through the atmosphere like a hot knife. Paige released my arm and stepped back.

"Nothing, it's fine."

"I was worried when you didn't come back," he noted. "Samuel."

"Nathaniel," I answered.

Nate looked to Paige curiously. "Are you sure you're okay?"

She smiled weakly. "I am now."

"She was attacked," I interrupted, angry over her sudden blissful happiness after such an ordeal. "Prince had her pinned down and I think he hit her. She's not okay, she's shaken up. You should take her home."

Nate's pale green eyes bulged. "What?!"

"Don't Nate," Paige sighed. "I'm okay, really. Sam came in just in time."

"In time for what?" Nate growled. "What did Prince do?"

"Nothing, he just grabbed me, that's all," she exhaled. "Can we just go?"

Nate looked as mad as I felt. "Where is he?"

"Please can you just leave it?" she replied. "He was drunk and I'm fine. I just want to go home."

Nate looked at her for a long moment and seemed to diffuse.

"Sure, I'll take you home," he answered calmly.

I blinked in confusion—what'd just happened? If that was my girlfriend—hell, I still wanted to deck the guy—there was no way a pout would cover it.

"What's going on down here?" Ivy asked, walking towards us.

"Nothing, we were just about to go," Paige said. "Actually, Sam was about to come and find you."

Ivy's eyebrows lifted. "Oh?"

I frowned—maybe Paige was right. If I stayed I'd probably just get in more trouble than I cared to clean up later.

"Are you ready to leave?" I asked her.

She ran her finger down my chin. "If you are."

I glanced up at Nate who didn't seem to flinch at Ivy's affections towards me. Paige, on the other hand, looked as if she was trying to solve a hard maths equation.

"Okay, well, as long as you're all right," I added, glancing to Paige.

She nodded. "I am."

And that was it. We left and I dropped Ivy off before heading back to the house that used to feel more like home to me. I got ready for bed and rolled in, feeling my muscles loosen as I laid down. As I switched off my lamp, my phone lit up with a text from Paige: "*Turns out I need you after all. Thanks again for before. I just want you to be happy Sam.*"

I hit reply. "*I want the same thing for you too. Always prepared to come to your rescue.*"

159

I sighed and rolled onto my side as my phone glowed to life again: *"Ever the knight in shining armour."*

I smiled and closed my eyes. Guess I was more of a swordsman than I initially thought.

VIII

A Hard Place

Sunday morning I woke up to shouting downstairs and was surprised to hear my name thrown in the mix. What had I done now? I got out of bed and headed for my door, sauntering down the stairs to see what all the commotion was about. I almost headed straight back up when I saw who the voice belonged to. Police Commissioner Harvey Prince.

He looked up as I appeared and turned a shade of scarlet.

"You attacked my son!" he yelled. "We are pressing charges for assault and I'll only be too happy to add a restraining order to that!"

He was waving something around; it looked like a piece of paper. Artie was standing about three feet from him looking like he always did when my name was mentioned.

"Is this about last night?" I frowned.

"Last night? Of course it's about last night!" Commissioner Prince bellowed. "My Elliot is black and blue!"

Artie shook his head.

I tipped mine. "Assault *and* a restraining order?"

"You heard me!" Harvey shouted.

"Well in that case, why don't you speak to Paige Stewart about the assault and attempted rape charges that could be filed against *your* son?"

"I *beg* your pardon, young man?!" Harvey exclaimed. I fleetingly wondered if all guys in powerful positions used that phrase—it seemed a popular choice.

"Sure, I hit him *once*—I mean I barely touched him, because it was Paige who fought him off and knocked him out because he had her pinned to the bed against her will," I explained. "I take it Elliot missed out those details when he told you my part in all this?"

Harvey's face went from scarlet to beetroot. "Nonsense, Elliot wouldn't do that."

"And Samuel would not start a fight where there is no cause," Artie added. My mouth dropped open as he came to my defence and I quickly snapped it shut.

"Harvey, our boys have known each other a long time," Artie sighed, resting a hand on his shoulder as he walked him towards the door. "So why don't you have another chat to young Elliot before you come around here throwing accusations at my son?"

"He still admitted to hitting him!" Harvey replied.

Artie smiled his pleasant, yet exceedingly condescending smile. "It sounds more to me like a little disagreement amongst friends—or self-defence if you'd like to check all the facts. I'm on quite familiar terms with Miss Stewart's parents—good people; mother's a pharmacist and I believe her father is a philosophy lecturer—so I'd be happy to get in touch with them to discuss this like adults?"

Harvey's face drained white.

"No, no," he stuttered. "I'll—I'll talk to Elliot, leave it to me."

"I will. I have a hundred percent faith in your capabilities, Harv," Artie nodded. "So I take it the assault charges and restraining order can be put on hold until all the facts are uncovered? I'd hate for this to turn into something bigger than it is—after all, the boys are still young and you know as well as I do that criminal records don't just disappear with time."

Harvey blinked as the threat sank in. "Certainly Arthur, of course."

Artie opened the front door. "Thanks for stopping by."

"Good day to you both," Harvey nodded.

Artie smiled and closed the door, turning to me with an accusatory expression.

"Is it true?" he asked sternly. "About the Prince boy, what he did?"

"Yes."

I was a little miffed that he still didn't quite believe me but could hardy hold his doubt against him after he'd displayed none when standing up to the police commissioner. Plus he'd practically Jedi mind-tricked him out of pressing charges against me.

"Did you put your weight behind it?" Artie asked, taking me by surprise.

"You mean the punch?" I frowned. "Yeah, I did all right."

Artie pressed his lips together into the shadow of a smile. "Good."

He walked off in the direction of his office and I couldn't help but laugh before making my way back up to my room.

I spent the rest of the day fishing with Bryce and it was a much-needed change of pace. I headed home around dusk, which seemed to be getting earlier these days, and made it just in time for the family dinner. It was a lot quieter than normal with Artie not doing his normal domination over the conversation, so Amelia did most of the talking. I didn't know where things stood between Artie and Angela but I didn't want to ask. They were civil to each other at least—further backing my theory that my mother was an angel.

Monday morning I headed off to uni and had to put up with a fresh wave of people whispering as I walked by. I had to admit, it was a little bit refreshing that they weren't talking about my private life for a change but considering they were most likely including Angela in their bickering, I wanted to personally punch every single one of them.

163

"Hey," a quiet voice said as I walked with my head down back to Louis' car at three thirty after my four-hour workshop. I looked up and sighed.

"Hey Paige."

"How are you?" she asked, giving her cute mashed smile.

I tipped my head. "I can safely say that I've had better months."

She laughed. "Right."

"How are you?"

"Me?" she replied. "I'm fine, why wouldn't I be?"

I began walking again and she followed. "I had a visit yesterday morning from Commissioner Prince about Elliot pressing assault charges and a restraining order on me."

Paige frowned. "What?"

I shook my head. "Artie talked him out of it but he was pretty fired up."

"I'm so sorry, Sam."

I blinked. "Why are you sorry?"

"Because it's my fault—"

"No," I interrupted. "Just no. It's all Prince."

Paige gave a light laugh. "Actually, I was going to say that it's my fault he got knocked out. I think I did more damage to him than you did."

I burst into laughter and she grinned. I liked Paige like this, relaxed, carefree, smiling. She was beautiful when she smiled— who was I kidding? She was always beautiful, but when she smiled, there was something else on top of her normal beauty.

"So how are things with your parents?" she asked.

I exhaled. "I don't know, they don't really talk about it. They seem okay."

"Can't be easy on you and Amelia though."

"I'm more worried about my mum," I answered honestly. "She's had to put up with a lot over the years."

Paige nodded and we stopped at the curb across the road from Louis' car. She looked up.

"Where's your car?"

"Sitting on my driveway."

"Why?"

"It died," I shrugged. "I was working for Austin at the garage to fix it but Artie paid him to do it all. I'm protesting."

Paige bit her lip. Lord, that lip.

"That makes perfect sense," she answered. "So you're driving Macca's car? Is he away again?"

I smiled. "Yeah, he let me borrow it."

"That was nice of him," she noted. "Though he is enabling your childish behaviour."

I rolled my eyes. "Childish? Artie started it."

Paige breathed a laugh and bit her lip again. I looked away to control myself.

"Well I'd better go," she murmured. "I'm supposed to be meeting Nate."

"Right," I nodded. "Is he still coming to training?"

Paige blinked. "Right, football training. I really should remember that by now."

I glanced at my feet.

"Hang in there with your folks, Sam," she whispered. "Family is important."

"Yeah," I breathed.

She mashed her lips together and brushed my arm, walking away without another word. I watched her go, watched the way her red hair bounced as she walked, her finger weaving their way around the ends.

"Hello you," a voice interrupted as Ivy bounced up in front of me, her hands moving around my neck to pull my face down to hers. Her lips encompassed mine, taking me by surprise as her body arched, forcing mine to lean over hers. I can't say it was an unpleasant surprise but it was a little awkward in the ways of greeting.

"Ivy," I gasped as she pulled away. "Um, hi."

Her eyes flickered behind me and she grinned, brushing my cheeks with her fingers. "Hi."

I glanced to the side but she stopped me from turning my head. "What are you up to?"

"Nothing," she smiled. "What about you?"

"About to head home before footy training."

"Great, sounds like fun."

I blinked. "What does?"

"All of the above," she smiled.

I frowned. "You want to come to football training with me?"

She shrugged. "I've got nothing else to do."

My eyebrows rose. "Okay, if you want."

She lifted her hand gesturing for me to lead the way and as we turned, we were face-to-face with Isobel and Liam.

"Oh, hi," I stuttered.

Isobel looked like she'd just swallowed a teaspoon of wasabi. "Hello."

"Hey Liam," Ivy waved. "Who's your friend?"

Liam blinked.

"I, um, this is Isobel," he answered. "Isobel, this is Ivy."

"Charmed," Isobel exhaled.

"Likewise," Ivy beamed. "Well we were about to leave, weren't we Sam?"

I bit my lip. "Uh, yeah."

"How do you two know each other?" Isobel interrupted. I wasn't sure whether she meant me and Ivy or Ivy and Liam.

"Sam and I met in the library," Ivy answered, glancing up at me. The look on her face made my heart quicken—then I remembered that I was there and nothing suggestive had happened at all. "And Liam and I know each other because I used to date his best friend."

Isobel pulled a face. "Paige?"

Ivy's eyebrow rose. "Now there's a thought."

I tried to hold my laughter but a chuckle slipped out. I didn't want to embarrass Isobel but even she knew that Ivy wouldn't be talking about Paige.

"She means Nate," Liam murmured almost in Isobel's ear.

"Right, Nathaniel," Isobel nodded. "Who is *currently* dating Paige."

Ivy tipped her head, her blonde hair falling into the contours of her chest. "Is he?"

"We should go," I said, moving my arm around to rest on Ivy's hip. Isobel's eyes dropped and she rolled back her shoulders.

"Us too," she replied, taking hold of Liam's hand. Liam glanced around self-consciously and I smirked at the thought that he was wary of Elliot—then I remembered that I hated Elliot more than I hated Liam.

"See you guys," I nodded, towing Ivy across the road. I opened the passenger door for her and waited for her to get in then closed it, as I walked around to the driver's side; I glanced back at where Isobel and Liam had been and saw Isobel's blue eyes peer over her shoulder at us before quickly turning back forward. I guess I should give Ivy more credit—she certainly knew how to play games.

***

"Your house is a castle," she noted as I pulled up the driveway.

"I know."

"Whose car is that?" she asked, nodding towards the Morris Minor.

"Mine."

"Whose car is this?"

"A friend of mine's."

"Is it stolen?"

I huffed. "No."

"So why do you have it?"

"Long story," I sighed, opening the door. I walked around to get hers for her but she was already halfway out. She stepped aside and I closed it for her.

"So when is training?"

"Five thirty."

She nodded. "So we've got just over an hour until we have to go."

I smiled and headed up the stairs to the front door. "Yes."

"Well."

"Well?"

"Well."

I pushed open the door. "After you."

"Thank you," she replied. "So chivalrous."

I raised an eyebrow and she breathed a laugh.

"Samuel, I—oh," Artie's voice bellowed. "Who's your friend?"

"Uh, this is Ivy," I answered. Great, meet the parents. "Ivy this is my father, Arthur."

Artie frowned at my introduction.

"Mr Saber," she beamed. "Such a pleasure to meet you."

"Ivy," he grinned, thawing instantly at the use of a title rather than his first name. "It's nice to meet you too."

I pressed my lips together. "Did you need me?"

Artie looked over. "What? Uh, no son, it can wait."

"Okay," I nodded; resting my hand on Ivy's lower back to guide her towards the stairs. Artie looked unusually smug as we walked away. I couldn't be bothered trying to work out why.

"So your room is up stairs?" she asked. "Which level?"

"Third."

"Three?"

"Yep."

She glanced back at me and smiled. "Are you freaking out?"

"Me? Why?" I laughed.

"Because you hardly know me and I invited myself over," she replied, stopping at the top of the first flight of stairs.

"Why would that freak me out?" I asked, stepping up so we were eye-level.

He shoulder lifted. "Some guys get freaked out with girls who are forward."

"Really?"

"Mm."

I smiled. "I'm not freaked out."

She tipped her head back, glancing down at me.

"Okay," she sighed, turning on her heel and heading towards the next flight of stairs. I chuckled and followed her as Amelia's head popped over the top.

"Sammy?"

"Hey Millie," I called up. "This is Ivy—Ivy, my little sister Amelia."

"Ivy," she repeated. "Hi."

"Hello Amelia," Ivy answered. "Wow, you're so pretty."

Amelia blinked. "Um, thanks. You too."

Ivy smiled, standing a few steps from the top.

"Are you dating my brother?" Amelia asked, looking to me for an explanation despite the fact she was addressing Ivy.

"We're just hanging out," Ivy replied causally.

I frowned at Amelia and she shrugged, disappearing back into her room.

"My room is to the left," I said, pointing to the door.

Ivy turned and pushed the door open and I chuckled as she stepped over some obstacles on the floor.

"It's big," she noted.

"I get that a lot."

She laughed. "Sure you do."

I folded my arms.

"So do you bring many girls to your house?" she asked.

"To my house?" I repeated, considering the question. "No."

"Why not?"

"My family is a little intense."

She nodded. "They seem nice enough to me."

"That's because you're still a stranger to them, they're on their best behaviour."

She peeled off her sweater and draped it over my desk chair. "I'm still a stranger to you too."

"I suppose."

"But we can get to know each other better."

My brow rose. "What did you have in mind?"

She smiled. "What's your mother like?"

I frowned. "Why?"

"I haven't met her yet."

"She's like a mum," I shrugged.

Ivy nodded, looking around at all my crap strewn everywhere. "How long were you and Paige together for?"

"About a year."

"What about the Isobel?"

"Isobel and I never dated," I replied.

Ivy looked over at me. "That's not what I asked."

I shrugged. "A couple of months."

"Did you sleep with her?"

"What's with all the questions?"

"I'm getting to know you better," she answered innocently.

"What about you and Nate?" I asked. "How long were you together?"

"Five months," she replied. "And yes, I left him for a guy which turned out to be a mistake."

"What do you see in him?"

Ivy blinked and her eyes unfocused. "He's different than he seems. He might appear to be a bit rough around the edges but he's really thoughtful."

"Why did you leave him then?" I asked.

She shrugged. "I didn't think I saw a future with him."

"But now you do?"

"Now I think maybe I was a little too dismissive of our relationship," she answered.

I thought for a moment about that—about going back to exes when things didn't work out the first time. Did things ever really change? What makes people think that the reasons things fell apart aren't still there? I wasn't sure I could do it—or would do it. I thought back to Paige and frowned—but things had changed between us since we broke up. Paige had changed. She was more open and carefree; the walls that seemed impenetrable seemed somewhat easier to climb. Maybe I was being too dismissive of Paige too…

"Sam."

"Hm?"

"What do you want to do?"

I looked at her and tipped my head. "Why did you want to come here?"

She shrugged. "Like I said, I had nothing else to do."

"Nothing at all?"

"Maybe I just wanted to hang out with you," she replied, cocking a brow.

"Why?"

"You're interesting."

I blinked. "Not really."

"Why did you say yes to me?" she asked.

"Yes to what?"

"To me coming here, to me in general?"

I rubbed the stubble on my chin. "I don't know. You seemed cool."

"Cool," she smirked, sitting back on my bed. "Wow."

"I guess I also liked the idea of getting back at Blake," I answered. "And you're helping me out too so… if you wanted to come here, I figured why not?"

She nodded, considering that for a moment. "Which one do you want?"

"What?"

"Which one? The redhead or the brunette?"

I frowned. "You already know the answer to that."

"Do *you*?"

"Where is this coming from?" I sighed.

She smiled. "I saw you with Paige today. I saw the way she looked at you on Saturday night. She's not over you."

"Paige?" I asked. "She's with Nate, of course she is."

Ivy laughed. "You of all people know that you can be interested in more than one person at a time. You were yourself— you still are."

"I broke up with Paige," I replied. "I broke up with Paige so I could be with Isobel."

"Who is where?"

"With Liam," I frowned.

"Exactly."

"So?"

"So Isobel looked pretty uncomfortable seeing you with me too," she explained. "Apparently she only wants you when you're taken and the other just wants you."

I rubbed my head. "This is completely mental."

"Don't you know that it's because of guys that girls hate other girls," Ivy sighed.

I shook my head. "Girls are weird."

"But if you want a group of girls to get along, just throw a guy in the mix and they're best friends."

"That's nuts."

"Girls just want to be liked."

"Then why can't they just be themselves?"

"Oh Sam, you really don't understand women."

"I never pretended to."

She smiled. "I like you."

I gave her a look.

"Relax, I'm interested in someone else," she added. "Although, you are a great kisser."

I chuckled. "Warning would be nice next time you throw yourself at me."

"You didn't seem to mind," she shrugged.

I huffed. Guess I didn't—especially when it meant getting Isobel's attention.

Ivy and I grabbed some food from Marion then hung around the house until I had to leave for training. She came and sat in the stands, which didn't go unnoticed by the guys. Nate didn't look thrilled about it but didn't mention anything; he seemed to have other things on his mind. Wesley had us teamed up again but was running through different drills.

Elliot, on the other hand, seemed to be gunning for me from the second I stepped on the oval. I wasn't surprised really, considering what had passed, but taking into account my reason for throwing the first punch, I would've thought he'd be smarter about acting the victim. If anything, I should be the mad one but he wasn't worth the effort. Nate wasn't so forgiving though.

"How can he act like he's done nothing wrong?" Nate mumbled to me. It was a bit refreshing that I wasn't on the receiving end of his sneer.

"He's a Prince," I frowned. "As far as he's concerned he hasn't. He wants something, he takes it."

"That doesn't extend to people."

"*I* know that," I sighed. "But he's not used to not getting what he wants."

"He needs to be taught a lesson," Nate growled.

I huffed. "Don't be stupid. I punched the guy for what he did and his father came around trying to slap assault charges on me."

Nate looked at me as if to question my sanity. "You serious?"

"He's not worth it, just let it go," I answered.

Nate glared at me—ah, back to the Nate I knew.

Despite the fact he seemed annoyed with my advice; he seemed to take it seriously and stayed clear of Elliot... at least until ten minutes before the end of practice. Wesley had us playing a half game pinning Elliot and Nate against each other—we were rotating players to keep our legs fresh. I saw it coming before it happened: Elliot was poised to receive the ball, leaning hard against Nate as he waited, Nate shoulder's tilting causing Elliot's body to give way and tumble hard to the ground.

He landed on his shoulder with a crunch and a wail. Needless to say, training finished a bit earlier for the rest of us, though we all waited while Wesley stood by with the paramedics to cart Elliot to hospital. Whether it was a broken collarbone or a dislocated shoulder, recovery for him by the end of the season looked slim. So before we all were dismissed, Wesley named me captain in Elliot's place.

"Is training always that eventful?" Ivy asked as I drove her home.

I exhaled. "No, thank goodness."

"Guess you'd end up with no team if it did," she laughed.

I frowned. "Prince is a decent player. We needed him this season."

"You're not so bad yourself though."

"It takes more than one good player to have a good team."

Ivy sighed. "Nate is a rogue."

I huffed. "What's not to love?"

"At least he breaks a smile once in a while."

"Who are you talking about?"

"Paige needs to lighten up," she noted. "And Isobel needs to chill out a little more."

I laughed. "And I suppose you're perfect?"

"Hey, I have my flaws but no one ever accused me of taking life too seriously," she smiled.

"You shouldn't judge too quickly, you don't know their story."

"You don't know mine," she shrugged. "It's next left then number thirty."

It took me a moment to realise she was giving me directions so my left was a sharp one. I slowed as I turned and counted down the letterboxes in Hawthorn Court, passed a block of flats on the right and almost at the end of the street was number thirty. It was a block of six small, cottage-looking buildings. They looked quite cosy from the outside.

I pulled up the shared driveway.

"Thanks for the ride," she smiled. "It beats walking or the bus."

"You don't have a car?"

Her eyebrow rose. "We don't all have friends who fly-in-fly-out."

I breathed a laugh. "Well you're welcome."

I hadn't even thought about it the other day when we went to Elliot's party since she'd asked me to pick her up from uni and drop her back at Crescent. I guess it wasn't that far but still a decent distance in the dark.

"Are you at uni tomorrow?" I asked.

"No, Tuesdays are my day off—of sorts." She smiled, clicking open the door. "I'll see you around, Saber."

"Um, Ivy?"

She dropped her head back into view, looking through the open passenger side door.

I pressed my lips together. "It was, uh, cool to hang out today."

"It was," she nodded. "Night Sam."

"Night," I smiled, lifting a hand to wave as she closed the door. I couldn't help but think, as I drove home from Nate's ex-girlfriend's house, that if nothing else, he at least had quite good taste in girls.

***

Tuesday morning I dragged my feet to class, still waking up after a restless night. Dally seemed extra needy so decided to camp at the end of my bed. I normally wouldn't mind but aside from being scared of the thunder, he tends to snore. Fun.

"Sam," Isobel hissed as I rounded the corner. She was waiting outside our tutorial—seemingly for me.

"Hey," I sighed. "What's up?"

"I need to talk to you," she murmured, walking up and grabbing my forearm.

I frowned. "We've got class, can it wait?"

Isobel did a second take—I'd never made her wait before. Princess Isobel.

"Class?" she stuttered. "Seriously?"

I raised my eyebrows. "I think I'm failing philosophy, I shouldn't really miss it."

I wasn't really failing, but I wasn't excelling. Maybe Mr Stewart could help me; he was one of the lecturers here.

"I don't have long after class," she answered, her forehead puckering.

"Is it going to take long?"

"Well, no."

"Okay then," I nodded, heading inside. She hesitated then followed me. I felt pretty pleased with myself.

The whole tutorial, Isobel fidgeted. I was actually pretty curious as to what she was going to tell me bit I liked the fact she was anxious about it. Normally the shoe was on the other foot.

When class was dismissed, Isobel was the first up. I made sure I took my time to pack my things before following everyone out.

"I'm meeting Liam in half an hour so we need to be quick," she sighed as I joined her. I was suddenly less interested in what she had to say.

"Fine."

She pouted and led me out onto the street. "Did you drive in?"

I glanced up at the almost black sky. "Yes."

"Where's your car?"

"I've got Louis'."

"Oh."

I scratched my stubble. "You want to go somewhere?"

She nodded.

"In half an hour?" I clarified.

"Yes, where is it parked?" she asked.

I started down the street and stopped three cars down, unlocking the door and holding it open for her. She got in silently and waited as I followed suit.

"Where to?"

"The bridge."

I exhaled and started the car. "Okay."

We drove in silence the short distance to the bridge, Isobel playing absently with the ends of her hair the whole while. When I'd parked the car, I sighed, resting my hands on the steering wheel.

"Well, what's on your mind?"

I knew it was a dangerous question to ask a girl but the reason we were here was precisely because she had something to say— plus as previously noted, we didn't have much time.

Isobel unclipped her seatbelt and climbed over the handbrake onto my lap.

"Wow, okay," I exhaled.

"Sam," she breathed, lowering her lips to mine. I was taken aback—it wasn't what I was expecting—so it took me a moment to participate. She pulled back, reading my surprise as something else.

"Don't you want me anymore?" she pouted. "Is this because of the blonde?"

The blonde, the brunette, the redhead—what was it with girls? Did they really all hate each other for no reason?

"No, I'm just surprised," I huffed. "I thought you wanted to cool things?"

"Is that what you want?" she asked.

I blinked—when had I ever said anything along those lines? I shook my head and reached up to tuck her hair behind her ear and she smiled. Lord, she was confusing.

Her mouth enclosed on mine again and she was kissing me fervently as the sky opened up and began pelting rain on the metal and glass shell of the car. Isobel pulled off her beige cardigan and threw it on the seat beside her, dragging my long-sleeved shirt off me and added it to the pile.

"How long have we got?" I panted as she unbuttoned my jeans.

She smiled. "Guess I can be a bit late."

***

Isobel straightened her top and replaced her cardigan as I drove us back to uni.

"So I thought we weren't going to do that," I smirked, glancing sideways at her. "Not that I'm complaining."

"I changed my mind," she smiled. "Plus, I'm not with Elliot anymore—and I already told you that Liam and I aren't a couple."

"You're not?"

"No."

I nodded. "Then what are you?"

"Just friends," she sighed.

"Friends?"

"Yes."

"Then why did you act like you were more than that?"

"When?" she pouted.

"Yesterday."

"When that blonde was all over you?"

I rolled my eyes. "Her name is Ivy."

"Whatever," she exhaled. "Why are you hanging out with her anyway? Has it got something to do with Paige?"

I groaned.

"Well it's too perfect to be a coincidence that she's Nathaniel's ex-girlfriend and he happens to be dating yours," Isobel shrugged.

"It's not a coincidence," I replied honestly. "She wants Nate back so I'm helping her out."

Isobel pulled a face as I pulled into park. "Why?"

"Because she's cool," I answered. "Why are you so bothered by it? You made it clear that we're not a couple."

"I'm not bothered by it," she smiled incredulously. "See who you want."

"I will."

She pulled in her lower lip and looked down.

"Well, today was…" I searched for the right word. "Fun."

She breathed a laugh. "Yes it was."

"Let me know when you want to do it again."

"Soon," she nodded, glancing around. It was still raining. "Goodbye Sam."

She leaned over and kissed me on the corner of my lips.

"Bye," I sighed.

Isobel got out of the car and danced undercover out of the rain. I watched her go and then checked my watch. Crap, my workshop had already started. I climbed out and darted for the path, fastening my jeans as I ran. There were definitely worse reasons for being late to class.

IX

Two to Tango

"Well you've certainly got a spring in your step," Marcus laughed as I let him in Tuesday afternoon. "Does this have anything to do with that leggy blonde you brought to practice yesterday?"

I felt my forehead pucker and smiled. "Leggy? She was wearing jeans."

"She has a set of stems on her," he answered. "Don't tell me you didn't notice."

I chuckled.

"So what did you want to do tonight? Crescent?" he asked.

"Nuh, I've got an example to set," I sighed. "Acting captain and all."

He grinned. "Right."

"We can go somewhere else though?"

"Nuh, it's no fun if we have to behave."

"We? You hardly drink anyway."

"What's that got to do with behaving?" he shrugged.

I laughed.

"Hey Marcus," Amelia said, sauntering down the stairs.

"Hey little lady," he nodded. "How goes it?"

"Fine," she shrugged. "How about you?"

Marcus winked theatrically. "You know me."

Amelia giggled and I frowned. She always acted jittery around Marcus; it was a little embarrassing—and concerning.

"Sax, want to grab a pizza? I'm kind of craving pizza," I said.

"Setting an example, huh?" he laughed. "Yeah, I could go for a pizza—what about you Millie?"

I looked at my sister as her cheeks glowed red. Ah crap.

"Are you ordering in or going out?" she asked.

"Out," I said at the same time Marcus said "in".

Amelia glanced at me. "No, it's fine."

Girls and their guilt-trips.

"Come if you want to, Amelia," I shrugged.

"You should see if the blonde wants to come," Marcus added, wiggling his eyebrows. I shoved him and pulled out my phone.

"Okay."

He gave a conspiring laugh.

"Do you mean Ivy?" Amelia asked. "She seems nice."

I looked up from texting and nodded.

Marcus cocked his head. "You've met her?"

"Sammy brought her here yesterday before training," she replied. Amelia—never knowing when to keep her mouth shut.

"So this is a thing now?" Marcus huffed. "I thought if anything you'd end up with Sadie."

"Who's Sadie?" Amelia frowned.

"The girl who talked him into getting the tattoo."

"Tattoo?" Amelia gawked.

"Shut up, Sax," I sighed. "Ivy will meet us there—are you coming or what Amelia?"

Amelia was frowning at me disapprovingly.

"Give me two seconds to grab my coat," she mumbled, disappearing up the stairs.

I turned to Marcus. "Honestly, you two."

He grinned. "Been holding out a bit, hey Sammy?"

I shook my head and started for the door as Amelia bounded down the stairs.

We pulled up at *Merlin's Pizzeria* as Ivy was walking up, sheltered by her yellow umbrella.

"Hey Sam," she smiled. "Hello Amelia."

"Hi Ivy," Amelia waved.

"I don't believe we've met," Ivy said, looking to Marcus.

Marcus glanced down at her legs and I smacked him in the arm.

"This is Sax—err, Marcus," I replied. "He plays football with me; you might have seen him at practice."

"Oh," Ivy nodded. "I don't really remember, sorry."

Marcus' smile faded and I laughed along with Amelia.

"Come on, let's eat," I chuffed, holding the door open. Ivy shrugged innocently, following Amelia inside as Marcus muttered something under his breath.

The evening was good. Ivy seemed to fit in with Marcus and Amelia like she'd known them for years—I guess that's just what she's like. After the initial bruising to Marcus' ego, Ivy was quite charming towards him. In fact, if we were a couple I probably would have been jealous. Amelia certainly looked it, though, as Ivy said, didn't *act* it with us two guys around.

"I think I preferred Paige," Amelia mumbled as I drove the three of us back to our place; Ivy had been quite happy to walk.

"Why?" I smiled, slightly amused at my little sister.

She just shrugged.

"I like Ivy," Marcus noted. "She's got spunk."

I caught Amelia roll her eyes and laughed, turning my attention back to the road.

When we got home, Marcus left and Amelia and I went inside.

"Hey kids," Angela sighed. "Did you go out?"

"Sorry Mum, I forgot to leave a note," Amelia blushed.

Angela smiled. "That's fine honey. Did you have fun?"

Amelia nodded, glancing to me as I did the same.

"Well, good night Mum," I yawned.

"Night Samuel," she murmured. "Night Millie."

"Night Mum, love you."

"I love you too."

I waved and made my way up, hearing Amelia behind me.

"Sammy, thanks for letting me come," she said with a small smile as we both reached the top.

"Yeah, no worries," I nodded.

She pressed her lips together, deliberating whether to leave.

My eyebrows rose. "What's up?"

She scratched her head, looking embarrassed. "Well, it's just that…"

I folded my arms, half expecting an awkward question about Marcus.

"I thought that you liked Isobel Armelle," she said. "And then Ivy showed up and Marcus mentioned something about a girl called Sadie?"

I frowned.

"I just hope you know what you're doing, that's all," she finished.

"Yeah, kind of," I nodded. "Things with Isobel are sort of complicated and Ivy and I are just friends."

Amelia shook her head. "You don't need to explain yourself to me."

"I know," I replied. "But I want you to know that I'm not playing them."

She laughed. "I know you're not."

I pressed my lips together. "Okay."

"Okay."

"Well, good night then."

"Night Sammy. Love you."

"Love you too, Millie."

"Hey Sam," Isobel said, putting her things down on the end of my table. I was sitting in the common room waiting for philosophy to start since I had an hour to burn between my morning lecture and the one thirty class.

"Isobel," I nodded. "Talking to me in public now?"

Amusement played in her pretty blue eyes. "Yes."

I bit my apple and huffed a laugh. "Okay."

"Can I join you?"

I frowned. "You need to ask?"

She shrugged.

"Yeah, of course," I answered.

She sat down and twirled her hair around her finger. I watched her warily, trying to dislodge the pieces of apple that had gotten caught between my teeth.

"You all right?"

She looked up. "Yes."

I folded my arms. "Sure?"

"Did you say something to Liam?" she asked.

"Me? No," I frowned. "Why?"

She shook her head. "He didn't show up the other day."

I pressed my lips together. "Well you were twenty minutes late."

"I know, but still."

I laughed. "I wouldn't stress about it."

"It's not like him to just not show up," she mused. "He's not answering my texts either."

I took another bite of my apple and then offered it to her. She shook her head.

"He'll come around," I shrugged, wondering why I was trying to encourage her not to give up on the guy who was trying to steal her from me.

Isobel glanced over at me. "What did you get up to last night?"

"Pizza with Sax and Millie."

"Marcus and Amelia," she smiled. "Third wheel?"

I pulled a face. "I hope not—no, Ivy came along too."

Isobel's blue eyes narrowed. "Ivy."

"Mm," I nodded.

"You two are spending an awful lot of time together," she noted.

"Not really."

She pulled out her notebook and a pen, flipping to a page. I watched her in amusement.

"Are you jealous?"

"What? No!" she snapped. "Like I said, I don't care who you spend your time with."

"That's what I thought," I smirked.

She wrote something and then put her pen down.

"It's just that you two seem close," she continued. "I saw you kissing her the other day."

I pressed my lips together. "Right, you saw that."

Her eyebrows rose as she waited for an explanation.

"She kissed me," I replied. "And we're not a thing; it was just… like an experiment."

"Experiment."

"Yeah."

"What experiment?"

"Erm, she was proving that she's not attracted to me."

Isobel scoffed. "Right, well I think she failed that one. She was all over you—and you were all over her, putting your arm around her."

I laughed, it all seemed very ridiculous.

"Don't laugh at me," she snapped.

"Sorry, it's just funny," I shrugged. "Because you're the one who started hanging out with Liam for whatever reason first."

"I told you, it was to protect you," she whispered.

"Whatever," I chuckled. "So call this protection for you."

Her forehead puckered. "I don't need protection from anyone."

"What makes you think I do?" I sighed. "And by the way, have you even considered that your man Liam might be staying away from you because of something Prince said or did to him?"

She blinked. "Did he say something to you?"

I shrugged. "The last I saw him he was in the back of an ambulance."

"What?"

"He went down at practice Monday," I sighed. "Dislocated shoulder."

"Oh my gosh, is he all right?"

I tipped my head. "I guess. Won't be playing for a bit though."

"Oh."

As far as I was concerned, Elliot had got his karma, it probably wasn't quite sufficient after everything he'd done, but it was a start. Clearly he had issues.

I finished my apple and threw the core at a nearby bin.

"Did Elliot ever hit you?" I asked.

Isobel looked up. "Sorry?"

"Elliot," I repeated. "Did he hit you?"

Isobel looked down, resting her hand on her neck. "I don't know what you mean."

"Sure you do," I replied, sliding up the bench so I was opposite her. "Tell me."

Her lips pressed together. "Elliot isn't a violent person."

I frowned. "But?"

"Where is this coming from?" she sighed.

I thought for a moment. "He attacked Paige the other night."

Isobel looked down. "He was drinking?"

"Yeah, so?"

"He loses control a bit when he drinks," she murmured.

"Isobel, did he hit you?" I repeated. She didn't look up so I reached out and took her hand. She looked around nervously.

"Sam, we're in public."

"I don't care."

She exhaled. "He… he hit me a couple of times, but it wasn't his fault."

I groaned. "Lord above."

"Don't Sam," she sighed. "Please don't do anything, it's in the past."

I stared at her incredulously. "Does anyone else know? Did you ever tell anyone?"

"Of course not."

"Why not?"

"It wouldn't change anything."

"Like hell it wouldn't," I huffed. "Your dad would kill him—*his* dad would kill him."

She shook her head, withdrawing her hand. "Don't say anything to anyone."

"Are you serious?"

"Sam, please," she begged. It reminded me of Paige when I'd found her. Why were they trying to protect him? Was he that frightening to them?

"Do you think Elliot did do something to hurt Liam?" she asked timidly.

I looked over at her. "No, how could he? He's injured."

Isobel nodded but didn't look convinced.

"Did he ever force himself on you?" I asked.

"Sam."

"I want to know."

She pouted. "It's none of your business."

I let out a steadying breath. "I will kill him."

"This is why I don't want to tell you."

"You just did," I huffed. "What else?"

She sighed. "Sam, just drop it."

"Did he ever verbally abuse you?"

"Samuel."

"Tell me."

"Not often," she answered.

"*What does that mean?!*" I near shouted.

Isobel shushed me and I looked around as people glared at us.

"Calm down," she hushed.

"I can't believe you never told me."

Her eyes looked sad. "How could I tell you? You would have done something stupid like you're considering now."

"Damn right I would."

She shook her head. "I'm fine. It was never anything too bad."

"Why did you stay with him if he was hurting you?" I asked. "I didn't think you were that much of a stickler for punishment."

"Nice Sam," she sighed.

"Well it's true, isn't it?"

She shook her head, looking to the side. "You don't know what he was like when we were alone."

"You're right," I replied. "But regardless, whatever he was like doesn't excuse what he did."

"I know."

"Do you?"

She shrugged. "I do now."

"Hey," a voice interrupted. Isobel and I both sat back.

"Liam," she sighed. "Where have you been? Did you get my texts?"

Liam glanced at me and I slid back down to my end of the bench. Isobel bit her lip.

"Yeah, sorry," he answered. "I was with Paige and Nate."

Isobel looked down. "Oh."

"I see you've found someone to keep you company though," he noted. I looked up in mild amusement at his annoyance.

"Sam and I were just discussing philosophy," Isobel replied.

"It was more ethics," I shrugged.

Isobel's perfectly carved lips turned down.

"Did you want to grab lunch or something?" she asked him.

"Don't you have class soon?" Liam asked, glancing at his watch. I looked at mine and saw we had twenty minutes until our philosophy lecture.

Isobel shrugged. "I can miss it, they put the notes online."

I frowned.

Liam looked up at me. "Sure, lunch sounds good."

I watched as she gathered her things and put them back into her bag. She glanced up as she stood.

"Bye Sam."

"Isobel."

She exhaled and walked away. I would never understand girls, but she was right about one thing—our lecture notes were available online—so I followed her example and skipped the lecture and headed home instead.

I took Dally for a long walk around the bridge and another nearby oval, trying to dodge the patchy downpours though we still ended up getting a bit wet.

After I dropped Dally home, I got a quick shower to thaw and changed for basketball. I was early getting there for once so just hovered around the entrance until someone else arrived. As luck would have it, that someone was Nate.

"Hey," he mumbled.

"Hi."

I kept pacing silently, turning my feet around so they stepped heel to toe.

"Have you heard anything about how Prince is going?" he asked after a few long, long seconds had passed.

I looked up and shrugged. "Nope, you?"

"Nope."

I continued stepping and then breathed a laugh. "I saw you do it."

"Do what?"

"Tip your shoulder," I replied. "He rolled right off."

Nate gave a half smirk. "Hearsay."

I stopped and folded my arms. "Karma."

"Or that," he huffed.

I nodded.

"Hey Saber," Bryce called.

"Hey Watson."

"You all right?"

I shrugged. "Can't complain. You?"

"Yep."

"How's the missus?"

He chuckled. "Good, yeah, she's good. Bub too."

"Are you married Bryce?" Nate asked. Bryce and I exchanged a look then both glanced at Nate.

"Yeah, four years."

"Huh," Nate tipped his head.

Bryce smiled. "I heard you've shacked up with Saber's ex."

I rolled my eyes at him.

Nate laughed. "Not shacked up just yet but we'll see."

Bryce lifted an eyebrow.

"Guess he didn't tell you he's dating mine then?" Nate added.
Dobber.

I forced a smile as Bryce turned slowly to face me. "No. No
he did not. This new?"

I shrugged. "Ish."

"Mm," Bryce nodded then laughed. "Geez, you two."

Nate and I exchanged a grin.

"So are we going to play nice today?" Bryce asked.

Nate shrugged. "We'll see."

"Right," I scoffed. "Because the Suns aren't going to struggle
enough with their captain out of action."

"Captain?" Bryce asked. "Something happen to Prince?"

I smirked. "Ask Blake."

Bryce turned and Nate lifted a shoulder. "I don't know what
he's talking about."

The door to the courts was unlocked and we followed the
other few guys in.

"Truce," Bryce sighed.

Nate and I glanced at each other in mutual agreement, not that
we'd ever admit it out loud.

***

"So you and Nate's ex," Bryce mused as we changed after winning
66-48. "When did this happen?"

I pulled my chin-length hair into a rough bunch and tied it. "She came to me; we're not really, actually, dating."

"I thought you were interested in someone else?" he asked. "Or was she the one that was *up-in-the-air*?"

"No, she's not the one."

"Oh man, it's not his sister is it?"

I laughed. "No."

"So?" Bryce fished.

I sighed. "Ivy and I are more for show purposes."

"Show?"

I shrugged. "She wants Nate back, she's using me."

"So what's in it for you?"

"Guess it's working that way for me too."

Bryce laughed. "Making Nate jealous?"

I elbowed him. "No. The one that's *up-in-the-air*."

"Man, I don't miss being single."

"Mm."

"Don't know what you're worried about," he smirked. "Sounds like you've got your pick of the litter."

I sighed. If only that was the case—but I suppose it's always the one you want that doesn't want you back. Not in the way I wanted anyway. Not yet.

"Got plans tonight?" he asked.

I pulled a face. "Family dinner."

"That's got to be fun after the news broke about Arthur," Bryce frowned. "How are things at the castle?"

"Eh," I shrugged. "I don't get involved. Everyone seems to be hanging in there."

"Good."

I patted him on the shoulder and pulled my bag on. "See you next week, Watson."

"Later, Saber."

I walked passed Nate on the way out. "Game, Blake."

He nodded. "Samuel."

"See you at football."

"Bring your armour."

I laughed. I really didn't want to like Nathaniel Blake. Damn.

When I got home, Angela and Amelia weren't there; it was Artie who greeted me—much to my surprise and horror.

"Evening son," he announced. "The girls have gone out to a movie. I thought we could have a guys' night."

Guys' night? Like the whole night?

"Oh."

"Figured we could go out for dinner at Constellation then have a nightcap somewhere," he continued. "So get changed, we'll leave in five."

I pressed my lips together. It didn't sound like I had much of a choice.

"Come on, hop to it."

Hop to it? Oh Artie. Who are you?

I headed towards my room and pulled on a shirt and the cleanest pair of pants I could find; grabbing my shoes, I sat on the stairs to lace them up.

Artie folded his arms as he waited. It was distracting.

"How was… err… practice?" he asked. It didn't surprise me he hadn't known where I was—guess my gym bag on entry gave that much away.

"Basketball," I clarified. "And good. We won."

"That's my boy."

I looked up. "What's going on?"

"What?"

"Why have Mum and Amelia gone out?" I asked. "It's family dinner night."

He exhaled. "They wanted to see a movie that was playing."

"Sure."

"For goodness sake, Samuel, don't read into things," he sighed. "Now come on, the car is waiting."

Great. Tonight was going to be fun.

On the way to Constellation, Artie was glued to his smart phone which suited me because I had a backlog of texts I had to answer from Marcus, Louis and Ivy. Marcus I wouldn't otherwise reply to, since his messages were just cannon fodder, but Louis wanted to know how his car was running and Ivy was just checking in to say hi.

"So, how's that lovely lady of yours going?" Artie asked as I typed a reply to her.

I scratched my cheek. "Who?"

"The blonde with good manners," he answered. Just couldn't resist.

I looked back down and hit send. "She's good. Not my lady though."

Whatever that meant.

"Not?" he asked. "Shame, she's a looker."

I lifted my eyebrows. You'd think he'd learn about cracking onto younger girls already.

"So are you seeing anyone then?" he pressed.

I shrugged. "No one specific."

"That's good I suppose," he nodded. "It's better not to get tied down when you're young."

I felt my forehead crease as I looked up at him. Artie and Angela had been together since they were seventeen. They were married when they were twenty-one. I wasn't sure what he was getting at.

"Everything okay Dad?" I asked, not actually wanting an answer.

His brown eyes traced to mine. "Hm? Oh sure son, everything's fine. No worries."

I nodded slowly. It was one "no worries" too much to actually sound convincing. But whatever, I asked.

We got to the restaurant and walked straight in, being ushered to our usual table, minus two settings. It was weird being here with just Artie. He sat down, unbuttoning his blazer and rolled his shoulders back—somebody get this man a throne already.

"So Mr Mayor, can I get you and your guest some drinks to start with?" the Maître D' asked. He sounded Swedish. I frowned—*guest?*

"I'll have a whiskey on the rocks," he answered. "And my son will have the same."

"Actually, I—I'll just have water," I interrupted. Man, Artie was a worse influence than Marcus.

"Nonsense," Artie bellowed. "Have a man's drink."

I frowned. "I'm in training."

"Hasn't stopped you before," he scoffed. "The two whiskeys thanks."

The Maître D' bowed and left and I sighed. Yeah, tonight was going to be real fun.

X

It Pours

I woke Thursday morning with a thumping headache and was relieved to find myself in my bed. How I got here remained to be seen though. The last thing I remembered was doing shots with Artie at one of the more upper-class men's clubs in South Coast City. The alcohol helped numb the crap that came out of his mouth.

I could barely move because each movement made me feel worse. I could still taste the sickening bitter sweetness in my mouth and on my tongue, down my throat and then there was the burning in the pit of my stomach. Nope, moving was not an option. I wanted to die. This was worse than the night out with Louis, Marcus and Demi.

Oh crap. I slapped my hand beside me and felt around on my doona. Fur. Dally. Thank the Lord I didn't do anything chronically stupid. Just reliably stupid.

My phone rang and the sound echoed painfully in my ears I moved my other arm closest to my drawers and located it, opening one eye to answer it.

"Yep?" I grumbled.

"Sam?"

I exhaled. "Paige."

"Are you okay?"

"No."

Silence.

"What's up?" I groaned.

"Um, you called me during the night, I was just… returning them," she answered a little more soothingly. "Oh, you were drinking, right?"

I rubbed my eyes. "Mm, sorry."

"Sax?" she sighed.

"Artie."

"As in your dad, Artie?" she asked, her voice rising an octave.

I groaned.

"Sorry, who else?" she laughed lightly. "So I guess you don't remember why you called."

"I'm really sorry Paige," I grumbled. "Really."

"It's fine," she answered, sounding amused. "Just, um, rest up. Lots of liquids, stay hydrated."

"No more," I murmured.

She breathed a laugh. "Take care, Sam."

"You too," I exhaled. "Sorry again for the calls."

"I'm sorry I didn't answer them," she huffed. "Sounds like it would've been an interesting conversation."

I gave a weak laugh—as much as I could manage. "Yeah."

"Bye."

"See you."

I hung up and dropped the phone and it fell on my head. I groaned and would've thrown it across the room if it didn't slip out of reach under my covers.

I don't know how long passed, but it didn't feel like long, it rang again.

"'Lo?" I grumbled.

"Sam."

Uh-oh. "Isobel."

"You're on the front page," she answered.

Uh-oh. That woke me. "Of the paper?"

"With your dad," she explained. "Did you go out drinking last night?"

Craaaaaaaap.

"Apparently," I exhaled.

"Sam, it doesn't look good," she sighed. "And you sound terrible."

"Thanks."

"I'm coming over."

I groaned. "You really don't need to."

"Don't bother arguing," she replied.

"No really—" I started. And dial tone. Perfect. Front-page news and that pretty much guaranteed I wouldn't start this week at football. Wesley had a rule about drinking during the on-season, rightfully so, it only really became an issue when we couldn't hide it—like making front-page news.

I fell back to sleep and woke to voices downstairs and then footsteps. My door opened.

"Samuel," Isobel gushed, walking to my side. "You don't look so good."

My eyes rolled opened. "You always look good."

She smiled, her eyes twinkled.

"Who were you talking to?" I murmured. I was half out of it. Probably still half drunk.

"Your parents," she answered, kneeling beside me as she placed a glass of water on my bedside table.

I frowned. "My parents."

"They're quite lovely," she smiled. That smile.

"Mm."

She rested her chin on the side of my bed.

"Are you okay, Sam?"

"Mm," I exhaled. "Don't you have to be somewhere?"

I felt her fingers brush my cheek. "No, I'm exactly where I need to be."

"I'm not going to be much fun," I sighed.

She breathed a laugh and stood up. "Shuffle over."

I blinked and carefully eased myself back as she peeled off her blue cardigan and kicked off her shoes before climbing into my bed, pulling the covers up over us both. She was cool compared to the warmth underneath and the clamminess of my skin. It was refreshing. She smelt incredible. I closed my eyes.

"Where's Liam?"

"Uni."

"Shouldn't you be there?"

"I'm fine here," she answered.

"What time is it?"

"Nearly ten."

I huffed. "I won't make it for my only class today anyway."

"Why did you get so drunk?" she asked, tracing my lips. It tickled.

My eyes opened. "I don't know. I didn't want to."

She waited.

"My dad practically poured drinks down my throat all night," I croaked. "How'd he look?"

I felt her shrug. "Fine."

Typical.

"What did the paper say?" I asked.

Isobel was silent.

"What?"

"It... kind of made him out to be this heroic family guy," she replied. "Like he was supporting you through tough times."

I frowned. "What?"

"I don't know," she sighed. "Maybe it's a media ploy for the bad press he's been getting?"

I thought about that for a moment. The guys' night, the dinner, the whiskey, refusing to take no for an answer even after I told him that I was in training. What better as a distraction than having the mayor's son go off the rails and have Artie save the day? Artie who is elbow deep in a sex scandal dropping all official business to spend time with his train-wreck of a son—if it *was* a ploy, he was more backstabbing than I gave him credit for. If it was a ploy, he might not have just taken me down with him, but ruined my football career and compromised my entire future too.

"Sam?"

"Do you think he set me up?" I murmured.

She pouted. "My dad does."

It was all I needed to hear. Isobel shuffled closer, burrowing into my chest. I could feel her heart hammering rapidly against her ribcage and felt a sense of victory that it was me who set it racing. It was probably going to be my only victory today.

We stayed there for a long time, until my head stopped feeling like it was a bomb about to explode, and then I headed in for a shower.

I was absolutely ravenous by the time I was up and dressed so Isobel and I went to get Marion to make me the most grease-filled breakfast she could muster. Isobel took it upon herself to go over my head and instead requested a ham, cheese and egg roll on my behalf. It still worked.

Artie was gone by the time we were up so I didn't feel the need to go to battle or make myself scarce. Regardless, there wasn't much to do around home and I desperately needed some fresh air, so Isobel and I went for a walk to our bridge.

"What do you think will happen with football?" she asked, glancing down at our joined hands. We'd never been like this before, like a couple, it was nice.

"I don't know," I sighed. "The best I can hope for is just missing this week."

She pouted. "Will it make a difference because Elliot is out?"

"Not to coach's decision; his hands are pretty much tied. Rules are rules."

"That really sucks."

"Yes it does."

She let go of my hand when we reached the bridge and went to sit on the swing. It hadn't rained overnight so for once it was relatively dry. I walked over behind her and gently nudged her seat to sway.

"What are you going to do?" she asked.

I exhaled. "There's really nothing I can do. It won't change anything."

"Surely you can't just let him get away with it?"

"If he did do it on purpose," I shrugged. Though knowing Artie, it was exactly something he would do.

"Sam," she sighed. I caught the seat as she swung back.

"Yes?"

She smiled, turning her head back, and kissed me. When she pulled away, I let her go and she giggled.

"What if you talked to Coach Wesley?" she continued.

Why were girls so dead-set on fixing everything?

"What can I say? The evidence is on the front page," I replied.

"But if you just explained that it was your father—"

"Isobel, I'm twenty-one, I don't think blaming Artie is going to have much pull," I chuckled. "Don't worry about it."

She shook her head and jammed her feet in the sand below to stop. I took a deep breath as she walked around towards me.

"I just want you to be happy," she frowned.

"I am—don't believe everything you read."

She grabbed the collar of my shirt, the weight of her hands dragging my shoulders down towards her. Normally this would thrill me but there was something in her eyes that looked sad. Like bad news was coming.

"What?" I asked.

She looked down, confirming my suspicions. "I just don't know if I'm good for you."

"What?"

She pulled her lower lip in. "You have a lot of complications in your life at the moment; I don't want to add to it."

"You're not," I replied. "You're like the one thing keeping me going right now."

"Don't say that."

"It's true."

Her forehead creased. I knew what was coming. I had seen that look before.

I pressed my lips together. "This was goodbye wasn't it?"

She didn't look up.

I ran my hands through my hair, it was tangled but I didn't care.

"You wanted to make sure I was stable before you walked away?" I guessed. "Suppose the article gave you a pretty good excuse."

She reached up and began to play with the ends of her hair, still not looking at me.

"Isobel."

Nothing.

"Is it Archer?" I asked, hoping to spur some sort of response from her. I didn't actually want to know if it was yet another guy she wanted more than me. I wasn't sure if my ego could take it.

She exhaled. "I'm really sorry Sam. I never planned this."

I shook my head and lowered to my heels. Way to kick a man while he's down.

"It's just never going to be easy with us," she explained. "Not with who we are and who our families are."

I frowned at the comment. She was bringing in the families. How was that fair? I couldn't choose who I was born to. This was complete crap.

She shook her head. "I don't know what else to say but I'm sorry."

I covered my mouth with my hands and wondered when the punches would stop.

I sighed. "So the other day was just...?"

"I still have feelings for you Sam," she murmured. "I just can't be with you."

"Can't?"

"Won't."

I exhaled and stood. "Got it."

I began walking away. I'd had enough for one... millennia.

"Sam, where are you going?" Isobel called.

I didn't reply. Anywhere was better than here.

"Samuel!"

I shook my head and was both relieved and disappointed that she didn't try harder to stop me from leaving. I couldn't believe her. I couldn't believe anyone. Artie, Isobel, everyone. What infuriated me the most was I had been warned about Isobel's crap. Ivy was right.

It started to rain and I couldn't even muster the energy to care. I didn't know where to go, I still felt a little seedy so I needed to go somewhere—but where? The bridge had always been my sanctuary but now that was ruined, home was stained with Artie's lies and Marcus and Bryce were no doubt at work. I racked my brain and was about to give up when it struck me. I grabbed my phone and scrolled.

"Sam?"

"Ivy."

"What are you up to?" she asked.

"Nothing," I sighed. "You want to hang out?"

"Sure."

I exhaled.

"I can meet you somewhere?" she offered.

"Actually I'm not far from your place," I replied, glancing around me. Hawthorn Court was just on the other side of uni from my house, more south but about the same distance away from SCU.

"You want to come to my house?"

"I'm a bit hung-over and not too keen on being in public right now," I answered honestly.

She laughed. "Okay. Are you driving?"

"No," I huffed. I didn't need a *driving under the influence* charge to add to my perfect month.

"Well I'll start walking and meet you."

I wiped the rain from my forehead. "Okay, but I'm bypassing the campus… sticking to the backstreets."

She breathed a laugh. "Got it Saber. See you soon."

Dial tone.

I slipped my phone back in my pocket and pulled up the collar of my jacket. I'd gone maybe five paces when it rang again. I didn't recognise the number.

"Hello?"

"Hello, is this Samuel Saber?"

"Who's this?"

"I'm calling from channel three news, I was just wondering if you'd—"

I hung up the phone. How on earth did they get my number? Crap. The article must've been bad. I switched it off and jammed it back in my pocket.

"Sammy, Sammy," Ivy called. Wow, that was fast.

"Hey," I frowned.

She smiled, despite the fact it was now raining in fat droplets around us.

"Where were you?"

"Uni," she answered. "Not all of us can sleep through class and still pass."

"I don't know about pass," I smirked, walking up to meet her. She stopped in front of me and rested her index finger on her pinkish lips.

"You look like hell."

"Naw, thanks," I smiled. "You look wet."

She shrugged. "As long as it's not acid rain I'll survive."

I laughed. "Are you missing class?"

"No, I was just in the library," she replied.

"Propositioning guys?"

Her eyebrow lifted. Despite my damp mood I had to admit, it was incredibly sexy. "Waiting out the rain."

I pressed my teeth together in an awkward smile. "Whoops, sorry."

"Its fine, I think it's here to stay," she noted, lifting her hands to the rain.

I exhaled. "You're telling me."

Ivy smiled and slapped her hand on my chest. I groaned and she gripped the corner of my jacket and tugged.

"Come on, let's go."

***

It took us about an hour to get back to Ivy's little cottage house because we wove around the streets, trying to avoid people. It was an adventure but we got completely soaked to the bone. At least now I felt well and truly awake.

"I need a cup of tea," Ivy gushed, peeling off her coat at the front door. She hung it up just inside on a hook and the water from it fell like it was linked up to a tap.

"Well, are you coming in?" she laughed.

I blinked. "But I'm dripping."

"So? This isn't exactly the royal castle," she answered. "Come on."

I stepped in cautiously as she pulled off her top.

"Wow," I breathed, turning to give her some privacy.

"What? Don't tell me you're shy."

"No but—"

"So what's the problem?" she shrugged. "I'm sure you've seen a girl's body before."

I breathed a laugh and took off my jacket, hanging it beside hers. She folded her arms and I looked up self-consciously.

"What?"

"T-shirt and pants," she answered.

I looked down. "Excuse me?"

"I'll put them in the dryer for you," she sighed. "Relax, you'll get them back."

I pressed my lips together contemplatively.

"What's wrong?" she asked. "*Are* you shy?"

I shook my head and pulled off my T-shirt before beginning to unbutton my jeans. She smiled tightly and I extended them towards her.

"Don't suppose you want your underwear dried too?" she asked, taking my clothes and resting them on a nearby chair as she pulled off her jeans.

I smiled. "I was just thinking the same thing."

She laughed and rolled them up, turning towards a hallway wearing nothing but her cotton bra and underwear. She had a killer body, like killer. I began to feel a little uncomfortable standing there mostly naked.

"Do you have a towel?" I called. "It's, uh, a little cold."

I heard her ghostly laugh and then something grey flew out the opening. I leaned over and picked it up, quickly drying my damp body before fastening it around my waist.

Ivy's house was cosy, a lot smaller than what I was used to, but seemed to have all the necessities. Her furniture looked second hand but homely. I realised that I wouldn't have a problem living somewhere like this.

"Better?" she smiled, returning to me wearing just an oversized black and white T-shirt which hung to the top of her milky thighs. She was drying her wavy blonde hair with a twin grey towel to the one I wore.

"Yep," I nodded, taking in the view. It still bemused me that she was so set on Nate when she could literally hypnotise any guy she wanted. She grinned at me, noticing the towel.

"Looks good on you."

"Thanks," I smirked.

She breathed another laugh and headed into the kitchen, throwing the towel on the back of the tan couch as she passed.

"Can I get you a tea or anything?" she called. I followed her voice and found her in the kitchen, reaching up into a high cupboard which made her shirt ride up to the bottom of her butt. She glanced around and raised her eyebrows expectantly.

"Sorry?" I stuttered.

"Tea?" she repeated, a smile playing on her lips as she held up the yellow box.

"Sure."

"How do you take it?"

"Uh, black with one."

She gave a nod. "So why the long face today?"

"Long face," I repeated.

She turned and gave me an incredulous look.

I pressed my lips together. "My dad got me drunk last night, jeopardised my football career and Isobel spent the morning with me and then suddenly ended things."

She frowned as she spooned sugar into the beige mugs. "Why?"

"Why what?"

Her gold eyes traced up to mine. "Why any of it?"

"Well, my dad's a jerk who, I think wants to detract attention from himself, and Isobel…"

"Is a game-playing little bitch," she finished.

"Don't call her that," I sighed. "She's just…"

"Young?" she fished. "Manipulative? Opportunistic?"

I exhaled. It was futile arguing with Ivy.

"You deserve better than her," she noted.

I looked down. "I don't want to talk about Isobel."

"Then what do you want, Sam?" she asked.

My eyes lifted to find hers. "I don't know."

"Why did you call me?"

"Because you were the only person I could think of that would answer."

She shook her head with slight amusement. "You're pretty messed up."

"So I've heard," I sighed, taking a seat at the table. The kettle clicked off and she poured the water into the mugs, adding a dash of filtered water before bringing them both over to me. She climbed on my lap so there was a leg on either side of me. I exhaled, turning my head to the side.

"What are you doing?"

She tucked a lock of my wet hair behind my ear. "Cheering you up."

"It won't work."

"You don't even know what I've got in mind."

I pulled my lower lip in. "I've got a pretty good imagination."

She rested her hands on my shoulders and I reached for the mug of tea, weaving it around her arms to take a sip.

"You're pretty decent, Saber," she mused.

"Why?"

"Most guys would take advantage of a situation like this," she shrugged. "I mean we're mostly naked and I'm straddling you in an empty house."

"Like you said, I'm pretty messed up right now," I replied. "I don't want to drag you into my complicated crap."

Her eyebrows pulled together in a pucker. "Then why did you call me?"

"I told you why."

"Okay," she nodded. "So what now? Why are we here? You want to talk?"

I shook my head. "No, I don't know."

Her hands moved down my chest to my abdomen and I stopped them before they reached the towel.

"Ivy…"

"Yes?"

"I've done a lot of stupid things lately," I sighed.

"So?"

I exhaled. "I don't know what I'm doing."

She gave a small laugh and pulled her hands free to smooth around my middle. "I find that hard to believe."

"That's not what I'm talking about," I murmured.

210

"Sam, whatever is going on with you is your business," she replied. "If you don't want to tell, I'm not asking, but I need to know what you want from me—I mean we started this arrangement to make other people jealous. Do you still want that?"

I hadn't thought about any of it, I'd actually completely forgotten about the *arrangement* as she called it. I just liked hanging out with her.

"I don't know, to be honest I think that Isobel is a lost cause," I sighed. "But I'll still help you with Nate. I gave you my word."

She dropped her hands to her thighs and rested them there. "And what about Paige?"

"Paige?" I frowned. "Why do you keep bringing her into it?"

"Because she's in it," Ivy replied. "If Paige and Nate break up she'll be available again."

She looked down. "Actually, something tells me the only reason why the two of them would break up would be because she still has feelings for you."

I frowned. "Why would you want to be with someone who doesn't want to be with you?"

"You tell me."

I exhaled and shook my head. "Ouch."

Ivy bit her lip and slid off my lap and onto the chair beside me. She grabbed her mug and took a mouthful of tea.

"Sorry," she pouted. "I guess we both know what it's like to be someone's second choice."

I glanced at her as she ran her finger around the rim of her mug, her usual confident facade falling away in front of my eyes. She was just a girl right now—a girl who wanted to be wanted by a guy who wanted someone else. We really were in the same boat. Why could we only see how pointless it was when it was happening to someone else?

"Hey," I murmured, reaching out to nudge her arm. "One day we'll be someone's first choice."

She looked up. "We already were though weren't we? And we took them for granted."

"Maybe we wouldn't have taken them for granted if they were our first choice," I shrugged. "Maybe we're just fishing in the wrong pond."

"You mean we should just move on?" she asked. "Find other people?"

I rubbed my forehead. "Yeah, maybe that's what I'm saying."

"Easy to say," she mused.

I nodded and gave her a weak smile which she returned—but then something shifted. The look between us lasted that little bit too long and morphed into that kind of pause that usually occurs before a first kiss. At the same time we both looked away as keys rattled in the door. I turned my head in the direction and Ivy sighed.

"Crap, that'll be Mira."

"Mira?"

"My roommate," she explained, looking to me and gnawing on her lip before breaking into a smile.

I frowned curiously.

"Ivy," the female voice called. "Are you home?"

"In here," Ivy replied.

I was suddenly quite self-conscious as the blonde appeared in the doorway, her light brown eyes popping as she saw me, and her jaw almost theatrically fell open.

"I—I—um…" she stuttered.

"Mira, this is Sam," Ivy smirked. "Sam, my roommate Mira."

I grabbed a handful of towel and stood, extending my hand towards the blushing blonde. She took it awkwardly, almost as if it was on fire and she was fearful of being burned.

"S-Sam Saber?" she stuttered. "Holy moley."

I glanced at Ivy who seemed to share my amusement at her discomfort.

"Nice to meet you," I replied.

Her eyes moved up and down my body as she tried to control her breathing. I felt a wave of embarrassment wash over me.

"Ivy," Mira whispered in a voice that wasn't quiet at all. "You didn't tell me you knew Samuel Saber."

"Slipped my mind," Ivy shrugged.

Mira couldn't stop her swift glances in my direction. "Why is he naked in our kitchen?"

I laughed. I couldn't help it.

"He's not entirely naked," she replied evenly. "We got wet walking back; his clothes are in the dryer."

Mira nodded in short bursts and I pressed my lips into a tight smile. Okay, now it was exceeding awkward.

"I might go and check on them," Ivy said, standing and moving swiftly towards the doorway.

"I'll help you," I added, pulling my hand away and following her out. Mira opened her mouth to say something but no words came. Phew.

Ivy was laughing when we reached the pokey laundry which was just one end of the bathroom.

"What's funny?" I asked.

"I thought her eyes were going to fall out," she whispered. "She's terrible."

"*You* are terrible," I corrected.

She lifted a devilish shoulder and smiled, pulling the clothes out. "Hm, they're still a bit damp."

"That's okay," I shrugged. "There's probably no point in drying them anymore since I'll have to walk home in them."

She handed them to me. "You don't have to go yet."

"Yes I do," I sighed. "I have football training tonight."

She nodded. "Right."

I put my shirt down and pulled my jeans on then handed her the towel and replaced my T-shirt. Ivy frowned.

"I think I liked you better in the towel."

I chuckled. "Sure you did."

"Thanks for a fun afternoon," she grinned. "It beat studying."

"Yeah," I breathed. "Thanks for hanging out."

She tipped her head. "I'll walk you to the door."

I gave a small smile and followed her out, down the short hallway and to lounge room and the front door. She unhooked my jacket and pressed it to my chest.

"Later Saber."

"Ivy," I nodded then frowned. "What's your surname?"

"Hunt."

"Ivy Hunt?"

"Yep."

"Miss Hunt."

She raised an eyebrow. That eyebrow.

"Well Miss Hunt, it's always a pleasure."

"Anytime," she breathed.

I smiled and opened the door. "Bye Mira, it was nice to meet you."

A blonde head popped out from behind the kitchen. "Goodbye Samuel, it was a pleasure to—to meet you too. Come back anytime."

I laughed. "Okay."

Ivy gave me a quick wink. "Hang in there Sam. Talk soon."

"Okay," I breathed.

"And Sam?" she called as I stepped out the door into the light drizzle. I turned and squinted through the rain.

214

"Don't be too upset about Isobel," she added. "She's a total idiot to walk away."

I smiled weakly. "I'll catch you later, Ivy."

***

I had to get home fast since it was already four thirty and at this rate, I'd cut it close to making it to training on time if I walked— so I ran. As I jogged up the driveway, Marcus' car was parked out front and he was pacing beside it.

"Sax," I called.

"Sammy, where have you been?" he yelled back. "Your phone keeps going to voicemail."

Oh crap, I'd forgotten to switch it back on.

"Sorry, reporters were calling," I replied, panting as I slowed in front of him. "What's up?"

"Have you seen today's paper?" he asked, holding it up. I tipped my head to read the headline:

Saber's Son's Sobriety Struggle it read, and below: *Why Mayor Saber's Guidance Extends Beyond the Office.*

"Oh, what a dick," I groaned, snatching the paper from him. "It *was* a set up."

"What?" Marcus snapped.

"He's trying to detract the attention from his scandal by creating one around me," I sneered, stringing a bunch of curse words under my breath. "This is not good."

"Damn right it's not good," Marcus nodded. "Coach is going to have a fit. You're our best player and Prince is out for weeks."

I scratched my forehead.

"Where have you been anyway?"

"At Ivy's."

"Ivy?" he frowned. "Really?"

"Long story," I sighed. "What's the time?"

"Almost five," he replied. "Grab your stuff."

I handed him the paper and nodded, running up the front stairs two at a time, kicked the door open, and headed straight for upstairs.

"Samuel, I need to speak to you," Angela called.

"Not now Mum, sorry," I muttered, continuing up. I got into my room and pulled off my damp clothes, replacing them with my training gear and grabbed my bag before tumbling back down the stairs.

"Samuel," Angela said sternly. I skidded to a stop.

"Mum, I'm sorry but I've got to go."

She sighed. "I know honey."

"What's up?"

She shook her head. "I didn't know, I promise."

My jaw clenched. "I didn't think so."

"I could kill him for dragging your name into it."

"Yeah," I exhaled. "Get in line."

"Please don't do anything impulsive, I'll deal with Arthur, okay?" she begged.

I groaned. "You know he's probably ruined my chances at getting drafted, don't you?"

"Samuel, I—"

"Sammy, let's go!" Marcus called.

I thrust a thumb behind me.

"You go," she nodded. "I'll see you later."

I gave a nod and pivoted towards the door, jogging down to Marcus' car which was already running. Hearing Angela confirm everything felt like I'd been stabbed in the back with a shard of ice. I wanted to hurt Artie for what he did, I wanted to call back the reporters and spill everything I could think of that might incriminate him—or at least explain why I am a bigger man than

216

him for *not* having a drinking problem despite his less than mediocre parenting skills.

When we got to practice, to use the term 'frosty reception' would probably be the biggest understatement of the year. My teammates felt let down, and I didn't blame them. I would be too if I was in their position.

"Sam," Wesley sighed as he saw me. "Sidebar."

I gave Marcus my bag and he headed into the change rooms with them. I frowned and walked over to Wesley.

"Coach."

"Sam."

"I don't know what to say," I sighed. "I'm not an alcoholic; I didn't even want to drink last night."

He folded his arms. "Are things okay at home, Sam?"

I looked at him incredulously. "Sorry?"

"It's a tough time for Sabers lately," he mused. "Are you all right, son?"

I blinked up at my coach and was surprised by his genuine concern. It was a foreign concept for me from a father figure. The word *son* was really used as a term of endearment when he said it.

"It's been tough," I agreed. "But I'll be fine."

Wesley pressed his lips together in assessment. "You said you didn't want to drink last night."

"No sir."

"But?"

I shrugged. "I've got no excuse, I'm a grown man."

He nodded knowingly, hearing the words he knew I couldn't say.

"Samuel, given the public nature of your night out, I can't let you play Saturday," he answered. "But for what it's worth, I wish we didn't have to do it without you."

I sighed, staring at my feet as I accepted my cross to bear. "Yes, sir."

"I want you alongside me though," he continued. "And I'll need you to prepare Blake for the game tonight. You're valuable, son, don't let this misdemeanour dictate the rest of your season."

I looked up—all hope wasn't lost?

"What about the RedBacks, coach?" I asked.

He nodded. "I'll talk to Jason, explain the situation. He's worked in the news so he's familiar with how stories can be embellished."

"Thank you," I replied almost incredulously. I couldn't understand how someone could be so helpful and understanding. "That's very cool of you."

"You're a good player, Sam," Wesley nodded. "Just try and keep your nose clean from now on, eh? There are only so many second chances that scouts are willing to hand out."

"Got it, dually noted," I answered.

He gave a hard nod. "Are you feeling okay for sprints?"

"Yes."

"Get started then," he murmured, tilting his head towards the tracks. "Chin up, son."

Chin up. I felt like I'd just found water in a hundred miles of desert.

"Thanks coach," I sighed, jogging around towards the lanes.

Maybe what they said was true: the night is always the darkest just before dawn breaks. If this was my second chance—my second sunrise—then there was no going back from here. I couldn't afford to be sucked in to Artie's war or Isobel's games, or be distracted by girls or alcohol or any of that stuff. This was my chance, my only chance, and I owed it to myself and to Wesley and my team not to let it slip through my fingers. It was the last chance I had to shine.

XI

Thicker than Water

"One week isn't so bad for an alleged alcoholic," Marcus noted as he drove me home after practice had finished. "We can't afford to lose you for longer."

I nodded absently, ignoring his jibe. A week was still costly considering we were one win to one loss already, had Elliot out and Louis away this week. But this we already knew.

"You okay about it?" he asked.

"Yeah," I sighed. "Like you said, it could've been worse."

There was a lull in conversation as Marcus hummed along to his music, bashing his steering wheel like it was a drum kit. Classic rock was constantly on repeat in his car—the song of the moment was Kansas, *Carry On My Wayward Son*. I rolled my eyes.

"So have you spoken to Artie since the story broke?" Marcus asked over the music.

"No."

"Are you going to do anything about it?"

I scratched my stubble. "Anything I do to him, I do to my mum, Amelia, and myself."

Marcus laughed a curse word. "He really is King Arthur."

"He's a jerk."

"Maybe you should move out?" Marcus mused. "Get out from under his iron fist."

I huffed. "Where and with what?"

"Ah," he nodded. "Right. Sucks."

I rested my head back, the reminder of my personal prison deflating me substantially.

"Hungry?" he asked.

"Starving."

"Lunar?"

"Lunar, really?" I frowned.

He shrugged. "Best burgers, bro. You should've slept with a waitress that worked somewhere crap."

"You know, Sax, I didn't really plan it."

He laughed. "Right—but Demi is pretty fit. Great set of—"

"Sax," I groaned.

"I'm just saying."

"Yeah," I sighed.

He chuckled and made a turn, heading towards Lunar cafe. Guess I had to face Demi eventually; might as well do it today while opinions on me were pretty low.

***

"Sam and Sax," Demi's pleasant voice sighed as we took our usual seat by the window. She stopped by the table and pulled the black pen out from behind her ear. "It's been a while."

"Hey Demi," Sax grinned. "How are you?"

She glanced up at him, her pretty brown eyes flickering to me. "Fine."

"I'll have my usual cheeseburger and chocolate shake please," he answered, bouncing in his seat. He was like a kid.

"And for you Sam?" she exhaled, staring intently at her order pad.

I waited until she looked up at me and frowned down at my menu. "Just a burger and lemonade."

"Sure," she replied, turning on her heel towards the counter. I drew in a breath and looked to Marcus who raised his eyebrows. Slipping off my chair I followed her over.

"Demi," I murmured.

She half turned but didn't stop until she reached the kitchen, pegged the order on the order wheel and spun it around to the chefs.

"Did you need something else?" she asked.

I nodded. "I need to apologise to you."

Her head tipped. "You already did."

"I know but I wanted to make sure you knew that I meant it," I answered. "I don't usually do that sort of thing so I don't want you to think—"

She shook her head. "I don't think."

I frowned. "Sorry?"

"It was just one night, Sam," she shrugged. "I'm a grown up, you know. I don't have any hired help to make my decisions for me. I've wanted it to happen for a while."

I blinked. "Okay."

She smiled. "You're an attractive guy, and trust me, the pleasure was all mine. Don't worry too much about it."

I lifted my head to nod but it seemed frozen in place. So, she wasn't a notch in my belt but I was a notch in hers. I wasn't sure whether to be relieved or offended. I guess I just wish I could remember this so called *pleasure*.

"You okay, by the way?" she asked. "I saw the paper today. I didn't really take you for an alcoholic."

"I'm not," I replied. "Despite my impressive imitation of one."

She gave a light laugh. "Right."

"Demi, order's up," someone called from the kitchen.

I glanced over and looked back to her. "I'll leave you to it."

"Sure," she sighed. "I'll see you around."

I nodded and turned to head back to the table. Marcus was creating a fort out of the sugar sachets. Apparently I can't leave him alone for five minutes.

"All good?"

"Yep."

"Sweet," he crooned. "We don't have to avoid this place anymore."

I shrugged. "We never did."

He glanced down at his phone. "Amelia is worried about you."

"My sister Amelia?"

"Yeah, know any others?" he laughed.

I didn't share his amusement. "How do you know?"

"She told me."

"When?"

"Just then."

"How?"

"What's with all the questions, bro?" he huffed. "She texted me."

"Why does she have your number?"

"I gave it to her."

"Why?" I frowned. "Are you interested in her or something?"

"Sammy, seriously, calm down," he sighed. "Amelia is like a sister to me too."

I nodded and sat back as Demi returned and set down our order.

"So what's the deal with Ivy? Nail her yet?"

"Sax," I sighed—he wonders why it would bother me if he was interested in my little sister.

"What? She's hot."

"Mm."

Marcus shook his head. "You're nuts if you don't move in on that soon. Girls like her don't stay single for long."

I picked at my chips and then took a long sip of lemonade.

"I think I just want to focus on footy right now, girls are too complicated."

Marcus took a bite of his burger and shrugged as he chewed. "But they're fun."

"Oh, okay and who is the last girl you were with?"

"Erm…"

My eyebrows rose.

"This isn't about me," he muttered.

I laughed. "It was Briony, wasn't it?"

"Sammy, focus."

"I am," I smirked. "I'm focusing on football. You, my friend, need to take your own advice."

He grinned. "About Ivy?"

"No."

"So you *do* like her?"

"Shut up," I sighed. "And stop texting my sister."

He rolled his eyes.

***

I didn't go home; Marcus and I hung out at his place with his roommates, Ash and Jonah. They were cool guys, tradesmen too, so the house was pretty trimmed with furnishings and everything was always in working order—well mostly always. Guys who work all day normally don't find much enthusiasm to work when they get home.

I ended up staying the night and crashing on their couch. I wasn't too eager about heading home to hear Artie's explanation, if I was even going to get one this time. Being ruler of all gave him a sense of entitlement to mess up other people's lives and not offer reasons why.

"Hey, Sammy," Marcus said in the morning, shaking my shoulder. "Call your sister."

"I hate you," I groaned.

"She's worried."

I sat up and hurled a pillow at him. "Stop texting her."

"I'll stop when you start," he snapped, throwing it back. Jonah and Ash chuffed as they ate their cereal.

I rubbed my eyes. "I'm not keeping tabs with her, she's my sister not my mother."

"She is as much trapped in that house as you are," he replied. "Only unlike you, she hasn't got a way out."

"Back off Marcus, I can take care of my own family."

"Can you?" he challenged. "Look at you."

I frowned and Marcus shook his head.

"Sammy, I've got your back so quit fighting me. I'm not the bad guy."

I rested my head in my hands.

"Family is more than blood," Marcus muttered. "You of all people should get that."

I looked up and exhaled.

"Right, well if that little lovers' tiff is over, I'm off to work," Jonah smirked, putting his bowl in the sink.

Ash raised his eyebrows and laughed, following Jonah out as Marcus turned back to me.

"Let yourself out whenever," he mumbled. "Just don't forget to lock the door before you pull it shut."

"Got it," I nodded.

Marcus turned to leave.

"Hey Sax."

"Mm?"

"Thanks for having my back."

He lifted his head in acknowledgement and left as I slumped back into the couch to put off dealing with the rest of the world for as long as I could—which didn't end up being long at all. Artie called and I let it ring out, then a private number called which I assumed was him calling from the home or office, then Angela's number rang. I switched it on silent and got up, gathering my stuff, and headed out to the gym on foot, regretting not driving myself to training last night—looks like it was going to be another day of wet clothes for me.

I only stayed at the gym for a couple of hours because I couldn't stand all the muttering of the guys there. It was crazy that people cared about what I did; I was nobody special—not yet anyway.

I called Ivy afterwards and she was at uni on a break so I went in to meet her. I headed to the library when I was on campus and ignored the tsunami of whispers as I passed. At least with the Paige email fiasco people only knew my name; being on the front cover of the *South Coast Courier* meant that people had a face to go with it. Thanks Artie.

"Hey Sam," Ivy smiled, glancing up from her notebook. I grabbed the chair opposite her at the table and turned it around to straddle, folding my arms over the top rail.

"What are you up to?"

She shook her head. "You're soaked."

"I'm taking a leaf out of your book and walking everywhere now," I shrugged.

She crossed her arms. "Really?"

"No, I'm just avoiding home."

"You haven't been home yet?"

"Just to pick up my training stuff," I replied. "Hence the casual look."

She bit her lip and I drew in a breath, feeling the compulsion to help her with it.

"I like the casual look," she sighed.

"Did you want to hang out later? We could grab dinner or something?"

"Dinner?"

I nodded.

"Are you going to change or should I dress down?" she asked, cocking an eyebrow.

I exhaled in a laugh. "You can dress down."

She laughed, twirling a soft curl around her finger, considering my offer.

"I was supposed to hang out with Mira tonight," she answered finally. "I've been neglecting her a bit lately."

"She can come."

Ivy laughed. "Like a third wheel?"

I pressed my lips together. "I could bring Sax?"

"Like a double date?"

I blinked. It certainly sounded that way. Huh.

"More of a hangout," I shrugged. "With two others."

Ivy looked to the side, her sparkling gold eyes searching. "Okay, I'll ask her."

"Okay."

She glanced at her watch. "I've got class in ten."

"Oh right," I frowned.

She tapped her pen on her notebook, looking around her with an endearing smile on her face.

"People are staring at you," she noted.

"I know."

"Doesn't it bother you?"

I shrugged. "You get used to it—not something I wanted to get used to really—but I kind of feel sorry for them."

Her head dipped. "Why?"

"I can think of better people to stare at."

She grinned, shaking her head. "Great line, Saber."

I breathed a laugh and stood up, turning the chair around the right way to push it back into the table. Ivy was frozen as she watched me, and then began packing her things away. I waited and she stood, slinging her bag over her shoulder.

"Where's your class?"

"You don't have to walk me," she laughed.

I shrugged. "I've got nothing else to do."

She stared at me in amusement as I mirrored her phrase from the other day, then shook her head, leading the way to the cloudy outside.

Ivy's class was practically next door to the library—rather it was above the library in a weird little room with doors that open to a sheer drop but had half-bars up the openings as lame balconies. I walked her up and told her I'd be in touch about tonight, and called Marcus to make sure he kept it free. He tried to object to my blatant set-up but eventually agreed. I talked Mira up.

I headed back down to the library to take advantage of the resources while I was avoiding home. I hadn't done much work lately so checked my email and outlines to catch up on readings. I ended up getting a decent few hours done before my reluctant procession home.

I walked in the door, determined to head straight up to my room and avoid a confrontation but Artie was waiting. He must've been working from home.

"Samuel," he bellowed.

I kept walking.

"Samuel, stop."

I took the first step to ascend to my room but he grabbed my arm.

"Son."

"Let go of me," I snarled, tearing my elbow free. "Don't you touch me."

Artie stumbled back in alarm.

"Samuel?"

"You are a vindictive, psychotic, control freak," I snapped. "You need help."

"Son, you need to understand—"

"Understand?" I huffed, stringing a bunch of curse words under my breath. "I don't understand any of this crap. You are a selfish bastard."

"I beg your pardon."

I started up the stairs. "Beg away old man, I'm done with this—I'm done with you."

"Samuel William Saber," he growled. "Don't you walk away from me—"

"Let him go, Arthur," Angela interrupted. "It's the least you can do after jeopardising his future."

Artie looked as if he'd been king-hit. I smiled tightly at my mother as she gave me a discrete nod and I continued up to my room.

Amelia popped her head over the stairs and frowned.

I exhaled. "Hi."

"Why do I have to go through Marcus to find out where you are?" she asked.

"Lord above, Amelia, you're not my mother," I groaned. "You don't need to know where I am every second of the day."

"I'm just worri—"

"Worried, I know," I sighed. "And quit texting Sax, it's weird."

"Sammy."

228

"I've got to get ready," I answered. "In case you're wondering, which I'm sure you are, I'm going out to dinner with Sax, Ivy and her roommate."

Amelia rolled her eyes and disappeared into her room. Good.

I finally made it to mine, dropped my bag and headed into the bathroom for a long overdue, much needed shower.

∗∗

Ivy, Marcus, Mira and I arrived at Constellation at peak hour but because of my new found fame, we were given a table almost immediately. The same Swedish-sounding Maître D' from the other night served us—I noticed his name was Heath—came up as we sat down to take our drink orders.

"White wine please," Ivy said. "House is fine."

"Same for me," added Mira.

"Um, do you do chocolate milkshakes?" asked Marcus.

I laughed and Heath nodded.

"Just water for you, right Mr Saber?" he smiled.

Ivy and Marcus looked between us curiously.

"Right," I huffed. "I mean it this time."

"What do you mean *this time*?" Ivy breathed.

I shook my head. "The other night I asked for water and Artie ordered a whisky for me."

"Are you serious?" Marcus frowned. "Dude, you've got to go to the media."

Heath suddenly looked terrified. "Oh, I—I—"

"What will it change, Sax?" I sighed. "What's done is done."

"Are you kidding me, Sammy? It will prove what he's like; it'll show everyone that he'd happily throw his own son to the gallows just to shift the attention off him."

"And then what?" I groaned. "He's still family and if he's thrown out, Mum, Amelia, we're all out."

"This is your future, Sam," he added. "This could help you."

Heath shifted uncomfortably. "I'll place your order."

I nodded and he disappeared.

"Me being selfish doesn't help anyone," I sighed. "I was still the one who got drunk regardless of who footed the bill."

"It's emotional blackmail, Samuel," Marcus said sternly. I glanced up at my full name—Marcus never called me *Samuel.*

I exhaled. "There's no point, Heath won't speak anyway; he doesn't want to lose his job. Artie is a powerful man."

"Who's giving him the power?" Mira quipped. "He sounds like he needs someone to stand up to him for a change to show that he can't bully everyone."

Ivy, Marcus and I turned to stare at Mira and her light brown eyes bulged. "Oh, I'm sorry. I didn't mean to—"

"She's right," Marcus huffed. "You're right."

Mira smiled.

"Just think about it, Sammy," he continued. "This comes out, your name, your reputation is cleared and coach might let you play."

I pulled a face. "Even if it did come out, what makes you think word would spread by tomorrow?"

Marcus cocked an eyebrow. "Still got that number in your call log from that reporter from channel three?"

I pressed my lips together. "This is a very bad idea."

"Nonsense, you look great," Mira smiled. "How's my hair?"

Marcus laughed and looked at me expectantly. It would certainly get back at Artie for what he did to me and it would make him think twice about how he treated people. Even as his family we were all pawns in his chess game. It might not change anything but it would reveal the truth and don't they say the truth always comes out? He'd brought this on himself. Game on, Artie.

I handed Marcus my phone and stood up. "Make the call, it's the unlisted number."

"Where are you going?" Marcus asked.

I lifted a shoulder. "I'm going to go and convince the Maître D' to talk."

Marcus gave a yelp as Mira clapped excitedly. I was about to light a match in a cave full of explosives; I just hoped I'd live to see the sunrise tomorrow. I'd gone three paces when I felt a hand on my elbow.

"Sam."

I turned. "Ivy, what's wrong?"

"This is," she whispered. "Just think about what you're doing."

"I have."

Her golden eyes looked worried. "Have you?"

I exhaled.

"Regardless of what he did, he's still your father."

"Father, right," I huffed. "He's a bully. He needs to be taught a lesson."

"At what cost?" she whispered. "I know you're mad and you're hell-bent for revenge, but Sam, what about your mum? What about Amelia? They've been through enough this past week without having you wage war against him."

I shook my head. Damn it, she was making sense.

"You said it yourself, what is it really going to change?"

I lifted a shoulder and bit my lip. "People will know the truth."

She frowned. "Sam, you don't need to do this. The truth will come out eventually anyway—people will see you're not the guy in the paper and will see you for who you are in the way you carry yourself. You don't need to stoop to his level, there's a better way."

"How?"

"By being the bigger man," she sighed, resting her hands on my forearms. "Take the high road and show them on the field who you really are—if that's what you want. Plenty of players have been in the news for this stuff and got passed it."

"Did I forget something, Mr Saber?" Heath asked.

"Please, call me Sam, Mr Saber is my father," I said, barely able to choke the words out. "And no, nothing for now—thanks Heath."

He nodded. "I'll be back to take your order in a few minutes."

"Thanks," I murmured.

Ivy exhaled. "You're doing the right thing."

"Maybe."

She reached up, brushing my cheek and then rose to her tip-toes to gently press her lips to mine. They tasted sweet, like strawberry.

I glanced to the table at Marcus as he mouthed the word 'hold' to me and I shook my head. His forehead creased.

"No go, bro," I called. "Hang up."

He pulled a face as if I'd just told him he'd been evicted and slowly removed the phone from his ear, glancing longingly at the handset.

"You are better than him, Samuel Saber," Ivy breathed. "So show them."

I frowned down at her, moistening my lips. "What are you doing to me?"

She smiled. "Bewitching you."

"Mm."

"Come on," she breathed. "Let's eat."

Dinner was pleasant but I could tell Marcus was seething that I wasn't going to push the media thing. He understood though; all I had to say was *Amelia* and he shut it. It bothered me that her name was all it took but in this instance it worked in my favour.

Marcus and Mira seemed to get along well but I could tell he wasn't into her despite the fact that she flirted with him like tonight was her last night on earth. He didn't mind.

After Constellation we headed to Crescent because the girls wanted to go out dancing. Marcus and I were happy to watch.

I dropped Ivy and Mira home first and then intended to take Marcus to his place on the way back to mine. I walked Ivy and Mira to the door since Marcus had dozed off in the backseat.

"Sam," Ivy whispered as Mira stumbled inside sleepily. I think she may also have been a little drunk.

"Ivy."

She smiled. "Thanks for tonight."

"Thank you," I breathed. "It was fun."

She nodded. "Are you dropping Sax home?"

"Yeah, or I could just leave him in the car," I laughed. "What do you think?"

"I think you should come back if you do," she shrugged.

"Here?"

"Here."

"Are you asking me to stay the night?" I smirked. "Because there's no one here to make jealous."

She shrugged. "There's Mira."

I pressed my lips together.

"Unless you're keen to get home," she added.

I laughed. "Give me twenty minutes, okay?"

"Twenty-one and I'm locking the door," she warned.

My eyebrows lifted. "See you in nineteen minutes then."

"Drive safe."

I gave a nod and headed back to the car.

Marcus was out cold so I had to drag him by the arm to his doorstep. He hadn't been drinking but he was the heaviest sleeper I'd ever known.

I rang the doorbell at his house and left him, when I got back to the car, Ash opened the front door and dragged him in before shooting me a wave—and I headed back to Ivy's. It was a seventeen-minute round trip.

The door was unlocked when I arrived back so I nudged it open.

"Ivy?"

"Sam."

I couldn't pick where her voice was coming from. I closed the door and locked it, searching around the darkened lounge room.

"Where are you?" I asked.

"Find me," her phantom voice whispered.

I laughed, glancing up the hallway. It was pitch black so I looked towards the kitchen where a shred of light glowed. I took a few measured steps in the direction and heard a creak so stopped. A heartbeat later, I felt hands on my shoulders as Ivy jumped on my back. I caught her before she slipped off.

"You found me," she breathed.

"*You* found *me*," I corrected. "You like games, don't you?"

"I like playing," she replied. "Not games."

I turned. "Playing games? Like the one we're playing so you can get Nate back?"

She slipped off. "You're not having fun?"

"Oh, it's fun all right," I shrugged. "For now."

"For now?"

234

"Well, you do want him, don't you?" I asked. "That's what this is all about."

Ivy frowned. "Is it?"

"Isn't it?"

"Maybe it started that way," she shrugged.

My eyebrows pulled together. "Okay."

Ivy blinked. "Okay?"

"Okay."

She sighed. "I like hanging out with you, Sam."

"I like hanging out with you too," I nodded. "But if Nate did want you back, just so we're understood, you would go, wouldn't you?"

She bit her lip and I almost forgot what I'd asked.

"Ivy?"

She glanced up at me with her twinkling gold eyes then rose to her toes to kiss me, her arms moving up to encircle my neck as she jumped up to wrap her legs around me. I moved my arms around her, holding her up as she breathed hot into my mouth, her tongue tracing my lips and massaging mine, forcing my blood to pump forcefully through my veins, reaching every muscle in my body.

"Down the hallway," she breathed into my mouth. "Third door to the left."

I started walking, obediently as a robot, and found her room, ignoring the light switch and heading straight to the bed where I leaned over and rested her down gently as we both began tearing off each other's clothes.

"Wait," Ivy panted. "Sam, wait."

We were mostly naked with the exception of underwear bottoms so it was probably about the cruellest thing she could have said in that moment. I dropped my head to her shoulder.

"What?"

"I don't want to ruin things," she sighed, cradling my head in her hands and tipping it up so I was forced to look her in the eyes. It was hard to keep them there.

"What?" I breathed. "What things?"

"I like you, Sam, I like what we've got," she whispered, looking forlorn. "If we do this, there's no going back."

"Back to what?" I asked. "Isn't it going forward?"

Her eyes closed and I knew that was a solid *no* so sat back as she covered her naked breasts.

"I'm sorry," she murmured.

I ran my hands through my hair. "What am I to you? What is this? You keep moving the goal posts, I can't keep up."

The shadow of a smile darkened the corners of her lips.

"I don't know," she breathed. "I'm sorry, I'm confused."

"Why?"

She looked down. "Things are getting complicated."

"You're making them complicated."

Her eyes lifted to meet mine. "I didn't—I don't…"

I shook my head. "I should go."

"You don't have to."

"But I should," I replied, finding my shirt and pulling it over my shoulders. Half the buttons had popped off in our haste so I didn't bother attempting to fasten them.

"You asked me earlier if I'd go back to Nate if he asked," she said slowly.

I considered that and realised that she'd never answered my question. I glanced back at her and nodded as she ran her fingers through her matted blonde curls.

"Right, and?"

Ivy sighed. "Would you go back to Paige?"

I exhaled. "Ivy, I told you—"

"What about Isobel?"

236

I pressed my lips together. "Isobel made it pretty clear that she wanted nothing more to do with me."

"But would you go back if they wanted it?" she asked.

I blinked—I hadn't thought about it since it wasn't really an option. If Paige told me she wanted me back, sure, I'd take pause because there was a point when I really felt something strong for her. But regardless, she never needed or trusted me the way I needed her to and there was no reason for that to change this time around. The problems that separated us still existed even if we had both changed since the breakup. At least I was fairly sure they did.

As for Isobel, that was a tougher nut to crack. There was no denying that I was attracted to her, I wanted her, and I would have done anything for her... but that wasn't reciprocated. How many times did I need to be kicked until I realised that it was a losing battle? Twice was enough.

"They wouldn't want it back," I answered a little belatedly. "Paige never needed me and Isobel never wanted me. I'm not putting my life on hold for something that could never happen."

"Nate doesn't want me back. He's moved on, he doesn't want me," she murmured then shrugged her naked shoulders. "To be honest, I don't even know if I want him back—I don't know if I was ever happy with him. If I was, I wouldn't have cheated on him the first time. You made me realise that, Sam."

I moistened my lips. "So what now?"

She breathed a humourless laugh. "I have no idea."

"So you don't want Nate anymore," I mused. "And you don't want me."

"I never said that," she replied.

I frowned. "Um, you told me to stop."

She bit her lip. "I don't want you to sleep with me then lose interest. Things change when guys get what they want."

"Not if you make it memorable."

237

Her eyebrows lifted then she laughed.

I shook my head.

"Ivy, I'm not that guy, I'm not the nail and bail type," I answered; then frowned as I thought of Demi. "Well, not on purpose."

"I don't know what that means," she huffed.

I let out a breath. "I wouldn't have slept with you then ignored you. You're probably the only girl who's been straight with me from the beginning."

She smiled and moved to her knees, peeling back my shirt to kiss me on the shoulder. I watched her curiously as she laid back down, my blood pulsing in my ears. Damn, she looked incredible. I had to leave now if she didn't want to cross a line. As much as I wouldn't say no, I didn't want to mess things up with her. She was right, we had a good thing—whatever it was.

I started to stand and she caught my wrist.

"Don't go," she whispered. "Stay with me."

Lord above, now she was begging me.

"Ivy."

"Sam."

I smiled wryly. "You're making this incredibly difficult for me."

She shrugged. "The best things in life don't come easy."

My lips pressed together and she rolled to her side.

"Come on, Sam, it's late. You might as well stay."

"To sleep?"

"And snuggle," she offered. "Maybe a little making out."

I raised an eyebrow. "A little?"

She laughed. "I'll let you get to second base."

"Second?" I groaned. "Come on."

"Take it or leave it, Saber," she smirked, slipping her blanket down to reveal more of her body.

I swallowed. "Fine, I'll stay."

"You were never going to leave," she whispered, sinking her teeth into her lower lip. I pulled my shirt off and lay down beside her as she shuffled around to face me, locking her lips to mine as she hitched her knee over my leg.

Oh man, I was in trouble. So much for no distractions...

XII

Out of the Bag

I woke in the morning tangled in Ivy's body, feeling as if I had barely slept—which I guess was true. A small part of me was glad that I wasn't playing today because my muscles felt overexerted after my gym session yesterday.

I glanced down at Ivy, still fast asleep, and brushed a piece of her hair from her face. She was a beautiful girl, more beautiful than I initially thought her to be having known her better now. Her skin was a flawless golden bronze with subtle beige freckles that speckled over her nose. She had a faint white scar that sliced across the crease between her eyebrows that I made a mental note to ask her about later. She was slim, but not skinny, with curves that you just wanted to climb and her golden hair was tussled and strewn around her face, like a sort of tainted halo. She stirred, rolling against my side, and subconsciously ran her hands across my abdomen. It sent prickles up and down my body.

"Hey," she exhaled, nestling into my chest.

"Hey."

"Have you been awake long?" she sighed, resting her chin on my ribs. Her gold eyes sparkled in the morning light. I moved my hands up to rest behind my head.

"Nope."

"Did you sleep well?"

I huffed a laugh. "No. You?"

"No," she giggled. "Hungry?"

"Always."

Her cute nose wrinkled. "Want to go out for breakfast?"

"All right," I nodded. "I might have to swing by home first to grab a change of clothes so I can go straight to the game."

"You still have to go?"

"Yep," I exhaled, moving my arm closest to her around her. "Want to come?"

"Do I get to sit with you?"

I lifted my shoulder. "If you like."

"Okay."

"Okay," I smiled weakly. "Should we get up now?"

"Probably," she sighed. "But I can't seem to move."

"Me neither."

Her eyes dropped and she frowned. "You're in really good shape."

I laughed. "Thanks. I sort of have to be."

"You must think I'm all kinds of lazy," she replied.

I frowned. "Why?"

"Because I'm all flabby and you're super toned."

Why did girls always do this? Surely they can't all be this self-doubting. I didn't think Ivy had a problem with how she looked, she always seemed so confident in her own skin.

"I think you have a great body," I answered honestly.

She pulled a face. "Thanks."

"Come on, you know you do," I laughed, sitting up. She rolled over to her back.

"I don't know if I have a *great* body," she replied. "I mean I try not to care what people think of me but despite that, I'm still an insecure girl who feels the need to compete with other girls."

"And girls think its guys who are the competitive gender."

She shrugged.

241

"Well I think you're hot," I answered, leaning down to kiss her neck. Her fingers combed through my hair as she let out a sigh which made my body clench.

"You're not playing fair," I murmured against her skin.

"You started it."

I pulled back and stood up. "Breakfast?"

Ivy drew in a breath and let it out. "Breakfast."

"Um, have you seen my pants?" I frowned.

"Not lately."

I searched the floor and found them underneath one of the blankets which had fallen off the bed. "Ah-ha," I smiled.

"Darn, I would have loved to see you go home pant-less and try and explain that to your folks," she grinned.

"Right, alert the camera crew," I nodded, throwing her one of her T-shirts. She caught it and sat up, pulling it over her head.

"I might grab a quick shower, want to join me?"

I froze. "For real?"

She shrugged. "Saves water, right?"

"Well, I am concerned about the environment."

A smile broke across her gorgeous face, like a sunrise over the ocean. "That's what I thought."

***

We ended up going to breakfast first because I found one of Louis' T-shirts in the back of his car that I wore with my pants. Ivy found it amusing that I was fine with wearing a surf-brand top with dress pants but I didn't care much—I reminded her it was because of her handy work that my shirt was now unwearable.

We had breakfast at Lunar because their breakfast burgers were almost as awesome as their regular ones, then headed back to Saber Manor to get my stuff together for football. Because I was sitting out, all that was really required was me wearing a suit with our team tie so it wasn't going to take me that long to change. When we got there, Angela and Amelia were out—Saturday mornings meant shopping for them so other than running into Artie, I didn't expect anyone to be home.

"Samuel," Artie bellowed as Ivy and I stepped over the threshold. I gave her hand a squeeze and released it.

"I'm not staying, I just came to change for football," I answered.

Artie stepped out from behind the wall separating the front entrance from the lounge room.

"Oh, you have company with you—hello Ivy," Artie nodded.

"Mr Saber."

Artie exhaled. "Samuel, we have a problem."

"Of course we do."

He glared at me. "Where were you last night?"

"Out," I shrugged.

"Where? Constellation?"

I blinked. "For a while."

"Who did you speak to?"

"Nobody," I shrugged. "What's the problem?"

Artie glanced at Ivy. "Can you excuse us, please?"

"No," I murmured. "Ivy stays."

Ivy slipped her hand back into mine as Perry stepped out.

"A news story has broken this morning regarding speculation about your night out the other evening with Arthur," Perry explained. "The waiter was interviewed and implied that it was Arthur who insisted on the alcohol."

My eyebrows lifted. "Well that's not entirely untrue."

"Samuel, be serious," Artie snapped. "Don't you know what this means?"

I shook my head.

"It means, *son*, that my reputation has received another blow and my future in office is in jeopardy," he hissed.

I exhaled. "Well, you should have thought of that before you set me up."

Artie's eyes darkened.

"*Who* did you speak to?" he growled. "Who else knows about this little theory of yours?"

I glanced sideways at Ivy who swallowed nervously.

"Was it you?" Artie snapped, thrusting a finger at her.

I pushed her behind me, blocking her from his wrath.

"Ivy hasn't left my sight," I answered. "It wasn't her that went to the media."

"Then who?" he shouted. "Someone you told must've taken it upon themselves to squeal."

"I don't know, Dad," I breathed. "Maybe the waiter did it himself after reading the lies Perry got published?"

"*This is not a joke.*"

"No one is laughing."

"Was it just you two last night?" Artie pushed. "Or were there others?"

I pressed my lips together, not about to throw my friends to the wolves.

"Marcus Saxon?" Artie fished.

I shook my head. "Marcus wouldn't say anything."

At least I hoped he wouldn't. No, he seemed ready to let it drop last night.

Artie folded his arms, his eyebrows lifting impatiently.

Ivy squeezed my hand and I glanced at her from the corner of my eye.

"I've got to go, I can't be late to football, I'm in enough trouble with Wesley," I said dryly, tugging Ivy towards the stairs. "If you'll excuse us."

"This conversation is not over," Artie called after me.

I should be so lucky.

Ivy and I didn't speak until we were in my room with the door closed. I opened my cupboard and took out my suit for the game; Ivy stood frozen with her back to my door.

"What's up?" I asked, taking off my T-shirt and shoes.

"Mira," she murmured. "What if it was Mira?"

I pulled off my pants. "What?"

"Last night, she was keen to call channel three as much as Sax was," she explained. "What if she made the call later on?"

I frowned and straightened after pulling up the clean suit-pants. "You think?"

She shrugged. "Who else would it be?"

I thought for a moment and grabbed my shirt, pulling it on. Mira had been pretty excited about the prospect of media attention but what benefit would it be to her to snitch?

"No," I replied, putting the tie around my neck. "She wouldn't have the number for starters."

Ivy pushed off the door and walked over, her fingers sliding onto the silk as she took over tying it for me.

"It's not hard to find the number for channel three," she explained. "Think about it. Sax wouldn't do it, he let it drop, but Mira might have thought she was helping. The only reason you gave for not pressing matters was that the waiter didn't want to talk and 'Amelia', which doesn't mean anything to her."

"Oh crap," I sighed. "Maybe you're right."

Ivy's hands fell away and she stepped back to appraise me. I sat on the corner of my bed to put my shoes on.

"I'm so sorry Sam," she pouted.

I tied the laces and looked up. "Why are you sorry?"

She shook her head, looking as if she might cry. Crap, tears were not a guy's friend.

"She's my friend, I should have said something to stop her," she whispered. "I should have—"

I stood up and rested my hands on her arms. "Done what? She's her own person, you weren't to know."

"I should find her, to be sure," she murmured. "And make sure she doesn't make it worse."

I frowned. "Okay, if you think that will help."

"You don't?" she asked, her gold eyes glossy.

My head shook. "Not now, the damage is done. Unless she knows anything else?"

Ivy shrugged. "I can't take that risk."

"Okay," I nodded. "Well I'll drop you home on the way."

She shook her head. "You'll be late—I'll just walk."

I moved my hands to cradle her face. "This is not your fault, okay? Don't blame yourself."

"I'm really sorry, Sam," she murmured. "Really. If this affects your family in any way—"

"Don't," I interrupted. "Don't even go there. We'll be fine, we always are. Perry will come up with something."

She leaned her cheek into my palm. It was strange seeing Ivy so upset; she normally wasn't bothered by much and it saddened me that it was because of my presence in her life that she was this way. Maybe Isobel was right to cut herself off from me.

"Good luck at the game," she murmured, pressing her lips into my hand. "I'll call you later."

"You don't have to go," I answered. "There's probably not much you can do."

She forced a smile—and it looked forced. "Come on, I don't want you to be late."

She reached up and took my hand, towing me towards the door. I let her drag me down the stairs and outside and was glad that Artie and Perry were nowhere to be seen.

"You look smashing," she smiled. "Seriously, you should skip games more often."

I laughed. "Thanks."

"I hope the Suns win," she sighed. Good, maybe she was over the whole Mira guilt thing.

"Me too, but I don't like our chances," I replied. "Are you sure you won't come?"

She leaned on my hands to lower my head so she could reach my lips and gave me a lingering kiss.

"I'll see you later, Sam," she whispered, then turned on her heel to walk down my driveway. My joints were jarred as I watched her, noticing the way her golden hair bounced and her hips wiggled as she walked, her hands finding each other behind her back as if she was imagining someone else was holding them.

I smiled to myself and turned towards Louis' car and began my drive to the oval. It was already packed when I arrived but there was still about half an hour until the game actually started. If I was playing, I would've had to be here at least an hour ago.

"Sammy," Marcus sighed as I walked in the rooms. "Oh man, I saw the news—did you change your mind?"

I shook my head. "Ivy thinks Mira made the call."

Marcus swore under his breath. "What did Artie say?"

"Ah, Artie," I laughed humourlessly.

"Right lads, gather 'round," Wesley announced.

I tipped my head and Marcus frowned as he moved to listen to Wesley's game plan and fighting words. I hated that I wasn't playing; it killed me that I had to sit on the sidelines while my brothers in arms went into battle. I felt like I was betraying them—in a way, I was.

"Sam," Wesley called.

"Coach?"

He gestured for me towards him. "Come, lad."

I slid my hands in my pocket and obeyed, wandering towards him. When I was close he patted my shoulder.

"You good, son?" he said, raising an eyebrow.

"Wish I was playing," I shrugged.

"Don't we all?" he winked. "Well, onwards and upwards, we've got a game to win."

I huffed. "Right."

The club song started and my teammates ran out onto the emerald green oval. It was great, the atmosphere of the games, the crowd cheering, the energy. I sometimes felt a little guilty for it all, because we were no one expect a bunch of guys who had an athletic skill and were praised for it. We didn't cure cancer or invent anything to help mankind, but we provided entertainment, so I guess that was something.

"Sam Saber, meet Jason Cobalt," Wesley said, half shouting as the guys warmed up on field. I glanced up at the older man; his eyes seemed to smile with the permanent creases around the dark blue irises. He looked kind.

"Nice to meet you," I smiled, accepting his hand. Jason Cobalt, the assistant coach of the South Coast RedBacks.

"It's a pleasure, Sam," he grinned. "You show great promise."

"Thanks, that means a lot."

"It's a shame you're not out there today," he noted. "The boys could use you after what happened to Prince."

I exhaled. "You're not wrong."

He patted me on the back as Wesley jogged onto the field to huddle, and a couple of minutes later, the siren bellowed and the game began.

Jason and I ended up chatting for most of the first half and he was a great source of information for everything football—he noticed things: handicaps and habitual techniques of players that I'd never picked before. I found myself looking inward at what he saw in my game but I was too engrossed with what he was saying that I didn't want to interrupt to ask him.

At halfway through the second half we were still two goals down. Jason had to leave so gave me his card and told me to call him tomorrow or Monday. I walked him up to one of the exits and on my way back spotted Paige in amongst the crowd looking utterly bored. I was impressed she'd lasted this long considering she didn't often stay for full games when we were together. But given it was Nate's first run, I figured she wanted to support him.

"Hey Stewart," I called. She was reading something; it looked like a textbook. Typical Paige.

She looked up curiously and blinked into the sun.

"Oh, hey Sam."

There were mutterings from the surrounding crowd that I ignored and made my way down the row to the spare seat beside her. She smiled as I fell to sit.

"How's it going?" I asked.

She mashed her lips together and breathed a laugh—it was like Paige's trademark.

"It's going great," she answered, shaking her head as her brow puckered incredulously.

I laughed at her. "Enjoying the game?"

"Yeah, it's very… riveting."

"You're not watching are you?"

"What makes you say that?"

"Because we're losing."

"Oh."

There was a short pause and she laughed and I couldn't help but chuckle with her.

"So how come you're not out there?" she asked, wedging the geology textbook between her legs. The gesture momentarily distracted me.

"Don't you follow the news?" I frowned.

She shrugged. "Did reporters start telling the truth?"

"Touché," I huffed. "Um, well you know how I went on that little bender with Artie the other night? Well it made the front page so it's more of an obligatory bye."

"Right, the missed calls," she nodded. "I can't believe you went out drinking with your father. You."

I shrugged. "It was involuntary."

"Okay," she breathed, shaking her head.

I looked at her carefully, she looked different, happier or something. The thought that another guy did that was a little bruising to my ego.

"So how are things with Nate going?"

The words were out before I could stop myself asking.

Her eyebrows lifted. "Uh, good."

"You seem happy."

She exhaled. "Yeah."

"Are you not?"

"Sam," she sighed.

I frowned. "Sorry, guess I don't have a right to ask."

She bit her lip. Ugh, that lip.

"No, it's okay," she shrugged. "Things are just different. They're different with Nate than they were with you. He's just…"

"Different?" I offered.

She smiled weakly. "He doesn't expect me to be anyone more than I am. Sometimes I think you wanted me to be this damsel but that's not me."

I looked down. "Yeah, you never were a damsel."

"Despite my altercation with Captain-Conceited last weekend," she added.

I huffed a humourless laugh. "Right."

"So how are things with Ivy?" she asked on a loud exhale. "Are you two still... whatever you are?"

My eyebrows lifted at her tone; if I didn't know any better I'd say she sounded jealous.

"We're good," I nodded. "She's won over Artie, and Amelia sort of likes her."

Paige seemed to pale. "Oh, she's met your family already?"

"Not Mum but the other two," I answered.

"Artie and Amelia like her, hey?"

"She is rather charming."

Paige mashed her lips together. Yep, it bothered her. Whoops.

"Mum still asks about you," I added. "I think she misses you coming around."

Her cloudy blue-grey eyes glistened. "Your mum is so nice."

I nodded in agreement and we fell silent as the crowd applauded and cheered around us. I glanced up at the score and saw we were catching up—only down by one now. Cool.

"I'm sorry," she said suddenly, catching me by surprise. Had she said something to offend me that I missed?

"For what?"

"Not telling you things," she shrugged; her head was shaking as she spoke. "It wasn't that I didn't trust you, it was more that I didn't want you to look at me the way they all did when they found out."

I felt my eyebrows pull together. Wasn't that the same? She didn't trust me not to judge her?

Paige pulled her lip in. "I wanted you to see me for who I am now—and you did. I just think that came at a cost because who I am now is only half of who I was."

The crowd roared and I cursed the fact we were having this conversation at a game. It wasn't the most ideal of surroundings.

"You're pretty great you know, who you are now," I replied. "I wouldn't have stayed with you if I didn't think that."

Her eyebrow rose. "But you wouldn't have cheated on me if it was enough."

"Ouch," I sighed. "And define cheating."

She shoved my arm. "Hooking up with another girl?"

I tipped my head, my shoulder lifting. "Well, technically…"

"I don't want to know," she interrupted, clasping her hands over the fiery red hair that covered her ears.

I laughed and looked up as the crowd erupted again. Even scores—the guys could really have this.

"How long to go?" Paige asked, noticing my distraction.

I glanced at the clock and frowned. "Maybe five minutes or so."

"So they could still stuff it up."

"Or win."

"Or stuff it up."

"Aren't you on our side?" I asked. "Where's your team spirit?"

She rolled her eyes. "Sam, you know me better than that."

I huffed. "Yeah, I'm floored that you're still here."

She lifted her book and gave an adorable chuckle that made me smile. I loved that sound; it used to be the most profound in my universe.

I wanted to tell her that I missed her but I couldn't get the words out. It wasn't fair to anyone for me to think them, never mind say them. She wasn't mine to miss anymore, she was Nathaniel Blake's, and I had my own tangled web of a life to sort out without involving someone else in the mix.

Paige mashed her lips together and looked down and I knew the moment had passed. We had our closure and it was the most we could hope for without crossing any lines that might lead to something more or something less than fair parting terms.

"I should get back," I said, leaning close to her so she could hear. "I'm glad you came. Nate will be too."

I sat back and her eyes fluttered, her head nodding in silent acknowledgment.

"I'll see you around," I finished, lifting my hand in some awkward half wave as I stood.

Her mouth opened as she formed the word 'bye' that I couldn't hear.

Walk away Samuel, walk away.

I shuffled back down the row, ignoring protests as I momentarily blocked people's view of the intense play and then cantered down the stairs back to where our interchange was. Wesley was a great coach—very involved—all others utilised the executive boxes behind the crowd but he sat with us, talked to us and got amongst the action. The officials even organised a floating screen where he could watch the action up close so he didn't miss anything vital. He really walked to the beat of his own drum but it worked for him, the guy was like a wizard with the team. Before Wesley, the Iris Cove Suns hardly ranked in the top half of minor league teams—now we were the ones to beat.

"Sam, son, did you get lost?" Wesley laughed as I reappeared. "Scores are even lad; I think we've got this."

I glanced up at the scoreboard.

"How long?" I asked.

"Minutes, son, minutes," he chortled happily. "Let's hope Blake learnt something from you, eh?"

I looked at Wesley then at the big screen, noticing that Nate had the ball and was heading for goal. This was his shot; if he got this, he would be a legend. Nate had played an impressive game: a lot of touches, a few assists and goal already today. If he won this in the dying moments, it would arguably be the best breakout performance in almost any player's career. I say almost because it's no coincidence it was me who had been given the task of prepping him and helping him train. Not many people knew that it was me that Wesley intended to make captain of the Suns before Elliot was offered the gig. I'd turned it down solely because all I wanted was to play and captain meant more responsibility, housekeeping and press releases. I had enough of that having Artie as a father.

Nate ran—and he was fast—dodging opposition and weaving his way through the mass of bodies creating human shields from goal. The clock counted down and you could almost hear Suns' fans inhale collectively as he did one of the manoeuvrers I'd taught him, spinning and kicking the ball off the side of his foot to bend back into the goals in a glory-almighty score. The siren sounded and the crowd went nuts.

The Suns had won their third game of the season without their captain, Elliot Prince, or me as the stand in-captain. I wasn't sure whether to cheer with them or kiss my rank in the team goodbye. So I did the only thing someone in my position could do: I ran onto the field to congratulate my team on a well-played game and absolutely nail-biting win.

***

'Saber Sabotages Son' today's headline read. No wonder Artie was in such a mood this morning. The reporters certainly didn't paint him technicoloured today. I picked up my glass of lemonade and took a long sip while Marcus sang to his burger. We were in Lunar after the game celebrations and it was mid-afternoon. I dropped the paper and stole a chip off his plate.

Marcus looked up.

"Can't say I'm sorry to see those words in print," he said, taking a bite. He said something else but it was a garble.

"This whole thing shouldn't have happened," I sighed. "It just makes everything worse."

Marcus shrugged.

"One good thing did come out of this though," he continued, mouth still full but at least he'd chewed most of his food this time so I could distinguish words.

My eyebrow lifted.

"Who knew Nate Blake had that in him?" he chuffed. "Amazing."

There it was again, that niggling jealousy. It was completely unreasonable.

"Right," I nodded.

"So Jason gave you his card?" Marcus continued. "We'll need Nate when you're drafted."

I took another chip. "No one is drafted yet. There's still time for me to stuff up again."

I sounded like Paige, it made me smirk.

Marcus pulled a face. "You won't stuff up; they've practically already printed your name in their line-up."

I exhaled, wondering who would want a guy who makes the papers for getting drunk with his father only to have it come out he was 'tricked into it'. Even for me that was too much drama.

"I don't know, bro, it just seems like a bit of a pipe dream," I shrugged. "I'm already older than regular rookies."

"You're better though."

"If I was I would have made it already."

Marcus shrugged. "He still gave you his card."

I took another sip of lemonade and groaned internally as Isobel walked in with Liam, Nate and Paige. Well this was cosy. All we needed now was Ivy to appear and the fun could really begin.

"Hey guys," Marcus called out before I had the chance to distract him.

Four sets of eyes looked over but it was Nate who replied.

"Hey Sax, Saber."

I lifted my head in a half-hearted nod.

"Hey Blake, Paige, Liam," Marcus replied. "It's Isobel right?"

Isobel looked at me then her eyes flickered to Marcus. "Yes, hello Marcus."

I looked down and began playing with my straw.

"Celebratory lunch, Blake?" Marcus asked. "Hey take a seat, we don't mind."

I looked up at him and wished slapping him upside the head would be a subtle gesture.

"Uh…" Liam and Isobel groaned, exchanging a glance. Paige drew in a breath and Nate sat down.

"Cool, thanks," he smiled. Ignorant rogue.

Paige sat beside him, between us, and Liam and Isobel filled in the gaps on our other side, Liam beside Marcus and Isobel beside me. My discomfort meter was at its peak.

"So where's Ivy today?" Isobel asked sharply. "Not here?"

I glanced over at her. "No, she had to meet a friend. We don't feel the need to spend every second together."

She rolled her shoulders back and moved her hand onto Liam's thigh and he straightened at her touch. I took slow breaths.

"Oh, is this what you were talking about Sam?" Paige asked, picking the paper up from the table.

I glanced down at it and frowned. "Yes."

"Did he really set you up?" she sighed. "I can't believe he would sink that low."

"The truth came out?" Isobel asked. "How? Did you tell?"

"No, not me," I answered, feeling as if I was caught in the middle of a tennis game. "It got leaked to the press."

"How's your dad taking it? Is he mad?"

"Furious," I exhaled. "Blames me, naturally."

"Oh Sam," Isobel said sadly, resting a hand on my arm. Marcus cleared his throat and both Isobel and I jumped. Crap, I forgot where we were—apparently she did too.

"There's more?" Demi's voice interrupted before it could get more awkward. "Can I take your order?"

I sat back as Demi looked between us, her head tipped.

"Hey, are you two back together?" she asked, pointing her pen between Paige and me.

"No," we answered in unison.

She nodded and her eyes swept to Isobel.

"Oh, sorry, you're with her now," she nodded. "Wait, was she the one on the phone?"

My eyes widened at her and I saw Marcus pull a face. Liam looked livid but Nate didn't look surprised—weird.

"I'll just have a green tea please," Paige interrupted.

Demi paused and then wrote it on her pad.

"Um, the burger looks good," Nate added. "And a red cream soda please."

Liam shook his head. "Nothing for me."

Marcus hadn't taken his eyes off Isobel and me. He stared, frowning, blinking, and looking as if he wanted to speak but knew this wasn't the forum for it. Crap. Double crap. I made a mental note not to tip Demi as much as I normally do.

My phone buzzed and I glanced down at it. It was Ivy: *Hey, spoken to Mira… she thought she was doing the right thing. I don't know what else to say but I'm so sorry Sam. x*

I sighed and hit reply: *Not your fault, don't blame yourself. Chat later.*

I put my phone back in my pocket and looked up, no one was talking—they were shifting uncomfortably in their seat averting their eyes. I needed to say something—this was nuts.

"So Nate, nice move there at the end," I said as lightly as I could. "You're a quick learner."

Attention was drawn back to the table.

"Yeah, thanks for the tip," he nodded. "I guess you know your stuff."

"Guess," I huffed.

"So are you back next week then?" he asked.

I exhaled. "Should be, hopefully."

"When is Macca due back?" Marcus asked, clearly thawing from his pouty pause.

"End of the week maybe?" I frowned. Guess he'll want his car back.

"Your silent protest will be over," Paige huffed, reading my mind.

I smiled at her. "Nah, I'll go back to walking everywhere again."

She breathed a laugh. "You're ridiculous, you know that. I remember when you were saving up for that boat trip we were going to go on and Artie—did he buy the boat or like rent it out for the week and said we could use it?—and you completely flipped and boycotted the whole thing."

I laughed at the memory. "He keeps doing it though, he pretends to do something nice but the second I accept it the strings appear."

Nate drew in a breath and I sobered.

"But yeah," I shrugged. "Maybe it's ridiculous."

"Well after this week, I wouldn't want to trust him either," Isobel added. "It's one thing to have power and another thing to abuse it against your own children. Mayor Saber should be more fastidious about his actions being in the position he's in."

I turned to Isobel, feeling the incredulous expression on my face that was mirrored on Marcus and Paige's. Nate looked bored and Liam looked a little annoyed and embarrassed—which was pretty amusing in itself.

"Right," I replied, not knowing what else to say. Sometimes I think Isobel tried to overcompensate for the fact she's a couple of years younger than the rest of us—and sometimes that doesn't entirely work in her favour.

Demi returned with the rest of the order and the distraction was almost a tangible relief. I glanced at Marcus as he finished off the last of his chips and raised my eyebrows. He lifted his head.

"So we might leave you guys to it," I sighed, pushing my chair out.

Marcus did the same. "It was cool to see you guys again."

"You too Sax," Paige nodded.

"All right then," Nate replied.

Liam didn't say anything and Isobel gave a polite smile.

"Um, so we'll see you later," I said, walking around to Marcus.

"See you," Paige and Nate said.

"Bye Sam, Marcus," Isobel added.

Liam gave a small nod. What a guy.

I walked over to Demi and gave her a twenty which would more than cover Marcus' burger and shake, and my lemonade, and still leave a little change for her. She nodded gratefully and gave an apologetic smile and we left.

We walked back towards Marcus' car—we'd dropped Louis' back at my place on the way out to save on parking—and Marcus stared absently at the concrete.

"So—Isobel," he mused. "When did that happen?"

I glanced at him—there was no point in denying it anymore. "Couple of months ago."

Marcus stopped dead in his tracks. "*Months?*"

I pivoted and pressed my lips together. "It's over now."

"*Now?*" he repeated.

I pulled a face. "Well as of Thursday."

"Like two days ago, Thursday?" he said in exacerbation. "You were hooking up with Prince's girlfriend for months and you didn't tell me?"

I tipped my head. "We didn't really tell anyone."

Marcus shook his head. "Oh crap, Sammy—months—you were cheating on Paige?"

I scratched my jaw. "It didn't go past second base when I was with Paige."

"I don't believe it," he groaned. "I just… it's not you to do something this crappy to someone."

I blinked. "I didn't plan it. Why are you acting like such a girl about this?"

"Paige was good to you," he said. "She really freaking loved you, you idiot. Breaking up with her because it's not working between you two is different to leaving her for some *princess* who has a superiority complex."

I recoiled. "Huh?"

Marcus slapped his hand to his head and began to pace. We weren't far from his car.

"So what happened then?" he asked. "You're not with Isobel because of Ivy?"

I shook my head. "Archer."

"Archer?" he repeated in disdain. "She picked him over you?"

I shrugged. "I'm too complicated for her."

"What a trollop."

"Don't call her that," I sighed.

He shot me a dark look but ignored the comment. "Does Ivy know about her?"

I nodded. "The thing with Ivy was a mutual back-scratching. She wanted Blake back and I wanted to make Isobel jealous. At least that's how it started."

"Started?"

I exhaled. "I don't know what it is now."

Marcus muttered a string of expletives under his breath as he shook his head.

"Does Prince know?"

My eyebrows lifted. "Are you kidding? He'd kill me."

Marcus huffed, making me frown.

"You're really mad that I didn't tell you?" I added. It wasn't really a question, it was pretty evident.

"Damn right I am," he snapped. "I thought we were bros."

"We are but... Sax I'm not going to sit down and talk about my feelings with you," I shrugged. "Bros don't do that."

He tipped his head. "Still... it's pretty messed up. Besides, if Prince did find out who would've had your back?"

"Sorry."

"Yeah."

I exhaled.

Marcus looked up. "You really make things more complicated than they need to be."

"I know."

He rolled his eyes.

"So are we good?" I asked.

"Yeah," he groaned, running his hands through his shaved brown hair. "We're good."

"Want to see a movie or something?" I shrugged. "My shout."

Marcus frowned in consideration. "Okay, but I'm getting popcorn too—the most expensive size."

I sighed. "Of course you are."

"Let's go."

XIII

To Riches

Marcus decided his forgiveness could be bought with a large popcorn, coke and a chocolate-coated ice cream cone. Movie prices are crippling so all together the little expedition cost me a fortnight's allowance. But hey, it's only money, right?

We didn't stay out late. I was still pretty tired from spending the night with Ivy and he was exhausted from playing close to a full game. Marcus is a good player but perhaps a little underrated at the Suns; it sucked but he didn't seem to care. He just liked the distraction and fitness that it offered for him—simple guy but salt of the earth.

Sunday morning I gave Jason a call and caught him on the way to Iris Oval for the RedBacks game in the early afternoon. The call paid off and he invited me to the game so I got myself organised and headed to the train station to meet him at the VIP entrance.

I got to hang out in the change rooms with him before the game, meet the coach, Gordon—one of the toughest and most notorious coaches in the country's football history—and have a chat to Tristan Holmes, the esteemed captain of the South Coast team.

My head was buzzing by the end of the day and with a rather convincing win by the home side. I walked back to the train station with an invitation to a closed RedBacks training session on Tuesday afternoon.

I hadn't checked my phone all day so when I boarded the Southward carriage I saw I had three missed calls and a text message. Artie, Marcus and Ivy.

I ignored Artie's attempt and checked the message Marcus had sent when I missed his call. Apparently he'd seen me on television when the station was filming the corporate box where I was sitting just below. Cool.

I hit the recall button on Ivy's call and waited while it rang. It took a while for her to answer.

"Sam?"

"Ivy."

"Hey."

"Hey," I sighed. "What's up?"

"Can I come over?"

"To my house?" I asked. "I'm not home at the moment."

"Oh."

There was a short silence.

"Is everything okay?" I asked.

"Yes," she exhaled. "I just wanted to see if you wanted to hang out."

I pressed my lips together. "I can come to yours?"

If I got off on the stop before mine it was a short walk to her house.

"No, Mira is there," she answered.

"You're not home?"

"No, I'm at Crescent."

"Really?" I frowned. "Okay, I'll come there then."

There was more silence.

"Ivy?"

"I'm here," she answered. "Okay, I'll see you soon then."

263

I paused and then was listening to dial tone so tucked my phone back in my pocket. Well that was weird. But hey, I never pretended to understand girls.

I got off at the stop I would have to go to Ivy's house and walked into town. It was closer to hers than it was mine and meant I wouldn't have to double back. I found Ivy in the front bar of Crescent, spinning a glass with clear liquid around in her fingertips.

"Hey," I said, sliding onto the stool beside her. "What's going on?"

She looked over and smiled weakly. "Hi."

I picked up her glass and smelt it—it was sweet, non-alcoholic.

"Lemonade," she noted. "I'm not a big drinker."

I huffed. "Me neither, these days."

"These last two days?" she quipped, raising a brow. "Sorry."

I laughed. "Why? It's true."

Her smile faded. "Thanks for coming."

"Everything okay?" I asked again. I hated how girls did this—practically begged for attention then played coy. Playing hard to get only worked if we were willing to take the bait.

"How are things at home?"

I shrugged. "Fine."

"Good."

"You're not still upset about the whole Mira thing are you?" I frowned. "Because really, it's not even close to the worst story that's broken about our family."

"No it's—I'm not still upset about that," she answered. "I'm sorry that happened though, I'm still mad at Mira."

"Okay," I nodded slowly. "So any particular reason why you wanted to hang out?"

She looked up at me shyly. "I just don't really have anyone else."

That surprised me. "Really?"

She blushed pale pink and the fact she was embarrassed was a little amusing. I didn't think Ivy ever got nervous.

"So did you want to stay here or go somewhere else?" I asked.

She turned and looked at me fully for the first time. "Where were you?"

"Football game."

"RedBacks?"

"Yep."

"Did we win?" she asked.

We. Cool. "Yep."

"You go with Sax?"

I shook my head. "On my own. I was asked by the assistant coach."

"Wow," she grinned. "That's pretty cool."

"Very," I agreed. "They even asked me to training Tuesday."

Her eyes shone. "Well look at you, Saber."

I shrugged and nodded.

"Can we go to yours?" she asked. "I'm still trying to avoid Mira."

My eyebrow rose. "Avoid? I hope that's not because of me."

"I'm having a girl moment."

"You are a girl."

"But I'm not a typical girl," she answered.

I laughed. "If you say so."

"So... your place?"

"Okay," I nodded. "Now or do you want to finish your lemonade first?"

She gave a laugh and threw it back. "Let's go, Saber."

"After you, Hunt."

She smiled and stood, brushing against my arm as she slipped off the stool. I pressed my lips together and followed her out.

"So, did you get to meet anyone exciting at the game?" she asked.

"Yes, I met the coach and a few of the players," I replied.

"Oh, did you meet Tristan Holmes?" she gushed. "I love him; he's so sexy and tall—is he tall? He looks tall."

I laughed. "Um, are you—you know the players?"

"Yes," she nodded. "Why?"

"It's just surprising, that's all," I shrugged. "I didn't take you for one of those fan-girls."

"Oh, I'm like a giant RedBacks nerd," she smiled. "When we made last year's finals, I literally camped outside the ticket box to make sure I got tickets."

I shook my head incredulously. "That's so cool."

Ivy folded her arms and tried to warm them as we walked. I shrugged out of my jacket and offered it to her.

"You'll be cold then," she answered, hesitating as she held it.

I gestured towards my torso. "I'm wearing wool, I'm fine."

"You sure?"

"Yes," I nodded. "So how come you missed the game today if you're such a die-hard fan?"

She pulled on my jacket and popped her little hands out the end of the too-long sleeves, tucking her curly blonde hair behind her ear.

"Um, well I left the house early this morning and went to the library and guess I forgot."

"Library?" I frowned. "You study so much."

She gave a weak shrug. "Like I said I'm avoiding Mira and I had an assignment that I needed to finish by tomorrow."

"Ah," I sighed. "Erm, what are you studying?"

She smirked, amusement twinkling in her eyes. "Psychology, criminology and justice."

"All at once?"

She laughed. "Yes."

"Lord above," I huffed. "No wonder you're always studying."

"What's your course?" she asked. "Sport science?"

I laughed. "No, mechanical engineering."

"What?" she gasped, annunciating the "t". "But you never show up to class! How are you passing?"

I shrugged. "I'm just really smart."

She burst into laughter that I should have found insulting, but it was rather amusing.

"Holy crap, Saber," she giggled. "You really are. What the heck are you studying that for if you want to be a professional footballer?"

"I used to want to be a mechanic but Artie wouldn't let me get an apprenticeship."

"For serious?"

I smirked. "Seriously."

"Why not?"

I frowned. "You have to ask?"

"He's not that much of a snob is he?" she asked incredulously.

I pressed my lips together she shook her head.

"Wow," she sighed. "My father... my father is a gardener at Iris Cove Primary, the fact that I got *into* university was an achievement in itself."

I glanced over at her and smiled.

Ivy laughed nervously. "What?"

"That's awesome; he sounds like a cool guy."

She huffed. "Not really. *Cool* and *Hector Hunt* aren't often used in the same sentence."

"You don't get along with him?"

She shrugged. "I don't really see a great deal of him. He was kind of glad when I was old enough to look after myself."

"What about your mum?"

"She lives in Almanbury with her new family," she replied. "I haven't seen her since I was ten. She and Hector separated when I was three."

"That kind of sucks," I mused. "So it's just you? No siblings?"

She exhaled. "Just me, thank goodness. I'm glad no one else got caught up in it."

"Bet you love hearing me complain about my overbearing parents then," I smirked.

"A father who's there and overbearing is just as bad as one who's absent," she replied. "What's your mother like?"

She'd asked me this question before—what did I say last time? *Like a mother*. Smooth, Samuel.

"She's pretty great actually," I answered honestly. "She's supportive and kind. If it wasn't for her I'd have left ages ago."

"And gone where?"

I looked at my feet. "Anywhere that's away from him."

"I know how you feel," she murmured. They were only words but they were enough.

I'd never voiced it aloud to anyone before, never had the compulsion or even the audience to speak about it. But why would I? Who would care? Poor little rich boy with a father with too-high expectations, living in a castle with everything he'd ever want or need and the money to do more. Yeah, I was someone to pity.

"You wanted to be a mechanic," she continued. "Was that before or after football?"

"After," I replied belatedly. "When I was told that I'd never even make it in the minor league. It was my plan B."

"So mechanical engineering was your default plan B?" she laughed. "Couldn't have picked something easier considering you're so good at football?"

"What? Like sports science?"

"Hey, it's not as easy as it sounds; the last guy I dated was studying sports science."

Must've been the one she left Nate for. Huh.

"If I was going to be made to study something, I wanted to be interested in it," I answered. "It was glorified mechanics. Artie chucked a fit but hey, it sounded smart."

Ivy smiled. "Fair call."

We continued back to the castle wordlessly with Ivy humming some pop boy-band song as we walked. It was comfortable being with her, effortless. It was like hanging with one of the guys but in a girl who was pretty hot at the same time. Ivy Hunt seemed to be a girl who strayed from complex and strived for uncomplicated despite her messed up childhood.

"Get your game face on, Hunt," I murmured as we walked up the driveway. "And don't mention anything about Mira, okay?"

"Got it," she nodded and then beamed a very convincing smile.

I smiled back and then felt her hand slip into mine. Apparently mine wasn't as convincing as hers.

"Samuel, honey, is that you?" Angela's heavenly voice hummed as I pushed the door open.

"Hey Mum," I answered as she appeared. "Um, this is Ivy. Ivy, my mum, Angela."

"Oh Ivy," Angela grinned, reaching forward to take her hand in both of hers. "It's so lovely to meet you."

"You too, Mrs Saber, Sam's told me a lot of nice things about you," she replied.

My mother rolled her eyes. "Please, call me Angela. Mrs Saber makes me feel old."

Ivy glanced at me as if to agree with my explanation of her.

"Are you two hungry?" Angela continued. "We already ate but there is some leftover steak pie."

I looked down at Ivy who seemed to share my expression.

"Sounds great, thanks," we both answered in unison.

Angela's eyes shone. "I'll get Marion to serve up. Take a seat, won't be long."

I ushered Ivy into the dining room as she took in the lavish surroundings and what I imagined would seem to her as a ridiculously oversized and expensive table.

"Woh, this really is a castle," she sighed. "I feel very out of place here."

I pulled a chair out for her. "You get used to it unfortunately."

"Feeling out of place or living like the rich?" she asked, cocking an eyebrow.

I smiled weakly. "Who said the two are mutually exclusive?"

***

We finished dinner and headed upstairs to my room and ended up watching a movie. Dally seemed to take a shining to Ivy and planted himself between us on the sofa. When the movie finished, he was snoring loudly.

Ivy smiled as she patted his fur. "Your life isn't all bad you know, Saber."

"I never said it was," I shrugged.

"I mean, Amelia, your mum, this house, Dalziel," she listed. "You've got what people spend their life trying to get: support and security."

I huffed. "And then there's Artie."

"Don't let him ruin your life," she replied, crawling up to sit on her knees. Dally woke and jumped off the sofa, heading to curl up in front of my desk.

I turned towards her. "It's not really a matter of letting him."

She thought about that for a moment and then shook her head, crawling forward to catch her lips on mine. It took me by surprise.

"Wow," I sighed. "My family are in the house."

"I can be quiet," she whispered, pulling my RedBacks jumper over my head.

"Ivy."

"Sam."

I ran my hands down her shoulders to rest on her forearms. "I thought you wanted to wait."

"Do you?"

I rubbed my forehead. "You're pretty confusing."

"Why?"

I shook my head. "Why do you want to do this now? What's changed?"

She tucked her hair behind her ear and sat back on her heels.

"I like you Sam."

"You like me," I repeated. "You mean you didn't before?"

"No I mean... *like* you," she breathed. "As in... more than just messing around and making people jealous."

"Oh, right," I sighed, pressing my lips together. Crap. What did that mean?

"You're freaking out, aren't you?" she answered. "I just freaked you out by saying that."

I frowned. "No, well, I mean, I don't really know what that means. Like, does that mean you want to start dating or... what exactly does it mean?"

Great. We were having the talk. I hated the talk.

"I don't really know yet," she shrugged, too casual about this little revelation.

"Well, um you know where I stand so..."

She bit the corner of her lip and began to play with my nut-allergy chain. "Where... um... do you stand?"

I looked down. "Oh, err..."

"Because I know you were hoping to be with Isobel but she ended things," she murmured, dropping her hands to run up and down her thighs. "And I'm not going to bring up Paige again since that always makes you mad."

Paige. I felt my stomach tighten and I frowned. I didn't think I'd miss her as much as I was starting to, especially now she was confusing me with being so cool about everything and actually talking to me like we should have when we were dating. Things weren't that complicated with Paige; I actually think it was me who made them complicated—and what the heck was Marcus saying about her loving me? I wonder if he was serious about that or just trying to make a point.

"Sam."

"Huh?"

She pressed her lips together.

I blinked. "What?"

"Where exactly do you stand?" she repeated.

"Uh, well," I mused. Crap, what was I going to say? That if it wasn't Isobel—or even Paige—that I wasn't willing to add the complication to my life? As much as I liked Ivy, and liked hanging out with her, I never really considered her as a girlfriend. That wasn't how she presented herself. That wasn't what I initially signed up for.

"I guess at the moment I was going to focus on football since recently my track record with girls has been pretty crappy."

She smiled. "So what you're saying is you're not looking for a relationship right now?"

"Right."

"But we can still hang out?"

I huffed. "Yeah, of course."

She looked down and cocked an eyebrow. "With clothes on?"

I shrugged. "Clothes are always optional."

"Okay," she laughed.

"Okay."

She drew in a breath and ran her fingertips over my chest. I pressed my lips together and caught her hand.

She grinned. "What?"

"Don't do that," I swallowed.

"Why?"

"Because I have a feeling in about a minute and a half you're going to get up and go," I replied.

Her brows pulled together. "Go where?"

"Do you want to stay?"

"Are you asking me to stay?"

I shrugged. "I'm not asking you to go."

"Is that the same thing?"

I sighed and tried to sit up, catching her wrists to stop her from falling back. She smiled as I cowered over her.

"You can stay if you want is what I'm saying," I answered. "If you want to avoid Mira some more."

She looked me in the eye thoughtfully. "You don't want a girlfriend at the moment... but what about a girl... friend."

I glanced down at her, watching how her quick breath parted her lips. "Huh?"

"So if we were friends," she mused. "Who fooled around..."

My brows pulled together. "Are you serious?"

"Well we've kind of been doing that already," she half shrugged. "Only now we're actually friends and before it was more for other people's benefit rather than our own."

I sat back and she moved forward over me again, leaning her arm above my head so her collarbone and chest were at my eye level. I lost all train of thought.

"So?" she prompted.

"What?"

She smiled, relishing in the effect she had on me. "No strings?"

"You're actually serious about this?" I half stuttered. Surely not—didn't all girls want substance? "Like just physical nothing else?"

"That's essentially what I'm getting at," she agreed.

"But I thought you said sex changes things?"

She shrugged. "If that was an option—but you just said it wasn't."

I breathed a laugh. Oh Lord.

"Do you think you can do it?" I asked. "I mean, you said you liked me—"

"I can do it because I like you," she answered. "And whatever, if you don't want to—"

"Oh, I never said I didn't want to," I chuckled. "I just wanted to state the obvious just so we were clear. I respect you enough to not want this to be hard on you."

She raised an eyebrow. "Saber, I'm the one who suggested it."

"Okay," I shrugged. "If you're sure."

She sat back and pulled off her shirt. Damn, what a body.

"Now?" I stuttered.

She lifted a shoulder. "Like I said, I can be quiet."

I huffed a laugh and sat forward, lowering her into the corner of the couch as her fingers fumbled to unbutton my jeans.

***

"What time is it?" Ivy exhaled, running her hand down my torso to settle on my hip. We were on the floor beside my bed and I could see the dim light around my window sill. I reached up to find my clock radio but couldn't locate it.

"Early I think," I answered.

She laughed, her frame shuddering with the motion. "Is that before or after eight thirty because I have class?"

"Hold on," I sighed, twisting to reach my jeans. I pulled my phone from the pocket. "Hm, seven thirty."

"Good," she mumbled. "There's still time."

I dropped my phone. "Is your class at eight thirty?"

"Nine thirty tutorial."

I laughed. "Plenty of time."

"Mm-hm."

"You hungry?"

She looked up at me and stretched her arms, rolling onto her back. "I could eat."

I propped myself up on my elbow and smiled. "Want to eat here or out?"

"You mean do I want to be served by your maid or pay someone to do it?" she asked. "Gosh this is weird."

"We still pay Marion," I shrugged. "It's all Artie's money, look at it that way."

She sat up. "Okay.

"Okay here or okay there?"

"Okay anywhere," she replied, pulling a piece of fluff from her hair. She laughed and tried to smooth it. "I must look a sight."

I handed her one of my T-shirts that was within reach. "You look good."

She breathed a laugh and looked around her. "Well, that was a fun night."

"Fun," I agreed.

"We almost made it to the bed."

"There's always next time," I shrugged. "If there is a next time."

Her eyebrow rose. "Oh, there will be a next time."

I chuckled and stood up, pulling my pants on.

"Breakfast?" I asked, offering her a hand.

"Breakfast," she agreed. She rose to stand, grabbing my shoulder as she found her feet. "I should find clothes first."

"Like I said, clothes are always optional."

"What if your parents are around?" she smiled.

I turned. "Oh look, here are your jeans."

"Yeah," she laughed, taking them and pulling them on.

We headed down to the kitchen but the house was relatively quiet. But that didn't mean much.

"Oh, good morning, honey," Angela said without turning. After a beat she glanced over her shoulder. "Hello Ivy."

"Morning Mrs—I mean Angela," she replied.

Angela glanced back to the paper in front of her as she took a sip of her tea. "Sleep well?"

"Uh yep," I answered. "But Dally was snoring."

She smiled. "Mm-hm."

Ivy glanced at me sideways and blushed.

I scratched my stubble. "So, we were going to grab breakfast."

"Sure thing," she nodded. "Your father is out so the coast is clear."

"Excellent," I sighed, resting a hand on Ivy's lower back as I guided her towards the kitchen.

Marion looked up as we entered. "Good morning Mister Sam."

"Morning Marion," I nodded. It took me close to nine years to get her to stop calling me *Master Saber*.

"Can I make you and your guest something?" she offered.

276

"This is Ivy," I said, turning to her. "What do you feel like?"

Ivy bit the corner of her lower lip. "What is there?"

"Anything," I huffed. "Everything, whatever you want."

"I kind of feel like a ham, cheese and tomato toasted sandwich," she answered slowly. "Is that too much trouble?"

Marion grinned. "Not at all Miss Ivy. What about you Mister Sam?"

"I'll have the same," I nodded.

"Coming up."

"Thanks Marion."

After breakfast Ivy had a shower and organised herself for uni. Marion packed her a lunch which put the most golden of smiles on her face and she started walking. I offered to go in early with her but she refused so I took the time to grab my own shower and ended up driving in for my eleven thirty workshop.

After class, I had a pile of readings and tasks to catch up on. I hadn't realised how behind I was so figured I'd follow Ivy's lead and head to the library for a while until I had to be at Suns football practice.

I was amped to get back out there with my teammates but it was definitely not as much fun as it was normally. Again, this was due in large part to Nate Blake, rogue turned wonder-boy hero, who strutted around like he'd just saved civilisation rather than win a game on a fluke. Sure, maybe I was a bit jealous because that used to be me, but it was one game—a good game—but it took more than one good game to make a player memorable. He needed to learn that.

Paige turned up to meet Nate after training and I was reminded of another title that used to belong to me that now belonged to Nate.

I was the first one out the change rooms because the guys were busy fussing about crap that didn't interest me, and as I crossed the car park to Louis' car, Paige mashed her lips together in her imperfectly perfect smile.

"Hey," she murmured.

I gave a small nod. "Hi."

"How are you?"

"Okay, you?"

Her brow creased. "What's wrong, Sam?"

She knew me well.

"Nothing important, I'm just being stupid," I smirked. "So the other day was a bit awkward with the six of us at Lunar."

She shook her head. "Wasn't it?"

"Mm," I nodded.

She bit her lip. I looked away.

"Isobel is really pretty," she noted. "A bit young but I can see what attracted you to her."

I looked up and found myself speechless as her cloudy blue eyes seared through me. She looked at her feet.

"She apologised to me," Paige continued. "For being there for you when I wasn't… it kind of bothered me at first but I realised she was probably right. I kept forgetting that just because I close myself off from people that other people don't. You needed me just as much as you wanted me to need you."

I listened silently and swallowed, feeling as if she was pulling threads of thoughts from my brain.

"Maybe if it wasn't her it would have been someone else," she shrugged. "But I guess she needed you too… she needed saving from her own relationship with that creep."

I pressed my lips together and glanced over my shoulder, noticing a few more of the guys had begun to emerge from the rooms. We were running out of time alone—I needed to find words, any words. Speak Samuel.

"I'm really sorry," I murmured. Oh really? That's the best I could come up with?

She breathed a laugh. "I wasn't looking for an apology but I accept it."

I blinked. "How are you being so cool about this? Any other girl would hate me for what I did."

"It takes two to mess things up," she shrugged. "I'm not thrilled about what happened because believe it or not, I really did…"

She stopped and looked down. I'd hit that wall.

"I get it," I nodded. "It's okay. I'm just glad we can be civil to each other. I still really care about you Paige. Really. You don't know how much I wish things could've been different."

Her eyes lifted. "But they weren't and I'm with Nate now."

Nate.

"Right," I exhaled. "Well, I hope you guys are going well. You seem happy with him."

She scrunched the front of her hair in her hand and brushed it to the side of her face. It was a small and inconsequential gesture but it still brought a smile to my face.

I half turned and saw Nate sauntering towards us.

"Well, I should go," I sighed. "It was good to see you."

"You too," she nodded. "And I hope whatever is bothering you works itself out."

I considered the irony that her boyfriend's success was what was bothering me and wondered if she'd still hope if she knew.

"Thanks," I smiled, ambling towards Louis' car. "I guess I'll see you around."

She glanced at Nate and sighed. "Guess so."

I huffed a laugh and turned, continuing to the car and climbed in, feeling as if it was a shield that defended me from whatever crazy that had erupted around me. The past few weeks had felt like

I had stumbled into some parallel universe. I could barely fathom how much had changed in such a short time.

I started the engine and pulled out, sitting just above the speed limit the whole way home. As I pulled up the driveway, my phone rang and I half expected it to be Ivy or Marcus but the number was blocked.

"Hello?"

"Hi, is this Sam?" the female voice asked. "Sam Saber?"

"Err, who's this?" I murmured. I'd learnt the hard way a few years ago about owning my name before I knew the caller.

"My name is Regan," she answered. "You may know me from the papers—I'm the one pregnant with your half-sibling."

Crap.

"So you say," I noted. "Why are you calling me?"

"I have a proposition for you."

I really wish girls would stop saying that to me. "What proposition?"

"Can you meet me?" she asked. "I'd prefer to talk in person."

"Why should I?"

"Because Arthur is ruining your name as much as he's ruining mine," she replied. "We could help each other."

"How?"

She sighed. "Meet me and I'll explain everything. I'll text you where. Are you free tomorrow?"

"No," I replied. RedBacks training. "Every day is pretty full until Friday."

"Friday it is then," she answered. "I'll be in touch."

Dial tone.

Crap. What had I just agreed to? My stomach felt like I had swallowed cement. I stared at my phone, wondering how she'd got my number and what on earth she meant by *help each other*. It may help me but what would it mean for Angela and Amelia? She sounded pretty confident about the whole affair story, too confident for my liking.

I glanced up as the front door opened and Angela stepped out in a halo of light.

"Sam, honey, are you coming in?" she called. "Marion's just serving dinner."

"Yep, coming," I replied, unclipping my seatbelt. That's just what I needed: a side serve of guilt to go with my cement. The next few days were going to be awesome.

XIV

Desperate Measures

"You agreed? Are you nuts?" Marcus hissed into the phone later that evening—he'd called since apparently I'd left a shirt in the rooms in my haste to leave.

"No, I'm allergic," I sighed. "I just want to see what it's about. I haven't agreed to anything."

"Sammy, I don't like this," he muttered. "What about Amelia?"

I frowned. "Let me worry about my little sister."

"I'm just saying, if you go with mutiny you'll drag everyone else in," he replied.

"I know, Sax, I'm not a total idiot."

"Oh really?"

"Whatever… this doesn't concern you anyway," I answered. "I just thought it was weird."

"No kidding."

I exhaled. "I should go anyway, I'm shattered."

"Yep," he sighed loudly. "I'll catch you Thursday if not before. Oh, let me know how the RedBacks thing goes tomorrow."

"Sure, will do."

"Cool," he replied—apparently appeased. "See you Sammy."

"Later Sax."

I hung up and dropped my phone, freefalling onto my mattress. Lord, I missed sleep.

When I woke Tuesday morning I had a text waiting from Ivy: *"Good luck this afternoon. Give Tristan Holmes a kiss for me."*

I rubbed my eyes and sat up, hitting reply: *"Thanks. Might settle for a high five though. Awkward."*

I yawned, looking around my room for any trace of clean clothes and spotted a couple of folded things on my desk.

My phone vibrated: *"Don't deny that the man is sexy. We could invite him over and befriend him in our deal. No strings."*

What? I began typing: *"Ha-ha, I don't share, sorry."*

Ivy replied almost right away: *"Not even with Isobel?"*

My eyebrows lifted. Low blow: *"Are you offering? I could see if she's free?"*

"Ha-ha," she responded: *"Now there's a thought."*

Lord above. She was… something else.

I dropped my phone on my mattress and grabbed the clean clothes, heading for a shower then down for a quick breakfast before the early philosophy tutorial.

Isobel was waiting outside again—or pouting was more like it. As I got closer she looked up, her blue-jewel eyes burning bright red. Ah crap, she'd been crying. My heart lunged.

"Isobel? What's wrong?" I frowned. "What happened?"

She shook her head in short bursts.

I sighed. Another thing I didn't understand about girls was their blatant attempt at covering up something that they obviously wanted to get out. I wanted to know. I wanted to stop the tears, to take away the pain, but forced myself into a different route. Isobel didn't want me; Liam should be the one consoling her—unless it was about him.

"Okay, well we can talk about it after the tute," I said, the words sounded off and her eyes traced to mine in horror. I almost broke so looked away towards the room.

"Are you going in?" I asked.

Her mouth dropped open then snapped shut and she turned on her heel to go inside. She sat at the desk furthest from the door and I slid into the closest one. It took every ounce of strength that I had not to go to her but I did it. She picked Liam. Focus Saber.

I didn't look at her. I took notes. I turned my gaze to the speaker. I didn't understand a thing.

After class she didn't move so I didn't move. The classroom cleared out and I allowed myself to look at her. Her stare was vacant, sad. Easy does it, Sam.

"Hey," I whispered. "Tell me what's wrong."

She looked over at me. "Liam left."

Ah, there it was. "Why?"

"You."

"Me?"

"Yes."

I pressed my lips together—I wasn't going to apologise because I knew that this time I'd done nothing wrong. She looked at me as if I was missing something obvious.

"He saw us together," she sighed. "He thinks I'm not over you."

"Are you?"

She scoffed.

I waited.

"I never said I didn't have feelings for you, I just said I couldn't be with you," she murmured. Not that it mattered what she said, it alluded to the same thing.

"Yeah, I remember," I groaned.

She exhaled. "He said he couldn't be with me when I wasn't over you."

Seemed fair. I wouldn't want to be with a girl who only had eyes for another guy. Call it pride or whatever, it would irk me.

"How are things with Poison Ivy?" she asked icily.

I frowned. "What's that?"

She rolled her eyes. "The blonde, you know."

"What did you call her? *Poison* Ivy?"

"Whatever, I don't really care anyway," she snapped.

I couldn't help but laugh.

She frowned. "Don't laugh at me."

"You're just acting so jealous, it's kind of funny."

"I'm glad you find my pain so amusing," she replied, standing up.

I rose to my feet. "Pain? Isobel, you walked away from me. I'm just getting on with things; you can't honestly blame me for that."

She exhaled. "I don't blame you, Sam. I miss you. I hate seeing you with her, it drives me crazy."

I blinked. Wow.

"Really?"

She shook her head. "Even seeing you talk to Paige, I just want to drag you away."

I pressed my lips together, scratching my neck. "Drag me where?"

Her eyes flashed up. "Under the bridge."

"The bridge?" I repeated, blocking out the last time we were there and focusing on the time before. "What are we doing under the bridge?"

Pink speckled her flawless cheeks. "What we do best."

I laughed weakly. This girl was nothing but trouble but unfortunately, she was also like an addiction.

"Would you ever go back?" she asked.

"Back?" I blinked. "Back to what?"

"How we were before?"

"Before when we were sneaking around you mean?"

She shrugged. "At least we were happy, right?"

She didn't get it.

"I don't know about happy," I answered. "But at least we knew where we stood with each other."

"Who would have thought it would get more complicated when we were both single?" she sighed.

Wow, she really didn't get it.

"You made it complicated the second you decided to use Archer as a decoy," I replied. "I was willing for it to be just us."

Realisation hit me like lightning.

"It was never my life that was too complicated for you," I added. "Maybe it wasn't complicated enough for you."

Her brow puckered. "What is that supposed to mean?"

"What you see is what you get, Isobel," I shrugged. "I don't like games, I hate all this drama; it's not me. My family might try and drag me into crap but that's not what I'm about. I don't want the limelight, I couldn't care less about the money and the prestige; I just want to get through a week without being implicated in a scandal."

"You don't want the limelight?" she repeated. "So you don't want to be a RedBack?"

I shook my head. "Not for the fame, I want it because they're the best and I want to know if I'm good enough."

Isobel's jewelled eyes looked glazed as she stared unseeingly at me, trying to comprehend what I was saying. What was I saying? That I didn't want her? No. That I didn't want the chaos and crap she brought with her? Perhaps. I wanted it to be easy—effortless like it was with Paige but with the openness that relationships should have... like the way Paige was being with me now. Oh damn, I was an idiot—and Ivy was right: Isobel liked games; she only ever wanted me because I was taken.

"I've got to go," I said, turning to leave. This was too much for this time of morning.

Isobel thawed. "Sam."

"Mm?"

"You're walking away from me?" she asked.

I thought for a second. "Yes."

"Are you serious?" she gasped.

I exhaled. "Maybe you should be alone for a while, Isobel. I think it might help you."

Her mouth opened but no words escaped her—I took my chance to go before she stopped me again. Man, what just happened? I'd just walked away from the girl I'd been chasing for months.

"Sam, don't walk away," Isobel's frantic voice echoed.

Crap, she was following me.

"Isobel, can we do this later—and maybe somewhere not so public?"

"No," she said sternly. "We're talking about this now."

I rubbed my forehead and dragged her by the elbow out of the middle of the path.

"What's going on?" I murmured. "You're acting hysterical."

Tears pooled in her glistening blue eyes, it was a little bit pathetic and frustrating as hell.

"Was it all about sex?" she asked. "Just because we slept with each other you don't need me anymore?"

"You know that's not true," I scoffed. "You walked away from me, remember?"

"Don't leave me," she cried.

I frowned.

"I'm sorry, Sam, I need you," she breathed. "I want you, don't leave me."

Lord above, now she was actually begging me.

"Stop, just stop," I sighed. "This is crazy. You're not acting like yourself."

"I don't have anyone else," she whispered brokenly as her lower lip trembled. She clearly wasn't used to being alone, it was actually pretty sad.

"Is that any reason to be with someone?" I asked. "Just to not be alone?"

"But I need *you*, Sam," she replied. "I've always needed you. You've saved me so many times. I need you to save me just once more."

She blinked, wide-eyed, seeming younger now than I'd ever thought of her. In fact, I looked at her and saw Amelia—or someone like her—and it made me uncomfortable. I finally saw it. She *was* very young. She needed someone her own age.

"I can't be the one to save you," I answered. "You need to learn to save yourself."

"But—"

"I'm letting you go, Isobel," I said clearly so she understood. "You need to let me go too. We had our chance and it didn't work out."

"No, that's just it—we never really got our chance," she sighed desperately, clutching my biceps. "But now we can have it."

I shook my head. "No."

"Why not?"

"Because I don't want it," I answered.

She stared at me as my words slowly filtered through, like sand falling through an hourglass.

"You don't want me?"

I pressed my lips together. This had to be the most ludicrous pseudo-breakup ever.

"I don't want us anymore," I repeated.

She nodded, reaching up to dry her eyes. "I see."

I waited.

"Well then," she exhaled. "I've clearly taken up too much of your time already."

"Isobel."

"No Sam, it's fine," she answered. "You've made yourself perfectly clear. I won't bother you again."

"Isobel," I sighed. She sniffled and walked away.

I groaned and turned, noticing the small crowd that had gathered that now looked awkwardly in different directions, too obvious to be oblivious.

Great, something else to make the rumour mill spin. If things weren't over with Isobel before, they certainly were now. I wasn't sure whether to feel relieved or mournful that we were finally and absolutely done. Oh well, regardless of how I looked at it, it didn't change the facts. Moving right along.

I ran my hands through the front of my hair and checked my watch. There was still over half an hour until my workshop but I decided to cut my losses and go straight there—at least I'd be out of public view for a while.

"Swordsman?" a familiar voice called.

I found myself smiling before I looked up. "Sadie."

She grinned knowingly at me. "Breaking hearts and taking names?"

"You heard?"

"Just now?" she asked. "Yes. Half the campus heard—well at least everyone in the admin building."

"Crap."

"Yeah," she agreed. "Was that the girl Liam was seeing?"

I tipped my head. "Well technically I was seeing her first but yes."

She laughed. "Samuel Saber the heartthrob. Nate said you were dating his ex—or are you?"

I scratched my cheek. "I wouldn't call it dating."

"Sly dog," she grinned.

"We have an understanding," I shrugged. "I'm not breaking any rules."

She nodded. "Are you going to Crescent tonight?"

"No," I sighed. "I'm trying to stay out of trouble."

She beamed. "You should probably try harder."

"Oi, Saber," a rough voice roared. "What's with you and Isobel?"

I glanced over my shoulder to see Elliot sporting a strapped and slung arm. Oh crap.

"I don't know what you're talking about," I shrugged.

"Try again," he snarled.

I shook my head. "Nothing, we were just talking."

"I heard," he gave a curt nod, his favoured hand flexing in the sling. Man, I was lucky he was injured; I had a feeling I'd otherwise be speaking directly to his knuckles.

I exhaled in a humourless laugh. "It's not what you think."

"I highly doubt that," he answered, his voice sardonic. "I suspected there was someone else and Archer didn't have the juice to blow her skirt up, the pretentious little tramp."

My fist flexed and his mouth arched in a wry smile.

"Hey Sam, we should go," Sadie interrupted. I glanced at her, forgetting she was still here. I wished she wasn't, what with the way Elliot regarded women.

"Stay out of this scrumpet," he said evenly, not wavering his death stare at me.

"Don't speak to her like that," I answered evenly.

"Or what?"

I glanced at his arm. "I don't think you're in a position for the alternative."

"I don't think you have the gumption, Saber," he murmured. "Daddy won't save you this time. Not after you slandered him. I'll end you."

He was right but every cell in my body rebelled against reason. I wanted to pummel him after what he did to Isobel and Paige and any other girl he treated like a punching bag.

"Sam," Sadie hissed, grabbing my balled hand. "Come on."

Elliot huffed, mumbling something under his breath that had the derogatory equivalent to "coward".

My arm moved to swing but Sadie caught it.

"No Sam, it's not worth it," she snapped. "He's not worth it."

I fumed and she shoved me back hard, her tiny fists on my chest. I let her win.

"Walk away," she murmured, turning my body and continuing to push me towards an exit.

"That's right, Saber, run away," Elliot chuckled annoyingly. I almost turned back but I was still at Sadie's mercy.

"Nope," she warned, nudging me outside. She backed me up against the wall of the building and I groaned as my spine smacked into the limestone.

"Stay out of trouble, huh?" she asked, her black eyebrows arching over her violet eyes. "Like I said, try harder."

I exhaled.

She smirked, it was pretty sexy. "Thanks for sticking up for me."

I pressed my lips together. "Thanks for stopping me from decking him."

She nodded and looked at her hands that were still flat on my chest. Neither of us made any attempt to move but I didn't trust myself to. I didn't know what her excuse was.

"Well," she sighed.

"Well?"

"What's going on here?" Nate's voice asked. Of course Nate was here. Of-freaking-course.

Sadie's hands dropped slowly and I flinched as they brushed my waistband before leaving my body.

"Hello little brother," she smiled. "Where's the redhead?"

Nate frowned. "Class. What's this?"

Sadie glanced at me reminiscently. "I was trying to stop Sam here from beating the disabled Prince."

"Prince?" Nate asked, his eyes flashing. "Elliot?"

I gave a curt nod.

"He's a bit of an arse," she answered.

"That's an understatement," Nate agreed. "He didn't touch you, did he?"

"No," Sadie replied, shaking her head. "He was more concerned with Sam."

Nate glanced at me but didn't ask why. I wondered what my expression looked like. I felt wrecked.

"What are you doing here anyway?" he continued. "I didn't think you had class until the afternoon."

"I had some housekeeping stuff to do," she shrugged. "If that's okay with you."

Her tone was brisk, which made me smile. Nate tended to treat her like a daughter rather than an older sibling. It was a little funny.

"Just curious," Nate sighed. "Where's Prince now?"

Sadie pressed her plump lips together. "Still inside."

"Then maybe we should go," he offered.

I lifted my head and Sadie grabbed a handful of my shirt, pulling me from the wall she'd near thrown me against. I let myself be led for a few steps and then she released me. I followed the two Blakes down the path since it was also the direction of my workshop.

"Did Mum find you to ask you about Dad's party Friday?" Sadie asked Nate. "She wanted to know if red was coming."

"Stop calling her that Sadie, she has a name," Nate groaned. "You're so rude to her."

I hid my smile. Poor Paige didn't seem to catch any more of a break from Nate's sister than she did mine. She'd had her fair share of moments with Amelia—not that Paige ever deserved it.

Sadie rolled her eyes. "Whatever, I mean it as a term of endearment. It's a nickname."

"It's still rude so cut it out."

"You're so sensitive," she sighed.

Nate glanced back at me and I kept my head lowered.

"I really like her, okay?" he murmured. "Don't make me pick sides."

My heart sank. Well, looks like Ivy was right about one thing. Nate would never leave Paige. I really underestimated the guy's feelings for her. At least with Isobel I knew that Elliot was a complete jerk so hating them together was easier. Paige and Nate seemed to be genuinely happy. So why did I hate him more for that?

"I've got class," I said, lifting my head towards the path I had to take. "Thanks again Sadie. I owe you."

"Ditto, swordsman," she grinned. "Coffee Thursday?"

"Sure, meet you in the library?"

She smiled, her eyes glistened. "Done."

I gave a weak salute and crossed the road, hearing Nate stutter a question to her that sounded like "what did you call him?" Geez, the guy was really uptight about nicknames; he needed to chill out more.

I could barely concentrate through the four-hour workshop. My mind kept running over what had happened with Isobel and where that placed things with Ivy now. I ended up leaving a bit earlier to try and clear my head before the RedBacks training. Training seemed like the last thing I wanted to do after my day, though focusing on the game seemed to simplify things. I just hoped that it would do the same thing for me tonight.

I arrived at Iris Oval ten minutes before training officially started and was met by Jason who led me through into the rooms. It was surreal walking through the doors with my heroes even if it was as a guest rather than an equal—it still felt like I was one step closer to my dream.

Coach Gordon and Jason let me run through the drills with the senior players and I was marvelled how well I kept up—so were they I think. By the end of it all, I'd put on a good show but I was still struggling a little. I may have been in-shape for the Suns but this was the major leagues. This was a whole new shape with bigger shoes to fill.

As the rest of the players headed for showers, Jason gave me an encouraging nod but it was Gordon who wanted to chat.

"Saber," he called, patting me hard on the back as I jogged over. My legs almost buckled beneath me, they felt as if they were made of straw.

"Coach."

"Good run today kid," he nodded. "You've got a bright future in the league."

"Thanks coach."

He rubbed his jaw contemplatively. "I do have my reservations though."

I folded my arms as he stopped, glancing up at me through his heavy brow.

"Your name makes you vulnerable; who your father is will ensure that your personal life is always on display," he explained. "I was disappointed to see you wrapped in the scandal last week regardless of the cause. If you're serious about becoming a RedBack—about being a senior league player at all—you need to order your priorities accordingly."

"Yes, sir," I nodded.

"The drinking stops," he said sternly. "I have a no tolerance policy during the on-season regardless of whether you're playing or not. No drugs, no enhancements, keep a clean diet. Four days a week of weight training and cardio five to six days. You think you can keep up?"

I blinked. "Yes, sir."

"If you really want this, Saber, you'll have to work hard for it. Opportunities don't come easy—I don't give a damn about who your daddy is or where you live or how expensive your sheets are."

I frowned—he *didn't* care who my father was? Wasn't that his main reservation?

"I'm willing to work hard," I replied. "Becoming a RedBack is what I've been working towards."

He glared at me. "Well, smarten up and knuckle down and we'll keep in touch. I'll get Jason to check in and track your progress and we'll see what happens."

"Yes, sir."

"Hit the showers," he finished, flicking his head towards the rooms. He walked off before I had the chance to answer so I began jogging towards the passage leading down, painting an even expression on my face even if my body wailed in pain of the over-exertion. Now that I'd stopped it was starting to hit me so when I made it into the rooms, my face buckled along with my knees and I near collapsed onto the benches.

"Pushing through it, rookie?" Tristan chuckled. "Tougher than you're used to?"

I glanced up and forced a laugh. "A bit."

"This isn't the minor leagues," he chuffed. "You're rolling with the real players now."

Wow, what an ego.

"Right."

"You'll have to clean your act up if you want in."

I sat back and ran my hands over my thighs, around to massage my stretched hamstrings. They were going to hurt tomorrow.

"No distractions," he added.

If this guy wasn't the captain and if I could move any limb of my body, I'd probably make more of an attempt to shut him up... but such is life.

"Holmes," Jason's voice cut in. "See the physio's about that shoulder. Saber, my office."

I glanced up at him both relieved and vexed at the same time. Move, I had to move. Come on body, move. Tristan huffed and disappeared and I clamped my jaw hard together and pushed up, feeling every muscle from my toes to my forehead prickle with lactic acid as I stood.

I couldn't hide my slight limp as I followed him into his office. It was pathetic really.

"Sam," Jason smiled, closing his office door and angling the blinds down so we were hidden. "Take a seat."

I gave a nod and lowered carefully into one of the chairs opposite his desk.

"How'd you go today?" he asked.

"I thought you were going to tell me," I replied with a light laugh.

He grinned, walking around to sit. "You're good, you're in good form—but you already know that. How do you think you went in keeping up with the team?"

I tipped my head. "I think I kept up all right. Just in a world of pain now."

He chuckled. "Ah."

"Coach Gordon ran through the rules," I noted. "What, uh, I mean do you think I'm cut out for this?"

"Do you doubt yourself?" he frowned.

"A bit," I shrugged. "I mean I'm older than some rookies and my record isn't exactly clean."

"Record?"

"He mentioned something about me being a Saber and warned me about staying out of the headlines," I mumbled.

He sighed. "What's in a name? You can't help who your father is. You can help how you prepare yourself for this though. He makes a point about the headlines—well the negative ones. No club wants someone who will detract from the game. Plus you give other players ammunition for heckling."

"Right," I huffed. "I know."

"Of course," he smirked. "Listen Sam, I've seen a lot of younger players starting out and I think you have a lot of potential in you. I'm here to offer my support where I can because I'm not going to lie: I think you'd be a great asset to the RedBacks. Obviously it's not a decision that solely falls on my shoulders but I want you to succeed with this team if that's what you want."

"It is," I agreed.

"Well okay then."

I glanced down at my dirt-stained hands. "Gordon mentioned something about weight training and cardio. Do you think I should up my regime?"

He pressed his lips together. "That's up to you and what you can handle but it wouldn't hurt if you were to follow a similar training schedule to our guys. That's just the calibre that is expected here."

"Right."

"But," he added with an exhale, "to be fair, we wouldn't be able to officially take you on until trading at the end of the season and anything can happen between now and then. My recommendation is just to bring yourself to a level that requires minimal transition. If you show the clubs that you're ready, they'll snap you up in no time. If you let yourself slip, you may risk not even being considered depending on the competition you're up against."

I frowned. "That sounds reasonable."

"But as I said, I'm here to assist if you need it," he smiled. "So keep in touch and I'll keep you in the loop. You've made yourself known now, Sam, make sure you leave your mark."

I gave a nod. "Thanks Jason. I'll do my best."

"I know you will," he replied, standing up. "I'm sure you'd like a shower so I won't keep you."

I bit my lip and pushed myself to my feet with a weak groan. Jason laughed, patting me on the back as he opened the office door for me.

"Shine bright, son," he nodded. "You've got the talent."

I smiled and raised my hand to pat his shoulder, hobbling back to the change rooms where a much needed hot shower awaited me.

The rooms were nearly cleared when I returned so I made it a quick rinse and changed back into my regular clothes. By the time

I left, there were two other guys: Silas Jones, a defender on the senior list, and a rookie I couldn't remember the name of. He was new though and hadn't had a run in a game yet.

"Hey—Saber, isn't it?" Silas said as I slung my bag over my shoulder.

I looked up. "Yeah. Jones, right?"

"That's right," he nodded. "Enjoy your time in wonderland?"

Wonderland?

I glanced to the side. "Erm…"

"Bit tougher than what you're used to with Wesley, eh?" he chuckled. "Gordon runs a tighter ship here."

Oh, that's right. Silas was a Sun before he became a key defender for the RedBacks. He used to play for us when he was dropped or injured in the earlier days but hadn't since I'd been on the side.

"I've noticed," I answered.

Silas tipped his head towards the exit and I joined him as we both headed for the car park.

"Got a bit of a limp there," he noted. "Pushing too hard or not warming up?"

I glanced at my feet and shrugged. "Both, neither."

"If this is how you cope with training, you're going to fold in a game."

I frowned.

"But hey, if you're serious about this, I might have something that will help. Just don't go spreading word around if you know what I mean."

"Something?" I repeated. This can't be legal.

He stopped and stared me square in the eye. His light brown eyes probing. "You cool, Saber?"

"Yeah," I nodded. "I won't say a word."

He considered that for a moment. "This something, it's undetectable to tests. Most of the guys use it," he continued. "But it all depends on how badly you want this."

I kept my expression even. I wanted this—but not this way. I could do this myself.

"Look," he murmured, grabbing my hand and pressing something into the palm. "Give it a try and see what you think. If you like it and you want more get back to me."

I blinked, ready to reject his offer on the spot.

"Don't knock it until you try it," he added, interrupting my thoughts. "But if you get caught with it, it's on you."

He wrapped the plastic into my fist and squeezed it hard, pushing it against my chest before he turned on his heel and left me standing there gobsmacked.

I hobbled over to Louis' car and climbed in gingerly, Silas' words racing through my brain at a million miles an hour. *If this is how you cope you're going to fold… undetectable to tests… most of the guys use it… how badly you want this… give it a try.*

What was going on at the South Coast RedBacks? *Most* of the guys used an undetectable performance enhancer? I felt like my entire childhood, my future, my world, was caving in on me. I threw the little snap-lock bag containing the two white pills into the glove box and started the snarling engine, flooring it all the way to Marcus' house.

When I was close, I called him, making sure that on the off chance he hadn't coaxed Ash and Jonah into going to Crescent. He picked up on the third ring.

"Sammy, what's up?" he asked, all business.

"Hey Sax, where are you?"

"Uh, why?"

I blinked. "What do you mean why? Are you home or not?"

"That depends, are you on your way to my place?" he replied.

I pulled around the corner and saw his rose-taupe ute out front. "What if I said yes?"

"Don't come over, I'm—I'm not there," he answered.

"You're not?" I said flatly. "Where are you then?"

"Out."

I stopped beside the curb and rested my elbows on the steering wheel. "Sax, you're a crappy liar, what's going on?"

He sighed. "You're out the front aren't you?"

"Yep."

"I'll be right out."

Dial tone.

I cracked the door open and climbed out, ignoring my protesting limbs as the flyscreen opened and Marcus danced across the wet grass to where I stood by the car.

"Hey buddy," he smiled.

I folded my arms. "Buddy?"

He chuckled. "What's up?"

"What's up with you?"

He shrugged. "Nothing much, just another quiet one."

"Quiet one? You?"

He gave a tight smile that made me instantly suspicious.

"Who's inside?" I asked.

"Inside?"

"Your house? Who don't you want me to see?"

He shuffled nervously. "I don't know what you mean, I don't have anyone inside, there's no one."

I pushed off the car and took two steps, finding his hand at my chest.

"Woah, where are you going?"

"Inside."

"Sammy," he sighed.

And then I saw her—who he'd been lying for, who he was hiding, her brown hair twisting around her finger as she peered out the door.

"You've *got* to be *kidding* me," I spat, seeing red as I looked to him. "My *sister?*"

Marcus took three giant paces back. "It's not what you think."

"It never is with you," I shouted at him. "Amelia, get out here now, we're going home."

She pushed the flyscreen open. "No Sammy, you can't make me."

"Get out here now before I drag you out," I yelled. "Do Mum and Dad know you're here?"

"They're too busy with their own problems to even notice I'm gone," she called.

I took another step and Marcus blocked my passage, making the building anger rise to my temples.

"Marcus, move," I warned.

"Sammy, you're mad, you're not thinking straight," he stuttered. "Millie is perfectly—"

"Don't, just don't," I growled. "Amelia, get out here, *now!*"

"No!" she snapped. "I'm not going home."

"Amelia!"

"Sammy, *back off*," Marcus said firmly, raising another hand towards me. "Amelia called me in tears, okay. Angela walked out and Artie was tearing strips off everyone, she called me because *you weren't there.*"

"Well I'm here now, so I've got this," I answered slightly calmer having had reality shoved down my throat. "Come on, Amelia."

"No, *I've* got this," he replied. "I'll take care of Amelia. She can stay here tonight; I'll take the couch and get her to school in the morning."

I looked up at my little sister and she pouted, dropping her gaze to her feet. She didn't want me now because I wasn't there for her when she needed me—and where was I? Killing myself to get ahead in a club that was apparently corrupt with untraceable illicit drugs.

"Where did my mum go?" I asked. "You said she walked out."

"Don't know, bro," Marcus shrugged. "Millie isn't sure; she was just caught in the crossfire."

That didn't sound like Angela. Something big must've gone down.

"You'll look after Amelia?"

"Of course."

I nodded. "Okay, I need to find my mum."

"Okay," he replied and I turned. "Hey, how was training?"

"Tough," I sighed. "Tell you later."

"Yep."

"Thanks, Sax."

"Later Sammy."

I climbed in the car and revved the engine. I had no idea where to start looking; the rest of our relatives had either moved over east, down south or up north. I didn't blame them; I wouldn't want to be around South Coast if I was related to the mayor and had the means to leave either.

I started driving and plugged in my hands-free, speed-dialling Lawson. I tried to not think of the irony that I had Artie's head of security on my speed dial.

"Master Saber," he said. He was well trained.

"Lawson, where is my mother?" I asked. "Is she still out?"

"She is not in the house, Master Saber."

I exhaled. "You know where she is though. I know Artie has you keep tabs on us."

Silence.

"Lawson, where is my mother?" I answered, controlling my rage. "Please just tell me or I'll call my father myself."

"She's at Eclipse, Master Saber," he replied dutifully. "Under the name Guinevere."

I huffed. At least she still had a sense of humour—she'd listed herself under the name of the Queen in King Arthur's classic tale.

"Thanks Lawson."

I hung up, giving the accelerator another nudge as I headed into South Coast City, towards the lights of the Eclipse Hotel.

***

Unlike when Artie stayed here, Angela hadn't booked herself into the penthouse suite but one of the lower, more modest rooms. I would normally take the stairs over the lift but was willing to compromise on this occasion. My quads and calves felt tight and overworked.

When I got to her room, I heard voices but didn't hesitate in knocking, despite the *do not disturb* sign that hung over the doorknob.

The voices stopped.

"Mum, open up," I called when I heard nothing. "It's Sam."

"Samuel?" she murmured in confusion. "Just a minute."

There was fossicking and then the door opened. Angela's glorious eyes looked slightly reddened. I wanted to kill Artie.

"Mum," I sighed, stepping forward to hug her. "Are you all right?"

She hugged me back. "I'm—I'm fine honey. How did you know where to find me?"

"Lawson," I near groaned.

She exhaled. "Of course."

My eyes caught a shadow move and I frowned, stepping back from her.

"Is someone here with you?"

It moved again and Lance Armelle stepped into view. "Hello Sam."

"Judge," I frowned. "What's going on?"

Angela shook her head. "It's not what you think."

I wish people would stop saying that to me. My eyebrows lifted as I waited, trying to stop my brain from jumping to conclusions about my mother being alone in a hotel room with Isobel's father.

"Lance was just giving me a friendly shoulder… and some legal advice," she explained.

"Legal advice," I repeated flatly. "Why?"

Angela pressed her lips together. Judge Armelle glanced up through a drawn brow.

"What's happened?" I asked. "Why'd you leave?"

She rubbed her forehead. "Arthur—your father—is refusing to insist that the girl making the claims gets a paternity test."

I nodded—this was not news to me, I had asked him about it as soon as the scandal broke. He'd said it would just make him look like there was something to hide. Maybe there was—not insisting definitely didn't make him look any more innocent.

"What did the lawyers say?"

"They suggest the test is taken," Angela whispered almost breathlessly. "Yet he, he…"

Lance stepped forward and rested a hand on her shoulder that I wanted to knock off.

"Your father refuses to pose the question," he explained. "He deems it irrelevant… and too risky to the girl's—erm—foetus."

"What?" I huffed. "You're kidding me, right?"

Angela blinked back tears. "He's more concerned about her than keeping our family together. So I left."

I ran my hands over my mouth and down the stubble on my chin. "Oh geez."

She gasped. "Oh gosh, Amelia?"

"Is with Sax—err, Marcus," I answered, shaking my head. "She's okay, he's looking after her."

"Oh good," she nodded.

I sighed. "So what's the legal advice for?"

She flushed and I wasn't sure if I was ready to hear what was coming next.

"I was curious about where we stood in terms of rights if it does turn out to be Arthur's child," she replied.

I nearly choked—not a divorce?

"What?"

"I love Arthur," she shrugged. "He and you kids are my whole world."

I clenched my jaw. "So you'd raise his bastard child?"

"Samuel, please," she sighed. "It might not even come to that."

"Angela," Lance interrupted. "If Arthur has been unfaithful to you, you will not part empty handed if that's what you're worried about."

Angela looked over at him, reaching up to brush his bicep. "It's not. But thank you."

I frowned. I didn't know that Lance and Angela were close—I hadn't thought she even knew him that well but the way they acted around each other... if I didn't know any better...

"So what now?" I asked, interrupting my thoughts before they got dangerous.

"Now I'm hoping Arthur will come around about the test and we'll take it from there," Angela murmured.

"You know that if she takes the test and it's positive, the best Dad can hope for is a pay-off for her silence," I replied. "South Coast will not look kindly upon its faithful mayor being unfaithful to his doting wife regardless of whether she wants to adopt the bast—"

"Samuel, please," Angela sighed. "Stop saying that word."

Lance glanced up at me. "He has a point, Angie."

Angie? Now she's Angie? What the holy Lord was between these two?

"It won't be in Arthur's best interest to take ownership of the child if he is the father," Lance agreed. "The public will not be as forgiving as you are."

Angela shook her head. "It won't matter anyway because the baby is not his. Arthur would not cheat on me."

Lance and I exchanged a look and I knew he trusted her judgment as much as I did.

"Are you staying here tonight?" I asked. "Do you have everything you need?"

Angela nodded. "I have an overnight bag."

I looked to Lance. "Erm, Judge?"

"I'm not staying, thank you, Samuel," he blushed. "Just making sure Angie was okay."

I pressed my lips together.

"I should actually be going," he smiled. "As long as you're settled."

Angela gave a weak smile in return as he headed towards the door.

"Samuel, honey, you don't need to stay," she murmured. "You must be tired, honey, you look exhausted."

I certainly felt it.

"I can stay if you want," I shrugged. "I'll take the floor."

"No honey, it's not good for your back," she sighed. "Go home, sleep. I'll be back in the morning. I just wanted to give your father some space."

I blinked. "You sure?"

"Absolutely."

XV

The Wrong Foot

I could barely move Wednesday morning when my alarm went off and I seriously considered just staying in bed all day. But unlike what Ivy suggested, I couldn't pass my classes in my sleep and if I wanted to spend my free time training and not fail, I needed to haul my sorry self out of bed.

Artie wasn't around when I had got in last night so I was hoping my luck would extend through to today—I couldn't be bothered dealing with him right now. No such luck.

"Good morning son," he said curtly as I crept downstairs. When I saw him, I relaxed my aching muscles and continued stomping down.

"Hey."

"I beg your pardon?" he replied. "*Hey?*"

I shrugged. "Hello?"

He exhaled. "I haven't seen you lately."

"Nope."

"Samuel," he warned. "Show some respect, I am still your father."

I forced a smile and grabbed a green apple, not even humouring waiting around for Marion to make me something. I'd prefer to starve.

"Right," I sighed belatedly. "Mum home yet?"

He blinked. "Uh, no."

I bit the apple. "Okay. Later then."

He cleared his throat but gave up—cool—so I left.

309

I made it to my eight thirty class as it was starting and regretting not grabbing a mocha beforehand. My brain was almost as exhausted as my body and two hours of mechanical engineering on a near empty stomach was brutal. But I somehow survived, as Sabers do.

On my hour break before my philosophy lecture, I went to *Café Excalibur* for food and stared at the menu for ten minutes, wrestling with my urge to buy the greasiest thing I could see versus adhering to the reminder from Gordon about clean eating. Eventually I settled for a chicken and salad roll on multigrain. It filled me up but it wasn't what I really wanted—seemed to be that way with things that were good for you.

Isobel wasn't in philosophy and I wasn't sure whether I was glad or not about not having to see her. I wanted to make sure she was okay but I couldn't deal with her drama right now. I couldn't even deal with my own. I couldn't stop thinking about Angela and how blinded she was by Artie. I guess it wasn't unlike how Isobel had been with Elliot—except that she was much more naïve though at least was smart enough to walk away in the end. I wanted to protect my mum but I didn't know how, and that frustrated me no end.

I hadn't realised the lecture was over until people started squeezing passed me as they filed down the aisle to leave. Crap. I could have stayed in bed for all the things I'd learnt here today.

"Sam," my name rang as I dragged my feet out.

I looked up. "Ivy."

"Are you okay? You didn't answer any of my texts."

Whoops.

"Yeah, just stuff at home," I shrugged. "What's going on?"

She shook her head. "Not a lot. Still avoiding Mira. What about you? How'd training go?"

I huffed a humourless laugh. "Interesting—pretty brutal actually. I'm pretty sore today."

She smiled weakly. "So what's happening at home?"

"Just the usual crap," I shrugged. "Are you finished now?"

She nodded. "I was heading to the library but I thought I'd see if you were okay since I hadn't heard anything."

"Oh, sorry."

"It's okay, I'm not mad or anything," she smiled. "I was just worried."

I stared at her, trying to figure her out. She was worried, but not mad I didn't reply to her... erm, what was the catch?

She drew in a breath. "Well, now that I know you're alive I guess I'll leave you to it."

She turned and I couldn't help but smile.

"You want to skip the library and hang out?" I asked. "I don't have basketball for a bit and I'll just go straight there."

She tucked a piece of golden hair behind her heavily pierced ear. "Or we could hang out in the library?"

I considered that for a moment—it probably wasn't the worst idea given my day.

"All right."

"Seriously?"

"Yep," I nodded. "I never joke about the library."

She laughed and held out her hand. I frowned at it curiously so she dropped it as I belatedly realised that she wanted to hold mine. Oh. She started walking and I caught up to her, catching her fingers with mine and lacing them through. It was only something small, but when she gently squeezed it, somehow things didn't seem so bleak.

"You really said that?" Ivy whispered, as her pen bobbled around between her fingers. "You actually told Isobel you didn't want her anymore?"

311

My eyebrows lifted in acknowledgement.

"Holy crap," she laughed quietly. "Did she go nuts?"

"Pretty nuts," I nodded. "Screamed down the admin building."

Ivy stifled her laughter, giggling into her palm. If it wasn't at the expense of Isobel I'd probably find it more endearing.

"Then Elliot showed up," I continued. "Of course, he'd heard everything."

"Crap," she sighed, though the amusement on her face contradicted her concern. "Did he go nuts?"

I looked at her incredulously. "Yes, he went nuts."

"Did he punch you?"

"His arm is in a sling."

"Did you punch him?"

"No one punched anyone."

Her shoulders dropped. "Well that's boring."

"I wanted to punch him."

"But you didn't."

"Well Sadie had to drag me away."

Her brow puckered. "Who's Sadie?"

"You know Sadie Blake."

"*Sadie Blake?*" she repeated too loudly. "How do you know her?"

I shrugged. "We have coffee every now and then."

Her mouth was hanging open. I reached across the table and pushed it closed. She shook her head.

"She—she's… you're friends with her?" she hissed. "Why? How?"

I pressed my lips together in a smirk and shrugged. "We met at Crescent, got drunk and she talked me into getting a tattoo."

She pulled her lower lip in. "Did you sleep with her?"

"No."

312

"I see," she murmured, looking down at her page and continuing with her work.

My eyes narrowed. "Are you jealous?"

"Nope."

"Really?"

She exhaled. "No Samuel, I'm not jealous that you're friends with Sadie Blake and got a tattoo with her and meet up for coffee with her all the time."

I pressed my lips together in amusement. "You're not?"

"Shut up," she muttered.

I laughed. "Ivy."

"Be quiet Sam, I'm working."

I grinned and rested my hand over my mouth.

Her gold eyes flashed up. "Stop smiling."

I shook my head. "Ivy."

"What?"

"You don't need to be jealous of Sadie."

"I'm not jealous," she snapped. "I just… she hated me."

I shrugged. "You did cheat on her brother."

"Of course you take *her* side."

"There are no sides," I chuckled. "Lord above, what is it with girls?"

She frowned. "I told you, we hate each other. We feel the need to compete regardless of whether there's a competition or not."

I rolled my eyes. "Well we're just friends—she's seeing some other guy anyway."

"I don't care Sam, you're not my boyfriend," she shrugged.

I felt like I'd just gotten whiplash by her mood change. "Right."

She exhaled, tapping her pen on the binding of her book. My eyebrows rose as I waited for her to snap out of her tantrum.

She looked up after a moment. "What?"

I didn't speak.

"Stop looking at me," she pouted.

I dropped my eyes back to my page, though they only stayed there for half a second before lifting to meet hers again.

She tried to hide her smile. "Stop, Samuel."

"Ivy."

"Sam."

"You're being a girl," I smirked.

She exhaled. "I know, I'm sorry. It happens sometimes."

I laughed. "It's funny that you feel the need to apologise for it."

"Sorry," she breathed, glancing to the side contemplatively. A beat passed and she dropped her pen and pushed her chair out to stand. I watched as she paced around the table, grabbing my arm as she passed and pulled me with her. My muscles protested but I conformed, struggling backwards and following her as she led me down the rows of books. Halfway down the library, she stopped, towing me down an aisle that smelled as though the books had started to mould and pushed me up against the rack. I groaned, it hurt, but I didn't care—it was incredibly hot.

"What now, Hunt?" I exhaled in mild amusement.

She smiled, her eyes glowing as her lips caught on mine, hooking me in as she mashed her body up against mine so I could feel her every curve. It was completely unexpected, spontaneous, but that somehow made it so much more exhilarating. I felt her hands creep down my abdomen and pull the belt loops of my jeans to draw me closer—if that were possible—and then she pushed me away suddenly, her cheeks as flushed as cherries as we both caught our breath.

Her eyebrow cocked.

I rested my head back, watching her curiously.

"I can be quiet," she whispered, leaning over to bunch up her long skirt. My brow creased as something pale fell to the floor— her underwear. You've got to be kidding me.

I swallowed. "You serious?"

She shrugged and picked them up, jamming them in my pocket before moving her fingers to unbutton my jeans.

She glanced up and down the aisle then grabbed the collar of my jacket, turning me around so her back was against the bookcase as she leaned on a stack of the old, decaying books.

"You're crazy," I chuckled.

"You love it," she breathed, pulling me towards her with an exhale as our bodies collided into one.

***

My head definitely felt clearer at basketball, thought I couldn't get Ivy out of it. It was only problematic because in addition to me moving like an old person, I responded about as fast as one so by the end of the game the guys were pretty peeved.

"Earth to Saber," Bryce chuckled, slapping a hand on my shoulder. We stepped through the change rooms after winning by a slim margin. But hey, a win was a win.

I blinked. "Huh?"

He laughed. "You've been zoning out all afternoon, what gives?"

"Just something that happened earlier," I answered vaguely.

He frowned. "Everything okay with your folks?"

I stared at him unseeingly and then remembered the crap that was going on at home. "Uh, not really."

"That sucks."

"Mm."

315

"So you haven't said how practice went yesterday," he noted. "I'm guessing it was pretty hard-core since you're moving like a wooden puppet today."

I pulled a face. "Hard-core."

Training, RedBacks, drugs. I think I preferred to think of Ivy.

"You family-dining tonight or did you want to come to mine?" Bryce asked. "Don't worry, we're getting take-out."

"I don't know," I frowned. "I don't know what Amelia is doing actually; she stayed at Sax's place last night."

Bryce nearly choked. "What? Are they...?"

"No," I snapped, too quickly. "No, he's just... helping out I guess."

Bryce pressed his lips together. "Things that bad at the castle?"

"Angela walked out."

He cursed under his breath. "I'm sorry Sam."

"Don't be," I shrugged. "She walked out in protest because she wanted to stay with him. She's hell-bent on making us all a happy family even if Artie ends up being the bastard kid's father."

"For real?"

"Mm."

"Damn."

"Right?"

"So Artie not happy about it?"

I sighed. "No, he's still denying everything."

"I see."

"Sax was going to make sure that Amelia got to school today but I don't know what's happening," I mused. Damn, I should have called her; I've really dropped the ball on this one. "Sax has tafe tonight for a few hours so I'm hoping that she just went home."

Bryce clutched my shoulder. "Raincheck then. Sounds like you've got a lot on your plate."

"Thanks Watson."

I headed straight home, calling Amelia's phone as I drove only to find that she was camped out at Marcus' place again. I wasn't pleased about it but I wasn't going to question it. Her being at home alone with Artie when he was not in full control was more damaging—I'd witnessed it firsthand.

I ended up crashing at Marcus' place too; upon hearing that Angela was heading home to talk things through with King Arthur. I wasn't sure whether I was glad or not about that—but whatever, it's her decision. Nothing I could say would change anything.

***

I borrowed some of Marcus' clothes for uni Thursday and coasted through until eleven thirty when I headed to the library to meet Sadie. Sadie looked a little worn when I found her draped over her usual desk like an old coat on a hanger.

"Hey," I sighed.

"Hey swordsman," she smiled weakly. "I'm so glad to see you."

I blinked. "Why?"

"You're here to distract me, aren't you?" she replied. "Please, I need a distraction."

"Okay," I shrugged. "What's going on?"

She exhaled. "Caffeine. I need caffeine."

I gestured towards the exit and she grinned, raising to her feet and sliding her books into her bag in one swoop before slinging it over her shoulder.

We started walking in the direction of Excalibur and she looked back at me, pouting a little pathetically.

I sighed. "So what's up?"

"I hate boys."

"Why?"

"They're stupid."

"Okay," I huffed, and of course girls weren't frustrating as hell either.

We stepped into the cafe and she slumped into the table we'd sat at last time. "Okay, maybe not all boys are stupid."

Progress.

I pressed my lips together. "Is this about your boss?"

"I don't want to talk about him."

"You brought it up."

"He's so frustrating," she groaned. "He either wants to be with me or he doesn't."

My eyebrows rose.

"He treats me like a call-girl."

"A call-girl."

"Yes," she sighed. "He calls me, I'll go like the fool I am, and he'll have his way and then go off with his friends. He said he didn't want a relationship with me and that's fine; I'm not looking for a husband and I know that we have to keep things quiet at work, but a little respect wouldn't go astray."

I blinked. So much for not wanting to talk about it.

"I just… I get so mad because he knows I like him but he still doesn't care," she murmured. "He'll still just use me for sex and then doesn't contact me for days."

I scratched my forehead. "Have you, err, spoken to him about how you feel?"

She scoffed. "Right."

"Then how is he supposed to know?"

She looked at me incredulously. "Seriously?"

I shrugged. "Well, if you said you're fine with it, how is he supposed to know you're not if you don't tell him?"

"I don't want to talk about Simon," she exhaled. "So what's up with you? You were dating that Isobel girl, right?"

"We never dated," I answered.

Sadie smirked. "But you slept with her; no wonder you're taking Simon's side."

"There are no sides," I groaned. "And it wasn't me who didn't want a relationship."

"Well I guess she changed her mind about that."

"Mm."

Sadie folded her arms. "So why don't you want to be with her now?"

I exhaled. "I just don't want the drama."

"So instead you start seeing Poison Ivy," she laughed. "Nice job on the no drama, swordsman."

"What do you mean?"

"I mean is it any coincidence that you start seeing my brother's ex after he starts dating yours?" she asked, cocking an eyebrow.

I shrugged. "South Coast is a small city."

"Not that small."

I smiled and picked up the menu.

"What sort of understanding do you have with her?" she asked.

"With who?"

"Poison Ivy."

I shook my head. "Don't call her that."

"Fine, *Ivy*," she said, making the name sound like an expletive. "Are you just sleeping with her too?"

I breathed an uncomfortable laugh.

"My, my, swordsman," she chuckled. "How many girls are you sleeping with?"

"Ivy and I are friends," I answered.

"With benefits."

I shrugged. "Sometimes."

"Your idea?"

"Hers."

"She's in love with you."

"What?"

"No girl would put themselves out there unless they felt something for the guy," she replied. "Sex is different for girls than guys. Girls use sex to get love, guys use love to get sex."

"I'm not using anything."

"Not consciously," she shrugged. "Boys are clueless."

"And girls are complicated."

"Keeping up?" she smiled.

I glanced back at the menu. "So coffee for you then?"

Sadie looked at her watch. "Better make it a take-away."

***

After half a coffee with Sadie, she headed to class while I went home to change into my own clothes then went to the gym. My muscles still throbbed but in true *hair-of-the-dog* fashion, the workout got my blood pumping and made them loosen up a little.

I tried not to think much about what Sadie had said about Ivy because I knew where things stood between us and so did Ivy—as long as we were honest with each other, then that was all that really mattered.

Football practice was better. I felt surprisingly stronger than I had and was almost back to form. It was noticeably different being back with the Suns as opposed to training with the RedBacks.

There was less of a boot camp feel to it and more of a team atmosphere. It was less rigid and more authentic to how football should be. Although there was a shift in the dynamics of the guys and the way Nate strutted around as if he'd grown ten inches since his winning goal. As time went by I wanted more and more to knock his block off and watch the arrogant smile mash into the dirt. It was unreasonable, but I couldn't help it. I still resented the fact he had my old life—my old girlfriend and practically my spot in the team—even if it was me who'd handed it over to him on a silver platter.

After practice finished, Marcus bailed straight away muttering something about needing to get home and clean for a rent inspection. Louis was back so I didn't bother asking why, after living in the place three years, that the owners had decided to check up on its condition.

"Hey Sam, thanks for looking after my car," Louis said, raising a hand towards me.

I gripped it and nodded. "Thanks for lending it."

"Did you want to grab some food?" he asked. "I'm starving after that run."

I laughed. "Actually I was supposed to meet Ivy; we were going to grab something."

"She can come too," he smirked, clearly wanting to say more but didn't.

"Okay, I'll ask her."

"Good."

"Good."

He looked down then gave a laugh. "Oh geez Sam."

"Shut up."

He nodded and tried hard to stifle a laugh. Apparently not hard enough.

"What's so funny?" I frowned, pulling my T-shirt down over my torso.

He shook his head. "I just didn't think you'd shack up with Nate's ex of all people. I thought you were after Isobel?"

"That's dead in the water," I huffed. "And we're not shacking up, we're just hanging out."

"And going on dates," he noted.

"It's not a date," I groaned, then blinked. "Well not really."

Louis dipped his head. "You're sleeping with her?"

I pressed my lips together.

"Geez Sam."

"Look, it's not like that, okay?" I murmured. "We—we've got an understanding."

He chuckled. "If you pull out a *friends-with-benefits* line, you know that never works. Someone always feels more."

I ran my hands through my hair. "I know, she—but she says she's okay with it. She wants it actually."

"And you?"

I shrugged. "I like her, she's a great friend. I don't want to lose her."

His eyebrows were almost in his hairline. "Well lad, you're going about it the wrong way."

"You don't know about it," I sighed. "It's fine."

He lifted his hands in defence. "Okay."

I glanced around and saw that most of the guys had dispersed and turned to sit.

"I've screwed a lot of things up."

Louis frowned. "Like what?"

I shook my head. "Paige."

He sat down. "What do you mean?"

"I don't know if breaking up with her was the right thing to do," I mumbled aloud for the first time. As I said it, I knew it wasn't even fair to think.

Louis chuckled incredulously. "You're a bit slow on the uptake. What brought this on?"

"Isobel," I sighed. "She went on a rampage the other day and I realised I threw away a good thing with Paige for something toxic with her. She just makes everything harder than it needs to be. Paige never did that."

"But Paige never made anything easy for you either," Louis noted. "Wasn't that the point? There was like, no depth?"

I considered that for a moment. Huh, maybe he was right. Paige didn't include me in any drama so there was no drama with her. That's what had drawn me to Isobel—her ability to open up to me, only Isobel seemed too inclined to turn everything into a soap opera.

"So cross out the brunette and redhead, what about Ivy?" he asked. "What's she like?"

"Blonde."

Louis laughed. "And?"

I blinked and looked at him. "She's impulsive and charming and…"

"And?"

I shook my head. "It's not like that Macca, she's just a friend."

"Okay," he chuckled. "But she sounds pretty perfect if she's willing to put feelings aside and keep it physical even if she wants more."

I rubbed my eyes.

"Look, heaven knows what on earth you do to these girls to get them following you around like puppies, but just look at what you're doing," he replied. "It's easy to get carried away so make sure you're not just making a sport out of it."

He slapped a hand on my chest and I groaned as he stood. That wasn't what I was doing—was it?

"Can we go to Lunar, or you want to go to Camelot instead?" he asked.

I barely heard him.

"Sam."

"Huh?" I sighed. "I don't mind. I'll ask Ivy."

Ivy.

"Okay, check with *Ivy*," he nodded, pulling his bag onto his shoulder. I glanced up and snapped out of my daze, dragging myself to my feet and grabbed my bag, following him from the change rooms. I looked towards the car park and saw her leaning against Louis' car. She must've walked.

"Sweet Jesus, please tell me that the blonde on my car is not the one you are talking about," Louis murmured.

"Yeah that's Ivy," I nodded. "Why?"

He swore under his breath. "Are you kidding me, Saber? She's—she—she's... how are you just friends with her?"

I shrugged. "With benefits."

"I officially hate you."

I chuckled.

Ivy's lips twitched in a smile as we advanced. "Sam."

"Ivy."

"Who's your friend?"

"The owner of the car," I said with a nod. "This is Louis McKenzie."

"Macca," Louis corrected. "But you can call me whatever you want."

Ivy smirked. "Nice to meet you Mr McKenzie."

Louis blinked. "I don't get that one often."

"So, uh, Macca suggested that we all go to Lunar for dinner," I said, scratching my neck. "Is that cool?"

Ivy blinked. "You mean the three of us?"

I nodded.

"Sure, sounds fine," she shrugged.

"Great," I sighed, raising the keys towards Louis. "Did you want to drive or do you want me to?"

Louis snatched the keys from me. "I've got it. You kids can cuddle in the backseat."

I slapped my palm lightly to his cheek. "Right."

"Hey," Ivy smiled, taking a step towards me.

I don't know why but for some reason I recoiled. "Hi."

Her forehead creased. "Everything okay?"

"Yep."

"Okay."

"Should we go?" I asked, opening the back door. "I'm starving."

Louis was looking at me curiously but Ivy seemed to have shut down.

"Sure," she shrugged, refusing the opened door and walking around to the other side.

"Okay then," Louis huffed, sliding in the driver's side.

I looked over to Ivy as she sat down and saw her exhale quietly, shaking her head.

Louis and Ivy got on well and dominated the entire dinner conversation. I actually don't think they would have noticed if I wasn't there and to make matters worse, Demi wasn't even working tonight for me to talk to. Instead, I zoned out, using the time to think about what Louis had said about Isobel being too much and Paige being too little but Ivy sounding perfect. I guess in that context she was a happy medium between the other two but unlike Isobel and Paige, Ivy showed her cards—if mystery was a spice then she didn't flavour. But even I couldn't deny that I loved hanging out with her—it was certainly never boring and she was definitely one of a kind.

Ivy's laugh broke my reverie and I frowned, dusting the flour from my wrap off my fingers.

"You two almost done?" I asked.

Both Louis and Ivy looked at me as if I'd interrupted an important business meeting.

"You in a rush, Sam?" Louis smiled.

I shrugged. "I haven't been home in a couple of days; I may as well not put it off any longer."

Ivy pressed her lips together understandingly.

"I guess you want me to drop you?" Louis asked.

I scratched my ear. "Nuh, I can walk. Thanks again for letting me borrow the car while you were gone."

"Have you even run your car since?"

"Nope, guess I'll need to jumpstart it."

I stood up and Ivy's mouth opened.

"Actually, I should be getting home too," she added. "I'll walk with you."

I felt a strange sense of unreasonable satisfaction that she chose to walk with me rather than stay with Louis—especially after he'd been holding her attention all evening.

"Why don't I just drive you both?" Louis offered. "Rather than sit here on my own."

We settled the bill and headed back to Louis' car as he and Ivy argued over who he should drop home first. Eventually Louis conceded and it was decided that Ivy's house would be the first stop. Good.

Her eyes were fixed on me the whole drive while she continued to answer Louis' questions. Mid-sentence she slid into the middle seat, clipping herself in as her hand found mine.

I didn't know what to make of it and as much as I wanted to let go, I found myself squeezing it back.

"Well, it was a pleasure, Ivy," Louis' said, shifting into park out the front of her unit.

"Yeah, it was fun," she nodded, side-glancing at me. "Um, Sam will you walk me to my door?"

I blinked. "Uh, sure."

I followed her out the backseat, not risking the glance back at Louis who was a little too silent behind the wheel.

We walked without words to her door, shielded by the brick wall encompassing her small courtyard.

"You're quiet today," she murmured, tipping her head so her blonde curls framed her face.

I sighed. "I've got a lot on my mind."

"Okay," she nodded, looking down as she reached across to run her finger over the back of my hand. "Did something happen at training?"

"No, not really."

"What's wrong Sam?" she asked. "You look… weird."

"Okay, there's something I need to say," I sighed. I looked down and took a steadying breath. "I think we should stop… the, uh benefits."

"Oh… kay," she answered slowly. "Why?"

I pressed my lips together. "Don't get me wrong, I mean it's been fun… but I think we should stop blurring the lines."

"What brought this on?" she blinked. "I mean, it's cool, I'm not going to force you to… but I thought you… liked it."

"I did—I do," I answered a little too quickly. How could I deny it?

"So what's the problem then?"

"I just don't think it's fair to you given the way you feel about me."

She smiled a little brokenly. "I know what I'm doing, okay. I don't care that you don't feel the same way about me."

"Ivy…"

"Sam."

"I can't."

"Why not?" she asked, reaching to take my hand.

I withdrew it. "Don't."

Her expression dropped, her cheeks flushing faint pink as her eyes pooled with tears. Crap, she was crying. I wanted to comfort her, to hug her, to kiss her or something, just make them stop, but my joints were jarred.

"I'm sorry," I whispered. "I didn't want to hurt you. I hope we can still be—"

"Friends?" she asked. "I mean, is that what you want?"

"I um…" I stuttered. Come on Samuel, speak. What do you want from her?

"You what?" Ivy asked. "What do you want from me? Just friends? Can you even do that now?"

"I don't know."

"You don't know," she nodded. "Where did this even come from? I mean yesterday you were fine with… the benefits and now suddenly you're worried about my feelings? Are you sure it's not your feelings you're worried about?"

"What?" I blinked.

She shrugged. "I don't know, maybe you're just afraid because you're starting to like me back."

"No," I scoffed.

She shook her head, staring at her feet. Crap, nice one Samuel.

"I mean, I just don't think of you that way," I amended.

Her head rose along with her eyebrows. "You don't think of me that way."

"Come on, Ivy, you said yourself that I'm not your boyfriend," I replied. "So why are you so shocked to hear that I don't think of you as my girlfriend?"

"You're right," she laughed humourlessly. "How silly of me to think that you could possibly give a damn about me."

"Lord above," I muttered. "This is what I'm talking about— this pseudo breakup thing, this is what I wanted to avoid. I mean for goodness sake, Ivy, it was all just some game to you."

She looked as if she'd just been slapped, but instead of her cheeks burning crimson, they drained pale as her head rocked to shake.

"You're right," she exhaled. "So shame on me for caring, huh?"

"Ivy," I groaned.

"Nope, you're right," she breathed, stepping back towards her door. "It was all just a game."

I pressed my lips together, fearing words would only make it worse. There was no point.

"Thanks for…" she stopped and scoffed. "Whatever. And goodbye I guess."

"We can still hang out," I answered, taking a step. "I mean, I don't want to lose you… as a friend."

She glanced at me, looking as if she wanted to say something but didn't, instead unlocking her door and stepping inside without saying anything more.

Crap. What did I just do? And why on earth did I do it?

I couldn't even think about it, not right now, so I turned and headed back to Louis' waiting car and headed to the front beside him.

I groaned, slamming the car door as I collapsed into the passenger seat. "I think I just completely messed things up—"

Louis wasn't moving so I looked over at him.

"What the hell is this?" he asked, holding the little snap-lock bag of pills towards me.

Oh crap.

"They're not mine."

Louis' brow drew. "Well they're sure as hell not mine so whose are they?"

I exhaled. "They were given to me but I'm not using."

"Who gave them to you?"

"I can't say."

"Are you serious?" he asked. "You didn't take any?"

"Louis, come on, it's me. You know me."

He huffed. "Yeah, but I don't know where your head has been lately. You said a little while ago that you've screwed a lot of things up lately—"

"Not that screwed up," I replied impatiently. "I meant with girls."

Louis nodded, his grim expression not lightening. "You're not in any trouble, are you?"

"Trouble?"

"This isn't about the RedBacks gig, is it?" he asked to my surprise and horror on how quickly he connected the two. "No one's pressuring you into anything are they?"

It wasn't often I was reminded of the age difference between Louis and I but right now, those four years that separated us were like an ocean.

"No, they're not pressuring me," I answered.

"Because no matter how desperate—"

"Trust me, I'm not that desperate," I interrupted. "I never even considered it. I meant to flush them but I guess I just forgot."

Louis looked at me long and hard. "Okay."

"Okay?"

330

"Yeah, okay," he nodded. "Geez Sam, what the hell is going on in that club?"

"I can't talk about it," I murmured.

He frowned but gave a nod. I wasn't sure if I had overstepped the mark and given away too much but I didn't care; Louis wouldn't say anything.

My phone rang and I moved slowly to answer it.

"Yep?"

"Samuel," Angela's voice sighed. "Honey, where are you?"

"I'm… on my way home, why? What's up?"

"Nothing, I'll see you when you get here," she replied.

"You're at home?"

"Yes, and Amelia is too, we're all back home again—as a family," she explained. "A united front."

"Right."

"Drive safe and we'll see you soon."

"Okay Mum."

Dial tone.

"All good?" Louis asked.

"Yeah, just my mum," I sighed. "She's back home."

"She moved out?"

"For a while," I shrugged. "It was nothing—more of a passive protest really."

He huffed. "Okay."

"I should get home," I frowned.

Louis started the car and pulled out. Nothing more was said. Louis was good like that.

XVI

What You Can't Have

We pulled up outside my castle of a house at the same time Marcus did and Amelia tumbled out of his ute.

"What?" Louis mumbled. "Is Sax doing your sister?"

I shot him a look. "No. She's been staying with him; he's been looking out for her."

Louis raised an eyebrow and glanced back at Marcus as he climbed out and carried Amelia's bags up the stairs.

"Are you sure about that?" Louis huffed.

I groaned and got out the car. "Thanks for the ride."

"Hey Sammy," Marcus called, halfway up the stairs. "You're just getting home too?"

"Yep." Home. "You finish cleaning?"

"Huh?" he frowned. "Oh, yeah, sort of."

I exhaled, pushing the front door open to find Angela and Artie standing either side of Amelia. Both looked up but only Angela smiled.

"Samuel, it's good to see you."

"Hello son," Artie nodded. "You're home."

I blinked. "I was only out one night."

"Marcus, thank you for letting Amelia stay with you," Angela said. "It was very kind of you."

Artie frowned.

"She was no trouble, Angela, Amelia is welcome anytime."

I frowned.

Marcus glanced over at me. "Well, I'd better bounce. The cleaning won't do itself."

"Right," I nodded. "See you Sax."

"Bye Marcus, thanks," Amelia added.

Marcus waved and left, leaving the four Sabers standing in silence. United again but somehow never further apart.

"So, who's hungry?" Angela asked.

"I already ate," I replied, edging towards the stairs.

"Me too, Marcus cooked…" Amelia started, and then trailed off as I turned to stare at her. As a general rule, Marcus didn't cook. He couldn't cook. The guy managed to mess up a cup-a-soup.

"I'm beat, I'm going to bed," I murmured. "Night."

"Good night, honey," Angela answered.

"Night Sammy," Amelia called.

Artie might have said something but I didn't hear. I was already up the stairs and nudging my door closed.

***

I woke up Friday to my phone buzzing and opened my eyes to see a text from Regan.

"*Sam*", it said. "*If you're still keen to meet up today I'll be at The Harlot Hotel, East Iris at eleven o'clock. I really hope you'll give me the chance to share my side of the story.-R.*"

I glanced at the clock on my phone—it was just after seven o'clock. I had plenty of time until I had to make a final decision on whether to go or not. I rolled over and exhaled. Crap, my car was probably a glorified monument on my driveway; if I was planning to drive it anywhere I'd most likely need to jumpstart it. I wondered if there was a government vehicle I could borrow, otherwise I'd have to find my portable battery booster to give it the boost. Eh.

I pulled my blankets up. It could wait. I was tired and my legs ached from yesterday.

My phone buzzed again, this time it was Ivy.

"I don't know what happened last night but I think we should talk about it. I don't want to stop being friends with you Sam. We can just hang out—no benefits. Please call me."

I pressed my lips together. I didn't know what to say to her. This was all getting too much. I dropped my phone on my mattress and rolled over. I'd deal with it all later on.

When I woke up again, it was nine forty-five and I didn't waste any more time before getting up and throwing on some clean clothes. I grabbed a banana and a nectarine and headed out the front to my car, not holding much hope for it starting but making sure it wouldn't before I had to resort to any methods to jog it.

It made a horrible choking noise that wasn't unlike the sound it made before I started fixing it—and before divine intervention in the form of the Saber patriarch stepped in. Crap, I'd need a jumpstart.

I looked around the vast yard and for once couldn't see any other vehicles so headed to the garage to find my booster. Inside, it was a total mess, looking like it had been ransacked and trashed. When was the last time I was here? The day my car was taken to Austin's garage probably. It was going to be impossible finding anything here and half my stuff looked like it was missing. My anger burned white hot, I bet it was Artie ensuring I had nothing further to do with working as a blue-collar. After he'd bankrolled the Morris Minor's restoration he'd probably done a clean out—or gotten one of his minions to do it. I fossicked through the remains for a while, noting the multiple tools and parts that were missing and eventually gave up. I'd have to catch a bus to East Iris to meet Regan and now, more than ever, I was eager to take him down. Amelia would be okay, she'd have Angela, me, and Marcus; and Angela would be fine too—if anything has come of recent events it's that she loves him more than he deserves.

I arrived just after eleven at *The Harlot Hotel* after taking a bus part of the way and walking the rest. The public transport system in South Coast left much to the imagination so I normally tried to avoid it, though today it was a necessary evil if I wanted to be punctual. I found Regan waiting in the restaurant part of the hotel which was set up with red booths and a crystal and chrome bar. She was more attractive in person than she had been portrayed in the media—and maybe that was the point. Artie had power over the papers and stations and would always be seen as the humble mayor. Regan sat up as I sat down, running her fingers loosely through her honey brown hair, her brown eyes bright but slightly reddened. Wow, I guess Artie had a type.

"Sam, thank you for coming," she said in a shaky voice. "I wasn't sure if you were going to make it."

"Sorry I'm late, car problems."

"You're fine," she breathed. "Thanks again for meeting me."

I gave a nod.

"Would you like something? The sandwiches and rolls here are nice and the coffee is awesome," she continued. "Although I've given up caffeine during my pregnancy."

I frowned. "I'm right for the moment."

"Okay," she replied.

I waited.

"You're probably wondering why I asked you to come," she mused.

"You want me to help you."

"Yes."

"Help you how?"

She looked around and leaned into the table. "Despite what the media seems to imply, I don't want to break up your family. I just want what's best for my baby."

"And what's that?"

She mashed her lips together.

Oh. "Money, right?"

She shook her head. "I just want to know that my baby, your sibling, will be okay."

I smiled ironically. "Well, with respect, we don't know that for sure."

"You think I'd lie about this? About an affair with the mayor? The most powerful man in South Coast?"

"You wouldn't be the first one."

"Sam," she sighed. "I'm not that girl."

They never are.

"So where would I come into it?" I asked flatly. "You want me to smuggle you money?"

Ha! The thought made me want to laugh out loud. When I wanted money, I had to undergo a cross-examination and Artie knew without doubt that I was his flesh and blood.

"No," she smiled. "I was hoping you would talk to them."

"My parents?"

She gave a nod. "Yes, they won't talk to me without a lawyer but I don't want to drag this through the courts, I fear it would end messy for everyone."

I leaned forward, capturing my hair in my hands and ran them through. This certainly wasn't what I was expecting from the meeting.

"I know it's a lot to take in," she noted.

I scratched my stubble. "You do know that my mum is pushing my dad to take the test? She wants to help you for some screwed up reason."

Regan blinked. "No, I didn't know that."

I shrugged.

"I don't want a test," she added.

"Why?"

"It's too risky to the baby."

"So wait until it's born," I replied. "You know that before Artie coughs anything out he'll need proof. The only reason he's resisting now is because it makes him look guilty."

Regan bit her lip. "I don't want to cause any trouble; confirming it for sure would bring shame on your family, on your mother and your sister... I just want my baby to be secure. I don't want anything else."

I frowned at her logic—*confirming it for sure?* "Is this actually his kid?"

"How can you ask me that?"

I shrugged. "It just seems like you're doing an awful lot to avoid confirming either way."

"I'm trying to protect you and your family," she whispered.

"Well that's odd," I replied. "Considering you went to the media to begin with."

"Only because Arthur wouldn't listen."

"Right, sure," I nodded, noting that none of her words confirmed the paternity of the unborn foetus.

"So this is sounding like you're not enthusiastic about what I'm asking," she sighed. "I just thought you of all people might understand—and might want to earn some respect back that Arthur has stripped from you."

"Respect," I huffed. "How'd he strip me of respect?"

337

"Sam, come on," she smiled ironically. "The tabloids, the accusations… everything he has done that has reflected on you adversely and tarnished your budding sporting career."

I breathed a laugh. "Right, well, you of all people bringing this little proposition or whatever it is to me, know that I don't really care what Artie brings on himself—that's his cross to bear. As for my sporting career—that's all on me. I make my own decisions, I call my own shots. My father's lifestyle choices don't affect my talent."

Regan lifted an eyebrow. "Okay, if you say so."

"Let's just say I do."

She exhaled. "Were you ever going to help me?"

"I don't know to be honest," I shrugged.

"Then why did you come?"

"To hear you out."

"Okay."

I pressed my lips together and her hand rose to stroke her ballooned belly.

"You're a lot like him, you know," she mused.

"Huh? Who?"

"Your father."

"How do you figure that?"

She glanced up. "Well, you're both strong-willed, determined and handsome. You know what you want, you know who you are and you don't apologise for it."

I frowned. Why did girls always read into everything? And why would I apologise if I hadn't done anything wrong?

"Right," I answered slowly—what more could I say?

She looked at me in a way that made me a little uncomfortable and I dropped my gaze, wondering if the offer for coffee was still on the table.

"Listen, Sam—" she started as the silence between us filled with my ringtone. I didn't remember taking my phone off silent mode—weird.

"Hello?"

"Sam, it's me—it's Paige," Paige said, sounding slightly stressed.

I blinked. "Hey, is everything okay?"

"Well, I um," she stuttered. "Are you at uni today? No, you don't have uni Fridays do you? You're not free by any chance are you?"

"What's going on? Did something happen?" I asked, barely understanding her nervous digress.

"I've got a flat tyre," she sighed. "And I could change it because I've seen you do it before but I'm—well I'm wearing a dress so I wasn't sure if…"

"You need my help?"

"Yes."

"Okay," I replied, glancing up at Regan. We were pretty much done here, right? "Where are you?"

"I'm at that hardware store near uni," she exhaled. "You know the one near—"

"Yeah, I know the one. I'm just finishing up something in East Iris at the moment but I can be there in about half an hour."

"That's perfect, I'll—I'll just hang out, take your time. Thank you so much, Sam."

"No problem. See you soon."

I hung up and looked at Regan who was picking at her fingers.

"You have to go?" she murmured.

"Yes," I sighed. "I figured we were almost done—what were you going to say?"

Her eyes rose to meet mine.

"Just that… I don't want to cause trouble for you and your family. If you believe anything I say, believe that."

I didn't believe her at all. "Right."

"Please… please think about what I said about everything," she continued. "If you were to get Arthur to agree to a one off payment without a test, I would disappear—you wouldn't hear from me again."

Hush money, that's all she wanted.

"If you knew anything about me and my family, you'd know that I have no pull with my father," I replied. "And look, I don't particularly want to be involved in this whole mess he seems to have gotten himself into—whether what you're saying is true or not. Regardless of what he's done to me, this isn't my fight so please just leave me out of it."

I shuffled to the edge of the booth, ready to stand. Regan's hand caught my wrist.

"Sam," she gushed desperately. "Whether it's your fight or not, this affects you. When the truth comes out, dishonour will surround you and everyone you love and you'll see that Arthur was the cause of all this and the one in the wrong. This isn't going to go away with you or him ignoring it."

"Maybe not," I shrugged, gently twisting my wrist free. "But at this point it's all hearsay—and it's still not my fight."

Regan sat back and I stepped clear of the table, turning to make my way out and down to the bus stop that en routed into South Coast University. The bus was pulling up as I arrived so was running in good time. I'd have to get off a couple of stops short of SCU and hike to the hardware store but it wasn't too far.

Paige was leaning awkwardly up against her little green Toyota hatchback when I arrived. She stood straight when she saw me, waving weakly.

"Thanks for coming," Paige sighed. "I couldn't get a hold of Nate and my dad is lecturing."

"It's fine, really," I smiled.

She rolled her eyes. "I cleared everything out the boot to get to the spare. I would have started trying to change it but I didn't want any random people to help."

I gave a nod—typical Paige, never wanting anyone's help. I was a little shocked that she'd called me and not just walked home.

Her lips mashed together and glanced towards the punctured tyre. "It's this one."

I crouched beside the sad-looking wheel. "You must have driven with it flat for a while, it's completely split."

"Oh."

"You'll have to get a whole new one; they won't be able to fix it."

She frowned. "Crap."

I rose and paced around to the back of the small car, pulling up the cover to remove the tyre, jack and other tools.

"You'd think someone would have told you it was flat."

She shrugged. "It was making a horribly loud noise."

I couldn't help but laugh. "I bet."

"Can I help?"

"No, I've got it."

"Are you sure?"

"Yes."

I knelt down and put the jack in place, attaching the allen key to raise the car.

"So you came from East Iris?" Paige asked, standing beside me. I glanced up the lengths of her long, material-covered legs and found her cloudy eyes watching me, momentarily forgetting her question. Paige rarely wore dresses, beats me why—she wore them well, they accentuated her every asset.

"Erm…"

"Did you walk?" she pressed.

"I caught the bus—from East Iris, yeah," I nodded, looking back to the tools—they were safe. "Then walked from the stop just up by the ice cream shop."

"Why didn't you get off at the furniture store?"

I blinked. "Oh right, that's closer."

She huffed a laugh. "A bit, yeah."

"So, uh, Nate not around?" I continued, loosening the lug nuts.

"No, I'm not sure where he is—his classes are in the afternoon," she said, sounding strange. I looked up and saw her pout, the familiar pucker creasing between her eyebrows.

"He's probably training or something," I offered, frowning at the thought. I should be at the gym.

"Probably, he's been doing that a lot lately."

I looked up and Paige bit her lip. I dropped my gaze.

"Nathan is taking the whole football thing pretty seriously," she mused. "Sort of reminds me a bit of you actually."

I huffed and loosened the last nut before removing the tyre. Paige crouched down, rolling me the new one.

"It's funny," she continued. "Since he became a Sun, he's changed… yet you seem to have changed too. Almost like the two of you have switched."

I felt my forehead crease. "But you and I aren't fighting."

She smiled her cute half smile. "No, we seem to be getting along better."

"So, uh, are things not going well between you and Nate?"

The moment I asked it, I knew it wasn't my place to—but I didn't care. I also didn't care that the hope in my voice was as obvious as a sunbeam at dawn.

Paige didn't miss it either; she sat back on the tyre and sighed.

"It's not that they're not going well," she explained. "They're just different now that he's better known."

I lifted the tyre up and lined up the holes, making sure the valve stem was accessible.

"Right."

"So what about you? I heard about the Isobel thing the other day," she frowned. "Are you—are you still with Ivy?"

"Ivy," I sighed, screwing the lug nuts back on loosely. "No, not really."

"Oh."

I glanced up and smiled at her feigned sadness. "Oh?"

She shrugged. "I—well I can't say that I'm disappointed to hear that."

"You're not?"

"Is that wrong?"

"No."

"Good."

I started tightening the tyre in place and huffed a laugh.

"What?" Paige smirked.

"Nothing," I sighed. "It's just funny that you and I can be like this after everything—and that we both hate seeing the other with someone else."

"Well…"

"As in looking out for each other," I mumbled, putting my shoulder into it. I secured the last one and spun the wheel.

"All set."

"Wow, you're the greatest, Sam," she gushed. "Thank you."

"No trouble," I smiled, beginning to lower the car off the jack. When it was safely down I gathered the tools together and rose to my feet, placing them back in the boot. "So I can take your tyre and get a new one if you like."

Paige's eyebrows rose. "You walked, remember?"

"Ah, right," I exhaled.

"I can replace it," she nodded, standing and attempting to pick it up. "I'll do it later."

I strode over. "I'll get it."

She stepped back. "Thanks."

I rested the broken wheel back in the boot and closed it. "You're all set."

"Thank you Sam, really," she answered. "I don't know what I would've done if…"

My brows drew. "Changed it yourself—or asked a random?"

She shook her head. "Walked?"

"Right," I nodded. Of course.

"Can I give you a lift anywhere?" she asked. "Were you heading home?"

I blinked. "Actually that would be great."

She smiled and I went around to the passenger door and climbed in.

"I'm not going to make you late, am I? Were you on your way somewhere?"

Paige looked at me curiously as she started the engine. "No, why?"

I huffed. "You're wearing a dress."

"Oh," she chuckled. "Right, that."

"That," I nodded. Paige never used to wear dresses, she was more of a jeans and T-shirt girl—she looked freaking beautiful in both, mind you.

"No, I just started wearing more dresses lately," she shrugged. "In winter… hence the tights."

I glanced down at her legs—she had great legs. "Fair enough."

A light blush coloured her features.

There wasn't a lot of sunlight filtering through the wintery clouds, but Paige looked beautiful bathing in it. Her usually hazy blue eyes looked almost silver, and her skin that was peaches and cream seemed more sun kissed rather than its normal pallor.

Looking at her I couldn't believe I gave up the privilege of calling her mine—even if things were never easy and there was no *depth*. What was that anyway? We got along just fine.

"Sam?"

"Huh?" Crap. "What did you say?"

"Have you heard any more about the RedBacks?"

Oh. "Not since training with them."

"You trained with them? That's awesome."

I frowned. "Yeah."

"Isn't it?"

"I guess."

She laughed. "You've certainly changed."

"Me? Why?"

"You're not the Sam Saber I remember, all football focused and knight in shining armour."

"Hey, just because I'm not—" I stopped midsentence. *Was* I not football focused anymore? Huh? I thought I was. "I mean, I'm still a knight."

"Sure," she smirked. "Guess you saved me yet again."

"When you let me," I groaned.

Paige mashed her lips together. We weren't too far from my house now.

"Why aren't you and Ivy together anymore?" she asked quietly.

Her question completely threw me. "Huh?"

"Just what I said."

"Why?"

"I'm curious."

I exhaled. "Guess she liked me more than I liked her."

"Is that true?"

"Why would I lie?"

She shook her head. "You know, despite the fact I never warmed to the girl, I can't deny that she seemed to make you smile."

"Oh… kay."

Paige looked over at me. "Were you scared?"

"Of what?"

"Of liking her back?"

I huffed. "Why would that scare me?"

She shrugged. "I just don't understand why you'd end things with her just because she liked you—unless you were scared of something."

I blinked. "Does it really matter?"

"Guess not," she sighed, breathing a laugh. "I suppose I shouldn't care about your love life but that Isobel girl treated you pretty crappy. At least Ivy didn't mess with your head by trying to hook up with Liam as well."

I frowned. "Right."

"It's none of my business."

"No, you're all right."

She exhaled. "I hope Nate gets a good run tomorrow. He's been working so hard this week. I think he's worried that his follow up performance won't be as impressive as his first one."

I glanced over at her and frowned at the concern on her face for the guy. I realised then that it was really over for us. Maybe I just didn't want to see it before. Regardless of how I felt or what I wanted, it didn't matter because she had moved on. She was Nate Blake's girl. The door was closed and I realised that I was okay with that now.

"He'll do fine," I shrugged. "He's in good form."

Paige smiled weakly. "I hope so."

"You mentioned he was training a lot before?" I asked. "Is he that worried?"

"It means a lot to him."

"So do you," I noted.

She blinked. "How do you know?"

"He told me—well he told Sadie and I just happened to be there," I answered. "Said something about not making him pick between you and the family since I guess it wouldn't end well for them. Sounds serious."

She blushed. "He—he's—he definitely surprised me."

"I'll say."

Paige laughed. "Sometimes love tricks you like that."

Love. Lord above.

She pulled up my driveway.

"Well thanks again for your help."

I unclipped the belt. "No problem. Don't forget to replace the tyre."

"I'll drop it in now," she nodded as her car rolled to a stop. "Listen, I want you to be happy Sam. Whether that's with Ivy or Isobel or whoever. Just… be open to things because you might be surprised."

Never in my wildest dreams would I have thought that Paige would ever be giving me relationship advice. I wondered if I actually had somehow fallen into a parallel universe where she was some sage Yoda-lady.

"Right," I laughed. "Will do."

"Seriously Sam," she smiled.

I gave a nod. "Bye Paige."

Paige waved and I returned the gesture, heading up to the castle wondering who would be home. Then I remembered my altercation with the garage this morning and I hoped Artie would be—he had some explaining to do.

I waltzed into the foyer, hearing voices in the lounge and sauntered in. Artie, Lawson and Perry. Artie was facing the window so was clearly expecting me when I appeared.

"Hello son," he nodded. "Was that Paige who dropped you off?"

"Where's my stuff?" I asked, burying the lead. I didn't have time for crap, my rage had resurfaced.

"What *stuff* are you referring to?" he answered, feigning shock at my outburst.

I rolled my eyes. "My tools and mechanical things in the garage. It looks like it's been ransacked. I want them back."

His eyebrows lifted. "I'm afraid I don't know—"

"Cut the crap," I sighed. "They're mine and I need them back. So either return them or replace them, I don't care."

Artie folded his arms. "Well, they were just taking up space."

I blinked. "I beg your pardon?" Crap, now I was even sounding like him. "Taking up space in this freaking castle? It's the garage; no one even uses that but me."

"Yes, okay, but you don't need them Samuel; whatever they were for, you can hire people to—"

"Are you serious?" I interrupted. "I'm a mechanical engineer; it's what we freaking do."

"I *beg your pardon*," Artie spat.

Lawson stood—great, that's all we needed, security.

I cursed at his ignorance, pacing away before I did something not so much stupid but something I'd probably regret… eventually.

"Well, if it's that important then you can just buy some more," Artie sighed. "Though, I doubt it is since it's already been days—"

"What did you do with it all?" I snapped. "Where is it? Did you sell it?"

348

He flicked his hand flippantly. "Oh, I don't know Samuel, I threw it all out."

HE. THREW. IT. OUT?!?! That stuff was worth more than my car when it was in running order. I focused on deep breaths as the capillaries in my eyes felt like they were going to burst. My hands balled into fists and Lawson shuffled uncomfortably from foot to foot. I noticed through my red-tinted vision that Perry was trying to disguise himself as a cushion on the couch.

Screw this; I wasn't going to be in the same room as someone who had so little regard for others. I turned on my heel, resisting the urge to throw a punch at him, and headed towards the door.

"Son?" he called.

Nope. Not having it.

I jogged down the driveway, determined to get off the estate before I was stopped. Not that he'd really come after me, he didn't care enough for that. I headed down a path, through some bushes so I was hidden from view and slowed, pulling my phone out and scrolling through my messages.

Regan.

Ivy.

Regan.

Ivy.

Revenge.

Ally.

Rival.

Friend. Friends. No benefits.

Ivy.

Crap, did I reply to her message from this morning? No. Crap. I hit call and waited while it rang. It rang for a while.

"Sam."

"Ivy," I sighed. "Hi."

"Hello."

"Are you all right?"

"Fine," she replied.

Fine. They didn't sound fine. "Are you sure?"

"What's up Sam?" she asked.

"Nothing, just wondering if you wanted to meet up?" I asked, and then exhaled quietly. "Since… we should talk about stuff."

Silence. "Okay. I'm in the library."

Typical. "Okay, I'm on my way. Be there in about ten."

"Sure, see you soon then."

I hung up and looked around, changing direction to make my way into uni.

Ivy.

Why the heck did I go and say we should talk? I didn't want to talk. What was I supposed to say? Hadn't we said it all? We were friends. Without benefits. Because I wanted to stop the benefits—because she was going to get hurt in the end and hurting her was definitely something I wanted to avoid doing. She was too good for that. She was too good for me. The people around me just got drawn into my drama and I didn't want that for her.

And then there was Louis who just kept on about it, the taunts, the blatant flirting—what was he playing at? It was right for me to stop it—she wasn't my girlfriend, it was never that way between us. Not really.

So what was I going to say?

I didn't want to lose her, I didn't want her to give up on me and I didn't want her to leave. I hated to think it, but I actually needed her. She was the one person who could make me smile even on my crappiest day.

And for some stupid reason that I didn't understand, she liked me.

Ah crap.

What if I went and ruined it?

What was I doing? This was a bad idea.

I dragged my reluctant feet onto campus, forcing one foot in front of the other. What was I going to say? What did I want to get out of this? What if she was still mad?

I walked into the library.

Bad idea, Samuel, bad idea…

Ivy looked up and smiled. I lost my train of thought.

"Hey," I exhaled, sliding into the seat in front of her. Why was I so nervous?

"Hi."

I swallowed. "I hope I'm not interrupting."

She dropped her pen, tucking a loose curl behind her ear. "It's a welcome interruption. I've been here for hours."

"Want to go somewhere?"

"Sure."

We both stood. I waited. She hesitated. We walked.

"So, are you hungry?" I asked.

"Starving."

"Any preference?"

She flashed a grin. "I'd kill for a burger."

A burger. This girl never failed to surprise me.

"Excalibur?"

"If you like, I don't mind."

I nodded and dropped my head to watch my feet step.

We arrived in silence and ordered, I barely read the menu—settling on the first thing my eyes settled on, some meatball thing—and we found a table just outside the door in the fresh air.

"So, you said you wanted to talk?" Ivy asked. "What about?"

I frowned. "Erm."

Her eyebrows rose.

The waitress came with our drinks. Ivy had ordered a strawberry milkshake. I had my usual mocha.

"I—what did you want to talk about?" I answered. "Your message this morning said you wanted to talk."

She nodded. "But you didn't reply to my message."

"I called you—the message said to call."

"And said you wanted to talk," she noted. "So talk."

She was going to make me say it—exactly what, I still wasn't sure about.

I took a sip of my mocha. It was hot for a change and burnt all the way down my throat. I coughed weakly and she nudged her milkshake towards me. I shook my head and she shrugged.

"Last night," I sighed.

She tipped her head, her golden locks tumbling over her exposed clavicle. "What about it?"

"I don't want to lose you in my life," I said before I could think—surprised at how true it was.

She nodded. "Okay."

"Okay."

"So what?"

"Huh?"

"What does that mean?" she shrugged. "As much as I hate this talk, I think we need to have it. What are we to each other? Just friends?"

The waitress rested our plates in front of us. We both murmured thanks.

I pressed my lips together contemplatively.

"Well you said something about not thinking of me as more than a friend," she replied, frowning at her burger.

I exhaled, stabbing a meatball with my fork.

Ivy looked up. "I'm guessing that hasn't changed?"

I barely chewed, feeling my heart squeeze as I swallowed the lump of meat. This was the question I had been dreading because I couldn't seem to wrap my head around any of it. Ivy didn't intrigue me like Isobel had, she didn't keep me guessing like Paige did. But she did do something to me.

I frowned, reaching up to my throat as my breathing grew shallow, tightening as I inhaled. My lungs felt constricted and my gaze dropped to examine my fork, the meatball that was on my plate. I thirsted for air that I couldn't seem to intake. Ah crap. Tree nuts.

I patted my empty pockets. Damn EpiPen: never on me when I needed it.

Ivy blinked, tipping her head. "Sam?"

I clutched at my allergy necklace, gripping it between my thumb and forefinger.

Her brow pinched for a moment before comprehension struck and she slid off her chair, tipping the contents of her bag out on the concrete as she rummaged through it. My eyes rolled back as I drowned on dry land, then felt a stab to my thigh followed by the release of oxygen and I gasped.

Ivy's hands tipped my head up, searching it as if she expected it to have changed.

"Sam, breathe," she whispered. "Breathe."

I exhaled. "Thanks."

"You scared me," she pouted.

"Sorry."

"What are you allergic to?" she frowned, glancing at my dog tag. "Tree nuts?"

I gave an infinitesimal nod and she laughed.

"Funny?"

She shook her head, raising her wrist revealing an allergy bracelet. "Peanuts."

I huffed a laugh—it hurt.

"Where's your EpiPen?"

I shrugged. "Other jeans?"

"You're an idiot."

"Yeah, so I've heard."

She turned and pushed my plate into the middle of the table.

"You saved my life," I murmured. "Thanks."

"Like I could let you die," she sighed. "You didn't answer my question."

"Curiosity saved my life?"

"Well, it killed the cat—I don't want to be next."

I smiled weakly, reaching out for my mocha. Ivy knocked my hand away and handed me her pink milkshake.

I glanced at her with amusement and took a sip. She rested her hand on my free one and I lifted a finger so she hooked it around hers.

"I don't think of you like that," I breathed.

She looked up. "As what?"

"I mean I don't *not* think of you like that," I amended. "I don't think."

"I don't follow."

"I—"

"Sam," she sighed. "Speak clearly."

I took a deep breath. "You're kind of perfect when I think about it."

She frowned. "Perfect?"

"That's supposed to be a compliment."

"How? You've just put me on an impossible pedestal."

I blinked. Girls really looked at things weirdly.

"Well, you've got an awesome personality," I replied, letting out a choke. "You're funny, smart, and incredibly hot—"

She made a face.

"What?"

"All cliché," she sighed.

"Well I was going to add *low maintenance*, but scratch that."

She smiled. "So why list my... attributes, or whatever? What are you getting at? Or is this your way of building me up just to say something stupid like I'm too good for you?"

"Well, you are but that wasn't where I was going with it," I croaked.

"Are you okay?" she frowned. "Do you want to see a doctor or something? I usually feel off for a few hours after a reaction."

I shook my head and the pucker between her brows returned. "Okay, but we're staying here for a while so you can regain your energy."

I shrugged. "By all means, make yourself comfortable then."

Ivy smiled, glancing back at her chair as she dragged it over by the legs and slid onto it beside me.

"So where were you going with it?" she asked.

I looked unseeingly at the pink milk beverage. "I think you were right."

"Yeah, I probably was," she agreed. "But about what specifically?"

"I think I freaked out a bit because of something Macca said, then something you said but I didn't want to believe it."

"Sam, for goodness sake, just speak clearly," she sighed. "What did Macca say exactly to freak you out?"

"Just something about you putting your feelings aside to do the benefits thing so you must really care—I don't know, it sounds stupid."

"Why?"

"Be... cause," I frowned. "I mean, is it?"

She glanced to the side. "Well, no. But you already knew that, isn't that why you ended the benefits thing? For my... erm, benefit?"

I nudged the milkshake towards her. "This leads me to where you were right."

Her golden eyes looked up. "Huh?"

"I do feel the same, sort of, I think," I frowned. "I mean, I don't know for sure, but what I do know is that I don't want to lose you, and when my day is crap, just seeing you makes it better."

"Stop, you're making me blush," she groaned, rolling her eyes.

I laughed. "It's actually a compliment."

"Sure," she smiled. "So what you're saying is that you do like me back, right?"

I glanced to the side. "I think so."

"You *think* so?"

"Right."

Ivy thought for a moment then shook her head, turning to scoop the crap from her bag off the concrete.

"Erm, what are you doing?" I mumbled.

"I'm leaving."

My heart pinched. "Why?"

"Because, I can't keep waiting for you to decide what you want from me, Sam," she exhaled. "It's not fair and you're actually driving me nuts."

I huffed at the pun and she scowled.

"Sorry," I breathed. "But seriously, don't go."

"Give me one reason to stay."

"I'll give you three."

Her shoulders lifted. "Fine, shoot."

I took a deep breath and sat forward. "You need me."

"*I* need *you?*" she scoffed.

"Sure—who else is going to save you from wasting your life away in the library?"

She gave me a fake smile. "What's number two?"

I shrugged. "You want me."

Ivy shook her head. "I don't—"

"Sure you do," I interrupted.

She didn't deny it. "Well what's number three?"

I smiled weakly. "I need you."

Her eyebrows lifted. "You need me?"

I nodded.

"Why?"

"Because you're awesome," I answered. "And all the things I listed before."

Ivy folded her arms. "I don't know if that's good enough."

I frowned. "It's not?"

"You needing me?" she breathed. "No. Needing and wanting are two very—"

"I do want you," I added.

"You do?" she asked flatly. "No you don't."

This wasn't exactly going as I expected.

"Yes I do."

"Why?"

"*Why?*"

"Yes, why?" she repeated. "Why now? Why me? Why any of it?"

I made a face. "How do I even answer that?"

She huffed. "You can't."

"Are you scared?"

"Me? What would I be scared of?"

"Of me liking you back."

"Do you?" she asked. "Because needing me or wanting me is not the same as liking me."

I blinked. Girls really were sticklers on technicalities.

"Erm, isn't that what I've been saying?" I asked.

"No."

"Right," I sighed. "Well, add that to the list then."

"What? That you like me?"

357

"Lord above, Ivy," I groaned. "I'm trying to speak plainly but you're really hell-bent on making this hard for me."

"I think you're doing that all on your own, Saber," she shrugged.

I ran my hands through my hair and stood up.

She squirmed. "You shouldn't be—"

"Relax, I won't break," I smirked.

She rolled her eyes and I stepped towards her. She shuffled her feet uncomfortably at my sudden close proximity.

"Ivy," I exhaled, moving my index finger to tip her chin up. "You want three reasons to stay? Well here they are: I want you, I need you, and I like you. A lot."

She pouted. "Why?"

"Stop questioning it," I breathed. "Just go with it."

She closed her eyes and I frowned.

"I want to believe you," she whispered. "You have no idea how much I want to believe you."

"Then why don't you?"

Her head rocked. "Because you know it's what I want to hear."

I ran my thumb over her slightly parted lips. "I still don't see a problem here."

"Sam," she murmured—more moaned.

"Ivy."

Her eyebrows puckered. "Sam."

I couldn't take it any longer; I didn't know what to say to make her believe me—so I didn't say anything. Instead I showed her. I breathed her. I tasted her. And she folded beneath me, surrendering to it all.

And nothing else mattered.

XVII

A Silver Lining

I stayed with Ivy—we stayed together in our own little bubble until the sun came up and the real world dawned.

"Have football today," Ivy murmured, running her index finger down my lower lip.

"Mm."

"Guess you can't miss it?" she sighed.

I chuckled. "Probably shouldn't."

"Okay."

My phone rang and I stretched to retrieve it from my jeans which were strewn on her carpet.

"'llo?" I groaned.

"Sam?"

I frowned. "Speaking."

"Good morning son, sorry to call so early, it's Jason—Jason Cobalt."

"Hey Jason, how's it going?"

"Good, son," he replied. "Actually I was wondering if you'd be free to meet up with me at some point today."

"Erm, today?"

"I know the Suns are playing but Wesley said it wasn't until around midday."

I glanced over Ivy to her clock. It was just after seven.

"Guess I could meet you this morning," I answered. "As long as I can make it to the rooms by quarter to eleven."

"Easy," he chuffed. "How about we meet… do you know where Lunar is?"

Lunar.

I laughed. "Yeah, I know the place."

"Say eight o'clock."

"Can do."

"Great, son, see you then."

"Bye Jason."

I hung up and dropped my phone, ignoring the other three missed calls that were also logged.

"You have to go earlier?" Ivy frowned, drawing her bed sheets up around her chest.

"Mm," I nodded, leaning down to lightly kiss her. "Jason wants to meet me—hopefully it's news about the RedBacks."

She squeaked. "That's exciting."

"Do you want to come?" I asked.

She blinked. "With you? To your meeting?"

"Sure."

"No, you go," she breathed. "I'll just meet you at the game."

"You're coming?"

"Of course," she laughed. "It's football."

Ivy.

"Awesome," I nodded.

She bit her lower lip. "This is crazy."

"What is?"

"You."

"Me?"

"Yes."

"Why?"

"Because," she squirmed, pulling the cover up over her head. "You're Samuel Saber."

"So?"

360

"You're going to be a RedBack."

I chuckled. "Maybe."

She threw them back. "What's with the *maybe*? You're better than at least half of those guys."

"Not sure if Gordon thinks so," I frowned.

"But Jason does," she whispered, sitting up and kissing my neck below my earlobe. I forgot what we were even talking about—none of it mattered, I only saw her. Ivy giggled as I moved over her, capturing her beneath my iron frame.

"You're going to be late," she breathed—panted.

"Everyone else can wait."

***

"Jason," I smiled, extending a hand towards him. "Sorry to keep you."

"Sam," he grinned, shaking it firmly. "Your time is more precious than mine."

The assistant coach of the RedBacks? I wasn't sure if that was entirely true.

"Have you ordered?"

"No, son, I was waiting for you," he nodded, handing me a menu. I didn't need it, I knew what I wanted.

"Oh, thanks."

Demi appeared to take our order but I hardly saw her or her short skirt.

"So why did you want to meet me?" I asked when we were alone again.

Jason exhaled. "You're a good player, Sam."

"Okay, erm, thanks." This sounded like it was heading for a *but*.

361

"I saw that from the start," he added. "And I told Wesley that I'd look out for you and make sure your best interest was the one that was being considered."

My forehead creased.

"Though in talking to Gordon, I'm not sure if that's *his* main concern," Jason frowned.

This didn't sound promising at all. "What does that mean?"

"It means that I'm not sure if—regardless of how hard you work, son—*if* he will put you on the RedBacks line-up—as a rookie maybe but not on the senior list," he explained. "I really shouldn't be telling you this since it could cost me my job, but I see a lot of talent in you and I'd hate for you to pass up the opportunity to shine elsewhere because you had your heart set on the RedBacks."

I didn't understand what he was saying. Did Gordon not want me to play? He seemed to be okay with it at practice as long as I kept my nose clean and trained hard.

"What makes you think he doesn't want me on the senior list?" I asked, my words catching like knives in my throat.

Jason leaned forward then back when our order arrived. He waited for Demi to disperse then leaned forward again.

"You're Arthur Saber's son," he answered.

Ah, Artie. Forever the sword in my spine.

"I see."

"With that comes a promise of scandal that he's not keen on," Jason explained.

"The promise of media scrutiny you mean?"

"Perhaps."

"I didn't know that was a bad thing when it came to sports," I shrugged. "Unless there was something he was afraid that they'd uncover."

Jason blinked then frowned. "You deserve more than what's on offer here."

So he knew about the crap that was going on at the club. Interesting.

"Thanks Jason, but that doesn't really help me," I sighed, stabbing my spinach omelette. I understood what he was saying but it didn't make it suck any less. Becoming a RedBack was something I'd dreamed about since I was a kid—now he was saying my dream wasn't good enough for me. Aces.

"I'm sorry, son," he sighed. "For what it's worth, I don't think you'll have any trouble catching the eye of another team."

Another team. Not the RedBacks.

"Right."

There was silence.

I took a mouthful of mocha.

"Is there any chance at all that could change?" I asked. "I mean, Gordon might get past it, right?"

Jason pressed his lips together sympathetically. "I suppose."

Means no.

"I'm not saying he won't take you in," he replied. "All I'm saying is you might not get a proper run—and then you'll spend the best years of your life in a great suit warming the bench. You're worth more than that Sam."

"Right," I murmured. "Well thanks for the heads up, I guess."

"Sorry son, I wish I had better news for you."

I scooped another forkful of omelette. "You and me both."

I didn't hang around after breakfast because there wasn't anything more to say. There was no future for me at the RedBacks. Over. Done. Finished. Another ending. Didn't see this one coming either.

363

Jason was cool though, we got along well. He was the type of guy I'd be honoured to call my father—his daughter, Ruby was pretty lucky.

I walked home to grab my football stuff and managed to avoid any traces of human life before catching the train to the oval. I was a bit early, it was just after ten and I was still stewing over how Artie had managed to make my football career go down in flames without even trying. In the past twenty-four hours, he'd literally demolished my entire future—though at least he'd be able to buy some of it back by replacing my tools.

***

"Hey, you're early," Ivy's voice echoed through the stands.

I blinked and found her sitting behind the interchange bench. "You too."

"Nothing else to do. How'd it go with Jason?"

I shook my head. "They don't want me."

Ivy dropped her notebook and leapt over the stand. "What? Why?"

"Artie."

"Your father? What does he—?" she stopped and sighed. "Paparazzi?"

"Yep."

She pouted. "That sucks."

"Yep."

"Well screw them!" she shrugged. "They'll be other offers, you're incredible, Sam."

"Maybe," I murmured. "But who's to say they all won't have a problem with who I am?"

"Then screw them all," she smiled. "Let's run away."

I laughed and she wrapped her arms around me. "If they can't see it, they aren't worth it."

"Thanks."

She buried her head into my shoulder and I held her tight against me. It felt right.

"Were you studying?"

"Trying to."

"You're such a good girl."

She laughed, pulling back to look at me, closing her eye in a suggestive wink. "You know that's not entirely true."

"Right," I chuckled.

She frowned. "You still look sad."

"I'm not sad, I'm just a bit annoyed," I sighed. "Feels like Artie is always messing with my life."

"He's a jerk."

"Yeah he is."

She glanced behind her. "Want to get out of here?"

I checked my watch. "I need to be in the change room in twenty minutes."

"Twenty minutes is enough time," she shrugged.

"For what?"

Her eyebrows rose.

I nearly choked. "Seriously?"

"You look like you need to de-stress."

I chuckled. "You are bad."

"If you want."

"Actually, can we just sit?" I asked, going against my better judgement.

Ivy smiled. "Of course."

My hand slipped down her shoulder, to her elbow, and caught her hand as she gave it a quick tug towards the interchange bench.

We sat down and she hugged my arm, resting her head against my bicep.

"It's not for nothing, you know," she said after a moment. "You've come a long way."

I sighed. "Yeah, maybe."

"*Maybe* nothing," she whispered. "Don't lose heart, Sam—you're a fighter. Don't let King Arthur break you—nothing is set in stone."

King Arthur.

Stone.

The sword in the stone.

Yeah, out of the stone and into my back.

"He hasn't broken me," I murmured. Not entirely.

"Good," she answered, looking up and turning my head towards hers. "Keep fighting."

I smiled. "Yeah, I will."

"You promise?"

"You believe in me that much?"

"Yes," she nodded. "You don't think the first time I heard about you was that email, do you?"

I blinked—I barely remembered that yet it was only a few weeks ago. "It wasn't?"

"I noticed you before that," she blushed. "But you were with Paige and then I saw you sneaking off with Isobel a couple of times…"

"Right," I breathed. That turned out well.

"I've been a Suns supporter since I was a kid too," she mused. "My dad used to bring me to games—he used to be a trainer when they first started but as time passed his drinking got bad so they let him go. He didn't have a job for a while so I had to support us both… then he sobered up and got the gardener job and I moved out."

"That really sucks," I frowned. "You had to support him when you were just a kid?"

She nodded. "I used to babysit for people in our neighbourhood; then when I was old enough word had spread so I got more jobs. Every Tuesday I still nanny for one of the families."

I thought for a moment. "Your day off—*of sorts?*"

She grinned. "Yes."

"Cool."

"Lemons out of lemonade," she shrugged.

I twisted my hand around to grip hers. "So if we were to run away, you wouldn't miss them?"

"Sure, I'd miss them," she whispered. "But they're getting older and they don't need me as much anymore. It's more for my benefit than theirs now I think."

I smiled. Ivy had definitely surprised me. She was almost the perfect balance between Paige and Isobel—how had I not seen it clearly before? She listened but she spoke, she was spontaneous but she cared. She wanted me when I was available—even more so—and I had been too stupid to see that it had been her all along who was actually the perfect girl for me.

"You're pretty amazing," I sighed.

Ivy looked up. "Me? Why?"

"Just because."

"You are."

I leaned in, catching her lips on mine—and everything else disappeared.

Despite how it felt, the rest of the world was still there—and I made it to the change rooms just in time to change before Wesley briefed us before warm-ups—I barely heard him.

Come on Sam, game face.

"Sammy, you good?" Marcus asked, nudging my arm.

"Hm? Yep."

He frowned but let it drop.

Louis was staring at me but I just shook my head. He turned away.

"Sam Saber," Wesley called at the end of his speech. "Stay behind lad."

Ah crap.

"Coach?"

"Did you speak to Jason, son?" he asked.

"Yes."

"Don't be too disappointed, there are other teams, son," Wesley said, patting my shoulder.

"Not in South Coast," I frowned.

"No, lad, not in South Coast," he mused. "Are you ready for today? Do you want to sit out the first change?"

"No, I want to play," I answered, slightly horrified that he'd humoured sitting me out.

"Okay, son, show them what you've got."

I nodded. "Coach."

We headed out to the oval for warm-ups as the stands began to fill with people still trickling in, and then headed back to the rooms for one final huddle before game time.

The oval was packed, but I found Ivy's face easily in the crowd and that made me smile. I saw Paige too, but she only saw Nate. Isobel was there as well, sitting beside Elliot Prince—or rather nestling into his side as he uncomfortably adjusted his sitting position. Guess I underestimated how much she needed to be with someone—even if he treated her like rubbish. It made me sad for her.

Then I saw Regan. What was she doing here? And was that Artie and Amelia? Perfect.

"Sam, you here?" Louis murmured, shouldering my side. "Where's your head?"

"I'm in the game, relax," I sighed. "We've got this."

The siren bellowed, snapping me out of my reverie and into my current reality. Football. That's what mattered right now. The game. When everything else didn't make sense, this made sense. I knew this, I was good at this. It didn't matter what was happening at home or even with the other teams or with girls, this was reliable. And I *was* good at this. No matter what anyone said or what Artie did. No one could take this away from me.

And they didn't.

It was arguably the best game I had ever played. I shone. I was untouchable. It felt great. It felt even better to play with my team and win with my team. For a player that was all you could hope for: a great game and an excellent win. Though I did feel a bit bad for Nate—well more for Paige since I knew she'd been worried about him—considering he barely got a touch in the first half then was benched for the second half. I did try to help but... guess it just wasn't his day.

"Holy hell Sam!" Louis hooted, ruffling my hair as we headed into the change rooms. "What just happened!?"

"Told you my head was in it," I chuffed.

"Four goals!" Marcus yelped. "Good to have you back Sammy!"

"Thanks Sax," I nodded.

"So what did you get up to last night?" he asked. "You didn't come home."

"Yeah I was hanging out with—what do you mean by *come home*?" I frowned. "Were you at my house?"

Marcus forced a smile.

"What were you doing at my house Sax?"

369

"Waiting for you to come home," he shrugged. "And hanging out with Millie."

I cursed under my breath. "I told you to stay away from my sister."

"And I told you that you've got nothing to worry about."

"She's still my little sister."

Marcus huffed. "She could do worse."

Louis' eyebrow's lifted.

I saw a tint of red. "What?"

"Nothing bro, I'm just saying—"

"Just don't say," I snapped, nudging him back against the wall. "Back off."

I shoved him and stepped back, feeling Louis' fist grab a handful of my jumper and pull.

"She was upset that you weren't there so I stayed with her—nothing happened," Marcus explained, stumbling to his feet. "If you were actually there—"

Snap.

I lunged to punch him but Louis caught my arm before my fist made contact, yanking me back from my best friend with the handful of my shirt he still held.

"Easy tiger," he exhaled as Marcus fell over his feet. "Sax, get out of here."

Louis pushed me back against the wall and I let him hold me there as a red-faced Marcus clambered to his feet and scooped up his things, heading towards the door.

The remaining guys in the change room slowly returned to their own business. Louis unhurriedly released my jumper from his grip.

"You all right?"

My head shook. "He deserved—"

"I know," Louis sighed. "But you'd regret it later."

I huffed. My best friend had just implied that I wasn't there for my family fresh off of telling me my little sister could do worse than him. It was highly unlikely I would've regretted it.

"He didn't mean it," Louis replied.

"Which part?"

Louis blinked. "The you-not-being-there part."

"I wasn't there last night."

"You're there when it counts."

I shrugged. "You think there's something going on? With him and Amelia?"

Louis brushed his hands through his dark blonde hair. "He said you had nothing to worry about."

"He also said that she could do worse."

"She could," Louis answered.

I grit my teeth.

"Hear me out," he sighed, lifting his hands in defence. "Even you have to admit the guy looks out for her. He knows you, bro, he knows your family—hell, he's practically part of the family—he'd be daft to mess with that."

I grabbed my towel and headed towards the shower. I didn't want to think about Marcus and Amelia right now, that was one issue that could wait. Right now I wanted to celebrate the fact that I was back on top at the Suns because judging by immediate history, it could be something short lived.

"Sammy," Marcus sighed as I stepped out the rooms after cooling down and changing back into jeans.

I groaned. "Not now, Sax."

Marcus frowned. "Why do you have such an issue with me and Amelia being friends?"

I huffed. "Friends?"

"Yeah, friends."

"You don't do friends with girls," I replied. "And Amelia is too young for that."

Marcus shook his head. "It's Millie, Sammy. She just misses you bro."

"Well that's between her and me," I mumbled.

Marcus exhaled. "Fine. Whatever."

"Quit doing that—quit turning this around and making it my fault," I exhaled. "I'm doing the best I can with everything."

"Yeah, I know," he nodded. "Sorry."

I pressed my lips together and caught Ivy at the corner of my eye. She smiled crookedly and waved and I couldn't help but smile weakly in return. Marcus followed my gaze and cleared his throat.

"We good?"

I looked back and knocked my fist against his.

"We're good," I murmured. "Just leave it to me, all right?"

He nodded and headed past me back into the rooms as I sauntered over to Ivy.

"Hey superstar," she grinned. "Great game."

"Why thank you milady."

She laughed. "Huh?"

"I don't know."

"Want to get out of here?" she smirked.

"Yes."

She looked behind her at Amelia. "I thought we could all go out for lunch?"

How was it that she read my thoughts before I even thought them?

"Sounds great."

"Awesome," she nodded, lacing her fingers through mine. "Let's go."

"Where are we going?" Louis asked suddenly behind us.

"Merlin's?" Amelia offered hopefully.

372

Louis gave a thumbs up. "Pizza? Count me in."

"Right," I sighed.

"Should we wait for Sax too?" Amelia asked.

Louis looked at me with raised brows while Amelia waited for an answer. Ivy gave my hand a gentle squeeze. She was here. She was on my side.

"Sure," I nodded. "Macca, you're driving."

***

I woke up Sunday in my own bed, tangled in Ivy's smooth legs and a strange ringing that I eventually identified as my phone.

"Sam's phone," Ivy's sexy morning voice hummed.

Crap.

"It's for you," she exhaled, dropping it on my head.

"Ouch," I groaned. "Who is it?"

"Wesley."

I was suddenly awake.

"Wesley?" I murmured, adjusting the handset to my ear. "Hello? Coach?"

"Sam," Wesley chuffed. "Sorry son, I hope I'm not interrupting."

"Uh, it's—no, err, not really," I stuttered, struggling to sit up with Ivy's vine-like legs pinning me down. "What's—uh—what's happening?"

"Actually son, I was hoping you could come down to the oval and have a bit of a chat," he answered.

"Everything okay coach?" I frowned. "I'm not in trouble am I?"

"No lad," he huffed. "When can you get here?"

I blinked down at Ivy who was rubbing her glistening gold eyes.

373

"Sam?"

"Huh? Oh, uh, I can be there in half an hour."

"Sure son," Wesley replied. "I'm just doing inventory."

"Right, well I'll see you when I get there."

"Great."

"Cool."

I hung up.

Ivy yawned. "Wah-dih-Weh-lee-wah."

I laughed. "He wants me to meet him at the oval."

"Ooh, why?"

"Not sure."

"Promising?"

"Well I'm not in trouble."

She made a cute noise of amusement and brushed the ends of my hair. "Promising, Sam."

"Do you want to come?" I asked.

She grinned. "No, you go. But I want to know all about it."

I nodded. "Are you sure?"

"Yes, Samuel Saber, I'm sure."

"Can I get Marion to make you some breakfast?"

She laughed. "No thanks. I'll go hunting for myself."

"Ivy Hunt."

"Samuel Saber."

"Ivy."

"Sam."

"Ivy."

I pressed my lips together as she traced them with her finger.

"Sam," she breathed. "You have to go."

"I'll drop you home if you like."

"Does your car start?"

I frowned. "No."

She chuckled. "I can walk."

"I'll walk you."

"You don't have to."

"I can catch the bus from uni."

"Okay."

"Okay."

She stared at me for a moment then laughed, jumping up to kiss me quick before reaching across for one of my shirts and pulled it on. I watched as she clambered out of my bed, her legs wobbly but glorious as she pulled on her jeans and threw mine at me. They collapsed over my right shoulder and I slowly got dressed as she propelled an orange coloured T-shirt at me that I let fall in my lap.

"You're going to be late."

I smirked. "I'll be fine. Wesley will wait."

"What are you looking at?"

"You."

"Me? Why?" a pink blush coloured her cheeks.

I shrugged.

She bit her lip and walked over, resting her forehead on mine.

"I'm happy," she whispered.

It was completely random—but I understood her saying it.

"Me too."

"You make me feel like summer."

"Summer?"

"Like sunshine."

I laughed. "That's... odd."

"Sunshine makes me happy," she breathed, dipping her head to kiss my neck and sending a tingle down my body. She stepped back and grabbed my hands, pulling me to my feet.

The T-shirt fell to the floor.

"Come on, Saber."

She released one of my hands and I reached for the shirt, grabbing my shoes in the same hand as she tugged me towards the door, stepping into her converse as she continued to tow me down the stairs.

"Morning Angela," Ivy smiled at my mother as we reached the bottom. She dropped my hand and let me pull on my shoes.

"Good morning Ivy, honey," Angela nodded. "Samuel, glad to see that you made it home for a change."

"Yep," I yawned. "Morning Mum."

"Are you kids heading out?"

"Wesley wants to see me and I'm walking Ivy home," I replied. "I'll catch you later, is that cool?"

"Cool," she smiled. "Sure thing honey."

I yanked the T-shirt over my head.

"Is that a tattoo?" Angela asked, catching me off guard.

I glanced at the sword on my inner bicep. It was completely healed now—not too bad really.

"Uh, yeah."

"And when did that happen?" she frowned.

"Remember when you found me on the doorstep a few weeks ago?"

"Hm."

"Yep, then."

"Marcus?" she sighed. "Oh well, it's quite a nice one at least, isn't it?"

I gawked at my mother and Ivy laughed as I walked over to grab a couple of apples off the table.

"See you kids later," Angela waved.

"Bye Mum."

"See you Angela," Ivy added. I passed her an apple and we headed out into the misty haze outside.

"So, erm, how are things with Mira? Are you talking again?" I asked as we walked down the driveway.

She took a bite of her apple. "Kind of."

"You're not still mad at her because of me, are you?"

"Not really," she shrugged. "I don't like that she snitched on your family."

I bit into my apple. "She probably did me a favour in a weird way. I mean, it more or less cleared my reputation. Artie will always be involved in some kind of scandal."

She smiled weakly at me. "I guess."

"Don't be hard on her, she's your friend," I answered. "Friends stuff up sometimes but that doesn't make them bad people—it just makes them human."

"Very wise, Sam," she chuckled. "Yes, I should let her off the hook."

"You should."

"What about Sax?"

I frowned. "What about him?"

"Are you going to let him off the hook?"

"What about?"

"Amelia."

"Amelia?" I asked. "What about my sister?"

She looked at me incredulously. "Come on, Sam, even you can't deny that little bond they have."

"Don't," I groaned. "I don't want to think about it. That's my little sister."

"He obviously cares about her—I mean the way he looks at her…"

"It's Sax."

"Right," she noted, stopping me and gripping the collar of my T-shirt as she rose to her toes to look me almost in the eye. The

377

clouds above tried to rain. "It's Sax—your goofy best friend but a fairly decent guy."

I pressed my lips together—as much as I hated to admit it, she was right. Marcus had really only had one girlfriend, Briony, and actually didn't have many random hook-ups despite his tendency to talk up the *talent* at Crescent—he was really pretty pathetic at chatting up girls.

"Besides, Amelia looks at him like…"

I shot her a look of discomfort. "Like what?"

"Like the way you look at me."

"Oh crap."

She laughed. "Don't look so afraid."

I shook my head. "I don't want to think about—you and I are different I mean, it's my little sister you're talking about."

"I get it," she nodded, hugging my arm. "You're protective."

I took another bite of my apple and she smiled.

"Maybe Sax is her sunshine like you're mine."

I chuckled. "Maybe."

Ugh. Marcus and Amelia. I was not equipped to deal with my little sister being interested in guys yet, never mind that guy being my best friend.

"Give Sax a break."

"I'll give him a break all right," I muttered.

Ivy giggled.

By the time I had walked Ivy home and doubled back to uni for the bus to Iris Oval, it was almost an hour after I'd hung up from Wesley. It was weird though, when I was with her it was like time had no meaning. It was a bit scary actually; things that used to matter to me just didn't anymore.

I actually didn't care about Artie and his crap anymore. I didn't even care about the RedBacks and Coach Gordon being a total douche about taking me on as a rookie. I guess it was because

I had this feeling like things might work out in spite of all of that. I wasn't sure how but I would be okay.

Samuel Saber. Arthur Saber's son. The mayor of South Coast's son. I would be okay.

"Sorry I'm late, coach," I called, walking up to where he stood in the equipment shed. "My car's dead and I had to improvise."

Wesley smiled. "No hassles, lad, I told you I'd be here."

Certainly a change from Artie's usual response of *everywhere in South Coast takes ten minutes*.

I exhaled. "So why did you want to see me?"

"Well, son, I got a call this morning from one of the scouts that was at the game yesterday," Wesley said. "Turns out he was impressed with you."

"Really?" I blinked, my heart squeezing like an orange in a juicer. "Which scout? I didn't even know there were any there yesterday."

Wesley nodded.

"What do you think about becoming an East Tiger, son?" he asked, raising an eyebrow.

"A tiger?" I repeated. "An *East* Tiger?"

He smiled. "I think you've well and truly earned your stripes."

"You mean I'd move east? Away of South Coast?"

"That's right, son," he answered. "You wouldn't be eclipsed by your old man anymore."

Eclipsed. Good word.

"Move east," I mused. "Be a tiger."

"What do you say?"

What did I say? Maybe my time in the west had well and truly set. But moving east would mean I'd be leaving it all behind—Angela, Amelia, Marcus, Louis, Bryce... Ivy. What about Ivy?

"Do you want to have a think about it?" he asked.

I could hardly order my thoughts.

East. Tiger. East. Tiger. *East Tiger.*

"How long do I have to decide?" I answered.

Wesley sighed. "That's the thing, lad, they'd need an answer as soon as possible—if you're keen, they'd fly you out sunset tomorrow."

Sunset.

Poetic.

"And what?" I choked. "That's it? I'm on the team?"

He tipped his head. "They'd train you up on one of their minor league teams that feed into the Tigers—they're shaping up for an early draft pick and that would be you, son."

I scratched my stubble.

Crap. This was huge. This was it.

"What do you think I should do, coach?" I asked.

"Son, I can't tell you what to do," he smiled. "But I can tell you that you've got a lot of talent and the Tigers are a decent team. Their coach is a straight up guy—unlike Gordon. Truth be told I've never really liked him lad, but I know you had your heart set on the RedBacks."

I frowned.

"It's ultimately your decision."

"Right," I nodded.

"So I guess you've got some thinking to do, son," Wesley smiled. "Where do you see yourself a year from now? What would make you happy, son?"

I pressed my lips together, glancing up at the sky as the sun broke through the clouds, sending a ray of light across the sky.

Happiness. Sunshine.

Epilogue

Till Dawn

I watched as dawn broke over the beach after my morning run, the sun greeting me with a warm welcome to the otherwise brisk morning. On the east coast, I encountered the sun as a beginning rather than an ending. I liked it better this way; it somehow shone brighter in the sky.

A year had passed since I met Wesley at Iris Oval and from that fateful day, I'd hit the ground running and never looked back. I'd met up with Ivy after the meeting and told her what had happened before heading home to break the news to my family. Naturally, Ivy harboured a little more enthusiasm than my Saber kin, though I could see Angela wanted to share in the excitement that was somehow masked with the sadness and dread of having me move across the country.

Amelia was quiet—she didn't speak to me for a couple of hours after I told her—then she realised that those silent hours were suddenly numbered. Artie hated the idea, naturally. After all, how could he showcase his family values with only one offspring? Guess he could've just waited a few months if Regan's baby had turned out to be his.

If.

That whole thing sort of erupted in her face. Artie had conceded to a test after speculations continued, making him drop down in the polls amongst the good people of South Coast. When the test came back negative, Regan was shamed into hiding and Mayor Saber had never been more popular as he was positioned as the poor victim of a crazy obsessed fan-girl. I read about it in the papers, it was pretty sickening. As a result, he was re-elected as mayor and all was right in his kingdom. How wonderful for King Arthur.

I headed up the path through the dunes and crossed the road to the cafe that was my east-coast Lunar, and sat down at my usual booth to wait for *her*. I glanced around the cafe at the now familiar faces and checked my phone for the time.

She was late. She usually beat me here.

I scrolled through my text messages and stopped on Bryce's name, smiling at the one I had received the day before: *'Ryder started walking today, few steps then toppled. Constance managed to get a photo. Jenny still loving the new baby to play with but always manages to steal the limelight.'*

Ryder Watson, now about nine months old. I'd made a special trip home for the christening—being Ryder's godfather. He was a pretty cute kid. I made an effort to send him regular letters and presents. Bryce said he had the East Tiger playing card I'd sent him of me framed in his room. It was pretty cool—though my time as a Sun had well as truly set in the west.

"Here's today's paper, Sam," a voice interrupted as a copy of the specially ordered *South Coast Courier* slid in front of me.

I looked up. "Thanks Portia."

She smiled. "Waiting for your girlfriend?"

"Yeah."

"Can I get you your drinks to start?" she offered. "The usual?"

"Thanks," I nodded.

She bowed and disappeared as I glanced down at today's headlines:

New Sports Stadium Begins Building: Mayor Saber Predicts Speedy Two-Year Opening.

Typical.

I turned the page and sighed—more good news I see: *Police Commissioner Prince's Protégé: Son Elliot's Second Aggravated Assault Charge.*

Both by-lined by Alex Marrone. I guess some things literally never changed.

"Hey Sam, sorry I'm late," her voice sang. Music to my ears. "I slept through my first alarm."

"You're not really," I smiled. "I ordered you your usual milkshake."

She grinned, biting her lower lip. "Thank you."

Damn. She was beautiful.

"How was your run?"

"Good."

Her bright eyes fell to the paper. "News from home?"

"News, yes," I huffed. "Nothing *new* though."

"Do you miss it?" she asked. "South Coast?"

"Do you?"

She shrugged. "Sometimes. Maybe."

Her hand reached across the table to run her soft index finger down my thumb.

Portia returned, placing our drinks in front of us.

The girls exchanged a friendly smile.

"Decided what you'd like to eat?" Portia asked.

I glanced over at her as she pouted at the menu.

"Actually can we have a couple more minutes?" I replied.

Portia nodded. "Sure."

She smiled. "There are so many choices. What haven't I tried yet?"

"I think you've tried them all."

"Maybe I should start from the beginning?"

"Or you could just pick your favourite and go with that?"

She tipped her head, her glossy hair falling over her shoulder as she absently picked up her straw, letting the thick liquid drain from the clear straw, back into the glass.

I still didn't understand why girls did that.

I took a sip of mocha and cleared my throat.

"Actually, there's something I wanted to say," I said slowly, rotating the glass in my fingertips.

She looked up, her bright eyes curious and clear, twinkling in the streaming sunlight. I nearly lost my train of thought.

"What's wrong Sam?" she asked. "You look… strange."

I took a steadying breath.

"I think we should get married," I answered. My words were louder than I thought they'd be, stronger, more confident. The silence that followed though was unnerving and I shifted uncomfortably in my seat, trying to read her expression.

She blinked in bewilderment, twisting the ends of her hair around her fingertips.

"You want to get married?" she repeated.

"Yes," I nodded. There was no going back now. The words were out.

She exhaled. "Why?"

"I love you," I shrugged. "And I don't want anything to change between us. When I think of my future, I can't imagine spending it with anyone else."

She bit her lip, staring unseeingly at the milk drops as they drained off her straw. I dropped my gaze as my hand fell beneath the table to the ring box in my pocket, popping the lid open.

"Listen, I—"

"Don't," she sighed. "Don't say anything."

I looked up. Crap, she was crying. I reached across the table for her hand, tucking the red velvet box in it.

"Marry me."

She exhaled, staring down at the ring. The stone was the exact same shade as her eyes. I commended my choice.

"Well, aren't you going to say anything?" I huffed. "I mean, way to leave a guy hanging."

"I'm sorry," she said helplessly.

My heart lodged in my throat as I rubbed my forehead. "Oh, right."

"No," she breathed.

"Yeah, I got it."

"No—Sam," she laughed.

She laughed?

I withdrew my hand.

She caught it.

I blinked in confusion.

"No, I mean…" she shook her head and took the ring out the box, extending it towards me.

"I meant I'm sorry for not saying anything," she answered. "And in answer to your question—"

I laughed, sliding the ring on her waiting hand. "I got it."

She exhaled. "Yes."

"Lord above," I groaned. "No wonder six percent of guys did this over the phone."

"What?" she laughed.

"Nothing," I smirked, sliding out of the booth. "Get over here."

She smiled and climbed out, wrapping her arms around me and kissed me, arching her body beneath mine.

"Seriously Sam," she exhaled, brushing her fingers over my cheek. "As if I'd say no."

"You had me worried for a minute there."

"I love you," she whispered. "How could you ever doubt that?"

I closed my eyes, feeling the sun's rays warm us as it streamed through the window. "Ivy."

"Sam."

"I love you too."

She sighed and I smiled.

Mistry by Moonlight
Claire Merchant
Vanguard Press, 2013

After a year in Europe, Taylor Mistry returns to South Coast a changed woman inside and out.

While some people barely recognise the person they have known for years, similarly Taylor doesn't recognise herself, finding it difficult to fit back into her old life.

The once overweight young woman who felt invisible to everyone is suddenly getting attention from all sides: an old infatuation and a mysterious stranger are vying for her attention, while the handsome man who quickly stole her heart back in Italy is still in her thoughts.

Life seems more complicated than ever, but Taylor is soon to find out that it's worse than even she realises. Her life is in danger but she's not sure why. Are her suitors more than they appear? And does it all have something to do with an act of kindness towards an injured wolf?